# AMBIVALENCE IN HARDY

# Ambivalence in Hardy

## A Study of his Attitude to Women

Shanta Dutta

palgrave

Published by PALGRAVE
Houndmills, Basingstoke, Hampshire RG21 6XS and
175 Fifth Avenue, New York, N. Y. 10010
Companies and representatives throughout the world

PALGRAVE is the new global academic imprint of
St. Martin's Press LLC Scholarly and Reference Division and
Palgrave Publishers Ltd (formerly Macmillan Press Ltd).

*Outside North America*
ISBN 0–333–74486–1

*In North America*
ISBN 0–312–22183–5

This book is printed on paper suitable for recycling and
made from fully managed and sustained forest sources.

A catalogue record for this book is available from the British Library.

Library of Congress Cataloging-in-Publication Data
Dutta, Shanta
Ambivalence in Hardy : a study of his attitude to women / Shanta
Dutta
p.   cm.
Includes index.
ISBN 0–312–22183–5 (cloth)
1. Hardy, Thomas, 1840–1928—Characters—Women.   2. Ambivalence
in literature.   3. Women in literature.   I. Title
PR4757.W6D87   1999
823'.8—dc21
99–13316
CIP

10   9   8   7   6   5   4   3   2
08   07   06   05   04   03   02   01

Printed and bound in Great Britain by
Antony Rowe Ltd, Chippenham, Wiltshire

To the cherished memory of my beloved father

# Contents

# Preface

Ever since Hardy published his first novel, readers and reviewers have puzzled over his contradictory responses to his women characters. Modern critics too have tended either to brand him as a misogynist or to appropriate him to the feminist cause. The truth perhaps lies somewhere between these two extreme views and this book attempts to explore Hardy's richly ambivalent attitude to women – both in his fiction and in his life.

What emerges is a conflicting picture of a man and artist who espouses certain revolutionary ideas on women's rights but who sometimes fails to transcend the gender-stereotyping so characteristic of his age. Thus, while his sympathy for the wronged, exploited, or marginalized woman is forcefully and unequivocally expressed, what is also simultaneously revealed are some of his fears, uncertainties, reservations, and tensions: the natural inheritance of patriarchal ideology and a predominantly male literary tradition.

In discussing the issue I have drawn liberally on the unpublished material in the Dorset County Museum, on Hardy's published letters, his disguised autobiography, his various literary 'notebooks', and the recently published letters of his two wives. Selecting the texts to support my argument presented a dilemma: I could either fall back upon Hardy's own categorization of the novels and select the 'Novels of Character and Environment' (which Hardy quite obviously privileges) or concentrate on the generally accepted 'major' texts, ignoring the 'minor' novels. However, I have tried to be as representative as possible by choosing one 'minor' and one 'major' text from each of the three decades of Hardy's writing career (in prose fiction), thus including both an early comedy like *The Hand of Ethelberta* and a late tragedy like *Jude the Obscure*. From the 1870s I have chosen *The Hand of Ethelberta* and *The Return of the Native*; the 1880s are represented by *Two on a Tower* and *The Woodlanders*; and in the 1890s the focus is on the short stories (*A Group of Noble Dames* and *Life's Little Ironies*) and *Jude the Obscure*. A word of explanation for what may seem an important exclusion: a study on 'Hardy and Women' which ignores *Tess of the d'Urbervilles* may appear strange, and the only reason I have not devoted a chapter to this novel is that

I cannot personally find any ambivalence in it. Despite modern readings of voyeurism and sado-masochism, Hardy's emotional commitment to Tess is so total, so personal, and so sincere (he even at one time thought of naming the novel 'Tess of the Hardys'), that it seems perverse to question his sympathy.

I take this opportunity of thanking the Commonwealth Scholarship Commission for awarding me the Commonwealth Academic Staff Scholarship. Without this generous three-year grant I would never have realized my long-cherished dream of doing research in 'Hardy' country. Thanks are also due to the Arts Budget Centre Research Committee of Leicester University for a grant-in-aid which funded one of my research trips to the Dorset County Museum.

I would like to record my appreciation and sincere gratitude to the Trustees of the Dugdale Estate, especially Mr Alan Gardner, and their solicitor Mr J. P. D. Wienand, for their generous permission to quote the following manuscript material: revisions in the manuscript of *The Woodlanders*; Hardy's marginal comments in his copy of Ernest Brennecke's *The Life of Thomas Hardy* (1925); Hardy's corrections to the unpublished typescript of Emma Hardy's story 'The Maid on the Shore'; Hardy's marginal comment in his copy of Rosamund Marriott Watson's *The Poems* (1912); and his marginal comments in his copy of George Egerton's *Keynotes* (1893). I am also grateful to Mr Gardner, Mr Wienand, and Professor Michael Millgate for their collective permission to make extensive quotations from the seven published volumes of Hardy's *Collected Letters* (1978-88) and from the published *Letters of Emma and Florence Hardy* (1996). I would also like to thank Macmillan Press for their kind permission to quote liberally from Hardy's published works, especially his posthumously published disguised autobiography.

I am grateful to Mr Richard de Peyer, Curator of the Dorset County Museum, for granting me access to manuscript material in the 'Thomas Hardy Memorial Collection'; and to William Hemmig and Vincent Giroud of the Beinecke Library, Yale University, for sending me a copyflo of Hardy's annotated copy of Egerton's *Keynotes*. Thanks are also due to the ever-helpful library staff of Leicester University, especially Mr Peter Woodhead, and all the wonderful ladies at the Inter-Library Loan desk.

I wish to express my heartfelt gratitude to Professor Norman Page for strongly recommending my book's potential to my publishers. My sincere gratitude also goes to Professor Michael Millgate for generously sharing his vast store of Hardy scholarship with a novice and for promptly replying to my many queries, despite his busy schedule. Thanks also go to Dr Simon Curtis for publishing a few of my contributions in *The Thomas Hardy Journal*. My greatest debt, however, is to my supervisor, Professor Joanne Shattock, for patiently and critically reading my drafts, for those delightful trips to Stratford, but most of all for her faith in me.

Finally, thanks go out to Dr Dilip Bhattacharyya and his family for their warm hospitality during my Leicester sojourn; and to Dr Nese Elgun for giving up her precious study hours to make me computer-literate.

Shanta Dutta
Calcutta, 1998

# 1
# Introduction: The Critics' Debate

In a 1918 review, Virginia Woolf sweepingly stated: 'no one will admit that he can possibly mistake a novel written by a man for a novel written by a woman'.[1] Perhaps she was forgetting the numerous anonymous and pseudonymous Victorian novels – like those by the Brontës and George Eliot – which puzzled the contemporary reviewer and reader alike, as regards the sex of the author. Faced with the anonymous *Desperate Remedies* in 1871 the anonymous reviewer in *Athenaeum* responded cautiously:

> We cannot decide, satisfactorily to our own mind, on the sex of the author; for while certain evidence, such as the close acquaintance which he or she appears... to possess with the mysteries of the female toilette, would appear to point to its being the work of one of that sex, on the other hand there are certain expressions to be met with in the book so remarkably coarse as to render it almost impossible that it should have come from the pen of an English lady. Yet, again, all the best anonymous novels of the last twenty years – a dozen instances will at once suggest themselves to the novel-reader – have been the work of female writers. In this conflict of evidence, we will confine ourselves to the inexpressive 'he' in speaking of our present author, if we chance to need a pronoun.[2]

Happily, the question about the sex of the author of *Desperate Remedies* has long been settled. What has not been either unanimously or conclusively settled is the attitude of this author towards the 'frail/fair sex'. While most readers would agree with the view that '[n]one of the male characters come quite up to these protagonists among the women',[3] the point at issue is whether these female protagonists are a libel on the sex or whether Hardy presents his female characters in a favourable, positive light. Given that most of the early reviewers were male, critical analyses of the novels soon revolved round the question of whether Hardy's women characters were 'lovable' or not.

Even a superficial survey of the critical response to Hardy shows a sharp schism: on one side of the critical fault-line, Hardy is held up as a champion of women, as a man who sympathized with their downtrodden condition and who fought to highlight the various socio-economic injustices of which they were victims. On the opposite side of the fence are critics who suspect Hardy of being a misogynist, a novelist who may have rejected institutionalized Christianity but who seems not to have outgrown the hereditary Christian notion that it is Eve and her daughters who bring 'woe' to mankind. Perhaps one of the earliest signed reviews to draw attention to Hardy's negative portraiture of women is that by Horace Moule, a friend and mentor of Hardy. Moule ends his appreciative 1872 review of *Under the Greenwood Tree* with this insight:

> The portraiture of Fancy herself conveys a kind of satire on the average character of a girl with good looks, capable of sound and honest affection, but inordinately moved by admiration.[4]

Later, Bathsheba comes in for more severe treatment in the 1875 review in *The Observer*:

> The first interview between Troy and Bathsheba represents the latter in so odious a light, if women in whatever rank of society, are supposed to retain any trace of modesty and reserve, that we confess we do not care one straw about her afterwards, and are only sorry that Gabriel Oak was not sufficiently manly to refuse to have anything more to say to such an incorrigible hussy.[5]

Similar sentiments had been voiced by Henry James in his 1874 review of *Far From the Madding Crowd* in *Nation*:

> But we cannot say that we either understand or like Bathsheba. She is a young lady of the inconsequential, wilful, mettlesome type which has lately become so much the fashion for heroines.... she remains alternately vague and coarse, and seems always artificial.[6]

Bathsheba is seen as being an 'arrant flirt over-flowing with vanity', as 'hard and mercenary', and the 1875 review in *Westminster Review* unequivocally stated:

We thoroughly sympathize with him [i.e. Oak] and pity him, and we must say that he deserved a far better woman for a wife than such a vain and selfish creature as Bathsheba Everdene.[7]

If the individualistic and unconventional Bathsheba aroused such (male) censure, Eustacia faced an even less sympathetic response. The 1878 review in *Athenaeum* shrewdly linked Eustacia with the 'Madame Bovary' type and expressed disgust at characters who 'know no other law than the gratification of their own passion.'[8] This same moral tone is heard in the 1879 *Spectator* review:

> His coldly passionate heroine, Eustacia Vye, never reproaches herself for a moment with the inconstancy and poverty of her own affections. On the contrary, she has no feeling that anything which happens within her, has relation to right and wrong at all, or that such a thing as responsibility exists... Hence, in her case, we never really reach the point of tragedy at all.[9]

Even such a toned-down heroine as Anne Garland in *The Trumpet-Major* had to face her share of critical ire. The 1880 review in *Athenaeum* is brutally frank:

> It is true, no doubt, that the heroine is, not to put too fine a point upon it, a fool, and the gallant Bob Loveday another; and that the reader cannot help feeling more regard for Matilda of the doubtful reputation than for the correct and ladylike Anne. But Mr Hardy has always inclined to the cynical rather than to the sentimental.[10]

The *Spectator* review (1880), conceding that Anne is 'personally lovely and attractive... amiable, innocent, generous, and tender hearted', expresses a sentiment that many readers have felt in reading Hardy's novels:

> and yet she makes woeful havoc of the heart of a worthy man. She is selfish, as Mr Hardy's heroines are selfish – not wilfully or intellectually, but by dint of her inborn, involuntary, unconscious emotional organism... It is Mr Hardy's delight to show his chosen woman doing these things; a hasty criticism might deem him cynical... We are appalled to see what harm these gentle, compassionate, sweet-tempered creatures can do.[11]

This focus on the ruinous potential of women is again evident in the 1881 *Athenaeum* review of *A Laodicean*:

> Mr Hardy would seem to have set before himself the task of illustrating in every conceivable way the Virgilian dictum about the nature of women. His heroines have their stations in many ranks of life; they are diverse in character and in attraction; but all have the common fault of their sex, they cannot make up their minds.[12]

This review ends with a remarkably modern insight:

> Without being in the least degree a 'fleshly' writer, Mr Hardy has a way of insisting on the physical attractions of a woman which, if imitated by weaker writers, may prove offensive.[13]

Modern feminist analyses of Hardy which highlight the author/narrator's delight in voyeurism and the reduction of woman to the object of male gaze were anticipated by early comments like the one just quoted and the more graphically expressed view of Mowbray Morris in 1892 in *Quarterly Review*:

> Poor Tess's sensual qualifications for the part of heroine are paraded over and over again with a persistence like that of a horse-dealer egging on some wavering customer to a deal, or a slave-dealer appraising his wares to some full-blooded pasha.[14]

However, it is with *Jude* that press reactions reached almost hysterical proportions. In her (in)famous 'The Anti-Marriage League' article (1896) in *Blackwood's Magazine*, Mrs Oliphant uses the sledgehammer to demolish *Jude*. Although the vehemence somewhat blunts the edge of her satire, she scores a few telling points:

> We rather think the author's object must be, having glorified women by the creation of Tess, to show after all what destructive and ruinous creatures they are, in general circumstances and in every development, whether brutal or refined...

> It is the women who are the active agents in all this unsavoury imbroglio: the story is carried on, and life is represented as carried

on, entirely by their means. The men are passive, suffering, rather good than otherwise, victims of these and of fate. Not only do they never dominate, but they are quite incapable of holding their own against these remorseless ministers of destiny, these determined operators, managing all the machinery of life so as to secure their own way... But it has now... become the method with men, in the hands of many of whom women have returned to the *role* of the temptress given to them by the old monkish sufferers of ancient times, who fled to the desert, like Anthony, to get free of them, but even there barely escaped with their lives from the seductions of the sirens, who were so audacious as to follow them to the very scene of the macerations and miseries into which the unhappy men plunged to escape from their toils. In the books of the younger men, it is now the woman who seduces – it is no longer the man.[15]

But it was not the attack of Mrs Oliphant, a rival novelist, that galled Hardy. He was more hurt by the criticism of a friend, Edmund Gosse, who wrote in an 1896 review in *Cosmopolis*:

The *vita sexualis* of Sue is the central interest of the book, and enough is told about it to fill the specimen tables of a German specialist... She is a poor, maimed 'degenerate', ignorant of herself and of the perversion of her instincts, full of febrile, amiable illusions, ready to dramatize her empty life, and play at loving though she cannot love. Her adventure with the undergraduate has not taught her what she is.[16]

Such negative views were not confined to the occasional articles/ reviews in the periodical press. Of the steady stream of full-length studies of Hardy that had been emerging since the 1890s, Samuel Chew's *Thomas Hardy* (1921) presents a representative summing up:

On the whole, however, Hardy's attitude towards women is unfavourable; his opinion of them is bitter. They have many good qualities of heart, but they are fickle and vain, insincere, conscienceless, and seductive.[17]

1928 saw a flood of articles and obituaries in the English and French press, most of which attempted to present a critical estimate of the recently deceased author. Daudet classified Hardy as a woman-hater, like Ibsen, and found in Hardy's rejection of Woman as a redemptive force the roots of his pessimism.

But it would be unfair to present only the negative side of the critical response to Hardy's achievement as a portrayer of women. Hardy had his supporters, even across the Atlantic, and F. W. Knickerbocker went so far as to assert that 'John Stuart Mill and Meredith alone anticipated him [i.e. Hardy] in claiming for women a large freedom to live and love'.[18] Recalling his personal association with the Hardys, T. P. O'Connor was convinced that *Tess* was 'the greatest plea for woman that was ever written. Hardy himself wrote the book with some such thought in his mind.'[19] Indeed, *Tess* marked a watershed and surely it won over that indignant female reader who, exasperated with Hardy's depiction of women, is supposed to have written on the margin of a circulating library copy: 'Oh, how I *hate* Thomas Hardy!'[20] That *Tess* represented a turning-point was evident from Richard le Gallienne's 1891 comment in *Star*:

> Mr Hardy has heretofore been more inclined to champion man the faithful against woman the coquette, but in *Tess* he very definitely espouses 'the cause of woman', and devotes himself to show how often in this world – all, alas, because the best of us is so conventionalized – when men and women break a law 'the Woman pays'. Of course it is a special pleading, because a novel might be as readily written to show how often a man pays, too.[21]

Perhaps the earliest general survey to speak positively of Hardy's presentation of women was the 1879 article in *New Quarterly Magazine*. While acknowledging the weaknesses of Hardy's women ('they never become thoroughly responsible creatures'), the reviewer is nevertheless appreciative:

> Though the vanity of his heroines is ever present and insatiable, they have none of the meanness which is imputed to feminine vanity by most male and by all female writers who take an exaggerated view of it. Their most universal desire for admiration will coexist with an honest passion for a particular man, and their utmost passion is never dissociated from a nymph-like and perfectly spontaneous purity.[22]

In a landmark 1883 essay, Havelock Ellis too recorded his fascination with Hardy's heroines and praised him for presenting:

> those instinct-led women, who form a series which, for subtle
> simplicity, for a certain fascinating and incalculable vivacity
> which is half ethereal and half homely, can hardly be matched....
> They are never quite bad... They have an instinctive self-respect,
> an instinctive purity. When they err, it is by caprice, by imagina-
> tion. Even Eustacia Vye has no impure taint about her.[23]

The most lyrical defence of Hardy's portraiture of women came, in
1887, from Coventry Patmore:

> It is in his heroines, however, that Hardy is most original and
> delightful... each has the charm of the simplest and most familiar
> womanhood, and the only character they have in common is
> that of having each some serious defect, which only makes us
> like them more. Hardy is too good an observer not to know that
> women are like emeralds and rubies, only those of inferior
> colour and price being without flaw; and he is too rich in human
> tenderness not to know that love never glows with its fullest
> ardour unless it has 'something dreadful to forgive'.[24]

Given these strikingly polar reactions to Hardy's presentation of
women in his fiction, a reader unacquainted with English literature
might be forgiven for assuming that there must surely be two
Hardys in question and hence all this confusion. The inability to pin
down Hardy and neatly label him is perhaps due to the author's
own lifelong claim that he was recording only 'impressions' and
not 'convictions'. Even in prose, which is less mood-dictated than
poetry, Hardy is constantly changing his stance, shifting his sympathies, so that it is difficult to freeze this protean artist into a fixed,
static attitude. Thus, recognizing both the cynicism and the tenderness in Hardy's attitude to women, Virginia Woolf wrote in her
1928 memorial essay:

> However lovable and charming Bathsheba may be, still she is
> weak; however stubborn and ill-guided Henchard may be, still
> he is strong. This is a fundamental part of Hardy's vision; the
> staple of many of his books. The woman is the weaker and the
> fleshlier, and she clings to the stronger and obscures his vision....
> His characters, both men and women, were creatures to him of

an infinite attraction. For the women he shows a more tender solicitude than for the men, and in them, perhaps, he takes a keener interest. Vain might their beauty be and terrible their fate, but while the glow of life is in them their step is free, their laughter sweet, and theirs is the power to sink into the breast of Nature and become part of her silence and solemnity, or to rise and put on them the movement of the clouds and the wildness of the flowering woodlands.[25]

This same recognition of ambivalence marks Abercrombie's entry on Hardy in the 1929 edition of *Encyclopaedia Britannica*:

> He is a fatalist, perhaps rather a determinist, and he studies the workings of fate or law (ruling through inexorable moods or humours), in the chief vivifying and disturbing influence in life, women. His view of women is more French than English; it is subtle, a little cruel, not as tolerant as it seems, thoroughly a man's point of view, and not, as with Meredith, man's and woman's at once. He sees all that is irresponsible for good and evil in a woman's character, all that is untrustworthy in her brain and will, all that is alluring in her variability. He is her apologist, but always with a reserve of private judgment. No one has created more attractive women of a certain class, women whom a man would have been more likely to love or to regret loving. In his earlier books he is somewhat careful over the reputation of his heroines; gradually he allows them more liberty, with a franker treatment of instinct and its consequences... His knowledge of women confirms him in a suspension of judgment.[26]

The debate continues; and in subsequent criticism the line dividing critics who see Hardy as misogynist and those who consider him an apologist for women has blurred somewhat as writers increasingly recognize the tensions, ambivalences and contradictions in Hardy's writing. H. C. Duffin is disturbed by the 'cynical' observations on 'the sex' which run counter to 'Hardy's pictures of womanhood [which] glow with love and admiration'. Nevertheless, defending Hardy against the charge of perversely willing suffering on his heroines, Duffin unequivocally declares:

> But a just view will not ascribe these melancholy facts to a special pleasure Hardy got out of inflicting torment upon women.

After all, he saw life as a very hard school, and if the women suffer more than the men it may be because woman is the weaker vessel. But surely some of the grimness may be due to a hurt idealism – to Hardy's sense of the gulf between woman's possible best and her actual achievement towards it. The pathetic deficiency seems to have come home to him with appalling force, and his ruthless pictures of woman's folly and suffering are the bitter cry wrung from him by grief… It is not Hardy who treats his women cruelly, but life – life as Hardy saw it. What Hardy could do for his women he did – he made them full of beauty, interest, fascinating and lovable qualities of all kinds, he gave them great parts to play, and let them (generally) play those parts well. His estimate of woman is high, but tempered and conditioned by keen observation of the realities round him. He has the necessary ideals of her as a creature nobly planned and bright with angelic radiance, but he knows also that it is only in rare cases that she is found free, undimmed, ideal… Hardy is no misogynist, but true lover in very deed.[27]

Giving Hardy credit for presenting us with 'a gallery of charming, impulsive, and dangerously contradictory women', Guerard considers Hardy:

a most cynical theorist de *natura feminae*. His attitude progressed…. from fascinated and unwillingly sympathetic criticism to almost uncritical sympathy, but his view of woman's incorrigible nature long remained unchanged… He looked upon his women from the outside coolly and as the sum of their illogical evasions.[28]

Aligning himself more with Duffin than with Guerard is another advocate of Hardy as a 'lover' of women, Irving Howe, who opens his chapter on *Tess* with the celebrated sentence: 'As a writer of novels Thomas Hardy was endowed with a precious gift: he liked women.'[29] While conceding that Hardy was 'quite capable of releasing animus toward his women characters and casting them as figures of destruction' (p. 108), Howe nevertheless claims for Hardy a rare 'gift for creeping intuitively into the emotional life of women' (p. 109). 'The feminine admixture is very strong in his work' (p. 109), and Tess's 'violation, neglect and endurance' show 'Hardy's most radical claim for the redemptive power of suffering' (p. 110).

Hardy 'hovers and watches over Tess, like a stricken father' (p. 131), and for Howe:

> Tess is one of the greatest examples we have in English literature of how a writer can take hold of a cultural stereotype and, through the sheer intensity of his affection, pare and purify it into something that is morally ennobling. Tess derives from Hardy's involvement with and reaction against the Victorian cult of chastity, which from the beginning of his career he had known to be corrupted by meanness and hysteria. (p. 110)

Ian Gregor speaks similarly about Hardy's 'overwhelming compassion' in *Tess*:

> In his novel, it is Tess herself who releases in Hardy a feeling that we can only describe as love – a love prompted, at least, by the fact that Hardy finds woman expressive, in the purest form, of the human capacity for endurance and the steadfast refusal to be overcome... In her, Hardy has invested his whole imaginative capital.[30]

Discussing the constant authorial revisions to the Ur-*Tess*, made by Hardy in an attempt to 'purify' Tess, Mary Jacobus too speaks of 'Hardy's compassionate identification with his heroine' and of the 'authorial allegiance to a living, breathing, sentient woman [which] evades external standards of judgement'.[31] Hardy's 'intuitive commitment' to Tess leads him to the 'character-assassination of Alec and Angel' (p. 325), and his 'imaginative allegiance to Tess does not flinch from her subsequent act of murder'(p. 334). In *Jude* too, Hardy 'is imaginatively generous towards both sides of the struggle, but as always his most intense feeling is for the loser',[32] and thus 'Sue's tormented consciousness haunts us more than Jude's bitter oblivion' (p. 324). Jacobus concludes:

> 'She was Sue Bridehead, something very particular. Why was there no place for her?' is indeed the question Hardy leaves us asking at the end of *Jude the Obscure*. This overwhelming sense of Sue's specialness is at once the basis of Hardy's protest on her behalf, and a measure of his imaginative achievement. (p. 325)

While Tess and perhaps Sue are obvious choices to argue Hardy's feminist sympathies, Elaine Showalter quite daringly chooses a self-confessed 'woman-hater', Michael Henchard, because it is 'in the analysis of this New Man, rather than in the evaluation of Hardy's New Women, that the case for Hardy's feminist sympathies may be argued'.[33] Arguing that Hardy 'understood the feminine self as the estranged and essential complement of the male self' (p. 101), Showalter charts the process of Henchard's 'unmanning' and shows how his humbling and loss of male power is really an 'educative and ennobling apprenticeship in human sensitivity' (p. 113) which forces him to recognize the 'long-repressed "feminine" side of himself' (p. 112) and to 'discover his own suppressed or estranged capacity to love' (p. 109). Thus Showalter confidently asserts:

> The fantasy that women hold men back, drag them down, drain their energy, divert their strength, is nowhere so bleakly rebuked as in Hardy's tale of the 'man of character'. (p. 103)

Henchard may be a woman-hater, but surely not Hardy! Quoting R. J. White's story of the tavern landlord who smilingly declared: 'Mr Hardy was fond of the Ladies', Rosalind Miles declares: 'Lord David Cecil observed that all Hardy's stories are love stories; and so they are; the story of Hardy's own endless love of women.'[34] Highlighting Hardy's 'poignant concern for women' and his 'guileless and ecstatic response to women in life [which] irradiated his writing at every possible level' (p. 26), Miles speculates:

> Despite the overspiritualisation of women which is undeniably a feature of Hardy's treatment it is through his female characters that Hardy mainly communicated his sense of that 'insupportable and touching loss', of the waste of human potential and the irrecoverable destruction of innocence. Heartsick at the world's cruelty, or worse, indifference, Hardy solaced himself by creating feminine softness and constancy. He found a recurrent consolation in rendering with loving exactness, through the medium of these imaginary women, the sensations of the castaway. (p. 27)

Claiming that in 'the female condition' Hardy 'discovered an objective correlative of his own emotional state' (p. 38), Miles nevertheless honestly admits in summing up that Hardy is 'alternately moved' by an 'agonised pity' and 'a lingering irritable suspicion of women's worthlessness' (p. 41). Hardy's whole tribe of 'crones' or 'anti-females' reveal 'his ambivalent, if not hostile, feelings about the sex' and this combined with his 'sexual pessimism' and 'native distrust of life' can 'sound like an abiding misogyny' (p. 33).

Such insights, characteristic of modern feminist readings, mark Boumelha's study of Hardy's treatment of women. Calling attention to the 'aphoristic and dismissive generalisations about women' and the 'images of taming' which 'pursue' Bathsheba, Boumelha suggests that 'there is an undercurrent of sexual antagonism towards her, expressed both in the action of the plot and in direct narrative comment'.[35] Later, Hardy's first attempt to write a tragedy (*The Return of the Native*), which is a 'double tragedy' turning upon marriage, will inaugurate a sexist pattern that will be repeated in the later novels: 'the man's tragedy is primarily intellectual, the woman's sexual' (p. 48). For all Hardy's attempt to approximate gradually to an 'androgynous' narrative voice, *Tess* will reveal:

> that all the passionate commitment to exhibiting Tess as the subject of her own experience evokes an unusually overt maleness in the narrative voice. The narrator's erotic fantasies of penetration and engulfment enact a pursuit, violation and persecution of Tess in parallel with those she suffers at the hands of her two lovers. (p. 120)

Rosemarie Morgan, however, contends that in Hardy's 'subversive method and intentions' 'we are invited to appraise the physical attributes, not only of the female, but also of the male' as in 'Bathsheba's pleasure in Troy's body'.[36] For Morgan, the 'authentic Hardyan voice' is heard in 'his close identification with Bathsheba and, consequently, his impulse to mourn her loss of vitality, sexual verve and bounding self-delight' (p. 49). In the final analysis, it is:

> upon Bathsheba's vulnerability, her pain, her passion, [that] Hardy's sympathies turn and turn again. The centre of caring feeling and intense emotion is quintessentially the flow between author and heroine, even at the last, where Bathsheba is but a ghost of her former self. (p. 56)

Morgan's conclusion about Hardy's attitudes is radical and unequivocal:

> For all his sympathies with the underprivileged male in his fiction, there is no doubt that for Hardy it is woman's social condition which requires reassessment and revision. His male characters may show individual strengths and weaknesses, but in their capacities as moral 'overseer', censor or watchdog they are uniformly vigilant in maintaining the conventional premise of the status quo. As such, Hardy treats them with an antipathy only thinly concealed by the narrative texture of the novel's structures. Where he, the author, takes pains to deny himself the right of standing in judgement upon his women, so too he refuses to vindicate their male censors – the pedagogical Knight, the spying Oak, the policing Venn. Each, as moral watchdog, partakes of a world of male domination bordering upon absurdity and menace, a world latently vindictive and tyrannical. (p. 162)

An interesting contrast is made by Maggie Humm between the male and female worlds in *Tess*, represented respectively by Angel's brothers and Tess's dairymaid friends who are all so supportive of Tess and self-effacing in their love for Angel. Humm pointedly remarks:

> the juxtaposition in *Tess of the d'Urbervilles* in the same chapter (44) of caring and supportive female groups with the actions of Angel's less than attractive brothers, 'their voices engaged in earnest discourse' fulminating against their brother's marriage, suggests Hardy's allegiance.[37]

Perhaps this allegiance developed due to Hardy's sensitiveness to rural tragedies centering around 'ruined' maids in his native Wessex. Highlighting the 'ruined maid' motif in Hardy's prose and verse (e.g. 'A Sunday Morning Tragedy'), Desmond Hawkins sees in it a proof of Hardy's intense sympathy for the suffering of women:

> The unhappy endings in real life, as Hardy witnessed it, were often tragic and brutal – public disgrace, suicide, crude abortions, infanticide, prostitution. When he visited Lord Portsmouth in Devon in 1885 Hardy's host showed him 'a bridge over which

bastards were thrown and drowned, even down to quite recent times'. The traditional price to be paid for the public disgrace of a maiden's ruin and unmarried motherhood was her banishment from the family home and the community, with the expectation that she would probably go 'on the streets' in some town or city. It was these disfigurements and mutilations of the natural sexuality of women that aroused in Hardy a deep feminist sympathy. Illicit unions and illegitimate births – to use the jargon of public morality – were a subject of his continuing meditation.[38]

Hardy's empathy for suffering creatures, human or animal, has been acknowledged, and this may account for his sympathy with women who receive a raw deal from patriarchal society. But another subtle reason may lie behind his identification with women, as Seymour Smith suggests in his biography. Hardy was:

> throughout his life resentful when he felt that his intellectual background was brought into question. This was undoubtedly a consequence of his extreme sensitivity, but it is also indicative of the great difficulties then faced by any writer who lacked a university background. Since all women were subject to this lack, it may well have put him into even stronger sympathy with them.[39]

While recognizing Hardy's 'emotional susceptibility' to women in general and his 'profound sympathy with the victimized women of the lower classes', Millgate realizes that this is not the whole truth. Discussing Hardy's literary friendships and collaborations with women, especially his marginalia in a gift copy of *Keynotes* by 'George Egerton' (pseudonym of Mary Chavelita Dunne, later Mrs Clairmonte), Millgate comments:

> The stories in *Keynotes* had created something of a sensation by the directness with which they treated of the relations between the sexes, and while Hardy's marginal annotations have to be read as contributions to the half-humorous debate being carried on with Mrs Henniker, they nevertheless indicate some hostility towards women in general or, at the least, a tendency to fall back upon the standard male attitudes of his time.[40]

This 'hostility towards women' is expressed surreptitiously through Michael Henchard who exclaims in exasperation: 'These cursed women – there's not an inch of straight grain in 'em!'[41] Even Irving Howe, who declared that Hardy 'liked' women, begins his chapter thus:

> To shake loose from one's wife; to discard that drooping rag of a woman, with her mute complaints and maddening passivity; to escape not by a slinking abandonment but through the public sale of her body to a stranger, as horses are sold at a fair; and thus to wrest, through sheer amoral willfulness, a second chance out of life – it is with this stroke, so insidiously attractive to male fantasy, that *The Mayor of Casterbridge* begins.[42]

If this 'male fantasy' is limited to Henchard/Hardy, then we need seriously to question Hardy's status as a 'lover' of women; but if this male fantasy is universal, secretly shared by half the world's population, then perhaps we can take a more generous view of Hardy *vis-à-vis* woman/wife/marriage. Based on textual evidence, the plot structure of *The Mayor* certainly seems to suggest, in the words of Frederick Karl, that 'a whole series of re-appearing women seem to doom Henchard, and each time he fails it is almost always over a woman or related to one'. Thus, women 'are rarely sources of consolation or Victorian mates, but furies and fates, temptresses, hostile creatures struggling to free themselves while entrapping males.'[43]

Similarly, Katharine Rogers speaks of '[w]omen's abuse of intelligent, unselfish men' in Hardy's novels, and she points out how:

> Jude and Sue re-enact one of Hardy's favorite situations, that of a worthy man snubbed and exploited by a woman. In each case, an unselfish man treats the woman he loves with devoted consideration, while she fails to appreciate him.[44]

In her book *The Troublesome Helpmate: A History of Misogyny in Literature* (1966), Katharine Rogers does not place Hardy in the misogynic tradition, and the only reference to him is in a brief footnote calling attention to the Biblical epigraph to Part First of *Jude*, which speaks of how men have 'perished', 'erred', and 'sinned' for women. But Rogers obviously revised her views on Hardy as a 'misogynist', because in her 1975 *Centennial Review* article she emphatically concludes:

> In short, these novels show the tenacity of sexist assumptions even in so humane and enlightened a man as Hardy. Rejecting the sexual mores of his patriarchal society, preferring unconventional women to the passive Victorian ideal, consciously sympathizing with women, Hardy still could not quite see them as human beings like himself. His primary sympathy remains focused on the sensitive rational man. Although glib anti-feminist generalizations are less evident in the novels after *Far from the Madding Crowd*, even *Jude* shows evidence of the traditional misogynistic stereotypes: that woman exploits deserving men, and that she is, as Aristotle said, an incomplete male ('a fraction always wanting its integer').
> [pp. 257-8; Rogers's parenthesis]

Such reductive gender stereotyping, argues Mary Childers, reveals Hardy's 'inadvertent, defensive misogyny' and results in artistic double standards quite blatantly in *Tess*:

> The intense and repeated eroticized descriptions of Tess' indecisiveness obscure the reader's sense of Angel as also indecisive. Though Hardy's novels often indicate that female indecisiveness is a response to continuously applied male coercion, it is more often fondly displayed as a function of female nature – with the consequence that the less dramatic appearance of male indecisiveness becomes almost invisible... The precipitousness of male judgements delivered against women is actually proof of the inconstancy of men, but Hardy shares the desire to disguise this fact which he dramatizes. He shields the men by generalizing about the inconstancy of women in a more accusatory way and by making the inconstancy of women one of the prominent structuring devices of his novels.[45]

Childers's conclusion about 'Hardy's uncontrollable wavering between delight and distaste with regard to women' (p. 332) perhaps best sums up Hardy's ambivalence as perceived by modern critics. Patricia Stubbs too highlights the:

uneasy co-existence between an intensely modern, even feminist consciousness and what are essentially archetypal patterns of feeling and relationship. This contradiction produces some of the strengths as well as some of the weaknesses both of his fiction and of his feminism.[46]

Echoing this is Judith Wittenberg's comment about how Hardy's 'sympathetic portrayals [of women] are subtly qualified by elements that are more ambiguous and problematic'.[47] 'Hardy's much-vaunted sympathy for women is covertly undermined' (pp. 50-1) not only by the 'narrator's intrusive generalizations about women' (p. 53) – a by-now familiar charge – but also by:

a recurrent pattern in Hardy's fiction – his tendency to 'punish', either with death or with chastisement, women who reveal somewhat masculine urges and a need to rebel against a purely feminine role, or who have extra-marital sexual experiences. (p. 50)

This employment of 'plot-as-punishment' mars even such a sympathetic novel as *Tess*, and as early as in Hardy's first published novel, *Desperate Remedies*, Wittenberg sees 'portents':

of the manipulative, even faintly sadistic narrative stance that would undermine his most splendid portrayal of a woman in difficulty – Tess Durbeyfield. Hardy's compassionate recognition and effective dramatization of women's psychological and socio-economic quest for autonomy is subtly contraverted by a covert need, revealed by aspects of his narrative method, to control and, not infrequently, to punish them. (p. 54)

Hardy's 'own way of looking' at Tess is 'yet another form of possession', and for Janet Freeman:

By necessity, then, Hardy himself is implicated in the very immorality he has watched and deplored. He cannot escape this fellowship. The grief that overwhelms the end of *Tess of the d'Urbervilles* ... is the expression of this guilt, futility, and loss.[48]

Kaja Silverman echoes this sentiment when she explores the consequences of the continuous subjection of Tess to what she calls 'a colonizing male gaze'. In the scene of Tess's rape/seduction:

> The narrator attempts to establish his own moral distance from what happens to Tess by inveighing against providence... However, since the narrator himself is the only transcendental agency on the horizon when Alec violates Tess, this outcry constitutes a classic disavowal, implicating him in the very action he abominates.[49]

This preoccupation with the 'supremacy of the male gaze' is an issue that George Wotton takes up in his chapter on Hardy's women:

> Trapped and captured by the masculine gaze each of Hardy's women is enmeshed in a conflict of perceptions, a complex of visions of herself. She is constituted as the observed subject whose existence is determined by her reactions to the conflicting acts of sight of the men by whom she is observed. Interpellated as as [sic] subject, subjected to the myth of being the weaker sex, internalizing and recognizing herself in that image, she behaves accordingly. Whatever Hardy's intention, the innumerable acts of sight which constitute the structure of perceptions put the ideological construction of woman into contradiction by showing that the perception of her 'essential nature' is always conditional upon who is doing the seeing.[50]

Wotton's awareness of the contradictions in Hardy's writing is representative of recent Hardy criticism and perhaps a more mature response than the earlier partisan labelling of Hardy as 'feminist' or 'misogynist'. Thus, Marjorie Garson warns the reader:

> While Hardy can be read as especially sympathetic to women and to working people, his sympathy is by no means unambiguous, and to see him simply as politically correct is to miss the anxieties, ambivalences, and ambiguities.[51]

A good example of such complexity is when 'politics of gender' clash with 'politics of class', as in the skimmington-ride episode in

*The Mayor*, where Hardy underplays the 'danger and malice' of the Mixen-Lane gang and obscures Lucetta's 'vulnerability as a pregnant woman':

By treating the Mixen-Lane machinations as social comedy and by metaphorically displacing the less endearing kinds of criminality from Mixen Lane on to Lucetta, Hardy loads the narrative against her in ways which seem motivated as much by misogyny as by sympathy with the underclass. (p. 107)

Although Garson highlights the 'author's real sympathy with women' (p. 20) in his descriptions of women wasting away under the labour of constant childbirth, the more powerful impression we are left with is of 'Hardy's instinctive terror of the woman who castrates and kills' (p. 121) and of the 'misogynistic streak in Hardy's eroticism' (p. 24).

On this combination of misogyny/sadism and eroticism/voyeurism, the most scathing attack on Hardy comes not from the 'critics' but from the creative writers – two novelists, one male and one female (so the question of gender-bias is irrelevant). In his witty interweaving of fact and fiction in *Peeping Tom* (1984), Howard Jacobson scores many telling points although he speaks not in his own narrative persona but makes his fictional characters voice his insights. Camilla, who organizes lectures for her summer school of Hardy enthusiasts, informs her audience:

'The ordinarily outgoing brute who beats his wife doesn't suppose that he is thereby providing for her needs while he is satisfying his own. Thus the violence done on Hardy's heroines is always essentially vicarious, connived at by the author but inflicted in another's name. The daemon, you see, must be free to watch and feel the pain himself. The seduction of Bathsheba, the rape of Tess, the subjugation of Elfride, are all observed as by an injured third party, jealously. And the more assured the rival's mastery, that's to say the more complete the woman's surrender, then the more exquisite the sense of injury... Hardy was using his novels to have the women he loved, real or imaginary – it comes to the same thing – violated by proxy.'[52]

The novel's 'hero', Barney Fugleman (the 'I' of the narrative), shrewdly opines:

> 'He [i.e. Hardy] hated them [i.e. women]. In his life and in his art. All his women characters are emanations of either guilt or grievance. He paid them out or he paid them back. The only women he ever cared about were dead ones and you don't need me to tell you that he only cared about them because he was hooked on the pain of missed opportunity.' (p. 40)

Isolated quotations fail to do justice to the witty pertinency of the sustained attack on Hardy, exploding the 'myth' of Hardy as a humane lover of women. But perhaps one more 'Camilla' outburst will suffice:

> 'The assumption of an advanced moral tone towards female impurity – that's not my word – when it's as clear as daylight that he's simply tossed, like a boat without ballast, between fascination and abhorrence. All that crap about natural Purity! He hasn't got the nerve to admit that Tess is interesting to him *because* of her experience, not *in spite* of it. If he'd been honest he would have given Tess to Alec on every page.' (p. 217; Jacobson's italics)

In her sombre retelling of the story of *Tess* (1993), Emma Tennant takes off from the bitter protest that Hardy's Tess expresses to Angel's suggestion that she take up a study of history. What is the use, Tess passionately asks, of learning that she is not the first woman in human history, and neither will she be the last, to know the meaning of suffering? The Tesses of this world, Tennant argues, in whatever country or century they live, have always been exploited and will continue to be exploited by patriarchal society. Her attack on Hardy, as a representative of patriarchal society, lacks the humour that tempers Jacobson's thrusts, and breathes of feminist polemic:

> For all Hardy's apparent compassion for Tess – and his description of her on the title page of the book that became him, overcame him and stayed more in the imagination of the world than anything else of him – as a 'Pure Woman', he was as guilty as the next man. His compassion was an exquisite cruelty. Hardy used

the execution of Tess for the crime of murdering her first and hateful lover as a final, tender way of killing the woman he loves; he shaped her, through all the ages of history that woman has toiled, died in the agony of labour, stood at the stake, fallen gagging on black water in the duckponds of witch persecution – through all the centuries of slavery and non-belonging, without even a name or a woman priest to turn to in the hours of worst desolation, Hardy led Tess to the last, inevitable punishment, the price she must pay as daughter of Eve. For her prime disobedience to man, her ruler, her father, her seducer, Tess must swing.[53]

On Hardy the individual, Tennant is no less damning. Exposing Hardy's 'incestuous obsession with his own creation', she comments: 'when Thomas Hardy falls in love, he falls in love with his own creation. His is the male controlling imagination that devours women in its lair: Monster eats the Muse' (p. 123). The unnaturalness is aggravated when this 'Monster' discards his fictional women and seeks flesh and blood ones to satisfy his hunger:

> For, by now, the Minotaur wants his victims to be real. No more webs to be spun, no more invented heroines, who become tiring to play with, as they trace and retrace the thread of his ideas in a labyrinth of his own making. Gertrude, the real, actual Gertrude who so resembles her beautiful mother, will be the next Tess.[54] (p. 126)

This is too extreme a note on which to end, and objective critical assessment must shed personal animus and recover a sense of balance. Thomas Hardy is neither monster nor messiah. A re-evaluation of his creative and critical writings, his correspondence, and his real life relations with women may reveal what his attitudes really were. Meanwhile, it is important to keep Widdowson's judicious warning in mind:

> There may be every possibility... for a modern critic to strategically reproduce a 'feminist Hardy', but it would be historically suspect, if nothing else, to hypothesize a male author in the second half of the nineteenth century as having a conscious and coherent feminist philosophy in view.[55]

# 2

# *The Hand of Ethelberta*

In *The Hand of Ethelberta* (1876) Hardy abandoned the vein of pastoral comedy that he had successfully exploited in *Under the Greenwood Tree* and *Far From the Madding Crowd*, and returned to the satiric mode of his first (unpublished) novel of high society – 'The Poor Man and the Lady'. The reason for this abrupt change of novelistic direction lay probably in his desire to escape being typecast as the writer of rural love comedies; also, there was the need to establish a distinctive voice of his own in order to put an end to the endless (often unfavourable) comparisons with George Eliot. However, *The Hand of Ethelberta* does not represent a totally radical discontinuity in Hardy's fiction: in having a secret 'past' which potentially threatens to blight her future marital happiness, Ethelberta has affinities with Fancy and Elfride before her and Eustacia, Viviette, Lucetta, and Tess after her.

Ethelberta is the first of Hardy's eponymous protagonists, and she is unique among the Hardy sisterhood in the sense that she is apparently in total control of her own destiny. Far from passively allowing her hand to be sought in marriage, she deftly plays her 'hand' in the game of social manoeuvring. The progress of her career from Berta Chickerel to Lady Mountclere is the result of her ruthless exploitation not so much of her looks as of her 'Mephistophelian endowment, brains'.[1] In her social climbing she learns to 'repress' the emotional side of her nature and her social triumph at the end represents the victory of reason over passion. Indeed, Ethelberta and her foil – her blushing and swooning younger sister Picotee – can almost be seen as a study in contrast of 'Sense' and 'Sensibility'.

Ethelberta shares with her creator her humble social origins, the individual talent which helps her to transcend her class, her consequent isolation, alienation and perhaps sense of guilt, and her literary aspirations which are threatened by financial insecurity. Like Hardy, Ethelberta is a poet by nature but, unlike him, she begins her career by publishing a volume of poems entitled *Metres by E.*[2] Like Hardy again, financial considerations force her hand and she reluctantly abandons poetry for prose narratives. She becomes a successful romancer, a public storyteller, and at the end of the novel we hear that she is engaged in composing an epic poem after having married a man forty years her senior. Her literary career closely parallels that of Hardy who began as a poet (although an unsuccessful and unpublished one), went on to become a major novelist and later reverted to his first love – poetry. Marrying, for the second time, a woman almost forty years his junior, Hardy would end his career by composing the epic drama *The Dynasts*.

At first sight, *The Hand of Ethelberta* seems to be almost a feminist novel, since Hardy allows Ethelberta to voice a trenchant critique of patriarchal society. Women, in such a restrictive and censorious society, are forced to have recourse to subterfuge, to adopt hypocrisy and not honesty as their policy for survival, to 'deny feeling in a society where no woman says what she means or does what she says' (p. 76). Ethelberta chafes at the constraints placed on her freedom of action as a woman in such a convention-bound patriarchal society. In the battle for survival the rules have already been laid down by men, and Ethelberta rebelliously tells her sister: 'don't you go believing in sayings, Picotee: they are all made by men, for their own advantages' (p. 153).[3] Men, by virtue of their sex, enjoy certain privileges denied to women, and Ethelberta feels this keenly when her London audiences thin away and Picotee suggests that she might take her storytelling performances to the provinces:

> 'A man in my position might perhaps do it with impunity; but I could not without losing ground in other domains… when it comes to starring in the provinces she establishes herself as a woman of a different breed and habit. I wish I were a man!' (p. 178)

What is unalterable in the world of reality can easily be altered in a world of make-believe. When Ethelberta authors her own fictional world, her heroine tries to gain a new freedom by cross-dressing. This desire to be a man, to arrogate the male privileges, makes Ethelberta herself almost 'masculine'.[4] The traditional equation of reason with masculinity and emotion with femininity is specially pertinent in Ethelberta's case as she tries to suppress all emotion and dispassionately plan her future. There are quite a few instances of gender reversal in this novel as when Ethelberta, 'immeasurably the stronger', presents a cool hand to her lover Christopher Julian whose hand is 'trembling with unmanageable excess of feeling' (p. 132). Also, as Mrs Petherwin, Ethelberta takes upon herself the paternal role of provider for her large Chickerel family and later, as Lady Mountclere, she becomes 'my lord and my lady both', controlling Lord Mountclere with an iron hand:

> ''tis a strange reverse for him. It is said that when he's asked out to dine, or to anything in the way of a jaunt, his eye flies across to hers afore he answers: and if her eye says yes, he says yes: and if her eye says no, he says no. 'Tis a sad condition for one who ruled womankind as he, that a woman should lead him in a string whether he will or no.' (p. 388)

For an aristocrat who once kept a series of resident mistresses on the premises, this is indeed a comedown. But Lord Mountclere's extreme dotage had already been prognosticated when he had ordered his fine elms (which he himself had planted as a boy) to be felled merely because Ethelberta had whimsically suggested that they blocked a potentially breathtaking sea-view. Ethelberta's power over Lord Mountclere had also been demonstrated in Rouen when she had marched haughtily up the 200-odd stairs of the tower with her elderly suitor slavishly following at her heels, despite his stiff joints and breathlessness. The complete reversal of roles in the Mountclere marriage is nowhere better symbolically anticipated than in the description of the archaeological expedition to Corvsgate Castle. After the lecture on the history of the ruined castle, most of the party disperse and:

> Lord Mountclere offered Ethelberta his arm on the ground of assisting her down the burnished grass slope. Ethelberta, having pity upon him, took it; but the assistance was all on her side; she stood like a statue amid his slips and totterings, some of which taxed her strength heavily, and her ingenuity more, to appear as the supported and not the supporter. (p. 245)

What is Hardy's attitude to such an '*un*womanly' woman? Does he approve of her assumption of male roles and her jettisoning of the traditional feminine virtues? 'Despite his apparent ambivalence as an impassive narrator,' says Richard Taylor, 'perhaps Hardy too was appalled by the possibilities latent in his creation.'[5] Finely balanced between identification and detachment, Hardy's ambivalence towards Ethelberta is perhaps best summed up by John Bayley:

> Hardy is too dispassionate about her, and in a curious way too much in practical earnest about what she might represent for him...[Ethelberta] is turned at the end into an enigmatic image of a woman who has become unknowable through her triumph. He has been too close to Ethelberta for her to be a proper heroine, but after her marriage to Lord Mountclere she is too far away to be imagined either by him or by us. Hardy seems to be wryly envisaging the possible effects on himself of his own social and literary success.[6]

Within the novel, the only indirect clue we have regarding Hardy's response to Ethelberta is the brief narrative comment: 'to have an unsexed judgment is as precious as to be an unsexed being is deplorable' (p. 84). Authorial judgement may also be obliquely reflected through a character such as Sol, who represents the native dignity of the honest workman. Hardy does not make Sol a butt of satiric ridicule, despite his inverted snobbery, as he probably secretly sympathizes with Sol's socialistic ideas. When Sol meets Ethelberta, after her hasty and secret marriage to Lord Mountclere, he is brutally outspoken:

> 'Berta, you have worked to false lines. A creeping up among the useless lumber of our nation that'll be the first to burn if there comes a flare. I never see such a deserter of your own lot as you be!...I am ashamed of 'ee. More than that, a good woman never marries twice.' (p. 366)

In the final chapter, when Christopher (a partial self-portrait of Hardy) catches a glimpse of Ethelberta in her Mountclere carriage, he stands 'a long time thinking; but he did not wish her his' (p. 389). Is this a case of grapes being sour or does it imply, at a deeper level, authorial censure and rejection of what Ethelberta has chosen to become? The question is pertinent because Hardy characterized himself as one who 'constitutionally shrank from the business of social advancement, caring for life as an emotion rather than for life as a science of climbing'.[7]

The Ethelberta who secretly visits Neigh's estate at Farnfield coldly to estimate his material worth as her suitor, or the Ethelberta who takes one look at Enckworth Court and dispassionately decides, 'How lovely!...His staircase alone is worth my hand!' (p. 293)[8] is admittedly not a very endearing specimen of womanhood. Her callous treatment of her suitors almost justifies D. H. Lawrence's comment that, in the end, 'she has nipped off the bud of her heart'.[9] But a careful reading of the text reveals that this is precisely what Ethelberta has been unable to do; and this is what ultimately saves her from being a Becky Sharp type of cold adventuress. The success of her schemes for her family's improvement depends on possessing a 'cold heart' (p. 217) but, much to her own surprise, she discovers that 'instead of being wholly machine [she] is half heart' (p. 295). This is something that Christopher too realizes as he has known her long enough to penetrate her mask of assumed indifference. When his sister Faith is critical of Ethelberta's public display of herself (as story-teller), Christopher defends her warmly: 'She has a heart, and the heart is a troublesome encumbrance when great things have to be done' (p. 130). Perhaps Christopher as a lover is a prejudiced and unreliable commentator, but Ethelberta's own actions speak louder than words. Although Christopher's gift of the musical score of 'Cancelled Words' (he has set one of her poems to music) is still capable of reducing her to sentimental tears, her 'jealous motherly guard' (p. 169) over Picotee prompts her to extract a promise from Lord Mountclere (as a precondition of agreeing to be his wife) that he will do all in his power to bring about a union between Picotee and Christopher.[10] Perhaps the most touching revelation of Ethelberta's failure to cut out her heart is the episode where she sits up at night hemming anew her sister Myrtle's damaged frock, after cutting out an inch all round at the bottom, because she has promised her young sister that the burn in the hem of her frock would disappear if only she would stop crying and go to bed. Buying a new dress would be an easy option; but not having the spare money for it, Ethelberta nevertheless has the tenderness of sisterly affection to sit up and patiently repair the damaged frock.

Is such a girl emotionally fulfilled in either of the two marriages – to a young boy and an old man – which frame her life story? Her marriage to young Petherwin is too cryptically narrated for us to form any clear opinion. Her love for him and his premature death do not seem to have left much of an impression on her. Her words of expostulation to her mother-in-law are admittedly quite cold:

'Dear Lady Petherwin – don't be so unreasonable as to blame a live person for living! No woman's head is so small as to be filled for life by a memory of a few months. Over three years have passed since I last saw my boy-husband. We were mere children…Two years will exhaust the regrets of widows who have long been faithful wives; and ought I not to show a little new life when my husband died in the honeymoon?' (p. 98)

There is also an air of ambiguity about her relationship with Christopher. Indications are that a romantic understanding between them predated her runaway marriage with young Petherwin. What caused the rupture between Ethelberta and Christopher is left deliberately vague and unexplained. Did Ethelberta shrewdly realize that Christopher, as a man lacking ambition and drive, was steadily going down the socio-economic incline and that the only son and heir of a 'just knighted' gentleman was a better social prospect? We are left guessing about Ethelberta's motives here, as elsewhere throughout the novel, because as Millgate points out:

her 'true' personality proves finally elusive – perhaps even to Hardy himself, though the deliberate indirection of the final view of her seems not so much an evasion of difficulty as a conscious choice of ambiguity, a decision to rest with the enigma.[11]

But there can be no ambiguity regarding the character of Lord Mountclere. A dissipated old aristocrat, with unnamed sexual secrets, he is repeatedly associated with the epithet 'sly'. Ethelberta's impression of him is that 'the dignified aspect which he wore to a gazer at a distance became depreciated to jocund slyness upon nearer view' (p. 240). Later, at the railway station, Ethelberta's earlier impression is confirmed as she notices 'an old yet sly' (p. 258) Englishman attended by his valet. When Lord Mountclere meets with a slight accident due to the overturning of his carriage, Christopher is at hand to help him. Christopher too characterizes the unknown gentleman as 'a sly old dog apparently' (p. 290). The narrator, describing Lord Mountclere's face, says that it presented a 'combination of slyness and jocundity' (p. 316) and when he silently follows Ethelberta through the streets of

Melchester, he is said to creep 'as stealthily as a worm into a skull' (p. 307). The unnaturalness of his pursuit and his ultimate marriage with Ethelberta is obliquely commented upon by the hostler in his rebuke to the milkman at the beginning of the novel:

> 'Michael, a old man like you ought to think about other things, and not be looking two ways at your time of life. Pouncing upon young flesh like a carrion crow – 'tis a vile thing in a old man.' (p. 34)

The image evoked by the last line strongly reminds us of Volpone's pursuit of Celia (*Volpone*, III. vii) but while Jonson leaves us in no doubt about the identities of the predator and the victim, Hardy is more ambivalent. In a remarkably proleptic image in the opening chapter of the novel, we first see Ethelberta forgetting her queenly bearing and running impulsively across the heath to watch the final outcome of a life-and-death struggle between a duck and a duck-hawk. The duck finally succeeds in escaping its pursuer by exploiting its skill in diving and staying under the water, and resurfacing at unexpected points of the pond, thus frustrating the duck-hawk. The image of the 'chase' is significant in a novel preoccupied with Ethelberta's 'man-hunt'. But here the identities are somewhat blurred: to see Ethelberta as the duck/victim and Lord Mountclere as the duck-hawk/predator would be too simplistic, and such a one-to-one equation would fail to do justice to a novel that explores the complexities of sex and class relations. As Boumelha shrewdly observes:

> it might be tempting to see here some exemplum such as how male strength can be evaded by the quick-wittedness of the female. But Ethelberta's active role in her own story forbids us such easy recourse to notions of predation and victimage, and we need in particular to remember that it is Ethelberta rather than her male suitors who displays superior strength.[12]

However, the temptation to see Ethelberta as the duck who *fails* to escape is very strong. When Ethelberta finally tries to withdraw her promise of marriage to Lord Mountclere, the terse narrative comment reveals how hopelessly (self?)trapped she is: 'Was ever a thrush so safe in a cherry net before!' (p. 305).

Ethelberta's belated attempt to extricate herself from Lord Mountclere's grasp takes the form of a desperate physical flight on the very
night of her wedding. Stung by the discovery that Lord Mountclere
has a resident mistress, she requests her brother Sol to wait at night
with a carriage to help her escape under cover of darkness. At the
appointed hour, Ethelberta quietly slips out and as the carriage
speeds away with her in it, she thinks she has made good her escape.
But, by a brilliant counter-move, Lord Mountclere has outwitted her
and Ethelberta discovers to her horror and dismay that the dark figure in the carriage, whom she had assumed to be Sol, is none other
than her 'sly' husband. Ethelberta knows herself to be checkmated
and she accepts her defeat with as good a grace as she can summon
under the circumstances. Adept, by now, at playing roles and hiding
her real emotions, she quickly recovers her composure and can even
congratulate Lord Mountclere on his 'masterly' counter-stratagem.
But the emotion that she represses is expressed in the unequivocal
narrative comment:

> Ethelberta might have fallen dead with the shock, so terrible and
> hideous was it. Yet she did not. She neither shrieked nor fainted;
> but no poor January fieldfare was ever colder, no ice-house more
> dank with perspiration, than she was then. (p. 381)

When Lord Mountclere then takes over her story-telling role and
gleefully narrates how he deftly intercepted her note to Sol, how he
cunningly changed the time and venue of the appointment and so
arranged matters that unwittingly the 'good wife rushed into the
arms of her husband', Ethelberta bursts out laughing.[13] But, as the
narrator tells us, it is 'laughter which had a wild unnatural sound; it
was hysterical. She sank down upon the leaves, and there continued the fearful laugh just as before' (p. 383). Does the duck escape
the duck-hawk after all?

Ethelberta herself has no illusions about her marriage to Lord
Mountclere. She tries to justify it to herself and sits up at night reading Mill's *Utilitarianism* in order to rationalize her decision. In her
earlier dithering over whether to accept or reject Neigh the question
that had haunted her had been: 'Would the advantage that might
accrue to her people by her marriage be worth the sacrifice?' (p.
212). That Christopher is the only man for whom she genuinely
cares is obvious enough. But to marry a struggling musician, who

barely keeps himself and his sister afloat, is out of the question. 'What she contemplated was not merely to ensnare a husband just to provide incomes for her and her family, but to find some man she might respect' (p. 212). Is Lord Mountclere such a man? Even on the eve of the wedding, Ethelberta herself has serious misgivings and makes a rare confession to Picotee: 'I have had a thought – why I cannot tell – that as much as this man brings to me in rank and gifts he may take out of me in tears' (p. 340). The reaction of Ethelberta's family and friends to this marriage is hardly encouraging. Her father, her brother Sol, her ex-lover Christopher, all react with horror because they have heard notorious reports of Lord Mountclere's past aberrations and excesses. 'I always said that pride would lead Berta to marry an unworthy man, and so it has!' (p. 356) is Sol's bitter comment when he arrives too late to prevent the marriage. Even more bitter are the words her father utters: 'I would almost sooner have had it that in leaving this church I came from her grave' (p. 356).

Despite Hardy's 'fundamental ambivalence in the presentation of his heroine',[14] it is possible to guess what he felt about this marriage. If we accept that Christopher is a partial self-portrait of Hardy, then Christopher's comment when he first hears of the projected union with Lord Mountclere has the added weight of authorial judgement. Disturbed on hearing news of the impending marriage, Christopher tells his sister: 'I should think her guardian angel must have quitted her when she agreed to a marriage which may tear her heart out like a claw' (p. 318). In a novel where Fate, Chance, Providence, or President of the Immortals are conspicuous by their absence, this reference to a suprahuman force controlling (or failing to safeguard) human life is very significant. But since the novel is a 'comedy', and since Ethelberta does not evoke 'the sympathy which Hardy extends to Bathsheba, Tess and Sue',[15] Christopher's comment lacks the passionate indignation and tragic resonance that a similar reference was to have in a later novel. Emotionally committed to his heroine, Tess's violation by Alec would move Hardy to question bitterly: 'where was Tess's guardian angel? where the providence of her simple faith? Perhaps...he was in a journey, or he was sleeping and not to be awaked.'[16]

If Ethelberta had not been framed by a comic narrative, then the near-tragic potential in her character would have been explored. There is in Ethelberta a bitter world-weariness that is very surprising in one so young and dynamic. Burdened with the self-imposed responsibility of caring for her large family, she is often weary of the constant struggle; and when 'the Hamlet mood [is] upon her' (p. 269) her lack of personal ambition is quite evident. As she confides to her mother:

> 'If I stood alone, I would go and hide my head in any hole, and care no more about the world and its ways. I wish I was well out of it, and at the bottom of a quiet grave.' (p. 175)

Quite often, when her plans go awry, the narrator tells us that:

> when the futility of her great undertaking was more than usually manifest, did Ethelberta long like a tired child for the conclusion of the whole matter; when her work should be over, and the evening come; when she might draw her boat upon the shore, and in some thymy nook await eternal night with a placid mind. (p. 210)

Frustration and the fear of failure breed in Ethelberta a defeatism that has a touch of Swiftian savagery:

> 'Yet I wish I could get a living by some simple humble occupation, and drop the name of Petherwin, and be Berta Chickerel again, and live in a green cottage as we used to do when I was small. I am miserable to a pitiable degree sometimes, and sink into regrets that I ever fell into such a groove as this...I begin to have a fear that mother is right when she implies that I undertook to carry out visions and all. But ten of us are so many to cope with. If God Almighty had only killed off three-quarters of us when we were little, a body might have done something for the rest; but as we are it is hopeless!' (p. 217)

In a rare moment of unburdening her soul, she confesses to her father:

> 'Father, I cannot endure this kind of existence any longer. I sleep at night as if I had committed murder: I start up and see processions of people, audiences, battalions of lovers obtained under false pretences – all denouncing me with the finger of ridicule...I am sick of ambition. My only longing now is to fly from society altogether, and go to any hovel on earth where I could be at peace.' (p. 282)

This concatenation of disturbed sleep, of seeing ghosts with their accusing fingers pointed at her, of a desire to escape from the battlefield of ambition, all remind us of a tragic protagonist who has indeed committed murder: Macbeth.[17] For Ethelberta, as for Macbeth, there is now no turning back, because: 'Returning were as tedious as go o'er' (*Macbeth*, III. iv. 137). Although in a light moment Ethelberta cavalierly compares life to a game of chess – 'there is no seriousness in it; it may be put an end to at any inconvenient moment by owning yourself beaten, with a careless "Haha!"' (p. 136) – in her more sober moments she knows that she has to carry on the fight till the bitter end: 'But, having once put my hand to the plough, how shall I turn back?' (p. 178). Even if she does desire to turn back and give up the struggle on her own account, there are others (like her father) to remind her: 'Having put your hand to the plough, it will be foolish to turn back' (p. 217). Thus Ethelberta, like Macbeth, is truly the bear tied to the stake. Being a successful illusionist herself, Ethelberta produces the illusion of free choice but she is as much a victim of the 'plot' that she herself has authored as Tess is the victim of the plot that Hardy has authored.

*The Hand of Ethelberta* does indeed anticipate *Tess* in the triangular relationship between Ethelberta, Christopher, and Picotee in the comic novel and that between Tess, Angel, and 'Liza-Lu in the tragic novel. Ethelberta's generous championship of Picotee's cause, when she discovers her sister's 'secret', foreshadows the famous Stonehenge scene where Tess urges Angel to marry 'Liza-Lu and begin life afresh. Picotee's feelings are far too complicated, because she is pulled in opposite directions between her one-sided (and undeclared) love for Christopher and her affectionate loyalty to her sister. As the narrator neatly sums up:

> What Picotee hoped in the centre of her heart as to the issue of the affair it would be too complex a thing to say. If Christopher became cold towards her sister he would not come to the house; if he continued to come it would really be as Ethelberta's lover – altogether, a pretty game of perpetual check for Picotee. (p. 148)

On the eve of Ethelberta's marriage to Lord Mountclere, Picotee has qualms of conscience which prompt her to put a crucial question to Ethelberta: 'Berta, I am sometimes uneasy about you even now, and I want to ask you one thing, if I may. Are you doing this for my sake?

Would you have married Mr Julian if it had not been for me?' (p. 340) Although Ethelberta (quite characteristically) returns an evasive and equivocal reply, we have the narrator's assurance quite early in the novel that Ethelberta's 'foremost feeling was less one of hope for her own love than of champion-ship for Picotee's' (p. 169). Thus, when Ethelberta and Christopher decide that their ways must part, her words of farewell to him are: 'Care for us both equally!' Unwilling to sever the last link,

> Ethelberta at once said, in a last futile struggle against letting him go altogether, and with thoughts of her sister's heart:
> 'I think that Picotee might correspond with Faith; don't you, Mr Julian?' (p. 182)

Here Ethelberta is playing a benevolent Providence for at the end of the novel when Christopher finally proposes to Picotee, he confesses that it 'has been an instance of loving by means of letters' (p. 392). He had read the letters Faith regularly received from Picotee and gradually 'got more interested in the writer than in her news' – which is perhaps what Ethelberta had hoped all along.

Although Picotee's own marriage will be rather humdrum and low-key, she vicariously enjoys the 'glory' of Ethelberta's grand marriage to a peer. She rhapsodizes over Ethelberta's future 'jewels', 'horses and carriages', and 'footmen', and is quite disappointed when Ethelberta tells her that she will live very quietly without the usual dinners, travels, and jaunts to the city common to one of her station. 'Will you not be, then, as any other peeress; and shall not I be as any other peeress's sister?' (p. 311) is a fairly disturbing question. Will Picotee, under Ethelberta's influence, develop into a second Ethelberta? There is an incipient snobbery in her words to Sol when he comes to visit Ethelberta immediately after her marriage to Lord Mountclere: 'You need not come near the front apartments, if you think we shall be ashamed of you in your working clothes. How came you not to dress up a bit, Sol?' (p. 363)

Picotee's assumption of the plural 'we' here identifies her with Ethelberta's social mobility. But although the gradient of Ethelberta's social climb is undoubtedly a regular upward graph, there is a deliberate ambivalence about her emotional/moral progress. Hardy himself tantalizingly raises the question through his narrator: 'Was the moral incline upward or down?' (p. 286) It is a crucial question but one which Hardy himself refused to answer; he 'deliberately left unresolved the question of whether, for Ethelberta herself, achieved ambition also represents achieved happiness'.[18] In the final chapter of the novel, Ethelberta is no longer centre-stage and we hear reports of her married life with Lord Mountclere from an anonymous driver and from Picotee. We are told that Ethelberta has succeeded in taming Lord Mountclere, in gaining control over his estates and finances, in short, of becoming 'my lord and my lady both'. But, surely, marital felicity is not just a question of who wears the trousers in the family or who controls the bank account. Hardy's non-committal attitude to Lady Mountclere almost prompts us to echo Auden's ironic questioning at the end of his poem celebrating 'The Unknown Citizen':

Was he free? Was he happy? The question is absurd:
Had anything been wrong, we should certainly have heard.[19]

But something is patently wrong, if only we pick up the right clues. Ethelberta after two years of marriage, Picotee informs Christopher, 'lives mostly in the library...She is writing an epic poem' (p. 391). Most critics have seen in this a comforting assurance that Ethelberta's cynical marriage of convenience has not dried up her literary inspiration, and her return to poetry after prose is seen as a welcome resurgence of emotion from the domination of reason. This, hopefully, may be the case; but what is vaguely disturbing is the earlier part of the sentence: 'lives mostly in the library'. That a young wife should find the library the most congenial part of the house and the company of books infinitely more preferable than the company of her viscount-husband insinuates that all is not 'plain sailing' on the marital/emotional front. We are reminded strongly of Jane Austen's Mr Bennet who, similarly, withdraws from life and (rather selfishly) makes the library his refuge after being bitterly disillusioned about marriage in general and his inane wife in particular. Does Ethelberta too shut herself up in the library in order to escape the company of Lord Mountclere? Before the marriage, expatiating on the richness of the Enckworth library, with its quartos and folios and 'literature from Moses down to Scott', Ethelberta had tried to reassure Picotee (and herself?) that 'with such companions I can do without all other sorts of happiness' (p. 311).

Hardy calls *The Hand of Ethelberta* 'A Comedy in Chapters' and it succeeds in being a comedy only because he persistently refuses to investigate 'the deeper implications of the conclusion'.[20] At one point in the novel, Ethelberta says: 'In a world where the blind only are cheerful we should all do well to put out our eyes' (p. 340). In this novel named after her, Hardy is doing precisely this: he is deliberately blinding himself to the near-tragic implications of his plot and protagonist because he knows that '[a]ll comedy, is tragedy, if you only look deep enough into it'.[21] As he later recorded in his disguised autobiography: 'If you look beneath the surface of any farce you see a tragedy; and, on the contrary, if you blind yourself to the deeper issues of a tragedy you see a farce.'[22] Again, in a letter to J. B. Priestley, Hardy showed his awareness of 'the tragedy that always underlies Comedy if you only scratch it deeply enough'.[23] In *The Hand of Ethelberta* Hardy chose to 'blind [himself] to the deeper issues' and he refrained from scratching the surface of the comedy to reveal the tragic substratum. In his next novel, *The Return of the Native*, despite the temporary physical blindness of Clym Yeobright, Hardy himself would remain unflinchingly clear-eyed as to the tragic possibilities of love, marriage, and social ambition.

# 3
# The Return of the Native

It is one of the ironies of Hardy's life that the phase he himself described as '[o]ur happiest time' and as the 'Sturminster Newton idyll'[1] produced the first great tragic novel of his literary career, *The Return of the Native* (1878). In this novel Hardy explores, in reverse direction, the problem of deracination. If Ethelberta is 'an uprooted native of Wessex' who seeks to escape from her native origins, Clym is the uprooted native who seeks to return. As a 'thinly veiled autobiography' (Hardy himself repeatedly returned to his native Dorset), *The Return of the Native* is 'an extension of the confessional impulse discernible in *The Hand of Ethelberta*'.[2] Thus the transition from urban comedy in *The Hand of Ethelberta* to rural tragedy in *The Return of the Native* is not as abrupt as it seems; and in the heroines of these two novels it is possible to detect a line of descent from Ethelberta's 'unmoral pursuit of power and wealth' to Eustacia's 'unmoral pursuit of pleasure'.[3] That Eustacia was originally conceived within a moral framework becomes clear from the plot outline that Hardy sent to Arthur Hopkins who illustrated the serial version of the novel in *Belgravia*:

> Perhaps it is well for me to give you the following ideas of the story as a guide – Thomasin, as you have divined, is the *good* heroine, & she ultimately marries the reddleman, & lives happily. Eustacia is the wayward & erring heroine – She marries Yeobright, the son of Mrs Yeobright, is unhappy, & dies.[4] Hardy's italic)

Hardy's polarization of Eustacia and Thomasin (continued by most critics) in terms of such rigid moral absolutes blurs some basic affinities between these two young women which are worth emphasizing. The critical tradition associates Thomasin with 'submissiveness not imperiousness, docility not fervour, amiability not anger, demureness not passion'.[5] Conversely, Eustacia is seen as the Promethean and Byronic rebel who is 'emblematic of the feeling and infinite desire which rebel against inevitable limitation'.[6] But what has not been recognized and therefore needs to be stressed is that passion and rebelliousness are not unique to Eustacia. Initially, at least, Thomasin is equally as capable of romantic defiance when she runs away to marry Wildeve after her aunt explicitly forbids the banns publicly in church. In her own quiet but firm way, Thomasin also rejects her aunt's cherished plan of a marriage between Clym and herself, although she is still living under her aunt's protection and although Wildeve's reluctance to solemnize their marriage has placed her in a compromised position.

Again, in the present form of the novel, both Eustacia and Thomasin are orphans.[7] Eustacia lives with her grandfather who seems unconcerned about her welfare, and Thomasin lives with her aunt whose domineering nature is equally damaging. Interestingly enough, in the original conception of the novel, Captain Vye (originally named Captain Drew) was to have been Eustacia's *father* and Mrs Yeobright was to have been Thomasin's *mother*.[8] By revising his original conception and making Captain Vye Eustacia's grandfather and Mrs Yeobright Thomasin's aunt, Hardy was not only in effect orphaning these two young girls but also, on the more positive side, freeing them from potentially tyrannical parental control. Both Eustacia and Thomasin are thus granted more individual autonomy, greater freedom of choice and, as responsible agents, they can now conduct their lives without constricting parental authority.

But, as one early reviewer pointed out, Eustacia 'has no feeling... that such a thing as responsibility exists'.[9] To Eustacia, the 'mockery of her hopes' seems to be a 'satire of Heaven'[10] and not the logical outcome of her own free choice. Thus when she fails to respond to Mrs Yeobright's knocking, due to a complex mixture of reasons, she refuses to recognize her moral culpability: 'Yet, instead of blaming herself for the issue she laid the fault upon the shoulders of some indistinct, colossal Prince of the World, who had framed her situation and ruled her lot' (p. 304). With her penchant for self-dramatization she can even see herself as a tragic heroine trapped in the toils of a sadistic super-power: 'Eustacia could now, like other people at such a stage, take a standing-point outside herself, observe herself as a disinterested spectator, and think what a sport for Heaven this woman Eustacia was' (p. 343). Her bitter words just prior to her drowning reveal the same frame of mind – that of a passive victim roused to indignant protest at the injustice latent in the scheme of things:

> 'How I have tried and tried to be a splendid woman, and how destiny has been against me!...I do not deserve my lot!...O, the

cruelty of putting me into this ill-conceived world! I was capable
of much; but I have been injured and blighted and crushed by
things beyond my control! O, how hard it is of Heaven to devise
such tortures for me, who have done no harm to Heaven at all!'[11]
(p. 357)

Eustacia's view of herself as victim of a cruel destiny is also echoed
by her lover Wildeve. Meeting her accidentally after her life is blasted by Clym's blindness and obstinate refusal to leave Egdon, Wildeve
commiserates: 'I sincerely sympathize with you in your trouble. Fate
has treated you cruelly' (p. 272). Later, when he visits her on the fateful day of Mrs Yeobright's visit, he reiterates his sympathy: 'The fates
have not been kind to you, Eustacia Yeobright' (p. 289). The narrator
too seems to endorse this view of Eustacia in a thinly veiled expression of authorial sympathy:

The gloomy corner into which accident as much as indiscretion
had brought this woman might have led even a moderate partisan
to feel that she had cogent reasons for asking the Supreme Power
by what right a being of such exquisite finish had been placed in
circumstances calculated to make of her charms a curse rather than
a blessing. (pp. 267-8)

But a total surrender of individual volition is inimical to genuine tragic status and Hardy, well versed in classical Greek and Shakespearean
tragedy, knew that 'anagnorisis' or (self)-recognition was indispensable for a tragic protagonist. Thus he grants Eustacia her rare
moments of insight, as when she warns Clym prophetically before
their marriage: 'Yet I know we shall not love like this always. Nothing
can ensure the continuance of love. It will evaporate like a spirit, and
so I feel full of fears' (p. 212). Fearing that she will only 'ruin' Clym,
she honestly admits: 'Sometimes I think there is not that in Eustacia
Vye which will make a good homespun wife' (p. 214). Later, when
Wildeve openly expresses his envy of Clym for his 'one great gift',
Eustacia has the grace not to pretend to misunderstand and fish for
compliments. With admirable directness, she says quietly: 'Well, I am
a questionable gift' (p. 289). Such moments of honesty bring Eustacia
down from the tragic pedestal to which both she and her creator arti-
ficially seek to elevate her; but, paradoxically, they also win for her
respect and sympathy as a tortured human being.

Throughout this novel, where Eustacia replaces the nominal hero Clym as the focus of interest[12] (anticipating Sue's displacement of Jude), there is a tension between two irreconcilable images of Eustacia. On one hand, classical allusions to Titans and goddesses, recurrent use of Promethean fire-imagery, self-consciously inflated rhetoric, all seek to build her up as a tragic 'Queen of Night'. Conversely, stripped of her grand pretensions, Eustacia is exposed as an essentially 'selfish and self-deceiving girl', 'an arrogant, willful creature, prey to unhealthy melancholy, self-pity and caprice'.[13] But this double perspective, far from being a flaw in conceptualization of character, actually represents Hardy's ambivalent feelings towards romantic aspiration. Eustacia represents the principle of 'individualism' and although 'something in Hardy approved of her', his 'feelings towards Eustacia were ambivalent, and he could not totally accept or reject her. He was unable, intellectually and emotionally, to commit himself for or against the principle he made Eustacia represent.'[14]

Eustacia, as Hardy originally conceived her, was a less complex character, calling forth a less complex response from her creator. As the demonic 'she devil Avice'[15] in the Ur-novel, Eustacia/ Avice was more the antagonist than the tragic protagonist, and her witch-like persecution of the 'good' Thomasin would not have made any great demands on the sympathetic interest of either author or reader. Vestiges of this original character conception survive figuratively in the novel in its final 1912 revised form. When her bonfire summons Wildeve to her side, Eustacia herself triumphantly compares her feat to 'the Witch of Endor call[ing] up Samuel' (p. 87). The rustic Egdon folk too think of her as 'the lonesome dark-eyed creature up there that some say is a witch' (p. 75). Although Susan Nunsuch limits herself to 'she is very strange in her ways' (p. 56), she will not only later prick Eustacia's arm in church but also burn her wax effigy because this over-anxious and ignorant mother superstitiously believes that Eustacia is bewitching her son Johnny and making him ill. Clym, too, in his frenzied state of guilt and remorse over his mother's death, compares her to 'a devil' (p. 330), and in that fatal scene of quarrel with Eustacia he bitterly laments: 'How bewitched I was! How could there be any good in a woman that everybody spoke ill of?' (p. 334). Determined to harden himself against her charms, he taunts her: 'Don't look at me with those eyes as if you would bewitch me again!' (p. 332)

This original Satanic Avice/Eustacia was radically transformed by Hardy's repeated textual revisions into a Promethean rebel whose titanic romantic aspirations drew forth Hardy's grudging sympathy and admiration. Investigating the implications of the several layers of textual revisions, Paterson sums up:

> The suppression of the diabolical Eustacia Vye and the emergence of the romantic heroine were clearly not essential to the bowdlerization of the Ur-novel. The modification of Thomasin's predicament could not have required, after all, so total a change in the nature of her antagonist. The truth seems rather to be that in the course of revising the Ur-chapters, Hardy discovered and indulged an *unconscious and even reluctant sympathy* with the demoniacal creature he had initially conceived. As the spokesman of a province whose roots were deeply imbedded in a traditional past, he was on the side of the Thomasin Yeobrights and Diggory Venns, who accepted the injustice of the cosmic administration without a murmur, but as the man who had gone to London and discovered the century of Shelley and Swinburne, he was also on the side of those who refused, like Eustacia Vye, to come to terms with it. Her transfiguration from satanic antagonist to romantic protagonist suggests, then, that what began as a bowdlerization developed spontaneously into a free and creative revaluation, the effect of which was to reverse the fundamental values of the novel.[16] (emphasis added)

Paterson's analysis of textual revisions gives us an insight into the process of creation and the shifts in authorial attitudes and intentions (although it is no longer fashionable to speak of 'authorial intention' in literary criticism today). Paterson's pioneering work has been supplemented by Gatrell's facsimile edition of the manuscript of *The Return of the Native*, which reveals that in the serial version, Hardy had affixed an epigraph to Chapter 10 of Book 1 which does not appear in subsequent versions of the novel but which is extremely significant as an index to Hardy's attitude to Eustacia in particular and womankind in general:

Woman oft has envy shown:
Pleased to ruin others' wooing,
Never happy in their own.[17]

Although Hardy removed this misogynic generalization, the attitude behind the lines survives in the narrative analyses of Eustacia's feelings towards Wildeve and Clym – the two men with whom she is seriously involved (for one can discount Charley with his one-sided boyish adoration). That envy and rivalry quicken her desire for Wildeve is something that Eustacia herself recognizes:

> Was it really possible that her interest in Wildeve had been so entirely the result of antagonism that the glory and the dream departed from the man with the first sound that he was no longer coveted by her rival? She was then secure of him at last. Thomasin no longer required him. What a humiliating victory!... what was the man worth whom a woman inferior to herself did not value? The sentiment which lurks more or less in all animate nature – that of not desiring the undesired of others – was lively as a passion in the supersubtle, epicurean heart of Eustacia. (pp. 121-2)

Again, apart from the seductive halo of Paris that surrounds Clym making him an object of infinite longing, Eustacia's infatuation for him is fanned by the thought of 'Thomasin, living day after day in inflammable proximity to him' (p. 163). Fears of being upstaged by Thomasin send a 'chill' through Eustacia's heart and make her regret that she had ever come between Thomasin and Wildeve. With Thomasin safely married to (a no longer desired) Wildeve, she would no longer pose a threat to Eustacia's romantic pursuit of Clym. Thus, on the night of the mumming, Eustacia feels:

> a wild jealousy of Thomasin on the instant. Though Thomasin might possibly have tender sentiments towards another man as yet, how long could they be expected to last when she was shut up here with this interesting and travelled cousin of hers? There was no knowing what affection might not soon break out between the two, so constantly in each other's society, and not a distracting object near. Clym's boyish love for her might have languished, but it might easily be revived again. (p. 161)

Here Eustacia is judging Thomasin by the yardstick of her own whimsical nature. In her case, the 'distracting object' Clym had displaced Wildeve in her affections, and she fears the same may happen with Thomasin because she cannot simply conceive of fidelity for fidelity's sake. To her, 'Love is the dismallest thing where the lover is quite honest' (p. 105). In fact, infidelity adds the necessary spice to her feelings for Wildeve initially:

The man who had begun by being merely her amusement, and would never have been more than her hobby but for his skill in deserting her at the right moments, was now again her desire. Cessation in his love-making had revivified her love. Such feeling as Eustacia had idly given to Wildeve was dammed into a flood by Thomasin. (p. 115)

The language of this narrative gloss ('amusement', 'hobby', 'idly') and the manifest irony at Eustacia's expense do not argue for much authorial sympathy. More damaging to Eustacia's status as a tragic heroine is a narrative comment which is passed off as being the articulation of Eustacia's consciousness: 'And the discovery that she was the owner of a disposition so purely that of the dog in the manger, had something in it which at first made her ashamed' (p. 123). Hardy's use of the reductive 'dog-in-the-manger' image is both conscious and deliberate. Equally deliberate is his use of Shakespearean echoes which he hoped his readers would pick up. In a conscious parallel with *King Lear*, not only does he provide Mrs Yeobright with a heath, a hovel, a fool (Johnny Nunsuch), but he also puts into her mouth words which recall two famous speeches from the play which also concerns itself with filial relationships. After Mrs Yeobright has been denied access to Clym's house, she bitterly muses on her homeward journey: 'Can there be beautiful bodies without hearts inside?...I would not have done it against a neighbour's cat on such a fiery day as this!' (p. 294). Mrs Yeobright's wonder at the complete disjunction between external physical beauty and internal moral/emotional bankruptcy echoes Lear's arraignment of Regan in the mock-trial on the heath: 'Is there any cause in nature that make these hard hearts?' (*King Lear*, III. vi. 75-6). Cordelia too is shocked that her sisters could turn out their aged father on such a violent night:

Mine enemy's dog
Though he had bit me, should have stood that night
Against my fire.(*Lear*, IV. vii. 36-8)

Hardy must have been aware that Mrs Yeobright's bitter words
would associate Eustacia negatively in the readers' minds with
Lear's 'pelican' daughters – Regan and Goneril – but at no stage did
he revise this speech to tone down its damaging allusiveness.[18]
Earlier in the novel, trying to warn Clym off Eustacia, Mrs Yeobright had offered an incisive glimpse into Eustacia's character: 'Miss
Vye is to my mind too idle to be charming. I have never heard that
she is of any use to herself or to other people. Good girls don't get
treated as witches even on Egdon' (p. 196). While making allowances
for the jealousy of a possessive mother, it is nevertheless true that
Mrs Yeobright's verdict is borne out by later events. Eustacia is
always isolated and alienated from the heath-people and, almost
hating her fellow-creatures, she is never shown as being of any use
to anyone. But she constantly uses other people, exploiting their
romantic weakness for her, in order to further her narrow personal
ends. She uses Johnny to tend her bonfire, which is a lover's signal
to Wildeve; she is not above trading on her physical charms and
using Charley to gain a role in the mummers' play in order to catch
a glimpse of Clym; she sees Clym not so much as a human being but
as a key to unlock the glittering world of Paris; and although her
pride is deeply mortified, she agrees to use Wildeve's services in
fleeing from Egdon when her marriage finally breaks down.

However, too severe a censure of Eustacia is disarmed by the fact
(often forgotten) that she is only 19 – an age when it is not too unnatural to have one's head full of 'romantic nonsense' (as Captain Vye
complains). In the famous 'Queen of Night' chapter, the narrator for
once abandons his impersonality and betrays his loyalties: 'And so
we see our Eustacia – for at times she was not altogether unlovable'
(p. 94). The inclusive 'our' seems to endorse Patricia Stubbs's reading of Hardy's 'essential sympathy for the way Eustacia feels about
her cramped, empty life' and his 'compassion for Eustacia in her
dilemma'.[19] However, in its present version, this transparent expression of authorial sympathy is but a pale shadow of the original manuscript reading where, in more positive terms, Hardy had boldly
declared: 'And so we see our Eustacia – for she was lovable after all.'

This was corrected to 'for she was lovable sometimes' and later, in the first edition (1878), retreating from such an open avowal of commitment, Hardy changed the positive phrasing to a negative one: 'for she was not altogether unlovable'. The double negatives do not add up to a resounding positive and it is further diluted by the revision of the 1895 Uniform Edition, which reads: 'for at times she was not altogether unlovable'.[20]

Hedged about by qualifications, authorial sympathy for the heroine is almost refined out of existence and, later in the novel, Hardy allows himself only the most indirect expression of sympathy. Thus when physical infirmity and surrender of social ambition on Clym's part lead to a considerable cooling in their marital relations, we are told that:

> Eustacia's manner had become of late almost apathetic. There was a forlorn look about her beautiful eyes which, whether she deserved it or not, would have excited pity in the breast of any one who had known her during the full flush of her love for Clym. (p. 266)

Readers of Hardy who are familiar with this indirect narrative strategy realize that 'any one' includes both author and reader in a common humanity. Later, on that fateful night of the storm when Eustacia meets her death, Hardy is not satisfied with just invoking the powerful emotional connotations of 'the agony in Gethsemane'. Drawing Eustacia within the fold of common human sympathy, in the same impersonal manner, his narrator says:

> Any one who had stood by now would have pitied her, not so much on account of her exposure to weather, and isolation from all of humanity... but for that other form of misery which was denoted by the slightly rocking movement that her feelings imparted to her person. Extreme unhappiness weighed visibly upon her. (p. 357)

Confronted with such extreme misery, our reaction can only be spontaneous sympathy; but there is a strange reluctance in Hardy to display any emotional commitment to his heroine. 'Hardy's ambivalent attitude towards her rebellion' produces 'the complex feelings of loss and waste, coupled with disapproval, which the reader experiences at her death'.[21] Hardy's ambivalence is reflected in his refusal to be explicit and to clarify two main issues relating to Eustacia: what is the precise nature of her pre-marital relationship with Wildeve and is her death an accident or a conscious suicidal choice? The prehistory of the Eustacia-Wildeve relationship is deliberately left vague and although, at their first meeting in the novel, Eustacia passionately accuses Wildeve of deserting her, later she acknowledges that he is not the sort of 'man to bear a jilt ill-will' (p. 306). Wildeve as deserter and Eustacia as jilt are impossible to reconcile and we assume that the truth lies somewhere in between. Again, Eustacia's bitter words to Wildeve during this meeting had been, in the first edition of 1878: 'deserted me entirely, as if I had never been yours'. This conveniently vague phrasing was elaborated by Hardy in the 1895 edition to: 'as if I had never been yours body and soul so irretrievably!' But fearing that he had been dangerously explicit, Hardy deleted the offending word 'body' and substituted the innocuous phrase 'life and soul so irretrievably!' in the 1912 edition.[22] Had this bowdlerization been occasioned by editorial pressure, for serial publication in a family magazine, Hardy's caution would be understandable. But in the relatively freer sexual climate of 1912, when his own reputation was already firmly established, why did Hardy change the bolder 1895 reading? One positive interpretation might be that Hardy deliberately chose to be ambiguous because he did not want his contemporary readers to take a judgemental stand towards Eustacia. If we know the precise nature of her past relation with Wildeve, then, in the scene of her bitter quarrel with Mrs Yeobright, we can decide whether her attitude of injured innocence and wifely indignation is genuine or just a clever pose. Perhaps Hardy wanted to secure for his heroine the benefit of the doubt.

Similarly, despite the opportunities offered by successive revisions of the text, Hardy refused to clarify the precise nature of Eustacia's death although it has important consequences in the evaluation of her character. Like Tess's violation by Alec (rape or seduction?), Eustacia's death by drowning could be variously interpreted. As a suicide, it can be seen as an act of Promethean defiance or as a guilt-ridden self-annihilation traditionally ascribed to the 'fallen woman'. As a tragic accident, it could signify the sheer futility of individual striving in an impersonal universe which finally triumphs over the non-conformists. Eustacia's death, like Tess's violation, occurs off-stage and Hardy is quite content to move:

back and forth between the traditional image of a vulnerable woman who drowns herself in despair and shame and the image of a strong, sexually-aware woman who, discontented with the cultural and moral *status quo* of her time, seeks death as a way out of social and sexual limitations.[23]

Unable or perhaps unwilling to decide whether Eustacia ranks with the 'Heloises' or the 'Cleopatras' of this world, the narrator compromises by suggesting that in heaven she will occupy a seat between these two prototypes. This same ambivalence can be seen in the presentation of Mrs Yeobright who is one of 'The Three Women' of the title of Book 1 of the novel. Her son Clym, obsessed by guilt and remorse after her death, almost canonizes her and nostalgically remembers her as a paragon of virtue:

'what goodness there was in her: it showed in every line of her face! Most women, even when but slightly annoyed, show a flicker of evil in some curl of the mouth or some corner of the cheek; but as for her, never in her angriest moments was there anything malicious in her look. She was angered quickly, but she forgave just as readily, and underneath her pride there was the meekness of a child.' (p. 333)

But the Mrs Yeobright who opposes Thomasin's marriage to both Diggory and Wildeve, and also Clym's marriage to Eustacia, does not exactly correspond to this sentimentalized and idealized portrait. As Paterson has demonstrated, Mrs Yeobright had been made of even sterner stuff in the original version but repeated revisions succeeded in softening down her unyielding rigidity and lack of charity.

Had Mrs Yeobright not publicly humiliated Wildeve by standing up in church and forbidding the banns, then perhaps Wildeve may not have retaliated by dragging his feet over his eventual marriage with Thomasin. Thomasin might thus have been spared a great deal of shame, misery and public gossip. There is also the suggestion that had she not opposed Diggory's original suit, Thomasin might have married him in the first place – as she eventually does – leaving the two romantic malcontents, Eustacia and Wildeve, to make a match of it. Thomasin's candid letter to Diggory in which she says 'I like you very much, and I always put you next to my cousin Clym in my mind' (p. 102) certainly suggests that a little more persuasion might have easily won her over, if only she did not have her aunt's displeasure to contend with.

Mrs Yeobright's interference thus changes the destiny of five young people who all seem to love at cross-purposes in typical Hardyan fashion. Her bitter opposition to Eustacia really hardens Clym in his resolve to marry her despite his mother's dire prognostications. Apprehensive of Eustacia's influence over Clym, Mrs Yeobright warns him: 'But when I consider the usual nature of the drag which causes men of promise to disappoint the world I feel uneasy' (p. 204). That these are not just the idle words of a jealously possessive mother is proved by the fact that the same idea was expressed in the narrative gloss which Hardy had prefixed to Chapter 1 of Book 3 in the serial version. In *Belgravia*, the prose summary of the action (or 'argument') of Book 3 read:

> The man & his scheme are fully described; & he begins his work. But a rencounter leads to emotions which *hamper his plans*, & cause a sharp divergence of opinion, ultimately committing him to an irretrievable step which a few months earlier he did not dream of.[24] (Emphasis added)

But Clym, in his refusal to listen to such prophecies of disaster, shuts not only his ears but also his eyes. If Eustacia is 'half in love with a vision' (p. 138), then so is Clym. He refuses to see Eustacia as the flesh-and-blood creature that she really is; instead he apotheosizes her into a semi-divinity whose dazzling radiance momentarily blinds him. Prefiguring his physical blindness is his figurative blindness, and the clear-eyed Mrs Yeobright bluntly tells him: 'You are blinded, Clym...It was a bad day for you when you first set eyes on her' (p. 209). Later, she laments to Thomasin: 'Sons must be blind if they will. Why is it that a woman can see from a distance what a man cannot see close?' (p. 228). The narrator too seems to endorse Mrs Yeobright's diagnosis and speaks of 'the first blinding halo kindled about [Clym] by love and beauty' (p. 216).

Although Clym is quite justly irritated and inclined to rebel against such a tyrannical matriarch, her death predictably reduces him to a state of uncritical adoration and he realizes that 'events had borne out the accuracy of her judgment, and proved the devotedness of her care. He should have heeded her for Eustacia's sake even more than for his own' (p. 404). Do we hear in these words of Clym (whom Casagrande calls 'a devastatingly critical self-portrait'[25]) the accents of regret of Clym's creator? For those who hold that Hardy's marriage to Emma was already deteriorating by 1878, these words might be an oblique reflection of Hardy's regret at having defied his mother in marrying Emma. This autobiographical speculation is not irrelevant because Hardy reportedly told Sydney Cockerell that Mrs Yeobright was modelled on his mother, Jemima.[26]

Also, when Hardy drew a map and published it as the frontispiece to the 1878 edition of the novel, the location of Clym's house as marked on the map of fictional Wessex almost exactly corresponded to the position of Hardy's birthplace at Higher Bockhampton.[27] Later, when busy revising his novels and correcting proofs for the 1912 'Wessex Edition', Hardy had commented: 'I got to like the character of Clym before I had done with him. I think he is the nicest of all my heroes, and *not a bit* like me' (Hardy's italics).[28] The very defensiveness of the comment should alert the reader to recognize how much Hardy invested in Clym – much more, in fact, than he would have liked to admit. Disavowals in Hardy are usually in inverse proportion to biographical truth and it is therefore reasonable to assume that in Clym, especially in his mother-obsession,[29] there is much of Hardy himself. Through Clym's love-hate relationship with Mrs Yeobright Hardy may be expressing his ambivalent feelings towards his mother: admiration, loyalty and gratitude for her devoted and protective care warring against suppressed resentment at her tendency to assume dictatorial control over her children's lives.

Although Mrs Yeobright's obstinate opposition to all marriage partners for Clym and Thomasin seems rather perverse, her instinctive wisdom – in recognizing Wildeve's unsuitability as Thomasin's husband and the essential incompatibility of Clym and Eustacia – is uncannily prophetic. Her motives may be suspect but her forecasts are accurate. In her Cassandra-like utterances of disaster, she goes unheard till events finally vindicate her. Sympathy for her starts building up after Clym leaves her; in her abandoned and lonely existence she might have pleaded, more justifiably than Eustacia, that the tragedy of her life is: 'want of an object to live for' (p. 145).

The centre of her life has always been her only offspring Clym (she regrets that she had not remarried and had other children to absorb her love), and after Clym marginalizes her, life ceases to have any meaning. Her movement towards death has a tragic inevitability which is heightened by the parallels with another child-forsaken parent, Lear. Sympathy for Mrs Yeobright's maimed existence is indirectly expressed through a remarkable piece of 'pathetic fallacy'. In her long journey towards Clym's house, in the hope of being reconciled, Mrs Yeobright sits down to recuperate her strength and courage:

> The trees beneath which she sat were singularly battered, rude, and wild, and for a few minutes Mrs Yeobright dismissed thoughts of her own storm-broken and exhausted state to contemplate theirs. Not a bough in the nine trees which composed the group but was splintered, lopped, and distorted by the fierce weather that there held them at its mercy whenever it prevailed. Some were blasted and split as if by lightning, black stains as from fire marking their sides, while the ground at their feet was strewn with dead fir-needles and heaps of cones blown down in the gales of past years…On the present heated afternoon, when no perceptible wind was blowing, the trees kept up a perpetual moan which one could hardly believe to be caused by the air. (p. 286)

Mrs Yeobright's transcendence of individual suffering in contemplating the blasted trees round her anticipates that famous scene where Tess forgets her own misery when confronted with the excruciating physical agony of the wounded pheasants. But within the novel, this scene echoes another powerfully symbolic landscape through which Clym passes when he sets out to find a separate house for himself and his future wife:

> Here the trees… were now suffering more damage… The wet young beeches were undergoing amputations, bruises, cripplings, and harsh lacerations, from which the wasting sap would bleed for many a day to come, and which would leave scars visible till the day of their burning. Each stem was wrenched at the root…. convulsive sounds came from the branches, as if pain were felt (p. 224)

This is not a gratuitous piece of nature description and we are meant to realize that Clym too is 'wrenched at the root'. His close relationship with his mother has been likened to 'the right and the left hands of the same body' (p. 205) and, when he tears himself away, this organic dismemberment is reflected in the mutilations in the world of nature. Garson, in her exhaustive analysis of the 'somatic imagery' in this novel,[30] fails to pick up these two powerful instances of bodily disintegration which are crucial in defining the mother-son bond at the heart of the novel. However, the rhetoric of these two passages is much in excess of the fictional situation and it suggests that in the Clym-Mrs Yeobright relationship Hardy was indirectly working out some private guilt over real or imagined filial betrayal.

Both Mrs Yeobright and Eustacia achieve through the heightened descriptions of their deaths a dignity and tragic grandeur that they had hardly attained in life. This transfiguration through death is something that is denied to Thomasin – the only survivor of 'the three women' at the novel's centre. Our first glimpse of Thomasin is when Diggory and Mrs Yeobright enter the reddleman's van and the lantern's rays fall on the face of the sleeping girl. Diggory has been accused of voyeurism but here, at least, Hardy is using Diggory and Mrs Yeobright as convenient camera lenses to focus on Thomasin, instead of using his usual formula of the ubiquitous and impersonal 'observer' who is made to notice and record things on behalf of the omniscient narrator. The light of the lantern reveals an 'honest country face… between pretty and beautiful' (p. 63). Diggory compares her to a frightened 'doe' in her distress after her failed marriage attempt, and the narrator compares her to birds in her various moods: a musing kestrel, a frightened kingfisher, a blithe swallow. To Clym 'that sweet voice of hers' (p. 316) comes like a soothing draught of fresh air after he recovers from his delirium, and this 'sweet' voice is heard repeatedly at crisis points in the narrative: urging Mrs Yeobright to forget the bitter quarrel and initiate a reconciliation with Clym and his wife, encouraging Clym to be more generous to Eustacia (her ex-rival) and prompting him to write a letter of apology and forgiveness in order to end their separation.

Even Wildeve, susceptible as ever to Eustacia's attraction, grudgingly concedes that Thomasin is a 'confoundedly good little woman', and he wishes he could be faithful to Eustacia without 'injuring a worthy person' – his wife 'Tamsie' (p. 105). Caught between two conflicting loyalties, Wildeve decides that it is possible to act generously towards his 'gentle wife' and with 'chivalrous devotion towards another and greater woman' (p. 369).[31] The grief of this 'gentle girl', in her widowhood, wakes Clym out of the stupor of apathy into which he had sunk following the deaths of Eustacia and Wildeve. Remembering his mother's cherished hope of a marriage between the cousins, Clym:

> could not help feeling that it would be a pitiful waste of sweet material if the tender-natured thing should be doomed from this early stage of her life onwards to dribble away her winsome qualities on lonely gorse and fern. (p. 392)

When Tamsin reveals to Clym her love for Diggory, after some initial reservations, he tenderly consents: 'I am only too glad that you see your way clear to happiness again. My sex owes you every amends for the treatment you received in days gone by' (p. 396).

Thomasin is thus obviously the 'good', conventional heroine of Victorian fiction and Lawrence's (rather patronizing) comment about her and Diggory is: 'They are genuine people, and they get the prize within the walls'.[32] As a symbol of renewal, Thomasin and her innocent self-reflection, the baby Eustacia Clementine, provide the much-needed stability of 'The Inevitable Movement Onward' after the tragic holocaust. For Thomasin the heath holds no terrors; it has never been a 'gaol' to her and although she leaves both the Yeobright home and Egdon after her marriage to Diggory, she is true to her roots and candidly admits: 'I am not fit for town life – so very rural and silly as I always have been' (p. 394). Raised to prosperity by Wildeve's inheritance and Diggory's new-found wealth, she assumes no airs towards the heath-folk and is moved to tears when they gather to wave her goodbye. Her popularity among the Egdon folk is attested by the fact that they gather together to make a mattress as a wedding present for her second marriage. Even on the occasion of her first marriage, as a gesture of goodwill, the heath-folk march up to Wildeve's inn to sing a few ballads to congratulate the newly-wed pair. Of course they do not know that Wildeve has bungled the marriage licence, and their friendly serenading is motivated not just by the hope of partaking of some good 'old mead' at the inn, but by the honest desire of 'pleas[ing] the young wife' (p. 54). As Timothy tells Wildeve, 'the woman you've got is a dimant' (p. 72); we realize that such community approval and congratulations are significantly absent in the narrative of the Clym–Eustacia marriage.

What is Hardy's attitude to this 'Agnes' figure in the novel – one who is almost his namesake? Millgate suggests that Hardy

> probably had his sister Mary in mind when creating the patient, unprotesting Thomasin, whose very name echoes Hardy's own and who in the manuscript was once cast as Clym's sister rather than his cousin.[33]

In so far as it is possible to recover the Ur-novel hidden under layers of revisions and afterthoughts, Thomasin probably was a more complex character and even perhaps the central figure in the novel. In her role as the 'ruined maid' (in the Ur-novel she was to have lived with Wildeve for a week before discovering that their 'marriage' was legally invalid), Thomasin obviously recalls Fanny Robin and anticipates Tess. Paterson speculates that

> Some ten years, then, before the appearance of *Tess of the D'Urbervilles*, Hardy may well have conceived in Thomasin Yeobright the figure of the pure woman caught in the toils of social law and convention and in her story the grounds for a direct attack upon the institution of marriage.[34]

But forced to bowdlerize his original conception drastically, Hardy abandoned Thomasin as 'the central figure of a drama of seduction and later replaced her domestic tragedy with Eustacia's cosmic tragedy'.[35]

Although Gatrell disagrees significantly with Paterson's interpretations of textual revisions, especially in attributing 'diabolism' and 'satanism' to the Ur-Eustacia, his reconstruction of Thomasin's original role is quite similar:

> If, however, it can be imagined that Hardy once thought of Thomasin living for a week with Toogood [as Wildeve was originally ironically named] under the impression that she is married to him, and then through the strength of her personality, her truth to herself, refusing to marry a man whom she no longer loves when he is driven to make amends, it would reinforce the still perceptible relationship between Thomasin and Tess Durbeyfield. It would

then be possible to consider this version of Thomasin in some ways a precursor of Tess. It might also indicate that one strand of *Tess of the d'Urbervilles* is a working out of an idea that he felt unable to pursue in *The Return of the Native*. Proceeding further into the realms of speculation, the comparison gives rise to the likelihood that Thomasin's child would, had her refusal to marry survived, have been illegitimate and thus akin to Tess's baby Sorrow. The relative insignificance of Thomasin in the surviving version – once she is safely married – may have been the direct result of Hardy recognizing that he could not examine her in the role that he had originally conceived for her, and thus losing interest in what had become a more commonplace personality.[36]

Traces of the complex role once envisaged for Thomasin linger in her indignant protest at the anomalous position in which she is left by Wildeve's 'stupid mistake' over the marriage licence. Aware of wagging tongues round her, and hurt and incited by her aunt's strictures, Thomasin replies with spirit:

'I am a warning to others, just as thieves and drunkards and gamblers are... What a class to belong to! Do I really belong to them? 'Tis absurd! Yet why, aunt, does everybody keep on making me think that I do, by the way they behave towards me? Why don't people judge me by my acts? Now, look at me as I kneel here, picking up these apples – do I look like a lost woman?...I wish all good women were as good as I!' (p. 132)

But with her marriage and motherhood, Thomasin is rescued from her ignominious peripheral position and brought within the folds of the community. Ultimately, she comes to represent the yardstick of the norm unlike Eustacia whose marriage with a 'native' fails really to integrate her to the Egdon community.

Although Hardy added a tantalizing note in the 1912 edition explaining that the Thomasin–Diggory marriage was not part of his original conception of the novel and that his hand was forced by the public demand for a 'happy ending', the marriage has its own comic appropriateness and inevitability. The additional 'Book Sixth' destroys the self-conscious five-act structure of the novel's action and the 'year-and-a-day' unity of time of the narrative; nevertheless it is entirely fitting that the novel which opened with Thomasin's misery at her failed attempt at marriage should end with the joyous celebrations of an achieved happy union. Her marriage acts as a necessary counterpoise to the lonely spectacle of a wasted Clym preaching his superfluous sermons to a congregation that merely tolerates and pities him. Without the suggestions of renewal and progress implicit in Thomasin's marriage, the ending of the novel would have been too bleak and negative, too much like the total nihilism and blankness of despair which makes *Jude the Obscure* such a painful and disturbing experience for many readers. At this stage, Hardy probably realized that after the Eustacias, Lucettas and Tesses have played out their tempestuous lives, it is the Thomasins, Elizabeth-Janes and 'Liza-Lus who survive to carry on the process of living – undramatically and unheroically. If Hardy the romantic idealist admired the passionate and uncompromising Eustacias, then Hardy the stern realist also recognizes that the world needs its Thomasins – those who quietly accept the tragic inevitability of things with wisdom, courage, and dignity.

# 4
## Two on a Tower

*Two on a Tower* (1882) deserves more critical attention than it has received. Appearing almost midway in Hardy's career as a novelist, it encapsulates most of the earlier Hardyan motifs and holds in embryonic form the thematic concerns of the tragic novels to follow. In this underrated novel, we have: humanity pitted against the vast, impersonal and indifferent universe; an agonizing struggle between the life of passion and the life of intellect; human love and happiness thwarted by the 'impishness of circumstance'[1]; a reworking of the almost obsessive 'poor man and the lady' motif; a rustic chorus that mediates the tragedy and puts it into perspective; overheard conversations, mistimed letters, accidental discoveries – in fact, all the typical paraphernalia of a 'Hardy' plot.

What is remarkable about *Two on a Tower* is the economy of its dramatis personae. Unlike the typical Hardy novel where the female protagonist vacillates or is offered a choice between two or more possible suitors, Lady Constantine is constant in her preference for the young astronomer, Swithin St Cleeve, although she is later forced to contract a marriage of expediency with Bishop Helmsdale in order to provide legitimacy to her unborn child by Swithin. This deception on her part roused the ire of contemporary reviewers who were indignant at what they considered an insult to the Church. The reviewer in *Saturday Review* found Lady Constantine's marriage to Bishop Helmsdale 'repellent',[2] while the *Spectator* reviewer characterized her passion for Swithin as almost 'repulsive'.[3] But, undaunted, Hardy defended his heroine in his 1895 preface to the novel where he unequivocally stated his sympathy for 'the pathos, misery, long-suffering, and divine tenderness which in real life frequently accompany the passion of such a woman as Viviette for a lover several years her junior' (p. 29). However, within the novel itself, there is a sustained tug of war between sympathy and censure, between tender, impassioned defence and cynical, almost misogynous, commentary.

Throughout the novel an interesting dialectic is set up within the narrative voice: on the one hand, Viviette's tenderness, sincerity, and noble sacrifice are highlighted; on the other hand, her corrupting

influence is repeatedly emphasized. Our introduction to Viviette
Constantine is hardly auspicious. Like a typical lady of leisure, she is
described as being in 'a mood to welcome anything that would in
some measure disperse an almost killing *ennui*' (p. 32). The italicized
word in the text (Hardy's) is the danger signal. A reader familiar with
the corpus of Hardy's novels immediately recalls Eustacia Vye and
Felice Charmond – two women who cause havoc in the lives of men
and women around them and who are ultimately self-destroyed.
When the first chapter ends with a reference to Swithin 'living on in a
primitive Eden of unconsciousness' (p. 39), it is easy to predict who
will play the Eve in the 'Fall' of Swithin/Adam from this prelapsari-
an devotion to science to the postlapsarian deception of clandestine
love affair.

Allusions to the 'Fall' are subtly strewn throughout the text in a
manner that squarely points the finger of responsibility at Viviette. As
her interest in the astronomer grows, she one day invites him and
gives him the free run of her well-stocked library. Immersed in the
world of books, Swithin forgets all about physical nourishment till a
footman brings him his lunch. When he has finished, Lady Constantine leads him to an adjoining room for dessert and the fruit that
Swithin eats in her presence is, significantly, an apple. More explicit is
Viviette's rueful admission – 'but that which is called the Eve in us
will out sometimes' (p. 116) – when she is slightly mortified by
Swithin's lack of gallantry in not protesting that her ten-year seniority
in age is really of little consequence. Later, when Viviette, despite her
anomalous social/moral position, nobly resolves to set Swithin free
by refusing to legalize their earlier (technically illegal) marriage, the
narrator too equates Viviette and Eve: 'Women the most delicate get
used to strange moral situations. Eve probably regained her normal
sweet composure about a week after the Fall' (p. 234).

The 'Eve' identification is adumbrated in that early scene where
Lady Constantine goes to Swithin's tower and finds her 'Astronomer
Royal' sleeping after the exhaustion of sitting up all night recording
astronomical data. As Lady Constantine stands contemplating the
beautiful sleeping youth, Hardy launches into a characteristic narrative aside disguised as her ruminations:

> He [i.e.Swithin] had never, since becoming a man, looked even so
> low as to the level of a Lady Constantine. His heaven at present
> was truly in the skies, and not in that only other place where they

say it can be found, in the eyes of some *daughter of Eve*. Would any *Circe or Calypso* – and if so, what one? – ever check this pale-haired scientist's nocturnal sailings into the interminable spaces overhead, and hurl all his mighty calculations on cosmic force and stellar fire into Limbo? O the pity of it, if such should be the case! (p. 65; emphases added)

The narrator's sympathy here is clearly with Swithin, who is a 'guileless philosopher', and Viviette is obviously the eternal 'femme fatale' – of Christian myth and classical legend. She is the woman who distracts, who is an impediment, who opposes sensual delight to intellectual pursuit, who traps the innocent man in the web of her female enchantment. The apparently rhetorical question, 'Would any Circe or Calypso – and if so, what one?', is answered in the next paragraph but one. Viviette, moved by some strange impulse, takes the scissors and cuts off one of Swithin's curls for a keepsake and then precipitately leaves the tower, half-ashamed of her own action. Hardy does not frame this telling episode within the context of myth and classical allusion which run throughout the text. But the reader is strongly reminded of the story of Samson and Delilah[4] and the suggestion is that by this rape of his lock, Swithin has somehow been betrayed, emasculated, castrated, and that it is Viviette who (in a reversal of gender roles) has taken unfair advantage of him.

As Swithin slowly wakes up to the truth of their relationship, he is transfigured from being a youth whose eyes shone with 'speculative purity' under the 'ennobling influence of scientific pursuits' (p. 65), to being quite an old hand at intrigue. As the narrator points out repeatedly, with an insistence that almost verges on misogyny:

St Cleeve's sudden sense of new relations with that sweet patroness had taken away in one half-hour his natural ingenuousness. Henceforth he could act a part. (pp. 110-11)

The master-passion had already supplanted St Cleeve's natural ingenuousness by subtlety. (p. 117)

Scientifically he had become but a dim vapour of himself; the lover had come into him like an armed man, and cast out the student. (p. 119)

'Is Lady Constantine at home?' asked Swithin, with a disingenu-
ousness now habitual, yet unknown to him six months before.
(p. 151)

Swithin's nature was so fresh and ingenuous, notwithstanding
that recent affairs had somewhat denaturalized him. (p. 196)

This almost overnight passage from 'innocence' to 'experience' is
summed up in a damning narrative comment which makes one
wonder where the authorial sympathy really lies:

The alchemy which thus transmuted an abstracted astronomer
into an eager lover – and, must it be said? spoilt a promising
young physicist to produce a common-place inamorato – may be
almost described as working its change in one short night. (p. 112)

Yet, just a couple of paragraphs earlier, the narrator, without any
apparent trace of irony, had spoken sympathetically of Viviette as
being 'fervid', 'cordial', 'spontaneous', and 'tender' (p. 112).

The misogyny implicit in the narrator is made explicit through a
character who does not enter the novel but who significantly affects
the lives of the two on the tower. Swithin's estranged uncle – Jocelyn
St Cleeve – leaves Swithin a handsome legacy on the condition that
he does not marry before he is 25. In the remarkably candid letter
that he (posthumously) leaves for his nephew, he expresses his
contempt for women in general:

Swithin St Cleeve, don't make a fool of yourself, as your father
did. If your studies are to be worth anything, believe me, they
must be carried on without the help of a woman. Avoid her, and
every one of the sex, if you mean to achieve any worthy thing.
Eschew all of that sort for many a year yet…Women's brains are
not formed for assisting at any profound science: they lack the
power to see things except in the concrete. She'll blab your most
secret plans and theories to every one of her acquaintance[5]…If you
attempt to study with a woman, you'll be ruled by her to entertain
fancies instead of theories, air-castles instead of intentions, qualms
instead of opinions, sickly prepossessions instead of reasoned con-
clusions. Your wide heaven of study, young man, will soon reduce
itself to the miserable narrow expanse of her face, and your myri-
ad of stars to her two trumpery eyes…the woman sits down before

each [man] as his destiny, and too frequently enervates his purpose, till he abandons the most promising course ever conceived! (pp. 138-9)

All this is no more than the familiar diatribe against women in literature written by men. But it is all so patently unfair, especially when we recall that it is Lady Constantine's generous gifts – of an object-glass for his telescope, of the even more expensive equatorial, and the lease of the tower itself – which contribute to make Swithin the competent astronomer he finally becomes.

The coercive effect of this collusion between the 'hardened misogynist of seventy-two' (p. 140) – Jocelyn St Cleeve – and the narrator is that Viviette becomes trapped in their language and she soon begins to see herself as these (unsympathetic) male viewers see her. Narrative commentary, Christian myth, classical allusion all powerfully combine to erect a moral straitjacket which imprisons Viviette and imposes on her a terrible burden of guilt. Had such a software been available, it would be tempting to feed the entire text of *Two on a Tower* into a computer and filter out all the negative words used to characterize the Viviette–Swithin relationship. But even a random sampling of such pejoratives will, hopefully, establish my point. Jocelyn St Cleeve's letter had been quite explicit:

> She is old enough to know that a *liaison* [Hardy's italic] with her may, and almost certainly would, be your *ruin*[6]...A woman of honourable feeling, nephew, would be careful to do nothing to *hinder* you in your career...An experienced woman waking a young man's passion just at a moment when he is endeavouring to shine intellectually, is doing little else than committing a *crime*.(p. 139)

Swithin, though far too loyal at this stage directly to point an accusing finger at Viviette, betrays himself in the argument he uses to persuade Viviette to marry him. Marriage, he says, will put an end to the danger and unease of their clandestine lovers' meetings: 'All this *ruinous idleness* and *distraction* is caused by the misery of our not being able to meet with freedom' (p. 120). When Viviette wisely counsels, 'Wait till you are famous,' she is stumped by the circularity of his logic: 'But I cannot be famous unless I strive, and this *distracting condition* prevents all striving!' (p. 121). That there is some justice in Swithin's complaint is recognized by Viviette herself when she tearfully acknowledges to Swithin: 'I am *injuring* you; who knows that I am not *ruining* your future...I am only *wasting* your time. Why have I drawn you off from a grand celestial study to study poor lonely me?' (p. 115)

Viviette's acute sense of self-reproach alternates with moments of rebellion when she is tempted to snatch happiness at whatever cost:

> At some instants she felt exultant at the idea of announcing her marriage and defying general opinion. At another her heart misgave her, and she was tormented by a fear lest Swithin should some day accuse her of having *hampered* his deliberately-shaped plan of life by her *intrusive* romanticism. (p. 212)

At one end of the pendulum swing of her moods, she feels she would 'perhaps be a nobler woman in not allowing him to *encumber* his bright future by a union with me at all' (p. 219). But '[t]aking brighter views, she hoped that upon the whole this *yoking* of the young fellow with her, a portionless woman and his senior, would not greatly *endanger* his career' (p. 219). However, Viviette is too intelligent to live in a fool's paradise for long, and the negatives pile up in this concentrated expression of her self-reproach:

> 'O, what a *wrong* I am doing you! I did not dream that it could be as bad as this. I knew I was *wasting* your time by letting you have me, and *hampering* your projects; but I thought there were compensating advantages. This *wrecking* of your future at my hands I did not contemplate.' (p. 226)

The narrator, closely reflecting Viviette's consciousness, tells of her regret at having '*blocked* his attempted career' (p. 226); her realization that '*bondage*' with an older woman 'would operate in the future as a *wet blanket* upon his social ambitions' (p. 231); her fear that marriage with her would only be '*depriving* him of the help his uncle had offered' (p. 231). The narrator sums up the situation:

> That she had *wronged* St Cleeve by marrying him – that she would *wrong* him infinitely more by completing the marriage – there was, in her opinion, no doubt. She in her experience had sought out him

in his inexperience, and had led him like a child…Without her, he had all the world before him, six hundred a year, and leave to cut as straight a road to fame as he should choose: with her, this story was *negatived.* (pp. 230-1)

Although a youth of 20 is hardly a 'child', it is surprising to note how often Swithin is conceived of as a 'child'. In fact, the turning point in Viviette's struggle to rise above the possessive nature of her love comes when she watches Swithin in church during the 'confirmation' ceremony:

How fervidly she watched the Bishop place his hand on her beloved youth's head; how she saw the great episcopal ring glistening in the sun among Swithin's brown curls; how she waited to hear if Dr Helmsdale uttered the form 'this thy child' which he used for the younger ones, or 'this thy servant' which he used for those older; and how, when he said 'this thy *child*' [Hardy's italic], she felt a prick of conscience, like a person who had *entrapped* an innocent youth into marriage for her own gratification. (pp. 168-9)

Realizing that the future will not exonerate her from having '*deluded* his raw immaturity' (p. 233), Viviette self-effacingly releases Swithin: 'I cannot *ruin* you…Take the bequest, and go. You are too young – to be *fettered*…I have vowed a vow not to further *obstruct* the course you had decided on before you knew me and my *puling* ways' (p. 239). Swithin takes her words at face value and leaves, and Viviette is released from her 'besetting fear' that her 'actions [are] likely to *distract* and *weight* him'. She is, in a way, relieved that she 'no longer *stood in the way* of his advancement' (p. 241). It is this sentiment that comes through in the final letter that she sends to Swithin, explaining why she married the Bishop:

The long desire of my heart has been not to *impoverish* you or *mar* your career. The new desire was to save myself and, still more, another yet unborn…I have done a desperate thing…The one bright spot is that it saves you and your endowment…I no longer *lie like a log across your path*, which is now as open as on the day before you saw me. (pp. 261-2)

Moralists might argue that Viviette's noble self-sacrifice is tainted by her cold inhumanity in duping the 'innocent' Bishop into marriage and passing off Swithin's child as his. But as Hardy was to argue very persuasively in *Tess*, it is not the purity of action but the purity of intention that is most important. Viviette's unselfish wish not to '*lime* Swithin's young wings' (p. 219) mitigates some-what our censure of her deception of the Bishop. The image, looking forward to the trapped animal images in *Tess* and *Jude*, anticipates Hardy's critical examination of the marriage bond in his later novels. Had Viviette not released Swithin to pursue his scientific career, he might well have questioned, like Jude, 'what he had done...that he deserved to be *caught in a gin* which would *cripple* him, if not her also, for the rest of a lifetime?'[7]

Hardy realized that it was at this crucial point in the narrative that he ran the risk of losing the reader's sympathy for his heroine. By the light of conventional morality, or even interpersonal honesty,[8] Viviette's action would be hard to defend. So Hardy the artist has recourse to a deft sleight of hand. Like Tess's rape/seduction, her hanging, Alec's murder, Eustacia's drowning, the triple hangings of the children in *Jude* – and one could keep expanding this list – Viviette's marriage to the Bishop occurs off-stage and is brought home to Swithin's consciousness by a newspaper report. Perhaps this is a lesson that Hardy learnt from his study of Greek tragedy: that anything unpleasant must occur off-stage and only be reported. As the 'whirligig of time' races by, nearly five years in the narrative – covering Viviette's marriage, the birth of her son, her husband's death – are slurred over in four or five pages. The narrative telescope which had swung away from England and faced the southern hemisphere with Swithin's departure for the Cape now swings back to focus on England with Swithin's return to his native village.

Hardy now makes every attempt to recover the lost ground of the reader's sympathy for Viviette. He chooses the parson, Torkingham, to be Viviette's indirect advocate. Torkingham enlightens both Swithin and the reader about the brief conjugal life of Viviette and the Bishop:

'His poor wife, I fear, had not a great deal more happiness with him than with her first husband. But one might almost have foreseen it...But the Bishop's widow is not the Lady Constantine of former days. No; put it as you will, she is not the same. There seems to be a nameless something on her mind – a trouble – a rooted melancholy, which no man's ministry can reach.' (p. 268)

This is not the first time that Hardy has used a marginal character to throw light on Lady Constantine's plight as a wife. Alongside the narrative commentary that sets up Lady Constantine as Eve/Circe/Calypso, there runs a parallel discourse of woman as deserted wife, as poor victim of a brutal husband, as a creature trapped by matrimony in an unfeeling patriarchal society and an equally inhumane and rigid Mosaic code. There is a significant moment when Lady Constantine enters the church and her incipient love for Swithin wrestles with her sense of guilt as a married woman:

> The rays from the organist's candle illuminated but one small fragment of the chancel outside the precincts of the instrument, and that was the portion of the eastern wall whereon the ten commandments were inscribed. The gilt letters shone sternly into Lady Constantine's eyes; and she, being as impressionable as a turtle-dove, watched a certain one of those commandments on the second table, till its thunder broke her spirit with blank contrition.[9]

> She knelt down, and did her utmost to eradicate those impulses towards St Cleeve which were inconsistent with her position as the wife of an absent man, though not unnatural in her *as his victim*. (p. 97; emphasis added)

Sir Blount Constantine – 'a notoriously unkind husband' (p. 218) – never features directly in the novel, but we hear enough about his cruel treatment of his wife to blot out any sympathy that we may be prompted to feel for him. Viviette's near-fainting fit when she suddenly beholds Swithin draped in Sir Blount's fur great-coat speaks volumes for the abject terror with which Viviette regards her first husband. Also, giving the lie to the general (male) conception that it is women's gossip that tears a woman's reputation to shreds, the young Tabitha Lark and the aged Mrs Martin discuss Lady Constantine quite sympathetically. Tabitha describes the deserted Lady Constantine as '[e]aten out with listlessness. She's neither sick nor sorry, but how dull and dreary she is, only herself can tell'. Mrs Martin responds with: 'Ah, poor soul!...No doubt she says in the morning, "Would God it were evening", and in the evening, "Would God it were morning".' When Sammy Blore concedes that 'the woman's heart-strings is tried in many aggravating ways', Mrs Martin again condoles: 'Ah, poor woman!...The state she finds herself in – neither maid, wife, nor widow – is not the primest form of life for keeping in good spirits' (p. 43).

In the course of the narrative we learn that Sir Blount has wrested from Lady Constantine a promise, prior to his departure for lion-hunting, that she will not go out in society but shut herself up like a nun. However, his jealousy does not prevent him from *knowingly* committing bigamy by marrying a native princess in Africa.[10] This is perhaps an early suggestion of Hardy's protest against the double standards of sexual morality which he was to voice more powerfully in *Tess*. Meanwhile, Lady Constantine has not heard from her husband for over two years and when he ultimately dies, he leaves her in severe financial straits. Sympathy for her financial and emotional impoverishment is voiced through yet another (male) member of the rustic chorus:

' 'Tis all swallered up', observed Hezzy Biles. 'His goings-on made her miserable till 'a died, and if I were the woman I'd have my randys now. He ought to have bequeathed to her our young gent, Mr St Cleeve, as some sort of amends. I'd up and marry en, if I were she; since her downfall has brought 'em quite near together, and made him as good as she in rank, as he was afore in bone and breeding.' (p. 107)

Thus, subterranean sympathy for Viviette the ill-used, deserted wife runs parallel to the more overt narrative censure of Viviette the seductive mistress. In the final, short-lived reunion between Viviette and Swithin, narrative compassion bursts to the surface and there can surely be no doubt as to where authorial sympathy lies. Swithin meets Viviette at the top of the tower and to all appearances it looks as if he and the widowed Viviette can carry on their romance from the point where they had left off – as Bathsheba and Gabriel or Cytherea and Edward had been able to do before them. But in the world of Hardy's tragic novels, the man for loving and the moment for loving do not synchronize. Swithin is so shocked by what he sees – Time's ravages on Viviette's beauty – that he involuntarily recoils in horror.

This scene has a tragic resonance that may best be explained by a complex welter of poignant memory, remorse, yearning, and guilt on the part of the author himself. Despite Hardy's strenuous denials of autobiographical elements in his novels, and his irritation with contemporary critics and thesis-writers who sought to read his life into his works, this meeting between the faded Viviette and the still-youthful Swithin may probably owe something to Hardy's subsequent meeting with Julia Augusta Martin, the local lady of the manor who taught 'Tommy' his alphabets and for whom the young Hardy long retained a boy's romantic infatuation. She was probably the original inspiration behind his recurrent 'poor man and the lady' plot pattern, and Hardy's meeting with Mrs Martin, years later in London, is best described by Hardy himself in his disguised autobiography:

> During the first few months of Hardy's life in London he had not forgotten to pay a call on the lady of his earliest passion as a child, who had been so tender towards him in those days, and had used to take him in her arms. She and her husband were now living in Bruton Street. The butler who opened the door... looked little altered. But the lady of his dreams – alas! To her, too, the meeting must have been no less painful than pleasant: she was plainly embarrassed at having in her presence a young man of over twenty-one, who was very much of a handful in comparison with the rosy-cheeked, innocent little boy she had almost expected 'Tommy' to remain. One interview was not quite sufficient to wear off the stiffness resulting from such changed conditions, though, warming up, she asked him to come again. But getting immersed in London life he did not respond to her invitation, showing that the fickleness was his alone. But they occasionally corresponded, as will be seen.[11]

As in his novels, so also in real life, Hardy could not resist focusing on missed opportunities and speculating on 'what might have been':

> Among the curious consequences of the popularity of *Far from the Madding Crowd* was a letter from the lady he had so admired as a child, when she was the grand dame of the parish in which he was

born. He had seen her only once since – at her town-house in
Bruton Street as aforesaid. But it should be stated in justice to her
that her writing was not merely a rekindled interest on account of
his book's popularity, for she had written to him in his obscurity,
before he had published a line, asking him to come and see her,
and addressing him as her dear Tommy, as when he was a small
boy, apologizing for doing so on the ground that she could not
help it. She was now quite an elderly lady, but by signing her letter
'Julia Augusta' she revived throbs of tender feeling in him, and
brought back to his memory the thrilling 'frou-frou' of her four
grey silk flounces when she had used to bend over him, and when
they brushed against the font as she entered church on Sundays.
He replied, but, as it appears, did not go to see her. Thus though
their eyes never met again after his call on her in London, nor their
lips from the time when she had held him in her arms, who can say
that both occurrences might not have been in the order of things, if
he had developed their reacquaintance earlier, now that she was in
her widowhood, with nothing to hinder her mind from rolling
back upon her past.[12]

In the world of the novels, Swithin's rejection of Viviette, though less
deliberate, is just as cruel as Knight's rejection of Elfride or Angel's
rejection of Tess. Stripped of its erotic content, it can also be com-
pared to Elizabeth-Jane's rejection of Henchard because all these
rejections reveal an essential lack of 'loving-kindness', the highest
Hardyan virtue. Having initially turned his back on Viviette, Swithin
is immediately remorseful as he realizes that:

> all her conduct had been dictated by the purest benevolence to
> him, by that charity which 'seeketh not her own'. Hence he did
> not flinch from a wish to deal with loving-kindness towards her
> – a sentiment perhaps in the long-run more to be prized than
> lover's love.[13] (p. 274)

This is not Hardy's belated attempt to whitewash the character of
his heroine, by drawing attention to her unselfish transcendence
of self-interest. Throughout the narrative, the sincerity of Viviette's
love – that strange compound of 'maternal', 'sisterly' and 'amorous'
feeling (p. 73) – is never questioned. When Viviette ultimately takes

the brave decision to separate from Swithin, the narrator unequivocally explains her motives:

> Nothing can express what it cost Lady Constantine to marshal her arguments; but she did it, and vanquished self-comfort by a sense of the general expediency. It may unhesitatingly be affirmed that the only ignoble reason which might have dictated such a step was non-existent; that is to say, a serious decline in her affection. Tenderly she had loved the youth at first, and tenderly she loved him now, as time and her after-conduct proved.[14] (p. 234)

Thus when Swithin, after his initial involuntary revulsion, turns back to claim her as his wife, Viviette utters 'a shriek of amazed joy', falls into his arms and dies: 'Sudden joy after despair had touched an over-strained heart too smartly' (p. 275). Surely it is unnecessary to enter a debate on the medical plausibility of such a death; what is more important here is the literary/poetic context that lends it both inevitability and credibility. In a novel that has called attention to its Shakespearean echoes, the description of Viviette's death surely recalls Edgar's description of the death of Gloucester in *King Lear*:

> ...but his flaw'd heart,
> Alack, too weak the conflict to support!
> 'Twixt two extremes of passion, joy and grief,
> Burst smilingly.         (V. iii. 195-8)

Lear's heart too bursts with sudden joy, after grief, when he mistakenly believes that life still stirs in the dead Cordelia.[15]

The narrator's reaction to Viviette's death is extremely ambivalent. The final words of the novel read: 'Viviette was dead. The Bishop was avenged' (p. 275). How are we to interpret these words? On the ironic level, they probably anticipate the narrator's sarcastic fling at 'Justice' and 'the President of the Immortals' in the more famous ending of *Tess*. On the more literal level, it reflects a narrator (and author?) trapped within a conventional patriarchal morality where, for women at least, the 'wages of sin' is inevitably death (Ruth, Hetty, and Tess all ultimately die). For, in a sense, Viviette is a 'fallen' woman because, despite Hardy's claim in his (1895) Preface that 'there is hardly a single caress in the book outside legal matrimony' (p. 29), Viviette's child is conceived when she is fully aware that her marriage with Swithin is legally invalid. This is something that Hardy went out of his way to emphasize in subsequent editions so that there is no scope for awarding Viviette the benefit of the doubt. Thus, within the narrow code of retributive justice, Viviette's death is a well-deserved punishment for her 'fall' and also her deliberate deception of the Bishop because, as Hochstadt claims, 'the book's concluding sentence manages to suggest that the early death of that deluded worthy [i.e. the Bishop] is not unrelated to his distress at being presented with a seven-months child'.[16]

While there is not much textual evidence to support this reading, there is no escaping the multiple ambiguities of the novel's ending. On the one hand, we have the unmistakable sympathy of the narrative gloss: ' "O Woman," might a prophet have said to her, "great is thy faith if thou believest a junior lover's love will last five years!" ' (p. 274). Readers familiar with the various disguises adopted by the Hardyan narrator (the 'an-observer-might-have-seen' or 'a-passer-by-may-have-noticed' formula) will immediately recognize that in this expression of compassion for Viviette, the author/narrator/prophet is one composite and unitary being. Thus, in Rosemary Sumner's opinion, the 'impressiveness' of Viviette's 'struggle is partly due to the success and sympathy with which Hardy has created her as a passionately emotional woman'.[17]

Despite such sympathy for the heroine, the overriding narrative anxiety seems to be for Swithin lest 'he should follow his father in forming an attachment that would be a hindrance to him in any honourable career' (p. 174). Fear of women and the narratorial animus against 'the sex' also clearly surface in that totally gratuitous gibe at Tabitha's expense at the end of the novel. Tabitha has blossomed into womanhood and has become a successful musician, playing at concerts and oratorios. She has, the narrator mockingly says, 'in short, joined the phalanx of Wonderful Women who had resolved to eclipse the masculine genius altogether, and humiliate the brutal sex to the dust' (p. 270).

Tabitha, 'the single bright spot' in the horizon, is the more natural mate for young Swithin, and the novel ends with a hint of a future union between Tabitha and Swithin which foreshadows Hardy's use of the sop ending in *Tess*. In a letter that Hardy wrote to Florence Henniker in 1920, he tantalizingly suggested:

History does not record whether Swithin married Tabitha or not. Perhaps when Lady C. [*sic*] was dead he grew passionately attached to her again, as people often do. I suppose the bishop did find out the secret. Or perhaps he did not.[18]

Hardy, who canonized his first wife Emma after her death through his poetical outpourings of grief and guilt, certainly knew all about how death renders a woman doubly well-beloved – because irretrievably lost.

# 5

# The Woodlanders

*The Woodlanders* (1887) is the quintessential Hardy story with its typical country-city conflict in the patterning of characters and their interrelationships. With the neat symmetry that critics associate with Hardy's stonemason's geometry, Marty South is seen as representing rural innocence, Felice Charmond the lure of the city, while Grace Melbury is precariously poised between her native rural moorings and the veneer of acquired urban sophistication. But this traditional interpretation needs to be re-examined because the categorization is too neat to go unchallenged.

One of the most haunting impressions left by a first reading of this novel is the poignant portrait of that lonely and devoted woodland girl, Marty. No reader can be left untouched by the description of her patient endurance, her dogged faithfulness, and her silent love that literally persists beyond the grave. Appropriately, the chorus of praise sung in her honour is rather deafening. The reviewer in *Athenaeum* hailed Marty as 'the really heroic woman, in her way the sweetest figure that Mr Hardy has ever drawn'.[1] Duffin echoes this when he debates whether Marty has not the stronger claim to being called the 'heroine' of the book because she is 'a figure of far greater beauty and interest' (than Grace) and it is 'a great loss to literature that Hardy did not make her the subject of a full-length study'.[2] In his elaborate chart classifying Hardy's female characters, Guerard places Marty alongside Tess as 'Two Pure Women' and he regrets that the 'solid worth and fidelity' of this 'unselfish child of the soil' goes largely unappreciated.[3] Millgate likens Marty to Elizabeth-Jane and sees Marty as 'a kind of moral touchstone of her world';[4] Lodge apotheosizes her as 'the personification of selfless, unostentatious heroism';[5] Stubbs sees in her a symbolic figure of 'the eternally faithful maiden who stands always by the tomb of the dead knight';[6] Brown sentimentally calls her 'the most moving' of Hardy's characters, one 'who incarnates the finest part of country attitudes'.[7] But a critical re-reading of the text makes it obvious that there are certain embarrassed silences, unanswered questions which gloss over those aspects of her personality which will not bear close scrutiny. Hardy tries his utmost to build her up as an asexual, almost disembodied creature, with no human desires or frailties, but the text simply does not bear out such an interpretation.

We first meet Marty in the second chapter of the novel where, in a situation of unrelieved poverty, the Mephistophelean intruder – the barber Percomb – tempts her with a lucrative offer if only she will part with some of her luxuriant curls. But Marty stubbornly refuses to comply because she shrewdly guesses that her trans-planted locks will go to enhance the charms of Mrs Charmond, whose reputation as a trifler has reached even a 'sequestered spot' like Little Hintock. 'I value my looks too much to spoil 'em', she declares with justifiable pride and the barber has to return empty-handed, but not before his triumphant rejoinder – '*you've got a lover yourself*, and that's why you won't let it go!' – leaves her blushing (p. 46; Hardy's italics).

In the next chapter Marty unwittingly overhears a conversation between Mr Melbury and his second wife regarding the marital prospects of his only daughter, Grace. Being an over-fond and anxious parent, Melbury is worried about Giles Winterborne's poverty but his wife reassures him with the homely wisdom that 'Love will make up for his want of money. He adores the very ground she walks on' (p. 50). At this point, there is a very interesting parenthetical insertion by Hardy: '(Marty South started, and could not tear herself away)'. What is important here is that Marty is *not* taken aback when she hears of this projected alliance between Giles and Grace, but the news that Giles 'adores' Grace hits her like a thunderbolt. Finally, she withdraws to her cottage with words of pained resignation: 'That, then, is the secret of it all… I had half thought so. And Giles Winterborne is not for me!' (p. 52). This is immediately followed by her 'mercilessly cutting off the long locks of her hair' and the motiva-tion is too transparent to require comment.

Successive re-readings of the novel raise awkward questions regard-ing Marty's role in the Giles-Grace relationship, questions which Hardy not only does not care to answer, but questions which he does not even dare to raise lest the sweet idyllic portrait should be cruelly shattered. For instance, what really prompts Marty to write those cruelly prophetic words:

'O Giles, you've lost your dwelling-place,
And therefore, Giles, you'll lose your Grace.' (p. 135)

on the wall of Giles's humble dwelling at a time when the sudden
reversal of fortune has made the social gap between Giles and Grace
suddenly seem all the more unbridgeable? Although Grace timidly
changes the word 'lose' to 'keep', the significance is lost on Giles
because – in keeping with the predominant role assigned to missed
chances in Hardy's novels – Giles never happens to notice the
favourably altered version. Weighed down by the sad truth of that
crude couplet, Giles sits down to write a formal letter to Melbury
withdrawing his claim on Grace and cancelling the tacit engagement
between them.

This is quite blatantly an instance of Hardy sacrificing character
to the requirements of plot. The plot requires a misunderstanding
between Giles and Grace, followed by estrangement, and Hardy
assigns to Marty the villain's role. Marty has just buried her only
parent barely a couple of weeks ago and, as a struggling orphan,
she surely has enough worries about keeping body and soul together,[8] to intrude uninvited into the emotional tangles of other people.
Or is it that she has not given up hope altogether and is angling for
Giles herself? It appears as if she is prompted by jealousy against a
more powerful and favoured rival and thinks everything is fair in
the war of love. Marty apparently knows Giles's weak point – his
delicate sense of honour – and through the warning she scratches
on the wall she is probably trying to open Giles's eyes to the social
disparity between him and Grace. Giles is too honourable to persist
in wooing his childhood sweetheart once he realizes that their
marriage will drag her down socially and financially. He would
rather willingly sacrifice his long-cherished dreams of marital
happiness with Grace than bring censure down on her beloved
head by any selfish act on his part. Thus Marty probably hopes that
although she may not gain Giles's love of his own free choice, she
might yet win him over by default.

Hardy does not ever state all this directly; indeed, he is strangely
reluctant to subject Marty's motives to close critical scrutiny. This
may partly be explained by Gittings's suggestion that Marty was
probably modelled on Hardy's much-loved sister, Mary.[9] Possibly,
too, Marty's dumb devotion to Giles draws on Mary Hardy's silent
loyalty to the memory of Horace Moule, whose tragic death (suicide)

had left a deep impression on Thomas Hardy. But the reader, lacking such personal and emotional reasons, is more sceptical. At the end of the chapter, when Giles taxes her about her motive in writing those words, Marty tersely replies: 'Because it was the truth' (p. 136). But who has appointed her the sole custodian of Truth in affairs that are surely not her concern?

If this appears to be an act of unwarranted cruelty – in demolishing the romanticized picture of loyal and suffering womanhood – then one has only to go farther into the text and take up an episode where she again plays a questionable role *vis-à-vis* the Giles–Grace relationship. With Fitzpiers increasingly playing truant from his lawful wife, Grace, and defecting to the alluring Mrs Charmond, Marty – like most Hintock folk – is apprehensive about the outcome. There is the distinct possibility that Fitzpiers's callous neglect of his wife will wean Grace's heart away from him and re-light the unextinguished embers of her childhood love for Giles. To forestall this possible re-attachment between Grace and Giles, Marty again acts as the self-appointed custodian of morality by handing Fitzpiers a letter to the effect that Mrs Charmond is merely a crow decked out in borrowed plumes. That this letter is crucial in the plot mechanism is obvious from its far-reaching consequences: it occasions a rupture between Fitzpiers and Mrs Charmond, leads to Fitzpiers's repentant return to English shores and his wife, and culminates in Giles's heroic self-sacrifice which in turn paves the way for a patched-up reunion between Grace and Fitzpiers.

What prompts Marty to write this momentous letter? Is it pure disinterested Christian/sisterly love which desires to repair Grace's ruined home and heart? Or is this yet another instance of Marty's 'playful malice' (p. 66)? In the words of the narrator, although she is 'so young and inexperienced', she sees the 'danger to two hearts, naturally honest, in Grace being thrown back into Winterborne's society by the neglect of her husband' (pp. 253-4). But the experienced woman of the world, Mrs Charmond (and the cynical reader) suspects otherwise. Helped by Marty's blushes and stammer, Mrs Charmond shrewdly divines that her idle amour with Grace's husband is indirectly 'involving the wreck of poor Marty's hopes' (p. 254). That she is not far from the truth is implied by the narrator in an earlier episode where Marty, rather unwillingly, has to act as a go-between during the midnight rites on Midsummer Eve. Much against her personal inclinations, but at the request of Grammer Oliver, the onus of contriving an accidental meeting between Grace and Giles rests on her. The narrator's comment on her predicament is revealing: 'Poor Marty, always doomed to sacrifice desire to obligation' (p. 170).

Similarly, the narrator's comments on Marty's motives for writing that letter to Fitzpiers hint at something that is never fully explored. That letter was 'poor Marty's only card, and she played it' (p. 261), (incidentally, 'poor' is the epithet that the narrator invariably uses when speaking of Marty); and the writing of the letter is not an impulsive gesture, but 'her long contemplated apple of discord' (p. 264). This is not to suggest that Marty is consciously playing the hypocrite; rather, both Marty and her creator are strangely reluctant to probe beneath the surface motives and light up the shadowy world of subconscious desires. Later, when Fitzpiers personally thanks her for that letter which facilitated his release from Mrs Charmond, the narrator says: 'Marty was shy, indeed, of speaking about the letter and her motives in writing it' (p. 343). Perhaps the darker springs of her motivation are really hidden from her; but, as critical readers, we cannot afford to be so naively blind.

That an unacknowledged rivalry in love accounts for many of Marty's actions is made clear in that encounter where Grace and Marty stand facing each other at the foot of the bed on which the long-suffering Giles has just breathed his last. In the distraction of grief, Grace murmurs: 'He died for me!' Being emotionally disturbed herself, Marty fails to comprehend the true import of these words. Not realizing the sense of guilt that prompted Grace's remark, Marty replies with a touch of bitterness:

'He belongs to neither of us now, and your beauty is no more powerful with him than my plainness...He never cared for me, and he cared much for you; but he cares for us both alike now.' (pp. 333-4)

Then both women kneel beside the bed and pray for his soul, and later they form a pact about going to his grave together, as they had 'both loved him'. A sadder but wiser Grace generously remarks to Marty: 'He ought to have married *you*, Marty, and nobody else in the world!' (p. 341; Hardy's italic). This idea has just been mooted in an authorial commentary:

Marty South alone, of all the women in Hintock and the world, had approximated to Winterborne's level of intelligent intercourse with Nature. In that respect she had formed his true complement in the other sex, had lived as his counterpart, had sub-joined her thoughts to his as a corollary. (p. 340)

For eight months after Giles's death, both Grace and Marty religiously keep up the practice of laying flowers at his grave every week. When finally Grace is won over by Fitzpiers, Marty waits for her in vain and finally goes alone to the churchyard to fulfil her sacred duty to the dead. The words she whispers while tending the grave are unconsciously self-revelatory:

'Now, my own, own love,... you are mine, and only mine; for she has forgot 'ee at last, although for her you died!... But no, no, my love, I never can forget 'ee...' (p. 375)

The accents here are unmistakable as, probably for the first time, Marty addresses the departed Giles openly as her 'love'. Giles had never given her a moment's thought when alive, at least not as a possible sweetheart; but now that he lies cold in his grave, and his Grace has returned to the lawful embrace of Fitzpiers, Marty feels that she can claim him as her very own, without any social or moral impropriety. In death, Giles has become hers as he never was when alive.

Most critics have eulogized this final elegy and, admittedly, this lyric lament *is* very touching. We are moved by Marty's sincerity and her tragic isolation. But even while acknowledging the beauty of this requiem for the dead, we cannot be deaf to the undertones of possessiveness and rivalry in love in the 'If-ever-I-forget-your-name' formula. Hardy (deliberately?) glosses over this aspect by presenting an almost etherealized picture of Marty as a creature quite removed from earthly desires:

As this solitary and silent girl stood there in the moonlight, a straight slim figure, clothed in a plaitless gown, *the contours of womanhood so undeveloped* as to be scarcely perceptible in her, the marks of poverty and toil effaced by the misty hour, she touched sublimity at points, and looked almost like a *being who had reject-ed with indifference the attribute of sex* for the loftier quality of abstract humanism. (p. 375; emphases added)

This is not the first time that the narrator has spoken thus. Earlier, in the scene where Giles accosts Marty for scribbling those cruel words, the narrator describes her as 'a slim figure in meagre black, almost without womanly contours as yet' (p. 136). But what about womanly jealousies? While describing Marty reposing beside the body of her father (awaiting burial), the narrator had tenderly called her 'a guileless soul that had nothing more left on earth to lose, except a life which she did not over-value' (p. 133). But surely a *guileless* soul, under such recent bereavement, would not have stooped to the gratuitous heartlessness of etching that couplet on the wall! Thus, despite Hardy's intention of refining her into a creature of pure air and fire, she comes alive as a normal human being of flesh and blood, with all the natural hopes, desires, and weaknesses that flesh is heir to. The problem with judging the character of Marty is that she is a half-drawn sketch and although, with our post-Freudian hindsight, we can easily divine her possible motives, Hardy declines his omniscient authorial privilege of delving deeper into her consciousness. The problem is aggravated by a sense of sadness, tinged with a sense of betrayal, at having to dethrone a universally beloved character.

In traditional analyses of this novel, Marty and Mrs Charmond fit very neatly into the Lily-Rose dichotomy so dear to Victorian novelists. Few critics have a kind word to spare for the unfortunate Felice. Commenting on the 'essential falsity' of her relationship with Fitzpiers, Merryn Williams says: 'Her interests are as futile as her emotions, and these are both artificial and shortlived.'[10] Stubbs, though finally recognizing Felice's 'victim' status, begins by calling her an 'emotional vampire'.[11] Jacobus rather surprisingly describes Felice as being 'at once Fitzpiers's "loadstar" and the "fiery sepulchre" which consumes the moth.'[12] This is quite the reverse of the truth because it is ultimately Felice who is *self*-destroyed, while Fitzpiers is the survivor who regains an estranged wife and a promising professional practice. Thus, to treat Marty as the unsullied Lily and Felice Charmond as the fatally seductive Rose would be an over-simplification. Although Felice *is* responsible for much of the tragedy in this novel where 'hearts are ill affin'd',[13] she is not a creature as dark as hell, any more than Marty is as white as the driven snow. Through very subtle touches, the character of Mrs Charmond is humanized till she becomes more a victim caught in the toils of her own passionate nature than a conventional seductress without either conscience or compassion.

We first hear of Mrs Charmond when the barber comes to Little Hintock to persuade Marty to sell her hair. With an arrogance born of wealth and social position, Mrs Charmond thinks that she can buy all the good and valuable things of life. No longer in her prime, her vanity makes her stoop to borrowed glory. She wears her false hair deliberately to ensnare the hearts of susceptible young men (like Dr Fitzpiers) in a way that makes her not much superior to Arabella, who uses the same artifice to entrap Jude. Mrs Charmond, with her languid idleness, her frustration at the tedium of rural life, and her frantic desire to escape to the excitement of the Continent, reminds us strongly of Eustacia, and we are apprehensive that this volatile woman will ultimately destroy both herself and those who come into contact with her.

Apart from being a heartless charmer (the narrator broadly hints that she had married the late Mr Charmond more for money than for love), she is also a heartless (and rootless) landowner, often wantonly reducing her tenants to homeless destitutes. Already inflamed against Giles because of his uncompromising behaviour during the Oedipus-like encounter of vehicles, she takes her revenge by refusing to renew his 'lifehold' leases. As a result, when John South dies, Giles is forced to leave the house that has been his family's for generations and ultimately all these cottages are callously pulled down. Such an introduction to the character of Mrs Charmond is hardly calculated to win the reader's sympathy, but the scales begin to turn halfway through the novel.

The scene where Mrs Charmond and Fitzpiers first encounter each other in the novel – ostensibly as patient and doctor – is richly ambivalent. Mrs Charmond has just suffered a minor accident and she summons the young doctor to attend her. The vision that greets Fitzpiers is described by the narrator with a fine touch of satire:

> by the light of the shaded lamp he saw a woman of elegant figure reclining upon a couch in such a position as not to disturb a pile of magnificent hair on the crown of her head. A deep purple dressing-gown formed an admirable foil to the peculiarly rich brown of her hair-plaits; her left arm, which was naked nearly up to the shoulder, was thrown upwards, and between the fingers of her right hand she held a cigarette, while she idly breathed from her delicately curled lips a thin stream of smoke towards the ceiling. (pp. 207-8)

Surely this is no patient, but a practised courtesan, a seductress, a vamp, complete to the last detail: a cigarette in hand. Every word, every gesture is rehearsed and every look calculated to entice. We are left cold by all this scheming and artifice but, midway through the interview, a note of sincerity creeps in as Mrs Charmond nostalgically recalls their first youthful encounter.

That this bygone meeting has left a deep imprint on Mrs Charmond's romantic imagination is obvious from the fact that she has recognized in Fitzpiers the young impecunious student to whom she had once lost her girlish heart. Fitzpiers's memory is not so fresh and needs to be goaded; neither is his regret at this early missed opportunity as keen and lasting as hers appears to be. He dismisses the experience as 'the merest bud...a colossal passion in embryo. It never matured' (p. 210). We are left speculating as to the probable course of events had this bud been left to flower in peace. Had this early romantic attachment not been frustrated, perhaps Felice would have grown to be a very different person altogether. Surely it is not fair to human nature to argue backwards (from our knowledge of her present character) and say that even in those innocent girlhood days she had not been in love with Fitzpiers, but in love with the concept of being in love.

As her renewed intimacy with Fitzpiers proceeds, it gradually turns out to be more than the idle recreation that it was initially meant to be. She even comes to regret having refused Giles a renewal of his house-leases because this has indirectly 'foredoomed [her] revived girlhood's romance' (p. 219). As she sinks uncontrollably into this abyss of infatuation, her better self struggles to assert itself. She is not completely without conscience and does not wantonly seek to destroy Grace's home and happiness by stealing her husband. This is proved by her hasty flight to Middleton – on the pretext of visiting an invalid relative – because she has no confidence in her ability to resist Fitzpiers if she stays on at Hintock. When she weakly confesses this to Fitzpiers later, the only emotion he experiences is the triumph of conquest, the thrill of knowing that 'the heart which others bled for, bleed[s] for me' (p. 233). The relationship had begun with Mrs Charmond toying with Fitzpiers; now, by a complete tragic reversal, it is Fitzpiers who has mastered the proud beauty of yesteryear. She, who had once 'smiled where she has not loved, and loved where she has not married' (Giles's comment, p. 246), is now completely enslaved by the whims of this philanderer.

This truth is recognized even by Grace, the wronged wife. In that memorable encounter in the woods, where the two women confront each other, lose their bearings in the maze of trees, cling to each other for moral and emotional support, and finally part with an almost conciliatory kiss,[14] Grace sizes up the real situation:

'I thought till now that you had only been cruelly flirting with my husband to amuse your idle moments – a rich lady with a poor professional gentleman whom in her heart she despised... But I guess from your manner that you love him desperately; and I don't hate you as I did before...since it is not sport in your case at all but *real* – O, I do pity you, more than I despise you! For *you* will suffer most!' (p. 255; Hardy's italics)

Mrs Charmond's pride prevents her from acknowledging the truth of this comment and she loudly protests her indifference. But Grace is not to be deceived by assumed appearances, and she goes on:

'I have called him a foolish man – the plaything of a finished coquette. I thought that what was getting to be a tragedy to me was a comedy to you. But now I see that tragedy lies on your side of the situation no less than on mine, and more; that if I have felt trouble at my position you have felt anguish at yours; that if I have had disappointments you have had despairs. Philosophy may fortify *me* – God help *you*!' (p. 256; Hardy's italics)

That Felice experiences moments of self-reproach is evident from the brief encounter with Marty which immediately precedes this crucial interview with Grace. Marty's embarrassment at the mention of Giles Winterborne's name tells her the hidden story that Marty is too tongue-tied to utter. Mrs Charmond is appalled: 'the picture thus exhibited to her of lives drifting awry, involving the wreck of poor Marty's hopes, prompted her yet further in those generous resolves which Melbury's remonstrances had stimulated' (p. 254). The reference here is to an earlier interview between Mrs Charmond and Mr Melbury, in which the anxious father had called on the lady of the manor, and 'appeal[ed] to her in the name of [their] common womanhood' (p. 239) in a desperate bid to salvage his daughter's marriage.[15] In fighting for his daughter's marital happiness, Melbury does not mince matters and Mrs Charmond is understandably indignant at first. To be lectured, on such a delicate matter, by a man so much her social inferior, cannot have been a pleasant experience. Predictably, she tries to assume the accents of injured innocence, but her consciousness of guilt soon reduces her to bitter tears. In this change of heart, what is significant is that 'the allusion to Grace's former love for her seemed to touch her more than all Melbury's other arguments' (p. 250). Thus, she is certainly *not* the heartless seductress that most critics have taken her to be. In fact, her helplessness is suggested by the narrator's comment:

A fascination had led her on; it was as if she had been seized by a hand of velvet; and this was where she found herself – overshadowed with sudden night, as if a tornado had passed. (p. 251)

Mrs Charmond does try 'her best to escape her passionate bondage' to Fitzpiers but finds that the 'struggle was too wearying, too hopeless, while she remained' (pp. 278-9). Conscientiously struggling against her 'infatuation', she makes two determined bids to escape Hintock and thus allow physical distance to cool her ardour. On the pretext of a relative's illness, she goes away to Middleton Abbey, but her attempt is foiled because Fitzpiers repeatedly pursues her even there. Later, moved by Melbury's remonstrances, she again determines to escape to the Continent because she is genuinely troubled by all the unhappiness that her liaison is generating for Grace, Marty and Giles. As an anonymous woodlander puts it:

'She's been all as if her mind were low for some days past – with a sort of fret in her face, as if she chid her own soul. She's the wrong sort of woman for Hintock...But I don't care who the man is, she's been a very kind friend to me.' (p. 263)

In the manuscript this speech, overheard by Fitzpiers, was radically different: the unknown speaker reports that Mrs Charmond's decision to go to the Continent is the result of a threat from her anonymous South Carolinian lover (now in the suicidal, rather than the homicidal, stage of his infatuation) to blow out his own brains if she fails to accompany him abroad.[16] By drastically revising this speech, Hardy changed Mrs Charmond's purely external motivation to an agonizingly internal one. The words 'as if she chid her own soul' suggest a tortured self-reproach that should demolish the image of Felice Charmond as a mere heartless coquette.

In fact, Mrs Charmond is in the act of packing some of her belongings, for her proposed Continental trip, when her pious resolution of severing all links with Grace's husband fades as a blood-soaked Fitzpiers, crawling on all fours for over a mile, taps on her window at midnight because it is the only sanctuary that he knows. With eyes blinded by tears, Felice does all she can to ease his pain and she ministers to all his needs with 'passionate solicitude'. She supports him up a narrow staircase, hides him in the lumber room, hauls out a bed for him to rest, fetches food and water for his nourishment, and finally washes the blood from his face and hands. All this selfless service wins from the narrator the tribute: 'While he ate her eyes lingered anxiously on his face, following its every movement with such lovingkindness as only a fond woman can show' (p. 281). No reader of Hardy can be unaware of the emotional value that Hardy attached to this Biblical word: 'lovingkindness'. To Hardy, it is the highest human virtue and it is significant that he uses it in this scene of extramarital love. What makes this loaded word doubly significant is that, in the manuscript, the sentence had originally read: 'with such solicitude as only a woman can show'.[17] 'Solicitude' lacks the Biblical overtones of 'lovingkindness', and the revision (along with the addition of the word 'fond') helps to lift Felice's passion for Fitzpiers from mere sexual appetite to something infinitely nobler.

Interestingly enough, in the scene which is an obverse mirror image of this one – i.e. Grace ministering to the dying Giles – the situational parallel is strengthened by a verbal echo that readers would fail to pick up from the printed text as it exists today. When Grace bathes Giles's hot head, moistens his feverish lips, sponges his heated body, the narrator says: 'All that a tender nurse could do Grace did; and the power to express her *solicitude* in action, unconscious though the sufferer was, brought her mournful satisfaction' (p. 325; my italic). Here, the word 'solicitude' which connects Grace with Felice (in the manuscript) remains un-changed, and Grace's tending of Giles is not described as an act of 'lovingkindness'. That the revising hand was ultimately sympathetic to Felice Charmond can perhaps be inferred from another textual revision in the manuscript. At Hintock House, when finally an exhausted Felice sponges the blood-stained railing with a trembling hand, the narrator rhapsodizes: 'What will not women do on such devoted occasions?' (p. 282). In the manuscript, this sentence had originally read: 'What will not women do on such desperate occasions?'[18] On second thoughts, Hardy struck out 'desperate' and replaced it by 'devoted'. The substitution of just this single adjective radically transforms the tone of the rhetorical question, and the transferred epithet 'devoted' signals, quite unequivocally, Hardy's final judgement on the character of Felice. The reader too is invited to take a generous view of Felice, a woman in whom 'there beat[s] a heart capable of quick, extempore warmth' (p. 70), who is 'not bad by calculation' (p. 240) as even Melbury readily concedes, and one in whose 'life' and 'love', the narrator solemnly assures us, 'there was nothing... to be ashamed of, and many things of which she might have been proud' (p. 215).

At the end of the novel, when Fitzpiers picks up a quarrel with Mrs Charmond over a trifle (her false hair) and abandons her, our sympathy for this 'devoted' woman is stirred even though she is not the deserted wife (like Grace) but only the discarded mistress. When we are told that she met her death while travelling in search of Fitzpiers, in the vain hope of effecting a reconciliation, the tide of compassion for her sweeps aside moral fences regarding the legality (or otherwise) of the relationship. Our pity for her is reinforced by the delicate hint – Victorian prudery did not allow Hardy to be more explicit – that Felice was pregnant at the time when Fitzpiers so callously abandoned her. In this novel where Hardy takes an honest and unflinching look at the Marriage Question, he does not fall into the conventional trap of glibly equating 'virtue' with 'wife' and 'vice' with 'mistress' (as Boumelha has rightly recognized).[19]

Hardy's concern to show how genuine emotion can transcend socially and morally accepted boundaries is illustrated also in the peripheral character of Suke Damson. On Fitzpiers's side, she is just a country girl of vitality who adds the necessary touch of spice to his jaded appetite. But for Suke, the initial tumble in the hay has led to a deeper involvement which is quite evident from her tearful reaction to the news of Fitzpiers's accident. The wildly exaggerated rumours about Fitzpiers's fall from his horse impel both Suke and Felice (who even forgets the discretion necessary to her social station) to rush to Grace's house to ascertain the nature and extent of the danger. Despite her initial sarcasm – 'Wives all, let's enter together!'[20] – Grace does not allow her wifely jealousy to blind her to the genuine emotion of these two women and a 'tenderness spread[s] over Grace like a dew'. The narrator's comment on the piquant situation is very candid:

> In their [i.e. Felice and Suke's] gestures and faces there were anxieties, affection, agony of heart – all for a man who had wronged them – had never really behaved towards either of them anyhow but selfishly. Neither one but would have well-nigh sacrificed half her life to him, even now. The tears which his possible critical situation could not bring to her [i.e. Grace's] eyes surged over at the contemplation of these fellow-women whose relations with him were as close as her own without its conventionality. (p. 275)

Although Hardy initially thought of naming this novel 'Fitzpiers at Hintock', and although the first 'woodlander' of any importance to whom we are introduced is Marty, the pivot of this story is neither the male intruder nor the female native. Fitzpiers's disruptive value is too great to be ignored and undeniably the book really begins and ends with the solitary figure of Marty. Nevertheless, it is Grace Melbury – the quintessential returned native like Fancy Day and Clym Yeobright before her – who is at the still centre of this storm of mismatched loves.

The tragedy in Grace's life is that she attracts, and dithers between, two men – Giles Winterborne and Edred Fitzpiers – who represent the two antipodal social hemispheres that come into conflict within her own personality. This conflict is nowhere better expressed than in the scene describing the homely entertainment to which Giles has invited the Melbury family and some of his neighbours. Intended to bring the young couple together, this ill-starred Christmas party, with its sequence of domestic mishaps, ironically widens the social gulf between Grace and Giles. Grace is uneasily conscious of the crude homeliness of it all and when the bandsmen strike up the old favourite melodies, the narrator says: 'Grace had been away from home so long, and was so drilled in new dances, that she had forgotten the old figures, and hence did not join in the movement' (p. 104). This is only to be expected of a born woodland girl whose city breeding has rendered her incapable of distinguishing between 'bitter-sweet' and 'John-apple' trees.

Apart from that one episode where Grace shows an independent will and timidly changes 'lose' to 'keep' in the couplet inscribed on the wall by Marty, there is an element of passivity in Grace. She acquiesces in her father's ambition for a socially advantageous marriage and does not even try actively to counter the strange fascination that Fitzpiers casts over her. She blows hot and cold towards Giles with a perversity which cynics would describe as being typically feminine. When Giles is relatively prosperous, she is not sensitive enough to hide her feeling of social superiority; conversely, when Giles is reduced to poverty, the narrator describes her sentiments thus:

> And yet at that very moment the impracticability to which poor Winterborne's suit had been reduced was touching Grace's heart to a warmer sentiment in his behalf than she had felt for years concerning him. (p. 131)

Such are the strangely unpredictable ways of the feminine heart, misogynists might exclaim!

Yet, to do her justice, the docile Grace's emotional confusion is worse confounded by her father who keeps alternating between his dream of a socially creditable marriage[21] and his long-cherished pious resolution of joining Grace and Giles in matrimony, as a reparation for the wrong he had done to Giles's father in stealing his beloved. This makes him encourage Giles and Fitzpiers by turns, although he very shrewdly guesses that 'somewhere in the bottom of her heart there pulsed an *old simple indigenous feeling* favourable to Giles, though it had *become overlaid with implanted tastes*' (p. 109; emphases added). Later, troubled by her husband's obvious infidelity, Grace too passionately regrets the fancy education which has left her neither crow nor peacock:

> 'I wish I worked in the woods like Marty South! I hate genteel life…Because cultivation has only brought me inconveniences and troubles…If I had stayed at home I should have married – ' (p. 240)

The tearful, broken sentence speaks volumes, especially since Grace has just made an 'appalling' discovery. She has courageously 'looked into her heart, and found that her early interest in Giles Winterborne had become revitalized' (p. 238).

While acknowledging that he liked *The Woodlanders* best as a story, Hardy expressed his misgivings about Grace. If we can credit the testimony of Rebekah Owen, Hardy is supposed to have conveyed to her that:

> Grace never interested him much; he was provoked with her all along. If she would have done a really self-abandoned, impassioned thing (gone off with Giles), he could have made a fine tragic ending to the book, but she was too commonplace and straitlaced, and he could not make her.[22]

While we certainly appreciate Hardy's respect for the autonomy of character, we doubt if Grace could have seized the initiative, given the moral strait-jacket which society imposes on her. She certainly gives all the encouragement necessary to motivate an average lover and cannot be held responsible for the fact that Giles is a laggard in love. On Midsummer Eve, for example, Giles – with his characteristic apathy and defeatism – disdains to reach out a restraining hand when Fitzpiers boldly steps forward and snatches Grace from under his very nose. After this symbolic usurpation, it is only a matter of time before Fitzpiers and Grace are declared man and wife.

Placing Grace in the tradition of 'Hardy women', an early reviewer astutely remarked: 'There is a little of Bathsheba Everdene in Grace Melbury – enough to make her marry the man of her fancy and not of her heart.'[23] But while Bathsheba had a providential escape from both Troy and Boldwood, and could finally settle down with Gabriel Oak, Grace is left with no other option but to return to a seemingly repentant Fitzpiers after Giles (rather selfishly?) courts death. Perceiving in Grace a rudimentary conflict between 'flesh' and 'spirit', Gregor comments that 'she provides Hardy with an opportunity to do a first sketch for Sue Bridehead.'[24] Apart from the very obvious fact that both Sue and Grace, like most Hardy women, vacillate between two contrasted male figures, other similarities are not hard to discover. Impelled by her 'Daphnean instinct' (p. 310), Grace may not have quite jumped out of her bedroom window like Sue, but her departure at the news of Fitzpiers's return (as the repentant husband) is no less precipitate. Grace's concern for social propriety which pushes the ailing Giles to his martyrdom is later recalled in the episode where Sue tantalizingly keeps the young Oxford student at arm's length, indirectly contributing to his death. Also, Grace's tame return to Fitzpiers is tragically echoed in Sue's humiliating final surrender to Phillotson. But the parallel cannot be pressed any further because, intrinsically, these two women belong to two opposite ends of the spectrum. There is a gulf of difference between Sue's morbid shrinking from physical contact and that part of Grace's nature which successive revisions of the text could only obliquely hint at.[25]

The narrator describes Grace as 'a woman who, herself, had more of Artemis than of Aphrodite in her constitution' (p. 325). This is a baffling comment because under her seemingly docile surface, wild passions smoulder. Although they belong to opposite sides of the marital fence, Grace is really more kin to Felice than is commonly realized. This is brilliantly suggested by the encounter in the woods where Grace, on accidentally meeting Mrs Charmond, 'stood like a wild animal on first confronting a mirror' (p. 254). Mirrors are self-reflecting, and this interview represents 'like meeting like' – Mr Melbury's shrewd comment on an earlier Grace-Felice meeting (p. 115). Both these women are susceptible to the 'fascination' of the 'coercive, irresistible Fitzpiers'. Grace experiences an 'indescribable thrill' (p. 151) when her eyes first meet Fitzpiers's, as reflected in the mirror, and later she is powerless to 'terminate the interview' because of 'the compelling power of Fitzpiers's atmosphere' (p. 155). The narrator's assessment of the Fitzpiers-Grace relationship is quite revealing: 'Fitzpiers acted upon her like a dram, exciting her' (p. 181); he exercised a 'strange influence… upon her whenever he came near her', but it was 'an excitement which was not love' (p. 184); the 'intoxication' that he produced lasted only during the brief period of physical proximity. This is as explicit as Hardy dared to be, without having the reviewers reaching for his throat. But what the Grundyites prevented Hardy from saying is rather crudely and openly stated by the uninhibited Melbury. When his daughter returns to her truant husband, Melbury accepts it with a shrug: 'Well – he's her husband…and let her take him back to her bed if she will!' (p. 372)

Even in her relationship with Giles, it is *her* 'agonizing seductiveness' (p. 303) that prompts Giles's first – and last – passionate embrace and kiss. 'Then why don't you do what you want to?'(p. 303) Grace archly asks, and Giles is just human enough not to be able to resist this open invitation. Earlier, it is *her* 'abandonment to the seductive hour' and the 'passionate desire for primitive life' as reflected in *her* face (p. 226) that lead to Giles absent-mindedly caressing the flower that she wears in her bosom. Even in the days of their 'childhood' affection, 'her mouth was somewhat more ready to receive a kiss from his than was his to bestow one' (p. 197). Towards the end, when she realizes the enormity of Giles's sacrifice, she repeatedly calls out to him to enter the hut. There is something more than common humanity or Christian charity in her final italicized appeal: *'Come to me, dearest! I don't mind what they say or what they think of us any more'* (p. 321).[26] This impression is strengthened by the wild, remorseful kisses she bestows on the dying Giles and the 'thrill of pride' with which she triumphantly tells her husband that he may draw 'the extremest inference' from their living together in the hut (p. 332).

That the Felice–Fitzpiers and Grace–Giles relationships are basically not very different is suggested by the question Fitzpiers puts to Grace on the death of Giles: 'Would it startle you to hear... that she who was to me what he was to you is dead also?' (p. 332). That these two relationships run parallel is dimly recognized by Giles too. Much earlier, when Grace had reacted rather sharply to his absent-mindedly stroking the flower on her dress, he had lamely muttered his defence: 'It would not have occurred to me if I had not seen something like it done elsewhere – at Middleton lately' (p. 226). This strange parallelism is nowhere more powerfully suggested than in the scene where Grace nurses the dying Giles. The scene is almost a mirror image of the previous one, where Felice had devotedly nursed the injured Fitzpiers, and no reader can miss the resemblance. Just in case (s)he does, Hardy is anxious to drive home the point through the consciousness of Fitzpiers. On entering the hut, Fitzpiers is:

> arrested by the spectacle, not so much in its intrinsic character... but in its character as the counterpart of one that had had its run many months before, in which he had figured as the patient, and the woman had been Felice Charmond. (p. 330)

A few pages earlier, in an authorial intrusion, Hardy had significantly commented:

> Six months before this date a scene, almost similar in its mechanical parts, had been enacted at Hintock House...Outwardly like as it had been, it was yet infinite in spiritual difference; *though a*

*woman's devotion had been common to both.* (p. 325; emphasis added)

No further explanation of the 'spiritual difference' follows, and the sentence remains quite ambiguous. If Hardy (who was certainly not a prude) is here trying to claim that the Grace–Giles relationship is on a higher plane because it is untouched by the physicality of the Felice–Fitzpiers relationship, then we have to find a satisfactory answer to a crucial question. Why does Hardy refrain from using the key word 'lovingkindness' in describing Grace's ministration to Giles, when he uses this value-loaded word to describe a relationship which should, by conventional standards of morality, remain beyond the pale of the reader's sympathy? But that is just the point. Conventional judgements of 'good' and 'bad', conventional stereotypes of 'virtuous wife' and 'false mistress' are simply irrelevant. Hardy's portrayal of women is very complex and ambivalent: the women themselves are a bundle of contradictions and conflicting impulses, inviting both our sympathy and our censure, and Hardy's attitude to his women is sometimes confused and shifting.

# 6

# The Short Stories of the 1890s

The short stories of Hardy really constitute the neglected area of his protean literary *oeuvre*. Although marginalized by readers and critics alike, some of these stories are significant in representing ideas in embryo, in tentative rehearsing of themes to be fully explored in the later novels. Thus, 'The Romantic Adventures of a Milkmaid' (1883), with its comic denouement, is an anticipation of *Tess* (1891) where 'Hardy looks unconditionally at the worst contingencies' because 'Tess is Margery carried to a frighteningly right conclusion'.[1] The writing of *Tess* seems to have sensitized Hardy to the pain and pathos of a woman's position in patriarchal society where it is always the woman who is forced to 'pay'. Despite modern critical readings of unconscious betrayals of voyeurism in Hardy's treatment of Tess, it is surely transparent to the average (and less sophisticated) reader that Hardy's emotional investment in Tess is both sincere and unalloyed. Hardy confessed to George Douglas: 'I am so truly glad that Tess the Woman has won your affections. I too lost my heart to her as I went on with her history';[2] to Thomas Macquoid he lamented, 'I am glad you like Tess – though I have not been able to put on paper all that she is, or was, to me'.[3] This is not merely the expression of a common artistic regret of execution failing to match the original brilliance of conception; it also reveals a personal commitment to Tess, who becomes for Hardy not just an imaginative fictional construct but an intimate flesh-and-blood acquaintance.

The experience of writing *Tess*, more than any other novel, helped Hardy emotionally to transcend gender boundaries; and in the wake of its (partial) composition,[4] he seems to have been left with a powerful, residual, intuitive sympathy for women which spilled over into the six short stories that he wrote for *Graphic*. These six stories ('Barbara of the House of Grebe', 'The Marchioness of Stonehenge', 'Lady Mottisfont', 'The Lady Icenway', 'Squire Petrick's Lady' and

'Anna, Lady Baxby'), along with four other previously published stories, were later gathered together as *A Group of Noble Dames* (1891). Although the ostensible narrators of these vignettes of the aristocratic past are the male members of the Wessex Field and Antiquarian Club, a powerful feminine point of view does emerge from these women-centred stories. This is hardly surprising in the context of a remarkable statement made by Hardy in his letter of 21 October 1891 to W. E. Henley, in response to the latter's editorial request for a story: 'Now – would you not rather wait till some time (late) next year? I am *pregnant* of several Noble Dames (this is an *unnatural reversal* I know, but my constitution is getting *mixed*) – I mean I have thought of several more sketches of that sort' (my italics).[5] For a male author to use the metaphor of 'mothering' a text is very unusual indeed because, as Gilbert and Gubar have pointed out, 'all-pervasive in Western literary civilization' is 'the patriarchal notion that the writer "fathers" his text just as God fathered the world', 'through the use of the phallic pen on the "pure space" of the virgin page'.[6]

In a majority of the stories of *A Group of Noble Dames* and *Life's Little Ironies* (1894) Hardy's major preoccupation is with the theme of marital incompatibility and the consequent loneliness and frustration of women trapped in emotionally sterile marriages. Having no other avenue of self-fulfilment, marriage becomes the be-all and end-all of a woman's existence. Sometimes, as in the case of Betty Dornell ('The First Countess of Wessex'), she is pushed into marriage by her ambitious and scheming mother at the tender age of 13 when she is too ignorant of its full implications. Even with the relatively maturer heroines, marriage seems to be a pressing economic necessity that does not take into account individual predilections. Revealing the naked economic compulsion beneath the decorous surface of love and romance (in a spirit that recalls Jane Austen) the narrator in 'An Imaginative Woman' tries to analyse Ella Marchmill's unthinking mismating. The dreamy poetic Ella has married the unsentimental 'gunmaker', William Marchmill, because:

> the necessity of getting life-leased at all cost, a cardinal virtue which all good mothers teach, kept her from thinking of it at all till she had closed with William, had passed the honeymoon, and

reached the reflecting stage. Then, like a person who has stumbled upon some object in the dark, she wondered what she had got...a clog or a pedestal, everything to her or nothing.[7]

This is a recurrent motif and Edith Harnham, in 'On the Western Circuit', is kin to Ella in being pushed into a marriage by well-meaning but insensitive parents whose limited visions can envisage no broader horizons for their daughters. As the narrator explains:

Edith Harnham led a lonely life. Influenced by the belief of the British parent that a bad marriage with its aversions is better than free womanhood with its interests, dignity, and leisure, she had consented to marry the elderly wine-merchant. (*LLI*, p. 97)

The obvious narratorial animus against such loveless life-bondages is a reflection of Hardy's own sentiments in the 1890s. Perhaps Hardy's personal disillusionment in marriage contributed not insignificantly to this state of mind but even without entering biographical speculation it is easy to gauge Hardy's sentiments from his contribution to a symposium in 1894. Answering a question on what he thought young girls should be taught before entering matrimony (a debate on sex education probably prompted by *Tess*), Hardy wrote:

As your problems are given on the old lines so I take them, without entering into the general question *whether marriage*, as we at present understand it, *is such a desirable goal for all women as it is assumed to be*; or whether civilisation can escape the humiliating indictment that, while it has been able to cover itself with glory in the arts, the literatures, in religions, and in the sciences, it has never succeeded in creating that homely thing, a satisfactory scheme for the conjunction of the sexes.[8] (my italics)

Hardy's questioning of the institution of marriage is fictionally reflected in Jude and Sue's hesitation and mistrust regarding marriage. More than twenty years later (in 1918) Hardy was to declare categorically to Florence Henniker: 'If I were a woman I should think twice before entering into matrimony in these days of emancipation, when everything is open to the sex.'[9] But this is precisely where the tragedy lies. Hardy's fictional women live out their frustrated lives in an age and society where opportunities for women were very limited and marriage was considered the only respectable maturation of self-hood. Hence for these lonely ladies, whether aristocratic or plebeian, marriage becomes a prison from which there is no escape since 'what's done can't be undone'. Hardy had used this phrase power-fully in *Tess* (Joan Durbeyfield's response to the news of Tess's deser-tion by Angel) and it echoes hauntingly through the stories of *A Group of Noble Dames* and *Life's Little Ironies*. After Barbara marries the penniless and socially inferior Edmond Willowes, her parents Sir John and Lady Grebe reconcile themselves to this misalliance because they realize that 'what was done could not be undone' ('Barbara of the House of Grebe').[10] Later, when her 'Adonis'-like husband returns from his Continental educational tour badly mutilated by fire, Barbara shrinks from him in ill-concealed horror and, despite her subsequent remorse next morning, she realizes that 'to undo the scene of last night was impossible' (*GND*, p. 264). Similarly, when Lord Quantock reacts with pained disapproval on learning of his daughter's runaway marriage, her husband coolly replies: 'The deed is done, and can't be undone by talking here' ('The Honourable Laura', *GND*, p. 358).

Unlike the world of *Jude*, where divorce is a practical possibility, the earlier novels and stories reflect a world where there is no prospect of release, save through death. Thus Mrs Dornell tries to argue the *de facto* nature of their daughter's marriage in pleading with her husband, Squire Dornell, to desist from sowing the seeds of rebellion in young Betty: 'Lord, don't you see, dear, that what is done cannot be undone, and how all this foolery jeopardizes her happiness with her husband?' ('The First Countess of Wessex', *GND*, p. 221). This irrefutable logic carries its weight with the hot-headed Squire and, when he later meets his son-in-law, he tries to suppress his paternal disapproval and grudgingly concedes: 'Well, what's done can't be undone... though it was mighty early, and was no doing of mine. She's your wife; and there's an end on't' (*GND*, p. 230). The tragic irreversibility of a course of action is brought home more achingly to Edith Harnham, whose initial charitable gesture of ghost-writing a love-letter on behalf of her illiterate maid,[11] Anna, boomerangs ironically on herself. Caught in a web of deception and vicarious romantic wish-fulfilment, Mrs Harnham cannot extricate herself from the position of Anna's 'amanuensis' to which she has so thoughtlessly committed herself. Despite her clear-eyed recognition of the emotional danger to which she is exposing herself, Edith

Harnham realizes that 'what was done could not be undone, and it behoved her now, as Anna's only protector, to help her as much as she could' ('On the Western Circuit', *LLI*, p. 96).

Woman as victim of her own (frustrated) sexuality is a recurring motif in these two volumes of Hardy's short stories. Mrs Harnham's growing 'infatuation' for the 'sensuous' Charles Bradford Raye (her maid Anna's lover) makes her passionately exclaim to herself on learning of Anna's pregnancy: 'I wish his child was mine – I wish it was!' (*LLI*, p. 98). Charles Raye's idle caress of Edith's palm at the fair (mistaking it to be Anna's, in the press of the crowd) has awakened a latent sexuality in one whose marriage 'contract had left her still a woman whose deeper nature had never been stirred' (p. 97). Unlike the 'unfledged' Anna whose innocent simplicity as a 'child of nature' makes her vulnerable to Raye, the maturer (30-year-old) Edith self-consciously 'indulge[s]' herself in the 'luxury' of her infatuation. In a startlingly frank analysis of female sexuality that must have shocked Mrs Grundy, the narrator says that Edith's passion for Charles is fanned by the fact that 'he had been able to seduce another woman in two days [which] was his crowning though unrecognized fascination for her as the she-animal' (p. 97).[12] But it would be grossly unfair to the 'lonely, impressionable' Edith to suggest that animality is her sole ruling passion. Behind her desire that Charles should have impregnated her and not Anna is surely her frustrated maternity, because the narrator clearly suggests that her taking up of Anna and her attempts to educate the country girl are the result of her 'being without children' (p. 88). Edith is staunch to Anna in her trouble and despite her private misgivings about 'ruining' the young barrister Charles,[13] she completes the business that she had so thoughtlessly begun by accompanying Anna (as witness) to the registry office in London. When she returns to Melchester and her sterile marriage, and her husband enters her apartment, all the agony of her situation is revealed by her broken whisper: 'Ah – my husband! – I forgot I had a husband!' (p. 106)

Edith's compeer, Ella Marchmill, indulging her 'tender' and 'passionate' feelings for the poet Robert Trewe,[14] similarly has to remind herself of 'how wicked she was, a woman *having a husband* and three children, to let her mind stray to a stranger in this unconscionable manner' ('An Imaginative Woman', *LLI*, p. 21; my italics). Later, in her deathbed confession to her husband, Ella admits: 'I can't tell what possessed me – how I could forget you so, my husband!' (p. 32) Both Edith and Ella 'forget' they have husbands because the emotional sterility of their marriages force their 'living ardours' into fresher channels. Ella's final self-justification – 'I wanted a fuller appreciator, perhaps, rather than another lover' (p. 32) – belies the erotic content of the earlier scene where Ella secretly contemplates Trewe's photograph with passionate tears and kisses.[15] Like Edith, Ella corresponds with her unmet 'God of Love' under her poetic pseudonym 'John Ivy', and she even sends him her votary's offering of some of her best poems. When Trewe (unknowingly) turns away from her very gates, Ella is prostrated by grief and disappointment and she 'trie[s] to let off her emotion by unnecessarily kissing the children, till she had a sudden sense of disgust at being reminded how plain-looking they were, like their father' (p. 27). Later, when she is expecting her fourth child, she must have often wished (like Edith), when she gazed at the poet's picture, that the coming child was the 'handsome' Trewe's rather than the 'plain-looking' Marchmill's. Her unconscious desire ironically triumphs at the end when by 'a known but inexplicable trick of Nature', the 'dreamy and peculiar expression of the poet's face' (and the colour of his hair) is reflected in the face of her little boy, like a 'transmitted idea' (p. 32).

A physical copy of their lovers, which Edith and Ella fail to achieve biologically, is attained by another 'possessed' woman, Car'line in 'The Fiddler of the Reels'. Car'line's almost epileptic reaction to the 'heart-stealing melodies' played by 'Mop' Ollamoor suggests that this 'weird and wizardly' fiddler robs her of her own volition, leaving her completely enslaved to his will.[16] Even after her marriage to the patient Ned Hipcroft (who accepts both her and her daughter by 'Mop'), Car'line is just as hopelessly vulnerable to the 'acoustic magnetism' of Mop's fiddle. The narrator's repeated use of words and phrases like 'hysteric', 'convulsively', 'paroxysm of desperation', 'excruciating spasms' suggest that when she dances 'slavishly and abjectly' during their final encounter, it is not just the gin and beer that she has drunk which is responsible for her complete surrender of 'independent will'. Like Margery in 'The Romantic Adventures of a Milkmaid' before her, Car'line seems to be trapped by an intoxication that has an element of 'witchery' about it. Mop and Baron von Xanten both carry a strong suggestion of the supernatural, and they seem to be, if not quite 'Mephi-stophelian' intruders, at least the type of demon-lover common to folklore and ballads. Their power over Car'line and Margery, who are like putty in their hands, cannot be solely explained in terms of sexual fascination, the allure of the exotic, the strange power of music, or a young girl's 'Cinderella' fantasies. But, surprisingly, the narrative sympathy that is so transparent in the case of Edith and Ella is more ambivalent in the case of Car'line, and the reader's sympathy at the end of the story is directed more towards the husband Ned than to Car'line. After Mop abducts his daughter 'Carry', it is the step-father Ned who spends sleepless nights in his anxiety that the 'rascal's torturing her to maintain him!' (*LLI*, p. 138). His love for a child not physically his own – 'But she *is* mine, all the same! Ha'n't I nussed her? Ha'n't I fed her and teached her? Ha'n't I played wi' her' (p. 137; Hardy's italic) – is contrasted with Car'line's strange unconcern: 'Don't 'ee raft yourself so, Ned! You prevent my getting a bit o' rest!' (p. 138). In her unnaturalness as a mother, Car'line forfeits the sympathy[17] that she deserves as a woman victimized in a sexual power-relationship by a man who consciously exploits his uncanny hold over her.

In fact, motherhood enters Hardy's short stories in a way unprecedented in the novels – despite Fanny's and Tess's illegitimate babies, Lady Constantine's technically illegitimate son, and the shadowy presence of Jude and Sue's children. Moreover, in these stories of the 1890s Hardy is very much ahead of his times and he seems to be advocating quite revolutionary ideas based on eugenic principles. For instance, the wife in 'Squire Petrick's Lady' suffers from a romantic 'hallucination' (like her mother and grandmother before her, so it seems to be an inherited nervous trait) and just before she dies after giving birth to a son, she makes a melodramatic death-bed confession. She enlightens her husband, Timothy Petrick, that their new-born son (the long-hoped-for heir) is not really his. Timothy Petrick's natural initial reaction as a widower is to sink into 'a hatred and mistrust of womankind' (*GND*, p. 317) and he sadly neglects the child Rupert. But gradually, through a perverse pride in his son's supposedly 'aristocratic blood' (the father is conjectured to be the young Marquis of Christminster), Petrick comes not only to dote on the allegedly illegitimate boy but also to completely reverse his earlier judgemental stand on his wife Annetta. Being a man 'of good old beliefs in the divinity of kings', his 'poor wife's conduct in improving the blood and breed of the Petrick family win[s] his heart' (p. 319). Completely ignoring what Hardy was to call, in *Jude the*

*Obscure*, the 'beggarly question of parentage',[18] Petrick's volte-face makes him admire and approve of 'his good wife' who 'like a skilful gardener' had 'given attention to the art of grafting' (p. 319) and improved the family stock. Petrick's reaction anticipates that of the nonchalant husband in Hardy's poem 'The Husband's View' (*Time's Laughingstocks*, 1909). In order to hide her 'sin', the girl in this poem hastily marries the first man who offers himself and when the 'untimely fruit' is discovered by the husband, instead of deserting or upbraiding her, he calmly approves of her action because the nation needs sturdy sons for 'soldiering'.

These radical impulses of the 1890s (perhaps influenced by Shavian ideas) hardened into convictions, and in 1906 Hardy was to write to Millicent Fawcett of his belief that the 'father of a woman's child' is entirely her own business.[19] Looking at it from the man's point of view, Hardy was to defend his poem and unequivocally explain his stance to Agnes Grove in 1909:

> In 'The Husband's View' to which you also allude, the husband's state of mind is preeminently a sane one, if you reflect on it. In fact he is the man of the future, though it did not strike me that he was till now. If our endeavours shd [*sic*] be directed to the good of humanity at large, & eugenic principles shd [*sic*] prevail, the husband of a century hence will say to his wife, 'Pray don't consider my feelings, if you shd [*sic*] meet with a healthier or more intellectual man than I am. The race is the thing.'[20]

This is a tall order for most average husbands, and certainly one which William Marchmill fails to live up to in 'An Imaginative Woman'. This story and 'Squire Petrick's Lady' form a diptych, an interesting study in contrast. Timothy Petrick ironically rejects his biological son when young Rupert's 'broad nostril' and 'bull-lip' finally convince him (along with a conversation with Annetta's family doctor) that the child is not really descended from the illustrious house of the Duke of Southwesterland. Conversely, William Marchmill no less ironically rejects his biological son because the child's physical resemblance to the portrait of the poet misleads Marchmill into a conviction that his wife has played him false with her (unmet) poet-lover.[21] That wives are often thus sorely tempted, especially when taunted with their failure to produce a son and heir, is illustrated in 'The Lady Icenway'. When Lord Icenway bitterly reproves his wife Maria that 'you could oblige your first husband, and couldn't oblige me' (*GND*, p. 314), Lady Icenway regrets that she had not 'sooner' thought of using her returned (and bigamously married) first husband to produce the much-desired 'lineal successor to the barony'. This first husband, the foreigner Anderling, is forced to live incognito (on his return to England after a long period of self-exile) because his love for his son makes him extremely servile to the imperious Maria's whims. As soon as Maria, now Lady Icenway, conceives of her plan of using Anderling, she goes to his cottage and unabashedly tells him, 'You must get well – you must! *There's a reason*' (p. 313; Hardy's italics), and she blushingly whispers her 'reason' into his ears. The dying man's sad response (recalling Tess's when Angel comes to reclaim her) is: 'Too late, my darling, too late!' The fact that Anderling has been employed as Lady Icenway's *gardener* is surely no coincidence, and when she goes to her 'gardener' for eugenic assistance, it recalls Petrick's praise of his dead wife as a 'skilful gardener' who had understood 'the art of grafting' to improve the family line.

Narrative sympathy for Maria as the unsuspecting victim of a deception (i.e. bigamy) is heavily undercut by the revelation of her arrogant social superiority and by her lukewarm maternal feeling, which makes Anderling's strong paternal interest in their boy appear ridiculously excessive to her. Her 'haughty severity', and the emotional coldness that her name suggests, make Lady Icenway one of the less amiable ladies in Hardy's gallery of 'Noble Dames'. Another not-so-amiable lady is Joanna Phippard of 'To Please His Wife' (*LLI*). This story is a ruthless exposition of internecine female jealousy,[22] and in Joanna we have an almost medieval personification of Envy and Covetousness. Joanna has no qualms about weaning the sailor Jolliffe away from her friend Emily Hanning to whom Jolliffe is nearly as good as engaged. But Joanna's 'green envy' is not assuaged even when she succeeds in becoming Mrs Jolliffe. In a spirit of competition, she resents that Emily, now married to the wealthy and 'worthy' merchant Lester, can afford to send her two sons to 'College' while Joanna's two sons are 'obliged to go to the Parish School!' (*LLI*, p. 114). Her constant nagging drives Jolliffe to seek his fortune afresh; and even when he returns from his first sea expedition with a bag literally bursting with gold 'sovereigns and guineas', it fails to satisfy Joanna, whose peevish response is: '*we* count by hundreds; *they* count by thousands' (p. 117; Hardy's italics). Joanna's social pride cannot stomach the fact that her 'boys will have to live by steering the ships that the Lesters own; and I was once above her!' (p. 117) In fact, Joanna's envy colours even the narrative voice, and we are told that '[t]races of patronage had been visible in Emily's manner of late' (p. 114) and that 'Emily's silks rustled arrogantly' (p. 119) when she entered Joanna's small grocery shop. That this is just a reflected expression of Joanna's jaundiced vision is made quite unequivocal when the narrator chooses to dissociate and distance himself from Joanna's all-consuming envy and state: 'To do Emily Lester justice, her assumption of superiority was mainly a figment of Joanna's brain' (p. 119).

'To Please His Wife' reads almost like a prose rendering of a morality play, with its pattern of Virtue (Emily) rewarded and Vice (Joanna) punished. The character contrast of these two women could not have been more stark, and the unexpectedness of the ending lies in the fact that it is so very inevitable. There is no final ironic twist such as one comes to expect of a short story in general and Hardy's short stories – dealing with 'life's little ironies' – in particular. Unlike Newson in *The Mayor of Casterbridge*, the sailor Jolliffe does not return to be reunited with his family, and the ship (appropriately named *Joanna* as a symbol of Joanna's inordinate 'ambition' which even stifles her genuine maternal instincts) presumably goes down with Jolliffe and their two young sons on board. Joanna ends up, half-crazed through remorse, grief, and long-deferred hope, virtually a pensioner in the generous household of Emily, 'the woman whose place she had usurped out of pure covetousness' (p. 113). The satiric portraiture of Joanna, however, mellows down in the final paragraphs of the story, where the 'wretched woman', moved by 'baseless expectations', hastens hopefully to the shop door every time that a fancied sound of footsteps in the street deludes her into thinking that her husband and sons have at last returned. It is easy to take a final judgemental stand on Joanna and say that she deserved her suffering, that her mental torture is indeed 'her purgation for the sin of making them [i.e. her husband and two sons] the slaves of her ambition' (p. 120). But narrative/authorial sympathy for this (self)-demented woman is expressed, indirectly, through the figure of the young man who, aware of her sad story, answers as 'kindly' as possible Joanna's eager question, 'Has anybody come?' (p. 122). This young man perhaps embodies that 'lovingkindness' in human relationships which Hardy felt made even the worst tragedies endurable.

Joanna's tragedy – reflected in the emptiness of the final words of the story 'No; nobody has come' – is largely self-invited; but this does not deprive her of authorial sympathy for her 'grief-stricken soul'.

Joanna's appropriation of Jolliffe had not been inspired by love; she had 'usurped' Emily's place 'out of pure covetousness'. Her 'dog-in-the-manger' attitude is reflected repeatedly in Hardy's fiction, notably in Eustacia's alternating attraction towards Wildeve and Clym, which is goaded by thoughts of Thomasin's real or imagined rivalry. Similarly, Grace's interest in her wayward husband Fitzpiers is rekindled when she sees how selflessly and passionately two other women (Felice and Suke) love him. When these two distraught women rush to Grace's house on hearing of Fitzpiers's equestrian accident, Grace's reaction is: 'How these unhappy women must have admired Edred!... How attractive he must be to everybody; and indeed, he is attractive.' The narrator comments on the possibility that '*piqued by rivalry*, these ideas might have been transmuted into their corresponding emotions by a show of the least reciprocity in Fitzpiers. There was, in truth, a lovebird yearning to fly from her heart; and it wanted a lodging badly' (my italics).[23] That a wife can be 'piqued' into renewed love and admiration for her husband, by learning how desirable he is to another woman, is illustrated in 'Anna, Lady Baxby'. Set against the background of the Civil War, the story domesticizes the conflict between Royalist and Parliamentary forces. Lady Baxby, responding to an emotionally charged appeal from her brother, is about to desert her Royalist husband and join the Parliamentary forces when she surprises an 'intriguing damsel' obviously awaiting a secret 'assignation' with Lord Baxby. But, instead of being repelled by her 'wicked' husband's 'faithlessness' and 'sly manoeuvrings', Lady Baxby's reaction is: '" How the wench loves him!"... She changed from the home-hating truant to the strategic wife in a moment' (*GND*, p. 328).

In the short stories female desire quite often seems to be inextricably linked with envy and covetousness rather than simple affection. Thus, in 'The Marchioness of Stonehenge', Lady Caroline, surfeited with the attention and flattery of young noblemen, chooses to bestow her hand on 'quite a plain-looking young man of humble birth… and guileless heart… the parish-clerk's son' (*GND*, p. 277).[24] Just as we are about to applaud her for her commendable lack of social pride and mature perceptiveness of innate human worth, there appears the deflating narrative qualification: 'It should be said that perhaps the Lady Caroline... was a little stimulated in this passion by the discovery that a young girl of the village already loved the young man fondly, and that he had paid some attentions to her' (p. 277). Later, Lady Caroline exploits the tender devotion of this simple village girl, Milly, by palming off her baby on her and thus removing all evidence of the 'mismated' clandestine marriage of which she is very soon heartily 'ashamed'. Continuing the same pattern of coveting what belongs to others, and now the Marchioness of Stonehenge, Lady Caroline's 'motherly emotions' are stirred years later when she sees what a fine young man and successful soldier her hitherto neglected son has become. In her determination to declare her true identity as his mother and reclaim him, she is again driven by a jealousy of Milly. Foolishly confident that her son 'would only too gladly exchange a cottage-mother for one who was a peeress of the realm', she resolves to tear him 'away from that woman whom she began to hate with the fierceness of a deserted heart for having taken her place as the mother of her only child' (p. 287). At this point the Marchioness conveniently forgets that *she* had initially used the threat of dire consequences in forcing Milly to assume the role of the parish-clerk's son's 'widow'. The Marchioness, like Joanna, meets her nemesis when her son chooses the 'dear devoted soul [pointing to Milly]' who 'tended me from my birth, watched over me, nursed me when I was ill, and deprived herself of many a little comfort to push me on' (p. 288; Hardy's parenthesis). Subsequently the Marchioness dies of '[t]hat anguish that is sharper than a serpent's tooth' (p. 289). The obvious allusion to *King Lear* is ironically double-edged, because while the son appears to be ungrateful to his biological mother (who had callously abandoned him), he remains unflinchingly faithful to his adoptive mother who cared for him when he was 'weak and helpless'.

In the final paragraph of this story, which obviously serves as the framing device to link the Dean's narrative to the following story which also deals with two women's rivalry over the possession of a child, the 'sentimental member' among the Club's audience voices what is perhaps an authorial sentiment: 'She probably deserved some pity' (p. 289). This line sums up the impulse behind many of the stories of the 1890s because they seem to suggest that woman, despite all her alleged waywardness, selfishness and occasional perversity, deserves pity and not censure. As the 'sentimental member' puts it, in his narrative gloss while relating the story of the 'Lady Mottisfont', '[w]hen all is said and done, and the truth told, men seldom show much self-sacrifice in their conduct as lords and masters to helpless women bound to them for life' (*GND*, p. 296). Hardyan accents are clearly audible behind this exercise in ventriloquism for, as Hardy acknowledged to J. W. Mackail: 'How much less regardful of self women are than men.'[25] Male selfishness is ruthlessly exposed in 'For Conscience' Sake' where Millborne re-enacts the 'old story' of promising a young girl marriage, seducing her, and then 'coolly' abandoning her because it would be 'beneath my position to marry her' (*LLI*, p. 49). Twenty years later, his conscience belatedly awakens and prompts him to 'rectify the past' by 'putting wrong right' (p. 50). In his reparative plan, Millborne seems to be impelled more by a desire to regain his own 'sense of self-respect' rather than to make amends to 'the poor victim herself, [who] encumbered with a child,... had really to pay the penalty' (p. 49). This 'poor victim', Leonora, is a Tess[26] who has come through triumphant because by her own determined efforts she has established herself as a respected teacher of music and useful member of society.

When Millborne belatedly offers her marriage, Leonora (who has passed herself off as a 'widow', Mrs Frankland) replies with admirable spirit and dignity: 'My position in this town is a respected one; I have built it up by my own hard labours, and, in short, I don't wish to alter it' (p. 53). Behind this speech lie twenty years of hard struggle as a single parent, and Hardy's admiration for such a woman comes out clearly from an anecdote that he incorporated into his third-person autobiography:

> In December Hardy was told a story by a Mrs Cross, a very old country-woman he met, of a girl she had known who had been betrayed and deserted by a lover. She kept her child by her own exertions, and lived bravely and throve. After a time the man returned poorer than she, and wanted to marry her; but she refused. He ultimately went into the Union workhouse. The young woman's conduct in not caring to be 'made respectable' won the novelist-poet's admiration, and he wished to know her name; but the old narrator said, 'Oh, never mind their names: they be dead and rotted by now.'

The eminently modern idea embodied in this example – of a woman's not becoming necessarily the chattel and slave of her seducer – impressed Hardy as being one of the first glimmers of woman's enfranchisement; and he made use of it in succeeding years in more than one case in his fiction and verse.[27]

One instantly thinks of Tess, who proudly refuses to pretend to love Alec (after her rape/seduction) although she knows that 'a lie on this thing would do the most good to me now; but I have honour enough left, little as 'tis, not to tell that lie'.[28] But consideration for her fatherless siblings finally forces Tess to submit to Alec and become his 'creature' again in the final 'phase' of the novel just as Leonora reluctantly accepts Millborne's offer of marriage in the hope that the consequent 'social lift' will smoothen the path for the marriage of her daughter Frances with the fastidious curate. Familial loyalties compel both Tess and Leonora to compromise their personal integrity, and Tess's bitter indictment of Alec – 'And you had used your cruel persuasion upon me.... O, you have torn my life all to pieces' (*Tess*, p. 403) – is echoed in Leonora's accusation of Millborne after their marriage ironically widens the breach between Frances and her lover: 'Why did you come and disturb my life a second time?... Why did you pester me with your conscience, till I was driven to accept you to get rid of your importunity?' (*LLI*, p. 58). If Alec keeps reappearing at Tess's side like the veritable 'Satan', Millborne returns 'as the spectre to their [i.e. Frances and Leonora's] intended feast of Hymen', turning 'its promise to ghastly failure' (p. 59). Ultimately, Millborne performs the only truly honourable act of his life – he disappears and leaves mother and daughter in peace to pick up the interrupted threads of their lives. In his letter of explanation for his self-exile he reiterates the 'what's-done-can't-be-undone' motif of these stories when he admits that 'there are some derelictions of duty which cannot be blotted out by tardy accomplishment' (p. 61).

Millborne is man enough to give the two women the deliverance they desire. Not so young Randolph in 'The Son's Veto'. Acutely conscious of his (precarious) social position, Randolph takes upon himself the male prerogative of ordering his widowed mother's life. He embodies the repressive codes of patriarchal society which stifle natural female aspirations. Poor Sophy, 'a child of nature', had stood too much in awe of her 'reverend and august' husband, and after his death their son Randolph arrogates to himself his father's authoritarian role. The sheer emptiness of Sophy's life is symptomatized by the elaborate braiding of her hair, which is intricately coiled up every morning, only to be 'demolished regularly at bedtime' (*LLI*, p. 33). This daily doing up and undoing of the cleverly woven braids is an index not of her vanity but of the emotional vacuum in her life, because her son 'seems to belong so little to me personally, so entirely to his dead father' (p. 43). Even after over fourteen years of marriage, Sophy is still a misfit in the social atmosphere to which she (the ex-parlour maid) has been raised by her marriage with a vicar. This is rendered painfully obvious when her son impatiently corrects her grammatical lapses, and also by her total sense of non-belonging at the grand event of the public schools' cricket-match where there is a parade of 'white collars' and 'great coaches'. Sophy's chance encounter with her teenage sweetheart, the market-gardener Sam, seems to offer her a new lease of life, but this hope proves illusory because her 'fastidious' son will not countenance a re-marriage that will socially 'degrade [him] in the eyes of all the gentlemen of England!' (p. 45)

Sophy had been introduced as a wheelchair-bound 'young invalid lady' and, as the story progresses, it becomes quite obvious that her lameness is psychosomatic in origin. When Sam reappears in her life and she goes down excitedly to meet him, she can perform this difficult task by 'sidling downstairs by the aid of the handrail, in a way she could adopt on an emergency' (p. 42). Sam is 'something to live for' (p. 42) and after her meetings with him she begins to 'revive' and is even 'able to leave her chair and walk about occasionally' (p. 44). But after Randolph tyrannically makes her promise, before an improvised altar, that she will not wed Sam without her son's consent, she 'seem[s] to be pining her heart away' and '[h]er lameness became more confirmed as time went on' (pp. 45-6). Her lameness thus becomes a metaphor for her enforced emotional crippling, and her wheelchair-bound existence speaks of her entrapment in a widowhood which denies her personal mobility and freedom of action. Narrative sympathy for Sophy is very transparent and authorial indignation on behalf of her wasted and stultified life comes through in the satire of Randolph, who becomes a 'priest' whose 'education had... sufficiently ousted his humanity' (p. 45) – a portrait that is reminiscent of the uncharitable and narrowly dogmatic brothers of Angel Clare.

Hardy himself considered 'The Son's Veto' his best short story,[29] and it is certainly one where his sympathy for a woman's position is expressed very unequivocally. Another story which speaks powerfully against man's inhumanity to woman is 'Barbara of the House of Grebe'. This story achieved notoriety because T. S. Eliot castigated it as introducing the reader to 'a world of pure Evil'. In Eliot's opinion, it is a story 'written solely to provide a satisfaction for some morbid emotion'.[30] Despite Hardy's lifelong interest in (admittedly) morbid details of hangings, this is a misreading; and Rosemary Sumner offers an alternative reading of the story as an 'experiment in aversion therapy' and as Hardy's intuitive anticipation of 'the use of conditioning as a therapeutic process' which began scientifically only in the 1930s.[31] This story, with its Browningesque exploration of abnormal states of mind, concerns Barbara's infatuation with the life-size marble statue of her dead first husband Willowes and the 'cure' improvised by her second husband, Lord Uplandtowers, who (like the Duke of Ferrara) determines that all smiles shall stop together.

Lord Uplandtowers's voyeuristic cruelty in forcing Barbara to repeatedly view the realistically mutilated features of the statue of her 'Phoebus-Apollo' husband is an elaboration of the earlier 'hints at sadistic practices in the bedroom'[32] in 'The Duchess of Hamptonshire' (1878; later collected in *GND*). Far from unconsciously betraying Hardy's covert indulgence in the sadistic delights of this 'perverse and cruel man' (p. 275), this story actually illustrates his continuing concern for the 'spiritual and mental suffering, for the most part undeservedly inflicted'[33] on vulnerable women by husbands/lovers/fathers/sons. The detailed narration of Lord Uplandtowers's brutality does not necessarily imply that Hardy either vicariously participates in it or condones it. Although Barbara's love for Willowes is culpable because it is a love engendered in the eyes only (a love based on external beauty, which dies when that perfect manhood is disfigured and is again brought alive when the statue reincarnates Willowes's bodily perfection), she does not deserve the psychological wife-battering to which Uplandtowers subjects her. Authorial sympathy for Barbara unmistakably filters through the words that Hardy puts into the mouth of the old Surgeon, the ostensible narrator of this tale. When Uplandtowers conceives his plan of 'fiendish disfigurement' of the immaculate statue in order to 'cure' his wife's infatuation, the narrator wonders at the obtuseness of a 'subtle man' who 'never thought of the simple stratagem of constant tenderness' (p. 270). That the pliant Barbara could be won over by love never occurs to Uplandtowers because he is simply incapable of such patient and nourishing love.

Randolph and Uplandtowers thus represent two faces of male repressiveness – the son's and the husband's – and authorial sympathy is evidently with the helpless victims of their oppression. Thus many of the stories in *A Group of Noble Dames* and *Life's Little Ironies* hark back to *Tess of the D'Urbervilles* in their spotlight on the victimization of woman and in their poignant 'what's-done-cannot-be-undone' refrain. These stories of mismatched loves bear the typical Hardyan signature in their plotting as they voice Hardy's indictment of a flawed universe, inimical to human happiness, where 'the call seldom produces the comer, the man to love rarely coincides with the hour for loving' (*Tess*, p. 67). They also anticipate some of the central concerns of *Jude the Obscure*, especially the interrogation of marriage as an institution and the revelation of the crushing weight of societal pressures to conform which constrict and ultimately deny individual volition. Hardy's main themes in these stories which bridge *Tess* and *Jude* seem to be woman's vulnerable position in patriarchal society, the frustration and isolation born of marital incompatibility, the coercive and irrevocable nature of the marriage bond itself, and the emotional sterility of lives denied the personal space in which to achieve self-maturation. Hardy's feminist sympathies – not to mention his radical ideas on eugenics – emerge obliquely, but unmistakably, through these woman-centred stories[34] which often read like powerful pleas against man's inhumanity to woman.

But it would be wrong to conclude that Hardy saw woman always as the 'exploited' and man invariably as the 'exploiter'. In 'The Lady Icenway', we have a reverse situation where Anderling – despite his original deception of a bigamous marriage – ends up being a victim of Lady Icenway's selfish manipulativeness. Similarly, despite his initial idle seduction of Anna, there is some narrative sympathy for Charles Raye ('On the Western Circuit') who is duped into a disadvantageous marriage by the collusion of two women. When Raye, at the end of the story, drearily resigns himself to a 'galley' where he is 'chained to work for the remainder of his life, with her [i.e. Anna], the unlettered peasant, chained to his side' (*LLI*, p. 105), it is not merely a case of self-dramatization or self-pity. It is a recognition of the inescapability from marital incompatibility – the barrister Raye and the illiterate Anna cannot even converse on the same intellectual wavelength – that will later prompt Jude (after his marriage with Arabella) to enquire of the powers that be what he had done to deserve to be caught in a 'gin' that would cripple him for life.

# 7

# *Jude the Obscure*

Hardy's novels sometimes had a long gestation period, and the embryo of *Jude the Obscure* (1895) is often traced to a note Hardy jotted down in April 1888: 'A short story of a young man – "who could not go to Oxford" – His struggles and ultimate failure. Suicide.'[1] But before working out this idea fully in a novel-length study, Hardy rehearsed it in a short story, 'A Tragedy of Two Ambitions' (1888). In this neglected short story Hardy portrays the struggles and frustrations of two brothers, Joshua and Cornelius, whose academic aspirations are thwarted by a combination of meagre financial resources, class prejudice, and family circumstances in the shape of a feckless and drunken father. While Hardy's sympathies evidently went out to the two brothers in their 'untutored reading of Greek and Latin', he was alive to the possibility that even the noblest intellectual aspiration could be both corrupt and corrupting.[2] Thus, the story strikes a balance between being an eloquent plea on behalf of deserving but deprived students who fail to make it to the University, and offering an unsentimental critique of the selfish pursuit of academic ambition.

When Hardy came to rework this theme of academic aspiration in *Jude* it was further complicated by the addition of the theme of marital mismatings. But what the reviewers of *Jude* took to be its central concern – the 'Marriage Question' – was to Hardy only incidental and of secondary importance. In 1895 Hardy clearly spelt out his thematic priorities to Edmund Gosse:

It is curious that some of the papers should look upon the novel as a manifesto on 'the marriage question' (although of course, it involves it) – seeing that it is concerned first with the labours of a poor student to get a University degree, & secondly with the tragic issues of two bad marriages, owing in the main to a doom or curse of hereditary temperament peculiar to the family of the

111

parties. The only remarks which can be said to bear on the *general* marriage question occur in dialogue, & comprise no more than half a dozen pages in a book of five hundred.[3] (Hardy's italic )

But a novel often outgrows its authorial formulation and, as Hardy himself recognized in his 1912 'Postscript' to *Jude*, 'there can be more in a book than the author consciously puts there'.[4] Thus, for most readers, the emotional histories of the criss-crossing lives of Jude, Sue, Arabella, and Phillotson tend to upstage Jude's Christminster obsession and the novel is a good example of an after-thought/sub-plot swamping the original impulse/main plot. Analyzing the evolution of *Jude* through its manuscript revisions, Paterson demonstrates how 'the novel's center of gravity shifted away from the university theme' and 'moved in the direction of the marriage question'.[5]

However, Paterson's reading of the novel's change of direction is challenged by Patricia Ingham who argues that 'the manuscript evidence does not show such a change, but rather that the story starts off already concerned with the relationship between Sue and Jude and with their possible marriage', and that 'from the earliest identifiable stage... the story is concerned with marriage as well as academic aspirations'.[6] Although Paterson and Ingham radically disagree on this issue, both stress that in the original version of the story, Sue played a more prominent role in what was later designated as 'Part First' of the novel. 'Sue is the focus of Jude's longing for Christminster', as 'the schoolmaster Phillot-son evidently did not exist when the first eighty-four pages of the manuscript were written'.[7] It is Sue, adopted by the Provost of a Christminster college, to whom Jude appeals for books, and it is Sue who provides the erotic touch to Jude's yearning for the 'city of light':

> [Jude] parted his lips as he faced the north-east, & drew in the wind as if it were a sweet liquor.

> 'You' he said, addressing the breeze caressingly 'were in Christminster city between one & two hours ago: floating along the streets, pulling round the weather-cocks, touching Sue's face, being breathed in by her; & now you be here, breathed in by me; you, the very same.'[8]

When Hardy erased Sue's presence from the opening section of the novel and systematically replaced her by Phillotson, this passage – with its transparent eroticism – is made to appear slightly ridiculous because of the discrepancy between the object of desire (Phillotson in Christminster) and the intensity of emotion inspired in the boy Jude.

Hardy not only erased Sue from the first part of the novel, but also effectively from the title he ultimately chose for it. It is interesting to consider his original titles for this novel while it was being serialized in *Harper's New Monthly Magazine* from December 1894 to November 1895. In the first instalment, the title reads 'The Simpletons', and in the second it was changed by Hardy (presumably because of its resemblance to Charles Reade's novel, *A Simpleton*) to 'Hearts Insurgent'. Dissatisfied still, Hardy wrote to the publishers in November 1894 and requested them to change the title to 'The Recalcitrants', although since the instalment had already gone to press, this title was never really used.[9] What has generally gone unnoticed is that these three early titles all employ the plural form, suggesting that Hardy initially conceived of the novel as having a binary focus. In finally choosing the title *Jude the Obscure* for the first book edition,[10] Hardy privileges Jude over Sue and erases her primary status as (joint) protagonist of this novel. But strangely enough, when in 1897 he made schemes for dramatizing *Jude*, the titles he provisionally selected were 'The New Woman' and 'A Woman with Ideas'.[11] Also, despite the close parallels between Jude's boyhood and his creator's, and despite the narrator's identification with Jude's point of view within the novel, Hardy confessed in a letter to Florence Henniker (1895): 'Curiously enough I am more interested in this *Sue story* than in any I have written' (my italics).[12] In referring to *Jude* as the 'Sue story' Hardy seems to be anticipating the impression of successive generations of readers who feel that 'Sue takes the book away from the title character, because she is stronger, more complex, and more significant'.[13]

Hardy's wavering and uncertainty about Sue's status in the novel is reflected yet again in the confusion regarding her prehistory. At one point we are told that when Sue's parents separated, her mother 'went away to London with her little maid' (pp. 93-4). Later, Jude's great-aunt Drusilla reports that Sue was 'brought up by her father to hate her mother's family' (p. 132). Hardy was an inveterate reviser and he usually took advantage of every new edition to improve his text, but this inconsistency regarding whether Sue was reared by her mother or her father remains even in the text of the 1912 Wessex Edition. All this suggests that despite Hardy's acknowledgement to George Douglas that he 'liked' Sue,[14] his emotional investment in her was not as all-consuming as it was in the case of Tess. A reader coming straight from *Tess* to *Jude* will at once be struck by the difference in the mode of presentation of Tess and Sue. In marked contrast to Tess's interiority, her transparent lucidity, we are confronted with the otherness of Sue, with what Boumelha calls her 'resistant opacity'.[15] Except on the rare occasion of her adventure in buying the pagan deities, Sue is hardly ever presented to us directly, but always mediated through the consciousness of either Jude, Phillotson, or the (male) narrator – or even Arabella, Aunt Drusilla, and widow Edlin. Sue thus remains a 'riddle' and a 'conundrum' to Jude; to Phillotson she is 'puzzling' and 'unstateable'; and the narrator too is baffled by 'the state of that mystery, her heart'. Extremely articulate, we do learn a great deal about Sue from Sue – through her endless self-analyses and her inadvertently revealing self-contradictions. But although we hear her, we never *over*hear her: we hear her public voice, but never that intimate inner voice that we can listen to in the case of Tess and even Jude. Thus we have monologues galore but no true soliloquies.

Within the novel, there is a persistent demand that 'Sue must be available to understanding',[16] and Hardy attempts to do precisely this in his 1895 letter to Gosse. Defending Sue, Hardy clarifies that 'there is nothing perverted or depraved in Sue's nature. The abnormalism consists in disproportion: not in inversion, her sexual instinct being healthy so far as it goes, but unusually weak & fastidious'.[17] This statement is significant because Hardy was probably aware that by 'the end of the century, sexologists were redefining the rebellious New Woman as an "invert" or lesbian'.[18] While taking care to protect Sue from the charge of lesbianism, Hardy however seems to be indirectly accusing her of playing a sexual power-game, because in the same letter to Gosse he further explains:

> One point illustrating this I cd [sic] not dwell upon: that, though she has children, her intimacies with Jude have never been more than occasional, even while they were living together (I mention that they occupy separate rooms, except towards the end), & one of her reasons for fearing the marriage ceremony is that she fears

it wd [*sic*] be breaking faith with Jude to withhold herself at pleasure, or altogether, after it; though while uncontracted she feels at
liberty to yield herself as seldom as she chooses. This has tended
to keep his passion as hot at the end as at the beginning, & helps
to break his heart. He has never really possessed her as freely as
he desired.[19]

In adopting this strategy, Sue reveals an 'impulse for power' as 'she
wants to be sexually attractive and powerful but to remain sexually
unavailable'.[20] Likening her to La Belle Dame Sans Merci, Robert
Heilman says that she not merely leaves her men 'palely loitering',
but '[s]ymbolically, she comes fairly close to husband-murder'.[21] In
less sensational but no less negative terms, Terry Eagleton sums up
the case against Sue and finds it remarkable that 'Hardy retains
some of our sympathy for Sue against all the odds. For there isn't,
when one comes down to it, much to be said in her defence.'[22] Value-
loaded words like 'hysterical', 'neurotic', 'sado-masochistic', 'narcissistic', 'frigid', 'morbid', 'perverted', 'abnormal', 'flirt', 'inconsistent',
'selfish' repeatedly crop up in critical analyses of Sue. Even Jude, in
his less tender moments, accuses her of being 'incapable of real love'
(p. 255), of having 'flirted outrageously' with Phillotson (p. 256), of
having a 'dog-in-the-manger' attitude to Arabella (p. 258), and of
ultimately being guilty of a mean save-your-own-soul-ism (p. 361, p.
381). However, revealing an interesting gender bias, Mary Jacobus
and Elizabeth Langland are more sympathetic to Sue. Rejecting D.H.
Lawrence's thesis that Sue was born with the female 'atrophied' in
her, Jacobus argues that it is 'precisely Sue's femaleness which
breaks her', her 'experience as a woman' which 'brings her from
clarity to compromise, from compromise to collapse' because the
'burden has been too heavy, the bearer too frail'.[23] Deploring both
the narrator's and Jude's tendency to 'evaluate Sue's behavior in
terms of sex rather than in terms of individual character', Langland
sees in Sue the expression of 'the passionate resistance of a cohesive
personality to the self-suppression and loss of identity traditional
love dictates'.[24] Defending Sue against the charge of frigidity,
Rosemarie Morgan maintains that it is not Sue who is sexually unre-
sponsive but rather Jude whose 'fantasies about the sexless "enno-
bled" Sue' imprison her latent passionate self, and Jude who ultimately disempowers Sue by 'denying her a sexual reality'.[25]

The complete lack of critical consensus about Sue lends point to Anne Simpson's claim that Sue 'occupies the site of unknowability in a text that challenges assumptions about the transparency and coherence of the feminine'.[26] It is certainly to Hardy's credit that he presents us a vivid, volatile and unpredictable human being rather than a clinical case which can be objectively analysed, neatly labelled, and conveniently filed away in a medical journal. Thus, Sue's 'inconsistency', 'contradictoriness', and 'elusiveness' are indirectly the greatest tributes to her living quality, her resistance to being reduced to a mere type. Hardy gives us a compelling sense of Sue's uniqueness and Sue herself contributes to this view of her specialness. After her marriage to Phillotson, when experience teaches her what marriage actually means, she confesses to Jude: 'I am certain one ought to be allowed to undo what one has done so ignorantly!'[27] I daresay it happens to lots of women; only they submit, and I kick' (p. 232). The 'they–I' opposition posits Sue as a Promethean rebel, distinct from the rest of her submissive sex. But, surprisingly enough, within the novel a high proportion of women do 'kick' against the bonds of matrimony. Arabella, after her sexual appetite is presumably satiated, runs away first from Jude and later from her (bigamously married) second husband Cartlett. In the careful geometric plotting of the novel, Arabella's desertions of Jude and Cartlett neatly parallel Sue's desertion of first Phillotson and later Jude. Although they may 'kick' for entirely different reasons, what is important is that both 'bolt' from their husbands. Though Sue blinds herself to this similarity with a woman whom she repeatedly calls 'low-passioned', 'too low, too coarse' (p. 278, p. 280), Arabella's shrewd comment is not lost on the reader. When Sue visits Arabella (as a penance for restraining Jude from going out to help her the previous night), Arabella bluntly tells Sue: 'you are a oneyer too, like myself...Bolted from your first, didn't you, like me?' (p. 283). Sue, of course, reacts with stiff dignity and refuses to acknowledge any such kinship, but Arabella's words are important because they remind the reader that Sue's aversion to marriage/Phillotson is not unique or pathological but is in fact shared by quite a few women in the novel. Sue is truly her mother's daughter because, according to aunt Drusilla, Sue's mother too could not 'stomach' her husband: 'Her husband offended her, and she so disliked living with him afterwards that she went away to London with her little maid' (pp. 93-4). From the prehistory of the novel, we hear of another such woman who was a common ancestress of both Jude and Sue. Her grim story is recounted by widow Edlin on the eve of Jude and Sue's attempt to solemnize their union at the registry office: 'She ran away from him, with their child, to her friends; and while she was there the child died. He wanted the body, to bury it where his people lay, but she wouldn't give it up' (p. 295). In a book of 400-odd pages, it is quite easy to forget such brief references which, nevertheless, are important in placing Sue's rebellion within a tradition of women who 'kick' and 'bolt'.

In fact, Sue's ultimate breakdown too can be somewhat explained in the light of this singularly mistimed narration, for Mrs Edlin continues:

'Her husband then came in the night with a cart, and broke into the house to steal the coffin away; but he was catched, and being obstinate, wouldn't tell what he broke in for. They brought it in burglary, and that's why he was hanged and gibbeted on Brown House Hill. His wife went mad after he was dead.' (p. 295)

This story is not an exact parallel of Sue's emotional history but the links are significant enough, although generally overlooked. Sue does not go 'mad', but her complete abdication of reason – which had hitherto made her intellect glow like a 'star' – is triggered off by the deaths of her children and her consequent feeling of guilt. This is not to suggest that Sue is a study in hereditary disposition, although heredity does play an important role in this novel and Sue herself is aware of the 'tragic doom [which] overhung our family' (p. 296). Hardy too drew attention to the 'doom or curse of hereditary temperament peculiar to the family of the parties', in his letter of 10 November 1895 to Gosse.[28] Writing on the same day to Florence Henniker, Hardy reiterated that the story 'is really one about two persons who, by a hereditary curse of temperament, peculiar to their family, are rendered unfit for marriage, or think they are'.[29] But such hints have largely gone unheeded, and critics who react with incredulity to Little Father Time's suicide tend to forget that the young boy is the child of a suicidally inclined father and the grandchild of a suicidal grandmother. Quite early in the novel, when Arabella's taunt provokes Jude into investigating his dead parents' history, his great-aunt Drusilla informs him:

> 'Your father and mother couldn't get on together, and they part-
> ed. It was coming home from Alfredston market, when you were
> a baby...that they had their last difference, and took leave of one
> another for the last time. Your mother soon afterwards died – *she*
> *drowned herself*, in short, and your father went away with you to
> South Wessex.' (p. 93; my italics)

Significantly enough, Jude's mother – i.e. Sue's aunt – is one more of the peripheral women in the novel (ignored by critics like John Lucas) who don't meekly 'submit' but actually 'kick' and 'bolt'.[30] Like mother like son, the narrative seems to suggest at this point, because on the very next page Jude attempts to repeat his mother's desperate act. He walks to the middle of a frozen pond and jumps twice, but the ice does not give way under him. Unable to literally drown himself, Jude drowns his sorrow in drink, and it is significant that his suicidal bid occurs (as in his mother's case) just after his final quarrel with his spouse. Earlier, the boy Jude, finding that 'Nature's logic was too hor-rid for him' and disillusioned because 'events did not rhyme', had desired to 'prevent himself growing up' (p. 42). Jude's son, who unfortunately inherits his 'despondency' and not Arabella's resilience, becomes the embodiment of 'the coming universal wish not to live' (p. 346) whose embryonic form is latent in Jude's desire 'that he had never been born' (p. 55).[31] Finally, when Jude does die, his death is self-willed and a direct consequence of his deliberately suicidal trip to Marygreen to visit Sue for the last time. The exchange between Jude and Arabella clearly brings out the suicidal theme:

> 'You've done for yourself by this, young man,' said she. 'I don't
> know whether you know it.'
> 'Of course I do. I meant to do for myself.'
> 'What – to commit suicide?'
> 'Certainly.'
> 'Well, I'm blest! Kill yourself for a woman.' (p. 397)

As if he has not already stated his intentions clearly enough, Jude goes on to elaborate: 'a fellow who had only two wishes left in the world, to see a particular woman, and then to die, could neatly accomplish those two wishes at one stroke by taking this journey in the rain' (p. 397). In the face of such textual evidence, it is surprising to find Terry Eagleton claiming: 'The factor of heredity certainly crops up from time to time, but in the end little is made of it, and it isn't an element in the final tragic catastrophe. It remains as an awkwardly unintegrated dimension in the novel, generating "atmosphere" but not much else'.[32]

Although in 1911 Hardy classified his 'major' novels under the heading 'Novels of Character and Environment', as an early admirer of *The Origin of Species*, he was surely not unaware of the role of heredity in determining character and action.[33] However, this is not to suggest that Sue's career is solely determined by her heredity any more than it is solely determined by her sex. Thus the vexed question of why Hardy allows Sue to break down remains. The narrator and Jude try to grope their way to an understanding of her tragedy by invoking an essentialist view of women. 'Strange difference of sex, that time and circumstance, which enlarge the views of most men, narrow the views of women almost invariably', Jude reflects (p. 405). While this may sound crudely sexist, there is some truth in it, because women cannot deny their bodies and the tragedy of a child's death will usually be more traumatic for the mother than for the father because of the undeniable fact of biology. Thus, Boumelha very rightly points out:

> Sue's 'breakdown' is not the sign of some gender-determined constitutional weakness of mind or will, but a result of the fact that certain social forces press harder on women in sexual and marital relationships, largely by virtue of the implication of their sexuality in child-bearing.[34]

The death of their children hits both Jude and Sue, but it hits Sue harder because, as Hardy reasoned, 'it was not so much the force of the blow that counted, as the nature of the material that received the blow'.[35] The 'nature' of Sue also accounts for the fact that Sue and Arabella react so differently to the tragedy. This cannot be explained away by arguing prosaically that Sue has lost three children while Arabella has lost only one, because the difference is not one of degree but one of kind. While the 'fragile', 'fine-nerved' and 'sensitive' Sue is completely undone, Arabella – as a 'woman of rank passions' – probably considers herself well rid of an encumbrance in her future marital adventures.

The 'deadly war waged between flesh and spirit', to which Hardy drew attention in his 1895 Preface to *Jude* (p. 27), has been a conveniently available paradigm in which to cast Arabella and Sue. Gosse, in one of the earliest reviews of *Jude*, was quick to pick up this polarity and state: 'As Arabella was all body, so Sue is all soul.'[36] Subsequent critics have continued in this tradition and Kate Millett sees in Arabella ('utter carnality') and Sue ('pure spirit') the familiar 'Rose-Lily' opposition which is so mutually exclusive that Sue almost becomes a 'victim of a cultural literary convention…that in granting her a mind insists on withholding a body from her'.[37] At the fulcrum of these two opposing forces, stands Jude, a representative 'Everyman'-figure, flanked, in Morality-play fashion, by his 'Good Angel' and 'Bad Angel'. Sue and Arabella become almost allegorical externalizations of Jude's inner conflict as he aspires to soar into pure realms of knowledge and is repeatedly (and rudely) brought down to earth by his bodily sensations.[38] Jude is humanity placed precariously between the angels above and the animals below, and this dualism is reflected in the vocabulary of the novel, where one set of terms – e.g. 'ethereal', 'refined', 'uncarnate', referring to Sue – are privileged over another set of terms e.g. 'low', 'coarse', 'gross', which all refer to Arabella.[39]

By the time Hardy came to use this form of the triangular love relationship, it had already established itself as a novelistic cliché, and one has only to look before and after to discover striking similarities in novels as diverse as *Tom Jones, Adam Bede, Jude*, and *Sons and Lovers*. Nothing can be more far removed from Fielding's blithely comic narrative than Hardy's bleak and pessimistic story; and yet Tom and Jude's courses run parallel, up to a certain point, in their amatory history. Tom is seduced by the gamekeeper's daughter Molly just as Jude is seduced by the pig-breeder's daughter Arabella. Both Tom and Jude find their ideal spiritual mates in Sophia and Sue (respectively), to whom they remain faithful in spirit despite their occasional backsliding in sleeping with 'coarse' women. The important difference is that while wedding bells finally peal out joyously for Tom, the Christminster Remembrance Day organ notes and hurrahs cruelly mock the dying Jude as he lies alone deserted by both Sue and Arabella. The comparison may seem somewhat arbitrary till one realizes that Hardy himself obliquely hinted at Arabella's literary pedigree in his letter to Gosse:

> As to the 'coarse' scenes with Arabella, the battle in the school room, &c., the newspaper critics might, I thought, have sneered at them for their Fielding-ism rather than for their Zolaism. But your everyday critic knows nothing of Fielding. I am read in Zola very little, but have felt akin locally to Fielding, so many of his scenes having been laid down this way, & his home near.[40]

Surprisingly, not many critics have taken up this clue, and in invoking Chaucer's proverbial 'Wife of Bath' as Arabella's progenitor they have overlooked a source much closer in both time and place. As Watts rightly points out, 'Arabella has an ancestor in the lusty Molly Seagrim'.[41]

Therefore, through Hardy's comments on Fielding's Molly, it is perhaps possible to guess his attitude to Arabella, whom the narrator describes as 'a complete and substantial female animal – no more, no less' (p. 62). Declining an invitation to write an 'Introduction' to a proposed Library Edition of Fielding's novels, Hardy wrote in June 1898: '[Fielding's] aristocratic, even feudal, attitude towards the peasantry (e.g. his view of Molly as a "slut" to be ridiculed, not as a simple girl, as worthy a creation of Nature as the lovely Sophia) should be exhibited strongly.'[42] In September 1898, Hardy reiterated his stand in a letter to Gosse:

> You just allude to F.'s [*sic*] 'aristocratic temper'. This temper of his always strikes me forcibly – more than it does most people I imagine: especially in his attitude towards Molly. His date has, no doubt, something to do with it: but I can never forgive him (as a youth, even, I never could) for regarding her as a grotesque creature, a slut, &c. – & my impression is that the shadowy original (or originals) of Molly were town girls with whom F. [*sic*] came into sensual contact, dressed up in peasant clothes; & no cottager. It would be too long to say why I have come to this conclusion; but I feel certain that F. [*sic*] never knew thoroughly the seduced rustic girl; or that, if he did, the 'aristocratic temper' you mention & the prejudices of his time, absolutely blinded him to her true character.

It is curious that such a woman of the people as George Eliot shd
[*sic*] have carried on the prejudice to some extent in her treatment
of Hetty, whom she wd [*sic*] not have us regard as possessing
equal rights with Donnithorne.[43]

Hardy's defence of Molly and Hetty would seem to suggest that his
sympathies lay with Arabella too. Thus, going counter to the long-
established critical tradition which holds that Arabella is probably
the only woman towards whom Hardy shows any animosity, Cedric
Watts sees in Arabella 'an affirmation of vitality' as she 'resourceful-
ly snatch[es] at life's few pleasures'. In her 'resilient selfishness
[which] has a degree of gusto and fighting spirit', she acquires 'an
almost Falstaffian positive value'.[44] This is persuasive rhetoric, but
the feeling persists that Arabella can embody a positive value only in
a world where all other (normal) positives have been eroded or
thrown overboard. The case against Arabella is not that she successfully exploits her sexuality (after all, any weapon is fair in the grim
battle for survival as 'Poor folks must live') but that she flouts, without regret, every norm of common human decency. Her treatment of
her son and of the dying Jude are equally callous and shows that,
more than Ethelberta, it is Arabella who has succeeded in completely
cutting out her heart. She allows Little Father Time to be handed
round like a piece of unwanted baggage, and the total atrophy of her
maternal instinct is revealed in her visit to Jude and Sue after the
children's deaths when she 'talk[s] with placid bluntness about
"her" boy, for whom, though in his lifetime she had shown no care
at all, she now exhibited a ceremonial mournfulness that was apparently sustaining to the conscience' (p. 356). The strongest indictment
of Arabella comes, however, not from Hardy's narrator but from
Little Father Time in his question to Sue: 'Is it you who's my *real*
mother at last?' (p. 292; Hardy's italic). In this piteous query is
summed up the poignant history of the boy's emotional starvation,
his quest for a mother's love and security, his bewilderment at being
passed from one substitute mother-figure to another, his bitterness
over the real mother who played him false, his childish despair of
ever reaching the end of his journey in search of a mother and permanent home. It is no wonder that this intensely lonely, unloved,
and unwanted child commits suicide, and yet his death seems to
leave Arabella with no perceptible signs of guilt or remorse.
Arabella's lukewarm 'I had often wished I had [my child] with

me...Perhaps 'twouldn't have happened then! But of course I didn't wish to take him away from your wife' (p. 356) contrasts very strongly and tellingly with Sue's complete prostration after her children's deaths.

In this late novel Hardy does not allow his narrator to indulge in those moralizing generalizations so characteristic of his early novels and therefore we have no authorial perspective on Arabella. But what the narrator refrains from expressing is often put into the mouth of other characters, and behind at least one of Jude's reproaches to Arabella it is surely not too fanciful to hear the voice of Hardy protesting against the indissolubility of marriage. When Jude discovers Arabella's ruse of pretended pregnancy which has trapped him into marriage, and when she defends herself by saying that 'Every woman has a right to do such as that. The risk is hers', Jude (without the hindsight of divorce) responds sadly:

> 'I quite deny it, Bella. She might if no life-long penalty attached to it for the man, or, in his default, for herself; if the weakness of the moment could end with the moment, or even with the year. But when effects stretch so far she should not go and do that which entraps a man if he is honest, or herself if he is otherwise.' (p. 90)

Jude here states the case fairly, recognizing that marriage could become a 'life-long penalty' for *both* the man and the woman, and this is the burden of Hardy's protest against marriage as an institution: 'the fundamental error of... bas[ing] a permanent contract on a temporary feeling' (p. 93). Fortunately however, in the world of *Jude* divorce seems to be quite readily available[45] and thus the 'penalty' need not be necessarily 'life-long'. Although in 1926, while considering a possible dramatization of *Jude*, Hardy speculated whether Arabella were not 'the villain of the piece',[46] it would be unfair to saddle Arabella with the sole responsibility for blasting Jude's life. Rather, Jude is destroyed by the collusion of two women who, 'antipathetic to one another though they are, are at some level working together to destroy the protagonist'.[47] The barely concealed misogamy of the novel shades off into implied misogyny in showing a 'gentle but pliable hero [who] is destroyed by two stereotypes of female sexuality – the scheming seductress and the fascinating, tantalizing prude'.[48] Caught between what Stubbs calls 'rapacious sensuality' (Arabella) and 'obsessive virginity' (Sue), Jude will become a prototype for D. H. Lawrence's Paul Morel who is torn between the virginal Miriam and the sensual Clara. The unstated but clearly implied thesis of both *Jude* and *Sons and Lovers* seems to be that Jude and Paul make a sorry mess of their lives not because they are inherently weak or culpable but because their women lamentably fail them. Thus, in presenting a 'lovable male protagonist [who] is destroyed between a sensual and a spiritual woman.... Hardy explicitly blames women for their contribution to [Jude's] ruin, as he never blames men collectively for that of Tess.'[49]

Therefore, despite Hardy's sarcastic reference in his 1912 'Postscript' to *Jude* to 'the screaming of a poor lady in *Blackwood*' (p. 30), Mrs Oliphant was not very far off the mark when she shrewdly observed that '[i]t is the women who are the active agents in all this unsavoury imbroglio' and the men are merely their 'passive' 'victims'.[50] Jude certainly sees his life's tragedy in these terms:

> Strange that his first aspiration – towards academical proficiency – had been checked by a woman, and that his second aspiration – towards apostleship – had also been checked by a woman. 'Is it,' he said, 'that the women are to blame; or is it the artificial system of things, under which the normal sex-impulses are turned into devilish domestic gins and springes to noose and hold back those who want to progress?' (p. 234)

Jude's equation of Arabella and Sue is valid up to a point because both are responsible for the destruction of, at least, his books. Arabella physically manhandles Jude's books, deliberately smearing them with her greasy fingers and angrily flinging them to the floor. Sue's effect is subtle and indirect but no less invidious as she destroys the very spirit enshrined in Jude's books. Her unremitting withering scorn of institutionalized religion ultimately leads Jude to make a huge bonfire of all his precious theological books. To a bibliophile and autodidact, nothing can be more tragic than such wanton destruction.

That women, generically speaking, *are* destructive is a discourse that runs throughout the novel as the negative vocabulary – 'checked', 'noose', 'hold back' – colours the language of the narrator, Jude, and even Sue in her guilt-ridden moments. The obvious symbolism of the 'Samson and Delilah' painting, which hangs on the wall of the inn that Jude and Arabella visit during their courtship, is underpinned by the reiterative use of negative terms as in *Two on a Tower*. When Arabella urges Jude to marry her soon by hinting that she is pregnant, Jude candidly tells her: 'It is a complete *smashing up* of my plans.... Dreams about books, and degrees, and impossible fellowships' (p. 80; my italics). This is merely a reformulation of the earlier narratorial comment, after Arabella's phallic missile has woken Jude out of his academic dreams, that the 'intentions as to reading, working, and learning, which [Jude] had so precisely formulated only a few minutes earlier, were suffering a curious collapse into a corner, he knew not how' (p. 65). When Jude later passes by the milestone on which he had carved his initials, he remembers that the act 'embodying his aspirations' had 'been done in the first week of his apprenticeship, before he had been *diverted* from his purposes by an *unsuitable* woman' (pp. 96-7; my italics). Jude's three-year 'coarse conjugal life' with Arabella is a 'disruption', and when he makes his way to Christminster, the narrator sees it as 'making a new start – the start to which, barring the *interruption* involved in his intimacy and married experience with Arabella, he had been looking forward for about ten years' (p. 101; my italic). Jude feels 'encumbered' and 'enchained' by this marriage and finally when he is drunkenly 'recapture[d]' into remarrying Arabella, he is explicitly referred to as 'her shorn Samson' (p. 384). But such negative language is not restricted to Arabella; Sue too unconsciously picks up this misogynic register, and after leaving Phillotson she voices her misgivings about having joined Jude: 'I fear I am doing you a lot of harm. *Ruining* your prospects of the Church; *ruining* your progress in your trade; everything!... O I seem so bad – *upsetting* men's courses like this!' (p. 253; my italics). The use of the plural – 'men's courses' – extends the implication of this speech to include Phillotson, who is made to suffer for his generosity in freeing Sue by being publicly humiliated and dismissed from his school job.

The novel repeatedly raises questions about the nature of women. After Sue is cowed into social conformity by the deaths of her children, Jude is totally at a loss to understand her 'extraordinary blindness now to your old logic. Is it peculiar to you, or is it common to woman? Is a woman a thinking unit at all, or a fraction always wanting its integer?' (p. 359). Much earlier, when Sue had requested Jude to give her away in church, during her first marriage to Phillotson, Jude had responded to her 'cruelty' by wondering: 'Women were different from men in such matters. Was it that they were, instead of more sensitive, as reputed, more callous, and less romantic; or were they more heroic?' (p. 193). Jude may flounder in uncertainty regarding women's essential nature, but the narrator is more confident in his generalizations on the sex whose 'every face bear[s] the legend "The Weaker" upon it' (p. 160). Although in this very late novel the incidence of reductive generalizations about women is much less than before, Hardy has not yet completely outgrown his early habit. For instance, when Jude sinks to his lowest depths in drunkenly reciting the Creed in a tavern, his subsequent bitter remorse is described by the narrator in these terms: 'If he had been a woman he must have screamed under the nervous tension which he was now undergoing' (p. 145). Jude ultimately does something better than scream like a woman; he commits suicide like a man. In a later episode, when Sue is understandably piqued by his belated confession about his marriage to Arabella, he is at a loss to comprehend her behaviour, which seems to him to be 'essentially large-minded and generous on reflection, despite a previous exercise of those *narrow womanly humours* on impulse that were necessary to give her sex' (p. 186; my italics).

However, despite the negative tenor of such reductive generalizations about women that pepper the text throughout – (which is why discussions on Hardy's misogyny tend to concentrate on *Jude*) – it is in this novel that Hardy voices his strongest pro-feminist position through Sue. Sue's indignation at the inferior status accorded to women comes out powerfully in her biting satire of the marriage service:

> 'I have been looking at the marriage service in the Prayer-book, and it seems to me very humiliating that a giver-away should be required at all. According to the ceremony as there printed, my bridegroom chooses me of his own will and pleasure; but I don't choose him. Somebody *gives* me to him, like a she-ass or she-goat, or any other domestic animal. Bless your exalted views of woman, O Churchman!' (p. 189; Hardy's italic)

The sexual inequality, the complete reduction of woman to the status of a commodity to be handed over from one owner to another, the absolute proprietorial rights of the husband over his wife – over both her wealth and her body – were a social reality in an age when a woman practically surrendered her legal existence on marriage. Also implicit in Sue's speech is her rebellion against a society which conditions women into accepting the passive role of being the 'chosen', instead of granting her the (equal) autonomy of becoming the active chooser. If women overstep their traditional passive roles, social anarchy will surely result: this seems to be the paranoia of those critics who were hostile to the New Woman's bid for independence. Fear of the New Woman's disruptive potential and ridicule of what was considered her inordinate demands, were widespread, surfacing even in such a popular thriller as *Dracula* (1897):

Some of the 'New Women' writers will some day start an idea that men and women should be allowed to see each other asleep before proposing or accepting. But I suppose the New Woman won't condescend in future to accept; she will do the proposing herself.[51]

In 1906 Hardy expressed his view that the father of a woman's child was entirely her own business, and Sue anticipates Hardy by a decade when she declares to Jude that 'in a proper state of society, the father of a woman's child will be as much a private matter of hers as the cut of her under-linen, on whom nobody will have any right to question her' (p. 255). A more subversive statement comes, surprisingly enough, from Phillotson when he is trying to justify his decision to grant Sue her freedom. Phillotson completely floors Gillingham (and surely Hardy's 1896 readership) by proposing 'Matriarchy': 'I don't see why the woman and the children should not be the unit without the man' (p. 247). For all her 'advanced' views, Sue does not go this far; but she gives authentic voice to the protest that conventional society imposes an identity on a married woman with which she often cannot emotionally relate: 'I am called Mrs Richard Phillotson, living a calm wedded life with my counterpart of that name. But I am not really Mrs Richard Phillotson, but a woman tossed about, all alone' (p. 223). That 'wifedom' can at times be totally annihilating is also acknowledged by Jude, indirectly, as he tries to convince Sue: 'No, you are not Mrs Phillotson... You are dear, free Sue Bridehead.... Wifedom has not yet squashed up and digested you in its vast maw as an atom which has no further individuality' (p. 206). Also, wifedom can imply inferior domestic status, and this is brought out in Arabella's ironic advice to Phillotson on how to tame a 'kicking' wife.

Though Arabella herself negotiates her different identities – from Miss Donn to Mrs Fawley, to Mrs Cartlett, and back again to Mrs Fawley (and possibly Mrs Vilbert next) – with blithe unconcern, even she is allowed to voice a valid criticism of social organization right from Biblical times. As far back as the days of Moses, the sexual double standard had flourished: '"Then shall the man be guiltless; but the woman shall bear her iniquity." Damn rough on us women; but we must grin and put up wi' it!' (pp. 328-9)

Jude, however, tries to argue that men are equally victims, and he scores a valid point when he insists:

'Still, Sue, it is no worse for the woman than for the man. That's what some women fail to see, and instead of protesting against the conditions they protest against the man, the other victim; just as a woman in a crowd will abuse the man who crushes against her, when he is only the helpless transmitter of the pressure put upon him.' (pp. 299-300)

If these are Hardy's views put into the mouth of his 'poor puppet',[52] then it certainly justifies the comment that 'Sue is at once Hardy's major contribution to feminism and the expression of his doubts about it'.[53] Ultimately, of course, Jude concedes that the 'woman mostly gets the worst of it in the long run!' (p. 362). What this 'worst' is has already been spelt out by the narrator in that notorious 'The Weaker'-sex passage: it is 'the storms and strains of after-years, with their *injustice*, loneliness, child-bearing, and bereavement' (p. 161; my italic). Seen in a positive light, as a protest against the 'injustice' of a woman's lot, this passage along with other statements by Sue, Phillotson, Arabella and Jude, can construct a truly feminist Hardy. But the case founders somewhat on the crucial issue of Sue's breakdown and volte-face. Hardy himself highlighted the issue, in his 1912 'Postscript' to *Jude*, by referring to a German reviewer who regretted that the portrait of Sue 'had been left to be drawn by a man, and was not done by one of her own sex, who would never have allowed her to break down at the end' (p. 30).

Why *does* Hardy allow Sue to break down? Perhaps Hardy was reflecting a social reality which his artistic integrity refused to sugar-coat. As Elaine Showalter has demonstrated:

For many late Victorian female intellectuals, especially those in the first generation to attend college, nervous illness marked the transition from domestic to professional roles.... From the pioneering doctor Sophia Jex-Blake to the social worker Beatrice Webb, New Women and nervous illness seemed to go together.[54]

Sue certainly seems to be a 'first-generation' college girl, and studies of other 'New Woman' novels of the 1880s and 1890s have shown that it was a common feature for these 'theoretically emancipated' women to make 'an initially successful bid for freedom and then collapse into crushing conformity.... Almost all New Woman heroines break down at the end, most go through some period of nervous prostration if not madness'.[55] Thus the German reviewer (if he is not totally Hardy's fictional construct) was certainly wrong, because most of the heroines of even female writers like Olive Schreiner, Mona Caird, 'George Egerton', and Sarah Grand suffer breakdowns, and Hardy was only sharing a 'common ambivalence in literature of the time' in his 'ambivalence of the treatment of Sue's revolt – a revolt which, though sympathetically depicted, is also shown to meet its nemesis'.[56]

But the more serious charge against Hardy is not that he allowed Sue to break down, but that he subordinated her so that 'she is made the instrument of Jude's tragedy, rather than the subject of her own'.[57] The novel never prompts us to 'ask what is happening to Sue; because it is rather a question of Sue happening to Jude'.[58] It is difficult to defend Hardy against this charge, especially since in his next novel, *The Well-Beloved* (1897),[59] the narrative further reduces women to object status. The three Avices – mother, daughter, and granddaughter – are even denied a personalizing name, and their emotional histories are relevant only inasmuch as they impinge on Pierston's consciousness. The rest of their life story is expunged from the text and their individual differences ignored and erased by the protagonist who tries to impose on them the uniform identity of the 'Well-Beloved' because (to rephrase John Goode) it is a question of the three Avices 'happening' to Pierston.

What, therefore, is Hardy's ultimate attitude to Sue and Arabella? The answer can perhaps be found in his successive textual revisions of *Jude*. Apart from the obvious restoration in the 1895 book edition of passages bowdlerized in the serial version, *Jude* underwent two textual revisions: in 1903 after Macmillan took over as Hardy's

English publishers, and again in 1912 for the definitive 'Wessex Edition'. Through the 'cumulative effect' of these successive revisions, Hardy tried to soften his original 'somewhat harsh' and 'too rigid' portrait of Sue by giving her 'more human sympathy': she is made less evasive about her feelings for Jude, and when she finally surrenders to his physical desire, the 1912 version has the significant additional words: 'I do love you' (p. 280).[60] Jude, too, is made to withdraw his 1903 accusation that Sue is 'cold', and he tones down his original harsh condemnation – 'you are *never* so nice in your real presence as you are in your letters' – to a moderate 'you are *often* not so nice' (p. 184; my italics). In the case of Arabella, however, Hardy's sympathy is much less in evidence, as is demonstrated in one crucial textual revision. The 1895 edition had described Arabella as 'a complete and substantial female human – no more, no less'.[61] In the 1903 Macmillan 'New Edition' (and all subsequent editions), just *one* word is changed, but it radically transforms the tone of the entire description as Arabella now becomes 'a complete and substantial female *animal*' (p. 62; my italic). In sliding down the evolutionary ladder – from 'human' to 'animal' – we suspect that Arabella forfeits some of her creator's imaginative sympathy, despite Hardy's genuine and repeatedly expressed concern for cruelly trapped rabbits and inhumanely slaughtered pigs.

# 8

# Hardy, his Wives, and his Literary Protégées

From the 1890s onwards book-length critical studies of Hardy began to appear and when these books found their way into the Max Gate library it was invariably their biographical sections that irritated Hardy. The worst offender seems to have been Ernest Brennecke's *The Life of Thomas Hardy* (1925) which is littered with Hardy's marginal comments: 'false', 'incorrect', 'untrue', 'conjectural', 'exaggerated', 'garbled', 'imaginary', 'impertinent invention'.[1] In a 1922 letter to Agnes Grove, Hardy refused to entertain a female thesis-writer whom she had recommended:

> I am sorry I am unable to be interviewed by the young woman. I have many such applications to obtain personal details, which are quite unnecessary for writing a 'thesis', that should be based on published works alone of course.[2]

Given such a clear warning that trespassers on his private life are unwelcome, it may seem a case of fools rushing in where saner critics have wisely refrained. However, to explore fully Hardy's attitudes to women it is necessary to take into account at least his relationships with his two wives – both of whom had literary ambitions – and with his literary ladies whom he protectively took under his wing, revising their work, urging reluctant publishers on their behalf, and even painstakingly correcting their proofs.

In her Hardy-baiting novel, Emma Tennant states provocatively: 'Yes, Thomas Hardy made of his wife that well-known Victorian phenomenon, the madwoman in the attic. His neglect and cold indifference alienated her, she became "scatty" and the housekeeping got beyond her capabilities.'[3] Behind the gross exaggeration in Tennant's accusation of Hardy there is perhaps a kernel of truth because when Emma Hardy retired to the attic of Max Gate she was frustrated and disillusioned at both personal and literary levels. Witnessing Hardy's susceptibility to younger, beautiful, (often aristocratic) women with literary aspirations – Rosamund Tomson, Florence Henniker, Agnes Grove, Florence Dugdale – it must have pained Emma to realize her husband's insensitive disregard of her own literary aspirations. When Emma and Hardy first met in 1870 it was perhaps her literary ambition that had drawn her to the unimpressive-looking architect who had 'a blue paper sticking out of his pocket' – the manuscript of a poem.[4]

Even biographers hostile to Emma Hardy concede that her emotional support was crucial to Hardy at a time when he was wavering between architecture and literature. Had she desired mere financial security she would have urged Hardy to stick to architecture, but her intuitive recognition of Hardy's literary potential made her supportive of his tentative efforts in that direction. Recalling those early years of indecision and struggle, Hardy paid Emma (then Miss Gifford) a warm tribute which deserves to be quoted at length if only to counterbalance the standard image of Emma Hardy as that of an eccentric, ego-centric, mentally deficient wife who was a social embarrassment to the long-suffering and uncomplaining Hardy:

> However, deeming their reply [i.e. Macmillan's] on the question of publishing the tale [i.e. *Under the Greenwood Tree*] to be ambiguous at least, he got it back, threw the MS. into a box with his old poems, being quite sick of all such, and began to think of other ways and means. He consulted Miss Gifford by letter, declaring that he had banished novel-writing for ever, and was going on with architecture henceforward. But she, with no great opportunity of reasoning on the matter, yet, as Hardy used to think and say – truly or not – with that rapid instinct which serves women in such good stead, and may almost be called preternatural vision, wrote back instantly her desire that he should adhere to authorship, which she felt sure would be his true vocation. From the very fact that she wished thus, and *set herself aside altogether* – architecture being obviously the quick way to an income for marrying on – he was impelled to consider her interests more than his own.[5] (My italics)

Emma's assistance took a very practical shape; she later recalled: 'I copied a good deal of manuscript which went to-and-fro by post, and I was very proud and happy doing this'.[6] This was the manuscript of *Desperate Remedies* which, unfortunately, has not survived.

Emma's service as Hardy's amanuensis continued right up to the early 1890s, and the painstakingly handwritten fair copies could only have been a labour of love. The full extent of her contribution is now a matter of speculation as much of the evidence was destroyed, often by Hardy himself, and it is only the reconstructive efforts of a few Hardy scholars that give us an idea of her erased work. For instance, when Hardy was composing *A Laodicean* he was totally confined to bed with an internal haemorrhage, and the publisher's deadline could only be met by his dictating a substantial part of the novel to Emma. In his autobiography, the normally reticent Hardy pays Emma a brief tribute: 'Accordingly from November onwards he began dictating it to her from the awkward position he occupied....She worked bravely both at writing and nursing, till at the beginning of the following May a rough draft was finished'.[7] But what happened to this manuscript in Emma's handwriting? When Hardy distributed his manuscripts to the various libraries, through Sydney Cockerell in 1911, the manuscript of *A Laodicean*, significantly, was missing. Hardy had himself burned it much earlier.[8]

A similar fate met those pages written by Emma in the manuscripts of the other novels. Often the bottom line or lines of a page are torn or cut away, and the subsequent pages missing, or the top of a page is torn or cut away and the previous few leaves missing, which seems to suggest that 'there was a deliberate and systematic attempt to suppress the fact of Emma Hardy's part in [the] manuscript'.[9] Simon Gatrell had similarly concluded that '[t]here is much circumstantial evidence to suggest that over a hundred leaves of the manuscript of *The Mayor of Casterbridge* were removed by Hardy... because they were all or part in Emma's hand.'[10] In the manuscript of *Tess* too,

> Thirty-nine leaves of the manuscript are missing, and recent research on other defective manuscripts... has suggested that Hardy probably removed them before allowing the manuscript to be presented to the British Museum because they were wholly or in part written in the hand of his wife, Emma.[11]

Emma Hardy's hand, however, does survive in the manuscript of *The Woodlanders*: while Purdy identified 106 sheets as being either wholly or partly in Emma's hand (out of 498 sheets), Manford makes a claim for 128 sheets, or nearly a fifth of the manuscript. This manuscript thus represents the largest number of leaves in Emma's hand that is extant and this fact, along with the nature of some of Emma's errors of transcription which suggest dictation (e.g. misspelling a character's name as 'Bocock' instead of 'Beaucock'), imply that by 1887 at least the Hardy marriage had not irretrievably broken down. Given the systematic removal of Emma's scribal contributions to Hardy's other manuscripts, the substantial number of pages in her hand in *The Woodlanders* manuscript which have survived seems somewhat of a puzzle. Significantly, *The Woodlanders* manuscript was not among those which Sydney Cockerell distributed to libraries in 1911, and Hardy seems to have lost control over it towards the end of his life, as it was purchased by Howard Bliss, one of the earliest private collectors of Hardyana. In 1924 Bliss pointed out that there were some pages in Emma's writing in the manuscript, and Florence Hardy replied conveying Hardy's reaction:

> I have been talking to T.H [*sic*] about 'The Woodlanders' MS. & he is appalled to think so many pages were not his. At first he suggested that they could be taken out, & he would write in the passages... but that seems unfair to the one who copied in so many pages with no thought save that of being helpful.[12]

Earlier, in 1921, when Bliss had reported the interesting find of a page of manuscript in Emma's writing, Florence Hardy had replied: 'She did indeed frequently copy for him any pages that had many alterations. She liked doing it. There are some pages of her handwriting in the MS. of several of the novels.'[13] Apart from making fair copies of the heavily revised pages of the manuscripts of the novels, Emma also copied out notes for Hardy in his 'Literary Notes' notebook. More than 200 entries (i.e. no. 21 to no. 249) are in Emma's hand[14] and this speaks volumes for her desire to be a willing 'helpmeet', especially since (unlike her successor) she did not have typing skills to lighten the labour.

Why Hardy removed evidences of Emma's contribution will remain a matter for speculation. Perhaps he felt that an 'adulterated' manuscript would not have authoritative value when donated to libraries; perhaps he was irritated by Emma's supposed claims that it was she who had really written Thomas Hardy's novels. Again, this wild exaggeration contains a tiny grain of truth. In 1911 Emma reminisced about their courtship days: 'The rarity of the visits [i.e.

Hardy's] made them highly delightful to both; we talked much of plots, possible scenes, tales, and poetry and of his own work.'[15] That this is not an idle boast, that Emma did have bright suggestions which Hardy readily incorporated into his work is proved by an instance as late as the 1890s. In Tess's confession of her past to Angel, the scene is lent an ominous quality by the firelight playing on Tess's jewels. Of this episode, Hardy wrote:

> Hardy spent a good deal of time in August and the autumn correcting *Tess of the d'Urbervilles* for its volume form, which process consisted in restoring to their places the passages and chapters of the original MS. that had been omitted from the serial publication. That Tess should put on the jewels was Mrs Hardy's suggestion.[16]

Characteristically enough, this crucial last line is missing from Florence Hardy's version of the text,[17] but as Millgate restores this line it now enjoys canonical status as the candid acknowledgement of the author of *Tess*. Confirmation is provided by Blathwayt in his 1892 article where he quotes Hardy as saying (pointing to a sketch): 'That is Woolbridge Manor house…In that house and on that same night… she tried on the jewels that Clare gave her. I think I must tell you that that was an idea of Mrs Hardy's.'[18] But several other unacknowledged graftings too occurred – e.g. snatches from Emma's courtship letters appear in Elfride's speeches,[19] vivid phrases from Emma's honeymoon diary recording their Continental trip surface in the description of Rouen in *The Hand of Ethelberta*, and passages from Emma's *Some Recollections* inspire some of the memorable poems of 1912-13. The edition by Evelyn Hardy and Robert Gittings makes the connections clear by juxtaposing Emma's prose passages with Hardy's companion poetic pieces, although Hardy himself rather disingenuously claimed that while composing 'A Man was Drawing Near to Me', 'he had either not read her reminiscence of the evening…or had forgotten it'.[20]

It was the fate of Emma's writing, whether merely scribal or more ambitiously creative, to be forgotten, suppressed, erased. Her voice was silenced, her achievement negatived. In those years of mutual estrangement Emma is supposed to have written the infamous 'Black

Diaries' about which Howard Jacobson acidly comments (through his fictional character, Camilla):

> 'After Emma's death Thomas Hardy found amongst her papers a mass of diary entries gathered together under the title, "What I think of my Husband". You won't be surprised to learn that he destroyed them. His remorse for his wife is famous, but it wasn't strong enough to allow her to have her say.'[21]

Perhaps of all the papers that fed the periodic bonfires in the Max Gate garden, these 'black diaries' deserved to perish. They were probably the safety outlet for Emma's bottled-up feelings of resentment and, if death had not forestalled her, Emma perhaps would have burnt them herself. While the suppression of these diaries is understandable, what is puzzling is a different case of editorial suppression in relation to the more sunny and romantic *Some Recollections*. Hardy was sufficiently impressed by the literary quality of this diary and he incorporated a fairly long extract from it in his own disguised autobiography. Allowing the pages of Emma's diary to take up the narrative of their courtship, he quotes Emma:

> I have never liked the Cornish working-orders as I do Devonshire folk; their so-called admirable independence of character was most disagreeable to live with, and usually amounted to absence of kindly interest in others, though it was unnoticeable by casual acquaintance.... Nevertheless their nature had a glamour about it – that of an old-world romantic expression; and then sometimes there came to one's cognizance in the hamlets a dear heart-whole person. (Hardy's ellipsis)[22]

What has been carefully edited out from this paragraph by the silent ellipsis – and in this instance the editorial scissors seem to be firmly in Hardy's hand – is the following sentence by Emma:

> One stands out [saliently] amongst them with worth of character and deep devotion though rather dumb of expression, a man gentle of nature, musical, christlike in guilelessness, handsome of face and figure, David-like farming his own land: he never married, and told after I had left of his disappointment, and [of his] attraction on first seeing me on the stairs.[23]

Even if this was mere romantic fantasizing on Emma's part, there was surely no harm in letting it stand. After all, Hardy's own output, in both prose and poetry, is replete with the tragedy of missed chances, with backward glances of yearning, and quite a few of his poems vocalize his regret for a 'lost prize': e.g. 'The Opportunity (For H.P.)' (Helen Paterson), 'Thoughts of Phena' (Tryphena Sparks), 'To Lizbie Browne' (Elizabeth Bishop), 'To Louisa in the Lane' (Louisa Harding), 'Concerning Agnes' (Agnes Grove), 'Wessex Heights' (Florence Henniker, among many others), 'An Old Likeness (Recalling R.T.)' (Rosamund Tomson). Unconsciously betraying the same double standards, against which *Tess* was so powerful a plea, Hardy here applies a double censorship: as the male editor, he silences this intransigent female voice; and as the husband, he discreetly draws the veil over his wife's verbal indiscretion.

A more insidious instance of the suppression of Emma's work relates to the other creative medium of her sketches. Emma's diaries are filled with lively pencil drawings, and probably after one of their visits to Tintagel Castle she did a painting of it in water-colour. Years after her death, in 1923, the Dorchester 'Hardy Players' produced Hardy's *The Queen of Cornwall* and the programme for the performance contained a photograph of Tintagel Castle. Actually, it was a photograph of the water-colour of the castle by Emma, but it simply bore the caption 'From a Water Colour Drawing in the possession of the Author'.[24] Emma's authorship of the painting is suppressed and her creative effort rendered anonymous.

Of Emma's purely literary efforts, her 'The Maid on the Shore' surely deserved a private printing. Although the narrative line is somewhat slack and there is some confusion about names and relationships, the story does possess a certain charm. There are powerful evocations of the Cornish seascape which are not unworthy of the hand of Hardy himself and the story is certainly richer in human interest than, say, 'Blue Jimmy: The Horse Stealer'. If, as Dalziel has demonstrated, Hardy had a greater hand in the composition of 'Blue Jimmy' than just editorial corrections on proof sheets),[25] then it was certainly one of his off days. 'Blue Jimmy', ostensibly by Florence Dugdale (later the second Mrs Hardy), is the dullest narrative to which Hardy ever applied his pen. 'The Maid on the Shore', by contrast, is full of surprises which nevertheless have an air of inevitability and the exploration of the psychology of love among the quartet of lovers is interesting. Hardy was presumably impressed by it because he preserved the typescript and even made corrections (typographical and stylistic) in ink in his hand.[26] But while he was busy improving the compositions of Florence Henniker, Agnes Grove and Florence Dugdale, he apparently did not give a thought to touching up Emma's story for publication.

Emma Hardy, however, did achieve publication. Her attempts at poetry were marginally more successful and one of her sonnets, called 'Spring Song', was published in *Sphere* in April 1900. Another, 'The Gardener's Ruse',[27] appeared in *The Academy* in April 1901, while three more short pieces appeared locally in *Dorset County Chronicle* in 1905, 1907 and 1910. In December 1911 a slim volume of her verse entitled *Alleys* was privately printed and this was followed in April 1912 by the private printing of her religious prose entitled *Spaces*. A couple of poems in *Alleys*, e.g. 'The Trumpet Call' and 'Dancing Maidens', are engaging in their simplicity and directness of appeal but by no stretch of sympathetic imagination was she a good poet. Earlier, drawing on the experiences of her journey across the Channel, she had written an article 'In Praise of Calais' which was published in *Dorset County Chronicle* in December 1908. Passionately opposed to any sort of cruelty to 'living creatures, even of the insect kind', she wrote to the Editor of *Dorset County Chronicle* and her letter was published in July 1910. Despite a literary misquotation, this short piece is remarkable for its sensitive statement: 'It must be remembered that minuteness of organism does not prevent agony, that size is of no account in the scheme of creation.'[28] The other passionate commitment in Emma's life was women's suffrage and she joined the 3,000-odd Suffragettes in their 1907 London march in such inclement weather that it came to be dubbed the 'Mud March'. Next year, she again joined the London demonstrations but this time, perhaps inhibited by her recurring lameness, she contented herself with riding in an open carriage at the head of the procession. She had contributed, in March 1907, to a symposium on women's suffrage (along with Millicent Fawcett) published in *The Woman at Home*, and in May 1908 she wrote a spirited letter to the Editor which was published in *The Nation* under the title 'Women and the Suffrage'. In it she makes a remarkable statement: 'The truth of the matter is that a man who has something of the feminine nature in him is a more perfectly *rational* being than one who is without it, though men who are not possessed of this supreme quality pour contempt on such rare ones as have it.'[29] This same insight is occasionally revealed in her personal correspondence. For instance, in 1894 she wrote to Mary Haweis about the move to clear London streets of prostitutes: 'I am interested in Mrs Ormiston Chant, her proceedings & her faith in the possibility of purifying London – if only she would organize a crusade to clear the young men from the streets – to attack them rather than the women – how she would do it!'[30] All this suggests that Emma was not as scatterbrained as she is generally made out to be, and if Hardy had only given her the same tutelage that he lavished on Agnes Grove perhaps she might have made a modest journalistic career for herself.

One of the ironies of Emma's literary aspirations is that she wrote a short story called 'The Inspirer', about a wife who serves as her husband's Muse. From Florence Dugdale's letters to Emma[31] (she was then typing it for the first Mrs Hardy) it is obvious that both Emma and Florence considered it her best work. Although this story itself does not survive, its creator does survive as indeed 'The Inspirer': for through her death, Emma inspired those poignant poems of 1912-13 with their haunting sense of loss. Another irony surrounding one of Emma's works – 'The Acceptors' – is that when Florence Dugdale was trying to place it with a publisher, she wrote to Emma (August 1910) saying that she had not disclosed Mrs Hardy's name as the author of the piece because she 'thought that it would be wiser to get a perfectly unbiassed opinion'[32] from the publisher so that the story could be published (presumably) on its own merit. As the publication of Hardy's letters now abundantly makes clear, Florence Dugdale's own literary attempts did not always achieve publication on their own steam. Hardy was solidly behind her, putting in a good word, egging on a reluctant publisher, and often heavily revising and polishing her drafts. As early as July 1907 (that is, much before her 1910 meeting with Emma Hardy when she could lay no claim to being 'for several years the friend of the first Mrs Hardy' which is how Hardy's autobiography rather disingenuously describes her[33]), Hardy tried to launch her on a writing career in order to spare her the 'drudgery of teaching'. Writing to Maurice Macmillan, Hardy warmly recommended Florence Dugdale as being 'well qualified to be of assistance to your firm in the preparation of school books & supplémentary readers' because of her 'strong literary tastes, & a natural gift for writing'.[34] The next day, Hardy wrote to Archibald Marshall, Editor of *Daily Mail*, ostensibly in response to his request for another poem, but making no effort to mask his true intentions:

> My immediate reason for writing is however of another kind – to bring under the editorial eye of the Daily Mail a young writer – Miss F. Dugdale, who has done research work for me at the British Museum to my great satisfaction, & whose growing practice in journalism & discriminating judgment in literature would render her, I think, of use in one or other department of the paper. She is a certified school teacher, & might, in my opinion, do good work in reviewing books for the young. She has already written a few things for the Daily Mail, but has not, I think, been sufficiently discovered by the Editors.[35]

Later, in September 1907, Hardy wrote to thank Reginald Smith for having accepted Florence Dugdale's story 'The Apotheosis of the Minx' which was published in *Cornhill* in May 1908.[36] This definitely suggests that Hardy had a hand in placing the story, if not in its actual composition. However, not all editors were so obliging and Herbert Greenhough Smith, acting editor of *Strand Magazine*, failed to respond to Hardy's recommendation of a story (in July 1908) by 'a modest young writer' which was 'somewhat lurid & sensational, but... well told & striking'.[37] The story, identified tentatively as Dugdale's 'The Scholar's Wife', found no better luck with Clement Shorter either and it was ultimately published in *Pall Mall Magazine* in January 1909. What means of persuasion Hardy used on this occasion is not known, but at times he was not above resorting to blatant arm-twisting tactics. For instance, in September 1910, Hardy wrote to James Milne:

> I am sending you for the Daily Chronicle a little topical sketch that was forwarded to the paper a year ago by the author, for publication on Oct 21. I have just read it, & have come to the conclusion that its rejection on that occasion must have been owing to oversight or press of matter, for it is about the only thing left to say in print concerning Trafalgar Day, & it is, moreover, said well, & with real literary art. If you & the Editor tell me that the Daily Chronicle does not want literature I have, of course, no answer to make.[38]

The article whose claims this covering letter urged was Florence Dugdale's 'Trafalgar! How Nelson's Death Inspired the Tailor', originally submitted (and rejected) in September 1909, but subsequently duly published in *Daily Chronicle* on Trafalgar Day, 21 October 1910. After all, very few editors could fail to respond to such a letter written by a man who had just been awarded the Order of Merit. In fact, Hardy's contribution in this instance was not just pushing the piece down a reluctant editor's throat; he seems to have had a hand in the composition as well, because in an earlier letter to Florence Dugdale (September 1909), he had written: 'The sketch reads remarkably well. If you feel you do not like my supposed improvements, rub them out; though I *advise* you to recopy the story just as it now stands' (Hardy's italic).[39]

In August 1910, Hardy again advanced the claims of 'Blue Jimmy' to Reginald Smith:

> At last I send the story – or rather record – I spoke about: 'Blue Jimmy the horse-stealer'. It seems interesting to me, &, if I may say so, worthy of the Cornhill, even if only from the novelty of its subject. I hope you will think the same. The writer has been at some pains to hunt up the particulars at the British Museum, & I gave her also a few traditional ones. I can guarantee the truth of the story – if truth has any virtue in such a case.[40]

'Blue Jimmy' was duly published in *Cornhill* (in February 1911) but Hardy was not always successful in promoting Florence's works. Earlier, a similar letter addressed to C. E. S. Chambers (March 1909),[41] accompanying an (unidentified) story of Florence, failed to produce the desired effect in *Chambers's Journal*.

Hardy's contribution to Florence Dugdale's literary output was sometimes more direct and yet covert. When Florence was preparing the prose and verse descriptions to accompany the illustrations in *The Book of Baby Beasts* (1911), Hardy passed off his own poem 'The Calf' under her name. Similarly, in Florence's *The Book of Baby Birds* (1912), the poem on 'The Yellow-Hammer' is actually Hardy's, and in her *The Book of Baby Pets* (1913) 'The Lizard' is Hardy's contribution. Purdy even speculates that Hardy probably had a hand in the revision of the other poems in all these three books.[42] That these three poems have subsequently found a place in the 'New Wessex Edition' of Hardy's *The Complete Poems* (1976) suggests that there is no serious scholarly challenge to ascribing these poems to the Hardy canon.[43]

Hardy's ghost-writing of his own (auto)biography was a brilliant strategy but it was nothing new. It was the natural culmination of a long period of ghost-writing Florence's articles /stories/poems, and when Florence Hardy acquiesced in this literary deception one suspects that wifely loyalty ran hand-in-hand with personal literary ambition. She perhaps saw herself in the tradition of Boswell-Lockhart, and her literary conscience did not urge her to reveal the secret as long as she lived. Already such subterfuges had been going on for some time, albeit on a minor scale. For instance, in June 1910, Hardy wrote to his friend Edward Clodd:

> I do not know if you saw in The Standard a sort of summary of my existence so far, which appeared there on my birthday. It was written by my secretary Miss Dugdale. She does work for that paper, & they asked her to do an interview; but I would not consent to that, so she wrote the article they printed, with which they were much pleased. The fact was that I knew they would print *something*, & I preferred to fall into her hands to being handled by a stranger, as I can always depend on her good taste.[44] (Hardy's italic)

Was this article, 'Thomas Hardy. Great Writer's 70th Birthday', really written by Florence Dugdale or did Hardy partly ghost-write it? The suspicion is confirmed by later events because in this same letter Hardy goes on to say:

> The Evening Standard... has now asked her to do a similar sketch of yourself for publication on your 70th birthday, & she wonders if you would mind. It would probably be quite short & general. I have told her that if you agree I will read the MS. before she lets it go, & I would not pass anything that you could possibly object to.

After Florence Dugdale's article on Clodd appeared in *Evening Standard* on 30 June 1910, Florence confided to Clodd: 'As for the purple patches, they were *all* his [i.e. Hardy's], I can assure you.'[45] If Hardy was responsible for the (omitted) 'purple patches' in Clodd's biographical sketch, then is it too much to imagine that he was probably responsible for many passages of his own '70th birthday' article?

Also, the final volumes of Hardy's *Collected Letters* contain quite a few letters drafted by Hardy but signed by Florence Hardy and sent out over her name. Hardy had become quite an adept in the third-person style and he seems to have realized his wife's potential as his proxy self. Disclaimers, letters of denial, letters expressing disapproval, are all sent out in Florence Hardy's name. For example, Hardy's lack of enthusiasm over Vere Collins's proposal to translate Hedgcock's book (because of the disproportionate space it devotes to his prose and the minor errors in the biographical section), is conveyed in a letter (22 June 1922), ostensibly by Florence Hardy, but probably composed by Hardy himself as even the words 'signed by F.E.H.' are apparently in Hardy's hand.[46] The same distancing strategy is adopted in subsequent letters to Vere Collins and Frank Hedgcock (July 1922).[47]

When Samuel Chew was working on the revisions to his book on Hardy he received a letter, ostensibly from Florence Hardy (17 September 1922), stating:

> I am enclosing herewith the notes for the new edition of your book as promised… they are sent on the understanding that they are kept private as to their present shape, & that you do not mention anything about how you came by the details they give, or that you state them on authority....
>
> Mr Hardy has looked them over, & says they are quite correct – indeed, they are based entirely on his own remarks.[48]

The caution expressed in these lines along with the presence of numerous additions in Hardy's hand in the accompanying typescript imply that although the list of suggested corrections is headed 'Notes on Professor Chew's Book by F.E.H.', the work was probably largely Hardy's own. Certainly this is the inevitable conclusion from the editorial decision to include it in Hardy's *Collected Letters*.

Perhaps the most revealing case of such ghost-writing is a letter of 24 August 1924 sent to T. H. Tilley regarding a possible dramatization of *Tess*. The letter, signed 'F.E. Hardy', states: 'Mr Hardy agrees to their performing the Tess play'. But in the pencil draft, for once the mask had slipped as the words Hardy had originally written were: 'I agree'.[49] Florence Hardy seems to have been passively acquiescent to such Hardyan intrusions into her own work, even her personal correspondence. Thus, in her letter of August 1918 to Sydney Cockerell there is a paragraph, on the 'fashion for obscurity' among contemporary young poets, which was actually dictated by Thomas Hardy and included by Florence as part of her own letter.[50] Also, Florence Hardy's comments on Crabbe as one of the 'potent influence[s]' on Hardy's 'realism' (rather than Zola) were dictated by Hardy and included (within quotation marks) as part of her letter of February 1919 to Cockerell.[51] Again, on 7 December 1919, in a letter to Cockerell, Florence Hardy complained of the 'flagrant' 'trickery' in the *Saturday Review* criticism of 'my husband's poems'; but as her subsequent letter (18 December) to Cockerell acknowledged, her comments were actually written at Hardy's dictation.[52]

Although Hardy continued to exploit his wife as a convenient mouthpiece to air indirectly his own opinions, he seems to have frowned upon Florence's independent literary efforts once she became 'Mrs Hardy'. Thus, as early as March 1914, just over a month after her marriage to Hardy, Florence lamented to Rebekah Owen: 'To my great grief I am just obliged to refuse to write, for my publisher, a book about dogs – to be illustrated by that splendid artist – Detmold. I have a pile of books, too, to review, but I suppose that it is unfair to my husband to take up so much outside work.'[53] On 22 July 1914, within six months of her marriage, Florence expressed her misgivings to Lady Hoare: 'Ought I – in fairness to my husband – to give up my scribbling?'[54] That this is not just a chance remark is obvious from her writing again to Lady Hoare only four days later (26 July 1914):

> With regard to my own writing I have a feeling, deep within me, that my husband rather dislikes my being a scribbling woman. Personally I *love* writing, poor though the result be, but I do realize that I can find plenty of domestic work to do, & I can also devote a great deal of time to him.[55] (Florence Hardy's italic)

That Florence Hardy did her best to sacrifice her personal literary ambitions and instead devote her energies to Hardy's domestic comfort and poetic productivity is suggested by Hardy's letter of May 1917 to Florence Henniker: 'She still keeps up her reviewing, but will soon drop it; not having quite sufficient spare time with the household to look after, & the garden also, which she has taken upon herself, much to my relief.'[56] The tone of this letter is complacent and prescriptive and suggests that, for all his feminist sympathies, Hardy did not take very kindly to a 'scribbling' wife. It is sad to think that a man who proudly wrote to friends on his second marriage that 'my wife is a literary woman' should, only four years later, be writing: 'F. [i.e. Florence Hardy] gets letters asking her to review books (since she reviewed Mrs Shorter's poems under her own name), but she does not want to, as the house is enough for her to attend to, she finds.'[57] Although Florence Hardy reviewed (anonymously) half a dozen novels for *Sphere* in July 1916 and continued with her occasional contributions to newspapers, she would lament to Rebekah Owen in 1920: 'All literary work of my own is put a stop to.'[58] The phrase is nicely ambivalent: was the termination self-willed or externally imposed?

As both the Mrs Hardys learnt to their cost, Hardy was singularly unenthusiastic about a 'scribbling' wife but when the 'dear fellow-scribbler'[59] happened to be a Mrs Henniker (or a Mrs Grove) of course the story was very different. Hardy had met Florence Henniker in May 1893 during his visit to Dublin where the Hardys had been guests of her brother Lord Houghton. Whether Hardy's increasing estrangement from Emma made him all the more susceptible to this 'charming, *intuitive* woman'[60] or whether his transparently passionate affair with Mrs Henniker resulted in the aggravation of marital disharmony is a classic 'chicken-and-egg' question. Within a month of this meeting, Hardy is 'keenly conscious' of the 'one-sidedness' of the relationship; later he expresses his wish that Mrs Henniker were more emancipated and 'free from certain retrograde superstitions'.[61] He offers to conduct her to cathedrals and give oral instruction in architecture; readily complies with her request to write down the true names of the places in her copy of *Tess*; suggests that they exchange copies of Swinburne's poems, annotate the volumes, and then restore each others' copies: in short, he seizes on any pretext to keep the correspondence alive. Mrs Henniker, perhaps not realizing the intensity of the emotion she has stirred, sent him her translations of three love poems[62] and later sent him her photographs (a pattern that had been enacted before with Rosamund Tomson and that would later be re-enacted with Agnes Grove). But there were limits beyond which she was not prepared to go, as she seems to have made clear to Hardy during their August 1893 trip to Winchester. Mrs Henniker had no intention of breaking her marriage vows for Hardy and no wish to see his name as co-respondent in divorce proceedings. However, she had no objection to their names being coupled in a joint literary venture because although she had already published three novels before she met Hardy, she realized that the Hardy connection would boost both her literary image and the sales.

It was probably Florence Henniker who suggested their collaborating to write a short story and, deprived of the fulfilment of his romantic hopes, Hardy ultimately agreed to this second-best literary substitute. The result was the story published in *To-Day* as 'The Spectre of the Real' (November 1894) and this is the *only* openly acknowledged collaborative work undertaken by Hardy. It is interesting to note that the story was originally entitled 'Desire' and referred to by this name in the letters that passed between the collaborators.[63] When Hardy later drastically revised the ending, making this title inappropriate, among the list of alternative titles that he asked Florence Henniker to consider were, significantly enough, 'A passion & after' and 'A shattering of Ideals'.[64] The complicated history of the writing of this story – with Hardy providing the plot outline, Mrs Henniker fleshing it out into a narrative, Hardy revising it and completely rewriting the conclusion, Mrs Henniker being hurt at her descriptive passages being cut out and Hardy reluctantly reinstating them against his better judgement, Hardy having the manuscript professionally typed and then correcting the proofs himself – all this has been discussed elaborately by Pamela Dalziel and it is pointless going over the same ground. What is important is that Hardy was determined to 'keep it a secret to our two selves which is my work & which yours', and since the manuscript does not survive it seems to have been a well-kept secret. Hardy's presentiment that 'all the wickedness…will be laid on my unfortunate head, while all the tender & proper parts will be attributed to you' was borne out by the reviews, one of which cautioned Mrs Henniker against 'the advancing pessimism of a collaborator, however illustrious' and another which lamented 'those deflections from good taste which seem to have become characteristic of Mr Hardy's later art'.[65] Hardy's revisions had emphasized the sexual nature of the heroine Rosalys's attraction towards her first husband Jim, and these apparently displeased not only the reviewers but also his co-author, because when Mrs Henniker collected the story in her book *In Scarlet and Grey* (1896) it was primarily these revisions that she bowdlerized.

Whether or not this collaborative venture cured Hardy's infatuation for Florence Henniker, it certainly decided him against such literary partnership in the future. Realizing Mrs Henniker's sensitivity to his implied criticisms in revising her draft, and perhaps hurt himself by the negative reviews, Hardy wrote to Mrs Henniker in 1896 advising her to 'keep better literary company in future'.[66] In the previous year, Hardy had sent Clement Shorter one of Mrs Henniker's stories, recommending it as 'an artistic & tender little tale'.[67] But when Mrs Henniker suggested that Hardy's name appear as co-author of this story, 'A Page from a Vicar's History', Hardy wrote to Shorter (March 1895) emphatically stating his objection:

> It is very good of Mrs Henniker to feel as she does about the story. But I should be manifestly wrong to put my name as joint-author, when it bears such clear internal evidence of the sex of the writer... my share having been editorial, my actual writing being limited to the rather commonplace incident of the last page or so. Possibly Mrs Henniker might be induced to reconsider her decision, or to write a new ending: otherwise I see no course left but to withdraw the story from publication.[68]

Despite Hardy's disillusionment with Mrs Henniker, at both romantic and literary levels, the relationship did *not* sour, and this is proved by the numerous long letters he wrote to her over a thirty-year period, i.e. 1893 to 1922. When she died in 1923, Hardy's notebook entry, later incorporated into his autobiography, read: 'After a friendship of 30 years!'[69] The genuineness of this friendship is brought out by an incident in 1915 which reveals the human touch that is always so endearing in Hardy. During those troubled war years, when even to have a German-sounding name rendered a person suspect in the eyes of the authorities and the common people alike, to be a German was tantamount to being a spy. Knowing that the one friend who would not fail her was Hardy, Florence Henniker appealed to him to provide a personal testimonial of trustworthiness for her old German maid Anna Hirschmann. Mrs Henniker's trust was not misplaced and Hardy promptly complied with her request thus possibly saving Anna from deportation by the Home Office.[70]

Hardy's friendship for Mrs Henniker expressed itself in various ways in the 1890s. It ranged from his early lover's solicitude about her health ('Don't fag yourself out at that dancing. Promise you won't') to offering advice on which photograph to use as the frontispiece of her collection of stories: 'If you do decide to put the portrait at the beginning of the volume take my advice & have the profile one – (the first you sent me.).'[71] In two letters of October 1893, almost exclusively concerned with professional advice on how best to deal with her publishers, Hardy attempted to teach her 'the tricks of the trade' and – perhaps remembering his own problems with *Under the Greenwood Tree* – he specifically warned her: 'Don't part with the copyright.'[72] On a more practical level, Hardy appointed A. P. Watt as Mrs Henniker's literary agent and wrote to him 'to stir him up' in his negotiations with publishers regarding her short stories.[73] Trying to bring her into critical notice, he wrote to Clement Shorter in April 1894 openly reminding him that he had not yet reviewed Mrs Henniker's book (*Outlines*); a review duly appeared in *The Sketch* in July 1894. Not satisfied with just this, he himself wrote a promotional paragraph about her in which he praised her 'emotional imaginativeness' and recommended her 'note of individuality, her own personal and peculiar way of looking at life' without which no writer 'has any right to take a stand before the public as author'. Hardy's brief survey of her literary career (slightly inaccurate), backed by a mention of her aristocratic credentials, appeared anonymously in *The Illustrated London News* (18 August 1894).[74]

On the purely literary level, Florence Henniker was the first of Hardy's three protégées. Although she was already a published author, with three novels behind her, Hardy felt free to revise her work when she sent him some of her stories. He must have used his red pencil somewhat liberally, because he sounds immensely relieved when he writes to her in 1893: 'I was very glad...that you received my scribblings for amendments on their pages without any of the umbrage you might have felt at the liberty I took in making them.'[75] However, Florence Henniker had an independent spirit, and was to prove less tractable than either Agnes Grove or Florence Dugdale, who often docilely accepted Hardy's suggestions and corrections. On this occasion, Mrs Henniker ignored his suggestion to rename the collection as 'The Statesman's Love-Lapse, & other stories' (the book was published as *Outlines*); neither did she heed his advice to include the story 'His Excellency' in the collection. Made wiser by his difficulties with the publishers regarding *Tess*, Hardy again anxiously wrote to Mrs Henniker in October 1893 about her projected collection: 'You must not *waste* the stories for the mere sake of getting them printed quickly. I hope you modified that one of them called "A lost illusion" as I suggested – & did the other things, as the changes were likely to affect a publisher's views' (Hardy's italic).[76] But Hardy seems to have soon realized that Mrs Henniker was just as thin-skinned as himself regarding criticism, even when it came from a genuine well-wisher. Thus, in December 1893, he solemnly reassured her about her story entitled 'Bad and Worthless':

> I packed up the type-written story, & sent it on to Mr Shorter, *without altering a line.* One *letter* I had altered, & did not remember till it was sealed up: in the spelling of 'Gawd' – which is Kipling's, & should decidedly be avoided. But you can restore it in proof if you care to. My defence of having thought of tampering with the sketch is that you said I was to get £50 for it, which of course you will not get as it stands.[77] (Hardy's italics)

This letter has an interesting postscript which suggests that Hardy was desirous of smoothing ruffled feathers: 'You must overlook the liberty I took in suggesting alteration of the tale. I am vexed with myself for it.'

Nevertheless, Hardy seemed chronically unable to refrain from offering constructive criticism. One point that he repeatedly stressed is that her stories were too brief, too skeletal, and they could well do with a little more fleshing out. Even in the first flush of romantic ardour, he bravely risked telling her (June 1893): 'Indeed I fancy you write your MSS. a little too rapidly.'[78] As late as January 1900 he repeated his point: 'I read your "Lady Gilian" with the greatest interest.... Like nearly all your stories, it makes one wish there were more of it. The opening scene is beautiful, & tender, & I don't know any woman but yourself who could have written it. It is this which makes me wish the latter part had been worked out at greater length.'[79] The same criticism is again implied when he refers to 'Past Mending' as her 'little – too little – story', and comments on 'A Faithful Failure' that 'as usual, I regretted its shortness'. Hardy of course immediately added the palliative: 'That suggestive style of writing is one that you have quite made your own.'[80]

By this time, however, Mrs Henniker was no longer his literary 'pupil'. Hardy had already congratulated her in December 1896 on

her graduation from a 'novice' to 'an experienced writer', although
even as late as July 1898 he is still offering to forward a story of hers,
with a letter of recommendation, to the American magazine 'The
Independent' – which he does, telling the editor that the story has a
sound moral![81] But, effectively, the year 1895 had marked a watershed in Hardy's role as literary mentor as is suggested by his letter of
4 August to Mrs Henniker: 'I am overwhelmed with requests from
Editors for short stories, but I cannot write them. Why didn't you go
on being my pupil, so that I cd [sic] have recommended you as a substitute!'[82] Exactly a month after writing this, Hardy met his next literary pupil on 4 September 1895. Amid a scene of 'extraordinary pic-
turesqueness and poetry', in the heightened atmosphere of music
and dancing, under 'thousands of Vauxhall lamps' and 'the mellow
radiance of the full moon', Hardy made his acquaintance with 'the
beautiful Mrs Grove'.[83] Agnes Grove was the married daughter of
the archaeologist General Pitt-Rivers, who had invited the Hardys to
visit Rushmore during the annual Larmer Tree Sports. Hardy's
meeting with this beautiful young aristocrat, with whom he promptly led off the country dances, certainly set his heart fluttering, and
this magical moment was poignantly recaptured thirty years later
(after Mrs Grove's death in 1926) in Hardy's poem 'Concerning
Agnes' (*Winter Words*, 1928). With his artist's vision, Hardy probably
had a presentiment of a pattern about to repeat itself, because only
days after his Rushmore visit he wrote to tell Florence Henniker
(September 1895): 'It was a pleasant visit,... the most romantic time I
have had since I visited you at Dublin.'[84] One wonders what Mrs
Henniker thought of this candid confession. Of course, moving in
the same social circles, Mrs Henniker and Mrs Grove were already
on visiting terms (they apparently first met in July 1895) and later a
genuine friendship developed between these two Hardy pupils.

   Hardy's romantic feeling for Agnes Grove was of lesser intensity
and shorter duration than that for Florence Henniker and soon he
settled down to an avuncular interest in promoting her literary
career. As he told Agnes Grove in 1907, while fondly recalling 'that
dance on the green at the Larmer Tree by moonlight': 'I have a
strong temptation to grow "romantical"... [but] I am not going to,
being long past all such sentiments.'[85] Agnes Grove's reaction to that
first meeting is recorded in her diary where the entry for 4 September
1895 reads: 'Went to Larmer Tree Sports, met & talked to Thomas
Hardy, found him interesting, dined there' (she does not mention

the dancing).[86] Subsequent diary entries reveal that Hardy visited her on 25 March 1896 and on 21 May she went to tea with the Hardys while on the following day the Hardys came over to tea. Meetings also took place at the houses of common social acquaintances, e.g. at the Asquiths' party and at Dorothy Stanley's wedding. In 1900 Mrs Grove visited Max Gate twice, in February and in March, and on the latter visit (when she stayed the night at Max Gate) Emma Hardy made the friendly gesture of meeting her at the Dorchester railway station. During 1906 and 1907 when the Hardys were in London for the 'season', Mrs Grove was a regular visitor at the tea-parties in their rented London flat, although the painter Jacques-Emile Blanche (who did a portrait of Hardy in 1906) presents an unfavourable picture of suppressed tensions, jealousies and resentments – with Agnes Grove usurping the role of hostess and Emma Hardy sitting fuming on the sidelines. There is probably some exaggeration in this account because as late as 1910 Hardy is warmly inviting Agnes Grove to visit Max Gate (which he could not have done if Emma were hostile to her): 'Why don't you motor over to see us on Monday (Bank Holiday)?... if you drop in here in the afternoon you will be a godsend.'[87] After Emma's death in 1912, replying to Agnes Grove's letter of sympathy, Hardy gives her a fairly detailed account of Emma's last illness saying that he has written of these 'painful details' because 'I gather from your letter that you cared enough for her to be interested in them.'[88]

Certainly there is every suggestion of an amicable relationship in the letter that Emma Hardy wrote to Agnes Grove in January 1906. Agnes Grove's young son Terence had fallen into the garden pool and been drowned and, like many a writer, his grieving mother had tried to find release from the pain through the cathartic act of writing. When the childless Emma Hardy read Agnes Grove's privately printed allegory on Terence's death, she was moved to write: 'I have read your lovely little dirge-tale with my woman's heart, twice over. Perhaps, never having had a babe I do not quite comprehend the grief, yet I believe I do too.... I feel I know & love your boy, & his sweet ways.'[89] In December 1907, Emma Hardy again wrote to Agnes Grove: 'I have been much entertained with your book "The Social Fetich" having observed many of the errors myself which you mention so felicitously & with such gentle consideration. And I have enjoyed the anecdotes'.[90] Emma then goes on to mention what she considers certain inaccuracies and infelicities in the book which she hopes Agnes will correct in a new edition. Mrs Hardy could not have been unaware of the fact that her husband had actually read and corrected the proofs of *The Social Fetich* (the book was openly dedicated to Hardy by Mrs Grove) and her criticism may thus be read as an implied criticism of Hardy himself. It is in certain passages in this letter that one can sense Emma's underlying sense of hurt, jealousy and resentment at Hardy's complete neglect of her own literary aspirations. If Agnes Grove's success as a writer had made Emma envious, what must have rankled even more was the knowledge of just how much Hardy had contributed to that success.

When Hardy first met her, Mrs Grove (unlike Mrs Henniker) was not a published author. Within two months of their meeting, Hardy adopted her as his pupil and frankly advised her to rewrite an article she had written in reply to a Bishop who had expressed his views on 'Why Women Do Not Want the Ballot' in *North American Review*. Hardy told Mrs Grove that her 'Reply' was 'a spirited & sincerely written' piece but that it bore 'evidence of inexperience' and a 'tendency to redundance'. This could be corrected by rewriting and Hardy characteristically offered: 'If you like, I will mark the places which I consider faulty, & send it back to you to revise & get recopied. If you then cared to return it to me I could despatch it.'[91] Agnes Grove must have acquiesced promptly because this 3 November 1895 letter is followed only four days later by Hardy returning her article with these explanatory words: 'I have marked it in a perfectly brutal manner; but I am sure that the person who had intelligence enough to write it will know quite well that, if she goes in for literature – where competition is so keen & ruthless – it is truest friendship which points out faults frankly at starting.'[92]

Presumably after making the suggested corrections, Mrs Grove sent the article back to Hardy who read it over again to see if he could improve anything, changed one 'flippant' word in it, and sent it to the Editor of *North American Review* with a covering letter (November 1895) which anticipates many similar letters to different editors that he would later write for his next pupil, Florence Dugdale. Mentioning Mrs Grove's aristocratic connections, in an attempt to impress the editor, Hardy wrote: 'The article herewith sent has come into my hands, & probably you will agree with me in thinking it a spirited reply to the argument of the Bishop in your pages. It is, besides, essentially *feminine* – typically feminine – &, as such has a value to students of the question, apart from its representations & reasonings' (Hardy's italic).[93] When the article was rejected, Hardy did his best to reassure her that the 'refusal has obviously nothing to do with the merits or demerits of the article' and advised her to 'shape the article into a general reply to the customary objections; & then wait for an opening for it when the question again comes to the front'. Hardy then went on to suggest a new essay topic at which, as a mother of young children herself, she might try her hand: 'Some remarks of yours about Sue's talk with the child in "Jude" suggested to me that an article might be written entitled "What should children be told?" – working it out under the different headings of "on human nature", "on temptations", "on money", "on physiology", &c. It would probably attract attention.'[94] By suggesting this topic Hardy at least ensured that the correspondence between them continued to flow.

An interesting sidelight on Hardy's relations with his two literary pupils – ex- and current – is provided by the publication of *Jude*. Florence Henniker had left her mark on the novel by contributing not only her name to the heroine (Susanna Florence Mary Bridehead) but also her essential character trait i.e. seemingly emancipated but ultimately quite conventional; also, in one letter Hardy calls Mrs Henniker 'ethereal' which is exactly the word Jude uses to characterize Sue in his thoughts.[95] Hardy delayed presenting a copy of the novel to Mrs Henniker, and when he finally did so he offered the lame excuse: 'My hesitating to send "Jude" was not because I thought you narrow – but because I had rather bored you with him during the writing of some of the story, or thought I had.'[96] On the other hand, he had earlier sent Agnes Grove a copy of the novel with the confident words: 'You are, I know, sufficiently broad of view to estimate without bias a tragedy of very unconventional lives.'[97] The opposition between the words 'narrow' and 'broad' in these two letters leaves the reader to draw his/her own conclusion. Far from being a pessimist, Hardy seems to have been, in this respect at least, an incurable optimist; and he believed that after his disappointments over Rosamund Tomson and Florence Henniker, he had at last found his 'enfranchised' woman in Agnes Grove.

One immediate consequence of Mrs Grove's reading of *Jude* was her writing of the article, on Hardy's repeated prompting, about what children should be told. Hardy, knowing her tendency towards prolixity (Mrs Henniker had erred in the opposite direction), offered

to read her MS and advised her: 'Above all, don't make it long –
quite the contrary, short: then, if it catches on, you can write a second paper on the subject – which is better than saying everything at
once. I would advise that you shorten the section headed "on religion" – reserving what you cut out for another utterance.'[98] After
reading her MS, he complimented her on revealing a 'sustained
power of reasoning not usual in women's arguments', but could not
refrain from detailed advice on revisions, pencilling his suggestions
and making 'inked corrections of obvious oversights'.[99] Telling her
that it would be wise to get the manuscript typed, Hardy cautioned
her: 'I have ruthlessly pencilled the MS. as you will see. The fact is,
you have grown too diffuse towards the end, with a consequent
weakening of your argument. To become a strong writer you must
keep a constant curb upon yourself in this respect.'[100] When she had
an afterthought and appealed to his judgement, his opinion was that
'this insertion will not improve the essay...though true enough, [it]
is quite commonplace beside the rest of the article'.[101] Finally, after
all the corrections had been made and the rewritten article had
reached Hardy again, he struck out two 'superfluous' sentences and
then sent it to the Editor of *Free Review*, reassuring Agnes: 'The trouble has been nothing. You are such a good little pupil that it is a
pleasure to offer you suggestions.'[102] The article was accepted and
published in two parts in July 1896. Agnes Grove's pleasure in seeing her work finally in print was slightly marred by her pique which
comes out in her diary entry: 'Received *Free Review*. [My] signature
wrong.'[103] The article had appeared under the name 'Mrs Walter
Grove' while she had obviously wanted the name to read 'Agnes
Grove'. Hardy consoled her: 'If you go on writing you will become
case-hardened to such accidents.'[104]

Agnes Grove's period of apprenticeship was clearly not yet over
because in July 1896 Hardy read another of her articles, suggested
changes in pencil, attached a forwarding note to the Editor of
*Contemporary Review*, and asked her to post it. On this occasion, however, their joint effort did not yield any result. In November 1896 she
wrote another essay as a continuation of her earlier series on 'What
Children Should Be Told' and submitted it on her own to *Free Review*
but it was not accepted. When she sent the essay to Hardy for his
opinion, he advised her to rewrite it as an independent article and
try the *Humanitarian*, adding his usual injunction: 'be sure you don't
make it lengthy.' He had marked the essay in pencil and alerted her

to the fact that 'some other sentences than those marked want looking to & shortening. Don't be afraid of full stops'.[105] The result of all
this schoolmasterly advice was that the revised essay was accepted
by *Humanitarian*, Hardy read the proofs, and it was eventually published in February 1897. Hardy's letter of congratulation to Agnes
Grove (January 1897) read: 'I think that upon the whole you may
congratulate yourself upon your advance during the year past: you
have obtained a firmer hold upon the pen, & are in a fair way of
being well known as a writer.'[106]

When Agnes Grove ventured into fiction and sent Hardy her
(unidentified) story, he found it 'distinctly promising' but, realizing
that nothing was 'so harmful to a young writer as deceiving him or
her by uncritical commendation', he frankly told her that her mad-
man was 'rather too melodramatic' and that some incidents, though
fine in themselves, needed to be better integrated to make them
'*indispensable* to the *ending* of the story' (Hardy's italics). Even after
over two years of being Hardy's pupil, Agnes Grove had obviously
not yet overcome her besetting fault because Hardy noted that he
had to change 'two or three passages where there is needless circum-
locution'.[107] Hardy sent the story to *Chapman's Magazine*, but it was
rejected, and the story does not appear to have achieved publication.
Hardy's advice to Agnes on this occasion was to tell her to 'think of
another tale about half the length of the present one' since what
seemed to matter most to editors was 'a convenient length'.[108]
Perhaps disappointed with the total lack of success in her maiden
attempt at fiction, Agnes Grove returned to her journalistic work
and to the topic closest to her heart – that of women's suffrage.
When her article 'Objections to Woman Suffrage Considered'
appeared in *Humanitarian* (August 1899), Hardy expressed his agreement with most of her opinions, praised the writing as a 'forcible
piece of rhetoric', and added: 'Indeed, I don't know any woman-
writer who puts such vigour into her sentences as you do, or who is
so dexterous in the conduct of an argument of that kind, & this
power of yours makes me feel that you should give your attention
exclusively to essay writing, & not to fiction, & also makes me proud
of you as a pupil.'[109]

In February 1900 Hardy again read one of her articles, made
'such corrections as I should make were the article mine', and suggested that she send it to a ladies' magazine because the writing is
of a 'delicate sort'.[110] Although this article does not seem to have

been published, her series of sketches entitled 'On Fads' appeared in *Cornhill* in April 1900. Hardy had read 'On Fads' in proof, with 'real appreciation of the delicacy & humour with which the situations are suggested',[111] and knowing him to be an inveterate reviser it is difficult to imagine him returning the proofs without pencilling in suggestions/corrections. This speculation seems to be borne out by Hardy's comment in a later letter: 'I thought "On Fads" read much better the second time, when I saw it in the *Cornhill*, than at first in proof: a good sign.'[112] In 1904 Agnes Grove successfully published a few articles and Hardy wrote to congratulate her on having 'passed your apprenticeship'[113] but, as in the case of Mrs Henniker, he simply could not let her go. Thus as late as 1907, more than ten years after their original meeting, he is still offering to read the proofs of her forthcoming book (*The Social Fetich*), which she plans to dedicate to him:

> I will certainly read the proofs with pleasure, if you would like me to. Two pairs of eyes are better than one, & it is extraordinary what things escape the writer – owing, of course, to his or her pre-possession with the real meaning, which has a blinding effect.... But if there are any passages I don't like you must not mind my saying so in horrid hard words.

> I shall feel much honoured by the dedication – you *know* I shall; & I am sure you will do it nicely – though you have a quite exaggerated opinion on what you owe to me. I shall be much envied by younger men.[114] (Hardy's italic)

But, apparently, Agnes Grove needed help even with the precise wording of the dedication, for in two letters of August 1907 Hardy advised her on whether to use the phrase 'aid & counsel' or 'help & advice':

> As it is a question of expression merely (the sentiments expressed being entirely your own, I am charmed to think) there is no reason why I should not make suggestions about it. It seems to me, then, that what comes most nearly to your feeling would be the words 'and in memory of old and enduring friendship' – the absence of the article before the adjective would also give more finish to the phrase in my opinion; while, on my side, it expresses exactly the truth. I have never ceased to bless the day on which we met at Rushmore.[115]

When Hardy read the proofs of the book, although he could find no fault with the 'Preface', the very first sheet of the text seems to have called forth copious comments and, somewhat apologetically, he wrote:

> You will be irritated, & no doubt rightly, at the masterfulness of my criticisms, but you need not adopt them; & I can assure you that they are such as I should have made on the writing of a person whose career was more to me than any other's in the world. (I have not thought it worth while to mark those passages for which I have nothing but praise.)[116]

That Hardy still looked upon Agnes Grove as a cherished pupil is suggested by his letter (December 1907) thanking her for sending him a copy of *The Social Fetich*: 'But though I find the book entertaining I am not going to agree to your always frittering yourself away on these whimsical subjects. You can do much more solid work, & no doubt will as you get older.'[117] More than two years later, when her selection of essays was published (*On Fads*, 1910), Hardy singled out three essays for praise but did not hesitate to tell her bluntly:

> When I read the more carelessly written after these I felt quite inclined to give you a scolding for not taking more trouble. But the fact is that your ideas come tumbling out in such a torrent that they make your sentences turgid & involved. You mustn't mind my saying this. The following slips are those I noticed more particularly: some are obviously accidental: some are *blameworthy*. (Hardy's italic)[118]

A list of mistakes and misprints accompanied this letter of April 1910 and in the following month Hardy admitted: 'I rather exaggerate your faults of style in criticizing you, to make you persistently careful, for you are, you know, rather inclined to let your pen run away with you at times!'[119] Agnes Grove had probably requested his opinion on the sentences in her book which had been singled out for attack by the critics, because in this same letter Hardy told her that a 'sentence may often be strictly correct in grammar, but wretched in style', adding rather disarmingly: 'But remember that I am no authority. I have written heaps of ungrammatical sentences I dare say'. Agnes Grove was intelligent enough to realize that behind all Hardy's criticism of her writing lay an affectionate interest in her career, for she could not have forgotten some remarkable lines that Hardy had written to her in August 1907: 'By the way, Swinburne told me that he saw in a paper "Swinburne planteth, & Hardy watereth, & Satan giveth the increase". If you are in any sense the "increase" you will be a remarkable seedling.'[120]

One book by Agnes Grove that won Hardy's unqualified approval was *The Human Woman* (1908), an inscribed copy of which she had sent him. After reading the book, Hardy wrote warmly:

> the whole is really a series of brilliant & able essays, which all who favour woman suffrage should be grateful for. I, of course, who have long held that in justice women should have votes, whatever may be said of the policy of granting them to the sex (from a man's point of view), have not needed convincing, though some of your ingenious arguments had not occurred to me.[121]

As an active member of the National Union of Suffrage Societies, Emma Hardy too must have welcomed this book, whatever the current state of her feelings for its author. Indeed, a passionate commitment to women's suffrage and an abhorrence of the violent stone-throwing and window-smashing tactics of the militants probably bound Emma Hardy and Agnes Grove together as allies in a common cause. While Agnes Grove felt that the militants were mistakenly encouraging the false idea of sex-antagonism, Emma Hardy expressed her disapproval of the violent 1908 demonstrations by temporarily withdrawing her membership of the London Society for Women's Suffrage.

Another interest that Emma Hardy shared with her two 'rivals' was Anti-Vivisection. Emma's love for animals and indignation at any form of cruelty practised on them led her to 'beard any man ill using an animal & amaze him into a shamefaced desistence'[122] and she wrote a letter to the Editor protesting against the cruelty of the methods used by animal trainers in circuses and hoping that an Act would be passed 'to prevent the exhibiting of performing animals'.[123] As Hardy informed Florence Henniker in March 1897: 'We – or rather Em [i.e. Emma Hardy] – had an anti-vivisection meeting in our drawing-room last week.'[124] Florence Henniker, an ardent anti-vivisectionist herself, seems to have suggested to Emma Hardy in

1897 that she persuade her husband to use his influence and get Zola to write a book on anti-vivisection.[125] Although this proposal fizzled out, Mrs Henniker's letters to Hardy reveal her concern for the suffering of horses wounded during the World War campaigns, her hope that more humane methods of slaughtering would be adopted, her delight at the passing of the Plumage Bill in America, and her fear that the newly set up physiological Laboratory at Cambridge would result in untold tortures to dumb creatures in private research rooms.[126]

Hardy shared many of these concerns regarding animal welfare and perhaps it was their common love of animals (personified in the numerous Max Gate cats) that formed the last bond between Hardy and Emma when all other links had snapped, probably under the strain of Hardy's involvements – romantic, literary, or purely social – with various other women. These relationships will be examined in the following chapter, on three distinct levels: first, an exploration of the correspondences between the works of two feminist writers and Hardy's late fiction, which suggests that they may have influenced his fictional portrayal of women in the 1890s; second, a survey of Hardy's literary and social interactions with some of his contemporary female writers, ranging from the intensely passionate (e.g. Rosamund Tomson) to the virtually non-existent (e.g. George Eliot); and third, an account of the homage paid to Hardy by the younger generation of women writers, some of whom made their pilgrimage to Max Gate, and Hardy's reciprocal warmth in encouraging and sometimes actively aiding these younger talents.

# 9

# Hardy and Some Contemporary Female Writers

In 1869 in the office of the publisher Frederick Chapman, an aspiring young writer was introduced to a novelist with an established reputation who gave the novice sober advice regarding the publication of his inflammatory first novel 'The Poor Man and the Lady'. This meeting between Thomas Hardy and George Meredith developed into a 40-year literary and personal friendship culminating in Hardy's obituary poem 'George Meredith' (dated 'May 1909') and the essay 'G.M.: A Reminiscence' (1928). More than a decade after this memorable meeting, in the early 1880s, and again in Frederick Chapman's office, a beautiful young writer – flushed with the success of her maiden novel – was introduced to the journalist and editor Frank Harris, who recalled her as:

> Distinctly pretty with large dark eyes and black hair... Her chief desire she explained to me at once. She wanted to know all the writers, especially the novelists. Would I introduce her to Thomas Hardy and George Moore? I promised to do my best for her. On the same morning she put forward something of the feminist's view...she was a suffragette before the name became known.[1]

Judging from contemporary photographs, this young feminist, Olive Schreiner, was certainly beautiful and a meeting with Hardy might have yielded interesting results, given Hardy's susceptibility to female beauty. If nothing else, a personal meeting would have produced at least a couple of euphoric poems; but there is nothing to suggest that such a meeting ever took place. The two writers, however, must surely have met through their works. The first edition of Schreiner's *The Story of an African Farm* (1883), with Hardy's autograph on the title page, features in a descriptive catalogue of books from the Hardys' Max Gate Library which were sold off in May 1938 (after Florence Hardy's death in 1937).[2] However, it is quite difficult to say with any amount of certainty when (if at all) Hardy read *African Farm*. With Schreiner's reading of Hardy we have evidence in the form of a letter she wrote to Havelock Ellis on 28 March 1884. Apparently, Schreiner was not too impressed by Hardy's early novels:

> I have just finished reading your article in the *Westminster Review* [on 'The Novels of Thomas Hardy'], and I have read *A Pair of Blue Eyes*. I think your criticism very adequate and just. I shall read *Far From the Madding Crowd* and then I shall better be able to make up my mind as to whether I like Hardy much or not. Now I hardly know – there seems to me a certain shallowness and unrealness about his work – no, that's putting it too strongly; it seems to me as though he was only fingering his characters with his hands, not pressing them up against him till he felt their hearts beat....It is very funny that in the book that I am revising now [*From Man to Man*] there is one character who reminds me somewhat of Knight in his relation to Elfride [*A Pair of Blue Eyes*]. The likeness is not strong, still it is there. He is a man who, when the woman he loves confesses to him, turns away from her; but my woman tells him that which he could never have known if she had not told him, and he yet turns away from her.[3]

In the absence of any further reference to Hardy in her letters, one wonders what Schreiner thought of Hardy's later novels, especially *Jude*, since the correspondences between *African Farm* and *Jude* are even more striking. Schreiner's fiercely independent heroine, Lyndall, anticipates Hardy's Sue in her frustration at the limited opportunities available to women, in her bitterness at blatant gender-discrimination, and in her refusal to commit herself to the iron contract of marriage. In fact, Lyndall's disillusionment begins quite early. Driven by an insatiable hunger for knowledge, Lyndall leaves her stagnant farm life and enters a boarding school through her own sheer determination. But her experience at the boarding school, instead of opening up wider vistas of knowledge, only reveals how hopelessly confined is a woman's lot:

> 'I have discovered that of all cursed places under the sun, where the hungriest soul can hardly pick up a few grains of knowledge,

a girls' boarding-school is the worst. They are called finishing schools, and the name tells accurately what they are. They finish everything but imbecility and weakness, and that they cultivate. They are nicely adapted machines for experimenting on the question, "Into how little space a human soul can be crushed?" I have seen some souls so compressed that they would have fitted into a small thimble, and found room to move there – wide room. A woman who has been for many years at one of those places carries the mark of the beast on her till she dies.'[4]

Lyndall's claustrophobic sense of being physically confined, of being denied the free space in which to develop her being, is echoed powerfully by Sue who is ultimately forced to run away from the rigour of the teachers' Training School. When Jude first visits Sue at the school, '[a]ll her bounding manner was gone; her curves of motion had become subdued lines' and 'she had altogether the air of a woman *clipped* and *pruned* by severe discipline' (my italics).[5] With 'all the bitterness of a young person to whom restraint was new' (p. 152), Sue confesses to Jude how they are 'kept on very short allowances in the College'. That Lyndall and Sue are merely reflecting the experience of many young girls of the time is confirmed by a letter that Hardy's sister, Kate, wrote to Emma Hardy in which she looked back on her Salisbury training college experience and bitterly declared: 'I don't mind if Tom publishes how badly we were used.'[6]

Lyndall's sense that 'to be born a woman [is] to be born branded' (p. 154) is echoed by the narrator in *Jude* in a passage describing the young girls asleep in their cubicles

every face bearing the legend 'The Weaker' upon it, as the penalty of the sex wherein they were moulded, which by no possible exertion of their willing hearts and abilities could be made strong while the inexorable laws of nature remain what they are. (pp. 160-1)

This biological determinism is something that Lyndall is forced to recognize at a very tender age. In words that will find an echo in the consciousness of many young girls even today, she bitterly says:

'They begin to shape us to our cursed end... when we are tiny things in shoes and socks. We sit with our little feet drawn up under us in the window, and look out at the boys in their happy play. We want to go. Then a loving hand is laid on us: "Little one, you cannot go," they say; "your little face will burn, and your nice white dress be spoiled." We feel it must be for our good, it is so lovingly said; but we cannot understand; and we kneel still with one little cheek wistfully pressed against the pane. Afterwards we go and thread blue beads, and make a string for our neck; and we go and stand before the glass. We see the complexion we were not to spoil, and the white frock, and we look into our own great eyes. Then the curse begins to act on us.... We fit our spheres as a Chinese woman's foot fits her shoe, exactly.... The parts we are not to use have been quite atrophied, and have even dropped off... We wear the bandages, but our limbs have not grown to them; we know that we are compressed, and chafe against them.' (p. 155)

Of course there are rebels who refuse to submit to this gender-conditioning and Sue can 'do things that only boys do, as a rule. I've seen her hit in and steer down the long slide on yonder pond, with her little curls blowing, one of a file of twenty... All boys except herself; and then they'd cheer her' (pp. 133-4). Sue's spirit of defiance would sometimes lead her to walk 'into the pond with her shoes and stockings off, and her petticoats pulled above her knees', saucily crying out: 'Move on, aunty! This is no sight for modest eyes!' (p. 132) But such youthful rebellion is crushed out of both Sue and Lyndall, by precisely the same emotional process.

Both Sue and Lyndall begin by rejecting marriage. As Lyndall declares: 'I am not in so great a hurry to put my neck beneath any man's foot' (p. 150). But it is not just a case of being emotionally unprepared; it is a radical questioning of the very nature of institutionalized marriage. When her lover tries to persuade her to marry him, Lyndall unequivocally replies: 'I cannot marry you... because I cannot be *tied*; but, if you wish, you may take me away with you, and take care of me; then when we do not love any more we can say good-bye' (p. 206; my italic). Sue too feels 'how hopelessly vulgar an institution legal marriage is' (p. 285), and that 'it is destructive to a passion whose essence is its gratuitousness' (p. 286). According to Sue, marriage is 'a sordid contract, based on material convenience in householding, rating, and taxing, and the inheritance of land and money by the children' (p. 227); it is a 'dreadful contract to feel in a particular way in a matter whose essence is its voluntariness!' (p. 230). Sue is afraid 'lest an iron contract should extinguish [Jude's] tenderness' (p. 273) for her and hers for him and, to the 'New Woman', a loveless marriage was no better than prostitution. When Sue pleads for freedom from a distasteful union, she does not shrink from telling her husband: 'For a man and woman to live on intimate terms when one feels as I do is adultery, in any circumstances, however legal' (p. 239). Later, when Sue decides to return to Phillotson and remarry him, Jude implores her to reconsider her decision: 'Error – perversity!... Do you care for him? Do you love him? You know you don't! It will be a fanatic prostitution – God forgive me, yes – that's what it will be!' (p. 368).

This equation of a loveless marriage with prostitution must have been startling to a society which idealized the sanctity of home and hearth, and insisted on keeping the 'good' and the 'bad' women socially segregated. But such an equation was common in the 'New Woman' novels and, as early as 1883, Lyndall had scornfully declared:

'With good looks and youth marriage is easy to attain. There are men enough; but a woman who has sold herself, even for a ring and a new name, need hold her skirt aside for no creature in the street. They both earn their bread in one way. Marriage for love is the beautifullest external symbol of the union of souls; marriage without it is the uncleanliest traffic that defiles the world.' (p. 156)

Lyndall vehemently rejects the 'separate spheres' theory, and she draws from nature her ideal of sex equality. Watching the ostriches on the farm, she notices the cock sitting brooding on the eggs and tells Waldo: 'I like these birds... they share each other's work, and are companions. Do you take an interest in the position of women, Waldo?' (p. 153) Although this is rather a clumsy way of introducing the long dialogue on the 'Woman Question', there is no doubt about Schreiner's radicalism and sincerity. Her narrative art here may lack sophistication but her feminist perceptions are strikingly modern and still relevant. To be equal with men, to be their comrades and to share in their intellectual labours is a dream with Sue too. Sue mixes with men like the young Oxford undergraduate 'almost as one of their own sex' (p. 167). She goes on walking tours and reading tours with the Oxford undergraduate, 'like two men almost'

(p. 168). With a 'curious unconsciousness of gender' (p. 169), she even lives with him for fifteen months till she realizes that such an ideal 'sexless' comradeship is not really what interests him. Being an 'epicure in emotions' (p. 191), Sue's 'curiosity to hunt up a new sensation' (p. 191) leads her into such experiments as living together with the Oxford undergraduate (and later Jude). Lyndall, too, when trying to analyse her motive for loving and living together with her unnamed lover, candidly confesses: 'I like to experience, I like to try' (p. 206).

But 'experience', for both Lyndall and Sue, is dearly bought. Both these nonconformists are finally broken by the weight of personal tragedy in the shape of the death(s) of their children. Although defiant to the end, in refusing to marry her lover, the death of her three-hour-old infant crushes all rebellion out of Lyndall and she almost wills her own death. Despite being very ill herself, Lyndall goes out one drizzly day and sits for a long time beside the grave of her infant. When she comes back, she takes to her bed and gradually wastes away, dying of what seems to be a psychosomatic illness. Although this wilful death reminds us more of Jude's suicidal trip, on a wet day, to see Sue for the last time, Lyndall's visit to the grave of her infant is echoed in Sue's visit to the cemetery and her pleading with Jude and the man filling in the newly dug grave to allow her one last look at her dead babies.

However, in the absence of any reference to Schreiner in Hardy's letters and literary notebooks, it is difficult to argue a case for conscious literary influence. If Hardy *had* read *African Farm*, he would have been consoled (in relation to the charge that *Jude* ends far too bleakly, especially with the gratuitous cruelty of the children's deaths), by Schreiner's comment, put into the mouth of the precocious Lyndall: 'It is a terrible, hateful ending... and the worst is, it is true. I have noticed... that it is only the made-up stories that end nicely; the true ones all end so' (p. 14). Perhaps unknown to each other, both writers shared a similar world-view. Schreiner's feeling that '[t]here is no order; all things are driven about by a blind chance' (p. 114) is an apt commentary on Hardy's novels where blind chance dominates the lives of the characters. Also, Schreiner's remark – 'If you will take the trouble to scratch the surface anywhere, you will see under the skin a sentient being writhing in impotent anguish' (p. 114) – although made in the context of (racial) oppression, has a universality which is distilled in Hardy's aware-

ness of 'the tragedy that always underlies Comedy if you only
scratch it deeply enough'.[7]

A better case for direct (mutual?) influence can be argued with regard to another female firebrand, 'George Egerton' (pseudonym of
Mary Chavelita Dunne/Clairmonte/Bright). When her *Keynotes*, a
collection of short stories, was first published in 1893 it created a
sensation – enough to prompt Hardy to write to Florence Henniker
in January 1894: 'I have found out no more about Mrs Clairmont
[*sic*], but if I go to stay with the Jeunes,... I may possibly hear something of her, though I am not greatly curious.'[8] Another reference to
Egerton comes in a letter Hardy wrote in 1894 to Emma Hardy: 'The
Speaker to-day quotes one of the candid sentences from "Life's
Little I." [*sic*] & adds – (*apropos* of women's novels, like *Keynotes*, &c)
"so that the old hands know a thing or two as well as the young
'uns" '.[9]

It was only in November 1895 that the two authors directly corresponded. Some unknown friend had given George Egerton a copy of
*Jude* and she enjoyed the book so much that she wrote to Hardy to
thank him for the pleasure provided by the novel, especially the portrait of Sue:

> Sue is a marvellously true psychological study of a temperament
> less rare than the ordinary male observer supposes. I am not sure
> that she is not the most intuitively drawn of all your wonderful
> women. I love her, because she lives – and I say again, thank you,
> for her.[10]

At a time when *Jude* was being vilified on all sides, and a bishop
even reportedly burnt the book for its immorality, such praise from a
fellow-artist, and a woman, must have been quite gratifying. Hardy,
as usual, was very generous in his response:

> My reading of your 'Keynotes' came about somewhat as yours
> did of 'Jude'. A friend had it presented to her, & after reading it
> with deep interest she sent it on to me with a request that I would
> tell her what I thought of it. I need hardly say what my reply was:
> & how much I felt the verisimilitude of the stories, & how you
> seemed to make us breathe the atmosphere of the scenes.

I have been intending for years to draw Sue, & it is extraordinary that a type of woman, comparatively common & getting commoner, should have escaped fiction so long.[11]

George Egerton's letter had an interesting postscript in which she laconically stated that 'the arrival of a little son' had delayed the posting of her letter. To this, Hardy responded: 'I congratulate you on the little boy. My children, alas, are all in octavo.'[12] Hardy's lifelong regret at his own childlessness, which may have contributed to his pessimism, is here transparently expressed to a stranger.

The 'friend' who had lent a copy of *Keynotes* to Hardy was Florence Henniker, and this copy, with Hardy's annotations and marginal emphases, is preserved in the Richard Little Purdy Collection of the Beinecke Library, Yale University. In view of the disclaimer – 'The notes in the margins are mostly *not* mine' – signed by 'F. Henniker', it is perhaps safe to assume that most of the marginal comments are by Hardy (the handwriting certainly resembles that of Hardy's surviving MSS). Hardy was so taken up by the first story in the collection, 'A Cross Line', that he not only wrote marginal comments on pp. 22-3, but also quoted a substantial portion of these two pages in his 'Literary Notes' notebook under the heading *'The key to woman's seeming contradictions'*. There are as many as five consecutive extracts from *Keynotes*, dated 3 January 1894, in this literary scrapbook[13] and that Hardy was, at this point, interested in speculations on women's nature is attested by the fact that the immediately following entry is headed *'Treachery of Women'*.

In 'A Cross Line', which reads somewhat like an Ur-*Lady Chatterley's Lover*, Egerton boldly plumbs the depths of woman's sensual nature:

The why a refined, physically fragile woman will mate with a brute, a mere male animal with primitive passions – and love him – ... They have all overlooked the eternal wildness, the untamed primitive savage temperament that lurks in the mildest, best woman.

This passage bears marginal emphasis, with a comment which appears to be in Hardy's hand: 'This if fairly stated, is decidedly the *ugly* side of woman's nature' (Hardy's emphasis).[14] Egerton's tearing aside of the decorous veil to reveal the frank sexuality of what she calls 'the female animal' (pp. 3, 63) perhaps prompted Hardy's description of Arabella as 'a complete and substantial female animal – no more, no less' (*Jude*, p. 62). But Arabella did not become a 'female animal' till the 1903 edition of *Jude* and perhaps of more immediate relevance here is a sentence that Hardy added to his story 'On the Western Circuit'. Analyzing the attraction that Charles Raye holds for Edith Harnham, the narrator says: 'That he had been able to seduce another woman in two days was his crowning though unrecognized fascination for her as the she-animal'.[15] This sentence was not present either in the manuscript or in the story as serialized in *The English Illustrated Magazine* in December 1891. When Hardy was collecting this story for the volume *Life's Little Ironies*, this sentence was still missing from the galley proofs which Hardy corrected from 8 to 12 December 1893.[16] It first appears in the book version of *Life's Little Ironies*, published on 22 February 1894. Therefore, it must have been added at some later proof stage, between 12 December 1893 and 22 February 1894. Interestingly, in December 1893 Hardy had been reading *Keynotes* because the five extracts from it in his 'Literary Notebook' are dated 3 January 1894. Therefore, possibly Hardy's reading of Egerton's frank treatment of female sexuality emboldened him to add this provocative sentence in his short story.

Some of Egerton's male characters are theoretically well versed in the ways of 'the female animal', and the narrator of 'A Little Grey Glove', the only story in the collection that is written from the man's point of view, 'pursue[s] the Eternal Feminine in a spirit of purely scientific investigation' (p. 93). But when confronted with a particularly maddening specimen of 'the female species' (p. 93), most of Egerton's men are bewildered by her inscrutability. To the average male perception (personified, for example, in the nameless husbands in 'A Cross Line' and 'An Empty Frame'), women are 'enigmas' (p. 21), 'as impenetrable as a sphinx' (p. 25), with an 'elusive spirit in her that he divines but cannot seize' (p. 29). The 'devilry' in her makes her a 'witch' – a word that Egerton's characters/ narrator use almost compulsively; and when she's not a 'witch', she's a 'gipsy'.

The nameless wife in 'An Empty Frame' thus reassures her unnamed husband: 'There, it's all right, boy! Don't mind me, I have a bit of a complex nature; you couldn't understand me if you tried to; you'd better not try!' (p. 123). Similarly, the male narrator of 'A Little Grey Glove' finds that although he devotes himself to everything 'in petticoats', 'the more I saw of her, the less I understood her' (p. 94). Against this sentence there is an interesting marginal comment by Hardy: 'a woman's view of herself: not a man's.' We must remember that when Hardy read and annotated *Keynotes* he was working on the final draft of *Jude* and, despite his disclaimer, the male perception of Sue is just such a baffled awareness of opacity. Sue is a 'riddle' to Jude (p. 154) and her conduct is 'one lovely conundrum to him' (p. 156). To Phillotson too, she is 'puzzling and unstateable' (p. 240), and the state of her heart remains forever a 'mystery' (p. 255) – to Phillotson, Jude, and the (male) narrator.

A characteristic that the 'quivering' and 'nervous' Egerton hero-ines share with Hardy's Sue is their love of being loved. As the fe-male protagonist of 'A Cross Line' confesses to her husband: 'It isn't the love, you know, it's the being loved' (p. 16). When Jude accuses Sue of being a 'flirt', Sue is equally candid in admitting that '[s]ome women's love of being loved is insatiable' (p. 222). Later, trying to justify her marriage to Phillotson, she explains it as 'a woman's *love of being loved* [which] gets the better of her conscience' (p. 256; Hardy's italics). Before she ultimately leaves Jude to remarry Phillotson, she quite gratuitously reveals to Jude that her love for him 'began in the selfish and cruel wish to make your heart ache for me without letting mine ache for you' (p. 361).

Sue's uncontrollable and involuntary physical shrinking from Phillotson is also anticipated by some of Egerton's women charac-ters. The wife in 'Under Northern Sky' betrays her revulsion when her sensual husband demands a kiss from her, and the housekeeper Belinda (in 'The Spell of the White Elf') laments: 'If one could only have a child, ma'm, without a husband or the disgrace; ugh, the dis-gusting men!' (p. 80). What this half-educated woman says is echoed by the more articulate Sue in one of her series of notes to Phillotson, begging for release from their marriage:

'I implore you to be merciful! I would not ask if I were not almost compelled by what I can't bear! No poor woman has ever wished more than I that Eve had not fallen, so that (as the primitive Christians believed) some harmless mode of vegetation might have peopled Paradise.' (p. 241)

Indeed, this physical disgust seems to be shared by quite a few women, as the female 'writer' who features in 'The Spell of the White Elf' tells us:

'It seems congenital with some women to have deeply rooted in their innermost nature a smouldering enmity, ay, sometimes a physical disgust to men, it is a kind of kin-feeling to the race dislike of white men to black. Perhaps it explains why woman, where her own feelings are not concerned, will always make common cause with woman against him.' (pp. 80-1)

Against the last sentence of the above extract is another marginal comment: '*No* they will *not*'.[17] Despite this categorical denial of women's potential for transcending their internecine rivalries, Hardy had illustrated female solidarity in *The Woodlanders* where Grace Melbury and Felice Charmond part with a kiss in the woods, despite the latter's devastating disclosure. That 'wife' and 'mistress' can meet on the common ground of womanly sympathy is illustrated by Egerton too. In 'A Cross Line', enlightened by her personal experience, 'the mistress, who is a wife, puts her arms round the tall maid, who has never had more than a moral claim to the name, and kisses her in her quick way' (p. 35). Here, social barriers are swept aside by the realization of a common female identity and experience: that of (illegitimate) pregnancy. Again, in 'Under Northern Sky', the wife generously allows the 'cow-girl' to kiss her dying husband good-bye, although it appears to be the common gossip that the cow-girl had once been her husband's mistress.

In their treatment of female relationships it is quite obvious that the 'old hand' knew 'a thing or two' as well as the 'young 'un'. Correspondences between Egerton's stories and Hardy's fiction are numerous enough to suggest a two-way imbibing of literary influence. For instance, the 'writer' in Egerton's story 'The Spell of the White Elf' relates how the child she adopts bears a striking resemblance to her:

'Well, the elf was born, and now comes the singular part of it. It was a wretched, frail little being with a startling likeness to me. It was as if the evil the mother had wished me had worked on the child, and the constant thought of me stamped my features on its little face.' (p. 81)

One is reminded of Hardy's story 'An Imaginative Woman' where Mrs Marchmill's innocent obsession with the (unseen) poet, Robert Trewe, leads to her son being born with a face that bears so striking a resemblance to the poet's photograph that the *un*imaginative Mr Marchmill (the child's legal and biological father) is misled into rejecting his own son.

In 'Now Spring has Come' Egerton's female protagonist is so moved by a book that she impulsively arranges to meet the unknown author who has so stirred her feelings. However, such soul-sympathy with an unknown artist brings only pain and disillusionment in its wake, and we recall Jude's similar impulsive journey to meet the composer of a hymn that has strangely affected him – only to discover that the writer of the divinely beautiful song is a prosaic and grossly materialistic man. In 'A Little Grey Glove', the male narrator of the story falls in love when his ear is pierced by the hook of the lady's fishing line, very much in the same comic and deflating fashion as when Arabella's love missile (the pig's pizzle) hits Jude's ear.

Some correspondences can be accounted for by the fact that both writers were drawing from a common stock of ideas current at that time. Egerton's description of a hawk swooping down and capturing a little brown bird is an image of Darwinian struggle that Hardy had earlier exploited in the description of the chase of the duck by the duck-hawk in *The Hand of Ethelberta*. The same Darwinism is again apparent in Egerton's description of nature where the trees 'fight for life in wild confusion' ('A Cross Line', p. 2). This passage is a pale echo of Hardy's more famous description of nature where the leaf is deformed, the fungi choke the trees, and the ivy strangles to death the promising sapling (*The Woodlanders*).

One image common to Schreiner, Egerton, and Hardy is that of the captive/caged bird which represents woman's sense of entrapment within the narrow role assigned to her by patriarchal society. A suggestion of claustrophobia, a passionate yearning for liberty, a frustrated chafing against the oppressive rigidity of the iron bars, all coalesce to create a powerful emotive symbol. Schreiner, through Lyndall, tauntingly questions:

'If the bird *does* like its cage, and *does* like its sugar and will not leave it, why keep the door so very carefully shut? Why not open it, only a little? Do they know there is many a bird will not break its wings against the bars, but would fly if the doors were open.' (p. 159; Schreiner's italics)

Egerton too uses this archetypal image to anticipate the liberation of the oppressed wife in 'Under Northern Sky'. Prophesying the death of the sensual husband, the old gipsy woman consoles the wife by holding out the hope that, after the rising of seven suns and seven moons, the cage will open and the bird will be free. Hardy too had used such a proleptic image at the beginning of *The Mayor of Casterbridge* where the swallow flying out of the furmity woman's tent anticipates Susan's release from Henchard (through the 'wife-sale'). Later, in *Jude*, when Jude and Sue decide to leave Aldbrickham and all their furniture (including Sue's pet birds) is sold off, Sue goes to the poulterer's shop, and, seeing her pet pigeons in a hamper, she impulsively unfastens the cover and allows them to fly away. Tragically enough, although Sue frees her pet birds, she herself ultimately remains (wilfully?) self-trapped in the cage of conventional morality.

In 1901 George Egerton married Reginald Golding Bright and although Bright later acted as Hardy's theatrical agent, and quite a few letters passed between them regarding possible dramatizations of *Tess*, there is no suggestion whatsoever that Hardy either met or corresponded again with Egerton.

Nor did Hardy try to establish personal contact with the greatest living novelist of his day – George Eliot. From his debut as a novelist right till the end of his career Hardy was upset by the constant comparisons of his work with that of George Eliot. He was not at all flattered when the anonymously serialized *Far From the Madding Crowd* was thought to be the work of George Eliot and throughout his life he tried to downplay what critics saw as his indebtedness to her. His 'rustics' were seen as inferior imitations of George Eliot's memorable creations; his tendency to indulge in *sententiae* and aphorisms was ascribed to the influence of her style; more specifically, his description of Fanny Robin's excruciating journey to the Casterbridge workhouse was seen as a pale rewriting of Hetty's 'Journey in Despair' in *Adam Bede*.

Understandably suffering from an 'anxiety of influence', Hardy tried to distance himself as much as possible from George Eliot. When Samuel Chew presented Hardy his book, *Thomas Hardy: Poet and Novelist* (1921), Hardy rejected Chew's hypothesis that George Eliot's 'success in delineating the peasantry of Warwickshire suggested to Hardy' the idea for his Wessex rustics, and insisted on tracing his literary ancestry not to George Eliot but Shakespeare.[18] In the

copious notes containing suggested corrections for the proposed revised edition of Chew's book, Hardy emphatically stated: 'It was
Shakespeare's delineation of his Warwickshire clowns (who much
resemble the Wessex peasantry) that influenced Hardy most. He
found no clowns i.e. farm-labourers or rustics, anywhere in G. Eliot's
books, and considered her country characters more like small towns-
people than peasantry.' To Chew's use of the phrase 'Hardy borrows
the theme', in comparing Hardy's story 'A Tragedy of Two
Ambitions' with *Daniel Deronda*, Hardy stiffly pointed out: 'If this
means that the incident of not attempting to save a drowning person
is borrowed from "D. Deronda" [*sic*] it is an error: kindred incidents
are common to hundreds of novels.' This attempt to deny any links
with George Eliot is also reflected in his autobiography where he
says he could not 'understand' why *Far From the Madding Crowd* was
mistaken to be 'from the pen of George Eliot' because: 'she had never
touched the life of the fields: her country-people having seemed to
him, too, more like small townsfolk than rustics; and as evidencing a
woman's wit cast in country dialogue rather than real country humour, which he regarded as rather of the Shakespeare and Fielding
sort.'[19]

In Hardy's opinion, George Eliot was undoubtedly the 'greatest
living' 'thinker' of his day but she was 'not a born storyteller by any
means', and this to Hardy must have seemed a serious artistic draw-
back, because he passionately believed that: 'We tale-tellers are all
Ancient Mariners, and none of us is warranted in stopping Wedding
Guests (in other words, the hurrying public) unless he has something more unusual to relate than the ordinary experience of every
average man and woman.'[20] Hardy also had reservations regarding
George Eliot's delineation of women, and he probably concurred
with the verdict in *Blackwood's Edinburgh Magazine* (April 1883) that
'George Eliot is the advocate of women; in Shakespeare we must
find their artist'. This is not just mean professional rivalry, because
Hardy also copied from the same *Blackwood* article the opinion:
'*George Eliot's women* – A truly magnificent revelation of the noble-
ness that is in women. But the other side is not fairly shown. The
mystery of feminine malignity is barely touched upon.... Art ought
to be impartially representative.'[21]

Had there been any inclination on Hardy's part, the opportunity
for a meeting between the two novelists would not have been too

hard to find, since George Eliot lived, until 1880. Had they met, a sympathetic chord might have been touched because George Eliot, like Hardy, was aware of the 'ever deepening sense of the pain of the world & the tragedy of sentient being'.[22] But the unpleasantness of being branded 'one of George Eliot's miscarriages'[23] made Hardy determined to keep his distance and later he declined William Blackwood's offer to write a volume on George Eliot in the proposed 'Modern English Writers' series, pleading that a 'fellow artizan' was not perhaps the one best suited for the task of 'sympathetic criticism'.[24]

However, one older contemporary that Hardy went out of his way to meet was Eliza Lynn Linton. In his late twenties he had read with interest the series of articles on the 'Woman Question' published anonymously in *Saturday Review* from 1866 to 1868 (later collected, under Linton's name, as *The Girl of the Period and Other Social Essays*, 1883). Like most readers, he assumed the writer of these critical articles to be a man, as he later confessed to Mrs Linton in 1888:

> If ever you come down into these parts, & I hope you will do so some summer, I shall be able to show you the exact spot – a green slope in a pasture – on which I used to sit down & read your renowned articles in the S. R. [*sic*]. In my innocence I never suspected the sex of the writer. I always thought that the essay which became most celebrated was not quite so fine & incisive as some of the others that you wrote in the series: but that's how things go in this world.[25]

Hardy ended his letter by lamenting that he was torn 'between my own conviction of what is truest to life, & what editors & critics will tolerate as being true to their conventional principles', and this is the tenor of his contribution to the symposium on 'Candour in English Fiction' in *New Review* (January 1890). The other two contributors were Walter Besant and Eliza Lynn Linton and there is much similarity in the views expressed by Hardy and Mrs Linton. Hardy felt that '[l]ife being a physiological fact, its honest portrayal must be largely concerned with, for one thing, the relations of the sexes' and therefore the 'crash of broken commandments' was a necessary 'accompaniment to the catastrophe of a tragedy'.[26] Mrs Linton too complained of the 'hypocritical' way in which the 'seventh commandment' was handled in English literature, and the combined tyranny of the 'British Matron' and the 'Young Person' which emasculated all fiction to a 'schoolgirl standard'. Casting her vote for the 'locked bookcase' rather than the current 'milk-and-water-literature', she pointedly asked: 'Must men go without meat because the babes must be fed with milk?'[27] Understandably, Hardy's article was the most trenchant of the three because by January 1890 he had already faced the full force of Grundyism in regard to *Tess* (it was rejected by three publishing houses); and later in the same year he would be compelled to tone down considerably for magazine publication some of the more outspoken stories of *A Group of Noble Dames*.

In Hardy's own words (in the 1888 letter), the 'ice [had] been broken' by his gesture of sending Mrs Linton a copy of his recently published story 'A Tragedy of Two Ambitions' (1888) as a Christmas offering. This gesture would later be repeated in reverse towards the end of his life when many eminent young poets and novelists, both male and female, would send Hardy their published works, with touching inscriptions, as a token of their admiration. Just as Hardy would later warmly respond to such literary homage, Eliza Linton too responded warmly, praising Hardy's story very highly in her reply. Their genuine mutual admiration resulted in Hardy paying Mrs Linton a visit in January 1891, when she was nearing seventy, and this first meeting is best described in Mrs Linton's vivacious epistolary style:

> Yesterday a stranger called on me. The boy said *Harvey*. I was in a fume – could not make out who it was – went round and round the central point, till the stranger said he was going out of town to-day. 'Where?' says I. 'To Dorchester,' says he. Then I ups with a shout and a clapping of my hands, and says I, 'Oh, now I know who you are! You are Thomas Hardy and not Harvey' – (the author of *Far from the Madding Crowd*, etc.). He was so pleased when *I* was so pleased, and stayed here for two hours. He is a nice bit manny, but of a sadder and more pessimistic nature than I am. It was very nice to see him. *We* have *missed* each other twenty times. He said his wife wants to see me, she had heard I was so handsome!!! Says I, 'Then tell her I am *not*.' Says he, 'No, I certainly cannot do that, because you *are*!'[28]

When a stranger drops in for a chance visit and then goes on to stay for two hours, it argues for a degree of mutual liking and instant rapport. For such a liking to develop at a first meeting, the lady did not have to be young and beautiful. When Hardy first met Mary Elizabeth Braddon in 1879, he described that encounter in his auto-biography thus: 'Hardy met there too... Miss Braddon, who "had a broad, thought-creased, world-beaten face – a most amiable woman", whom he always liked.'[29] Miss Braddon had been editor of *Belgravia* when Hardy's *The Return of the Native* was accepted for publication,[30] and if Hardy was aware of it he would have been doubly grateful, because his old friend and mentor Leslie Stephen had earlier rejected it for *Cornhill* as he feared that the relations be-tween the characters might develop into something dangerous for a family magazine. Hardy did not share Stephen's editorial timidity, and his liking for Miss Braddon seems to have continued despite her unconventional life (she had lived with the publisher John Maxwell from 1860 to 1874, marrying him officially in 1874).

If Mary Braddon and Eliza Linton (she had separated from her husband) were unconventional, Margaret Oliphant was convention-ality personified. At least this was the opinion expressed in *Saturday Review* (February 1877) and Hardy, perhaps with a certain relish, copied an abridged quotation from its pages: 'Mrs Oliphant always admires what public opinion has decided that it is right to admire, & patiently repeats the old estimates, & quotes the old stories.'[31] A per-sonal meeting with Mrs Oliphant in May 1885 did nothing to quell this impression for Hardy wrote to his wife Emma: 'Among others there was Mrs Oliphant, to whom I was introduced. I don't care a bit for her – & you lose nothing by not knowing her. She is propriety & primness incarnate.'[32] On the surface, there seems to be nothing to account for this hostile attitude on Hardy's part because three years earlier, in July 1882, Mrs Oliphant had written an extremely civil let-ter to Hardy suggesting that he write a sketch on the labouring poor of Dorset, for the publisher Charles James Longman. Hardy had replied equally cordially to her, explaining that he was very busy just then; but he did eventually follow up her original suggestion, because his article on 'The Dorsetshire Labourer' was later published in *Longman's Magazine*, in July 1883.[33] Although Hardy had courte-ously ended his letter to Mrs Oliphant by saying 'I welcome this op-portunity of a direct communication with a writer I have known in spirit so long', something must have intervened between July 1882 and May 1885 to change Hardy's attitude towards her.

What intervened was probably the publication of *Two on a Tower* in October 1882. Mrs Oliphant could well have privately expressed to friends her disgust at what she later publicly castigated as the 'grotesque and indecent dishonesty'[34] of Viviette Constantine in marrying Bishop Helmsdale to legitimize her baby by Swithin. Whatever the cause of offence, the breach between the two novelists widened as Hardy continued to publish one controversial novel after another. Although Mrs Oliphant grudgingly conceded some merit in *Tess*, her response to *Jude* – in 'The Anti-Marriage League' article – is now a legend. Hardy was so hurt by what he perceived to be her unfair criticisms, such as her accusation that he had made a ' "shameless" double profit' by publishing the story in magazine (expurgated) and book (restored) version, that although he referred to her as a 'fellow-novelist' in his detached, third- person autobiography, in the immediacy of personal letters she becomes the 'rival novelist' sneering at *Jude*.[35] In a letter to Grant Allen (January 1896) his anger at Mrs Oliphant's onslaught bursts forth with uncharacteristic vehemence: 'Talk of shamelessness: that a woman who purely for money's sake has for the last 30 years flooded the magazines & starved out scores of better workers, should try to write down rival novelists whose books sell better than her own, caps all the shamelessness of Arabella, to my mind.'[36] In the heat and hurt of the moment, Hardy forgot that Mrs Oliphant's prolific output was her only means of supporting her three fatherless children and also the children of her brother. Writing of this episode in retrospect, what emerges is a sense of personal betrayal:

> The unkindest cut of all, however, seemed to him at the time to come from his acquaintance and fellow-novelist Mrs Oliphant, who after abusing him shamelessly in *Blackwood* as aforesaid, wrote to the bishop commending his action. And yet shortly before this, on hearing that she was ill, Hardy had wasted an afternoon at Windsor in finding her house and seeing her. Now he, no doubt, thought how these novelists love one another![37]

Although Mrs Oliphant's comments continued to rankle, privately Hardy must have admitted to himself the justice of some of her remarks, such as the talk between Arabella and her friends which Mrs Oliphant considered 'a shame to the language' because it revealed a 'depravity' unworthy of even the 'darkest slums'.[38] Significantly, in his textual revisions to *Jude* it is just these coarse passages that Hardy toned down. All references to the 'slip of flesh', 'the limp object dangling across the handrail of the bridge', are removed from the description of Jude's first encounter with Arabella. Her friend Anny's comment, after Jude leaves, in the original 1895 Osgood McIlvaine edition had read: 'he's as simple as a child. I could see it as you courted on the bridge, wi' that piece o' the pig hanging between ye – haw-haw! What a proper thing to court over!' In the 1903 Macmillan 'New Edition', this is bowdlerized to the innocuous: 'I could see it as you courted on the bridge, when he looked at 'ee as if he had never seen a woman before in his born days.'[39]

A society hostess had once told Hardy that she used Tess as a litmus test to organize her varied assortment of guests into harmonious groups (based on the question 'Do you support her or not?' and depending on their positive or negative responses).[40] To Hardy personally, *Jude* must have seemed such a touchstone helping him to sift his friends from his foes. Hardy had received, among others, warm letters of praise for *Jude* from George Egerton, Ellen Terry and Pearl Craigie. Pearl Craigie had had a tempestuous life: in 1890 she had left her (syphilitic) husband, divorcing finally in July 1895, and for a brief period she had been George Moore's lover. As such, she was probably among those adult readers into whose soul the iron had entered[41] whom Hardy ideally had in mind as his true audience. Herself a writer of novels which focus persistently on unhappy marriages, she wrote to Hardy in November 1895, 'humbly as a student', to express her admiration of *Jude* which deals with the 'marriage question [as it] has never been so dealt with before'.[42] In her 'student's enthusiasm' she ranked *Jude* 'with Michael Angelo's "Last Judgment"' and hailed Hardy as 'the supreme master in Europe'.[43]

Hardy had met Pearl Craigie (writing under the pseudonym 'John Oliver Hobbes') in June 1893. Just before this meeting he wrote to Florence Henniker saying: 'I have a dreadful confession to make. In a weak moment I have accepted an invitation to lunch, to meet John Oliver Hobbes! She is very pretty, they say; but on my honour that had nothing to do with it – purely literary reasons only.'[44] That he was sufficiently impressed by Mrs Craigie is evident from the entry in his autobiography: 'met for the first time…that brilliant woman Mrs Craigie.'[45] This impression did not change, because after her death (in August 1906) his memories are of her 'intellectual brilliancy', and of her being 'entertaining & ebullient' and 'bright as ever'.[46] Hardy's high opinion of her is indirectly evident from the fact that when Gosse invited him in 1898 to join in signing a tribute to Meredith on his seventieth birthday and requested Hardy to think of more names of 'comrades in letters', Hardy confessed that the 'women seem the most ticklish business' and the *only* name he could immediately think of was 'J.O. Hobbes'.[47]

That their friendship was not merely a literary one is suggested by the entry for September 1893 in Hardy's autobiography. During his stay with Sir Francis and Lady Jeune, one 'Sunday morning Hardy took a two hours' walk with Mrs Craigie on the moor, when she explained to him her reasons for joining the Roman Catholic Church, a step which had vexed him somewhat. Apparently he did not consider her reasons satisfactory, but their friendship remained unbroken'.[48] That barely three months into acquaintanceship Mrs Craigie could speak on such a personal matter to Hardy argues for considerable mutual sympathy and trust. Indeed, Hardy seemed sometimes to invite such soul-confidences, and it is relevant here to remember that early in his career (in 1875) Leslie Stephen had invited him to be the sole witness to his signing of a deed renouncing his holy orders. Despite their differences in religious outlook, the friendship flourished, and in June 1894 Hardy and his wife went to see the first performance of a play by Mrs Craigie, followed by Mrs Craigie's visit to the Hardys in their London flat (June 1895) as part of a large lunch-party which included Florence Henniker. At Mrs Henniker's literary lunch the next year, Hardy again met Mrs Craigie, and – among others – 'Lucas Malet' and Rhoda Broughton.

Such social visits and occasional correspondence kept alive the relationship, and when in 1899 Mrs Craigie sent Hardy a copy of her one-act tragedy, *A Repentance*, Hardy wrote back complimenting her on her ability to 'do so much work without allowing it to sink below the highest intellectual & artistic level!'[49] Hardy was generally wary of indulging in insincere praise, even to beautiful literary women, and that he genuinely esteemed at least some of her work is suggested by the quotation from *Robert Orange* that he copied into his 'Literary Notebook': '*The passion of love* invariably drives men & women to an extreme step in one direction or another. It will send some to the Cloister, some to the Tribune, some to the stage, some to heroism, some to crime, & all to their natural calling.'[50] Hardy also probably agreed with her comment that '[a]n artist aims at the spirit of things'[51] because in his autobiography he says: 'My art is to intensify the expression of things... so that the heart and inner meaning is made vividly visible.'[52]

In 1904 William Archer published his conversation with Mrs Craigie in which she spoke of women being 'more complicated psychologically', of '[m]en's women [being] considered miracles' and 'women's men [being] regarded with smiling compassion', of women having the gift of psychological penetration because for centuries they have stood in 'a more or less servile relation to man' and 'slaves learn by very slight tokens to read the mind of their masters'.[53] Archer's *Real Conversations* also included a talk with Hardy who wrote to Archer thanking him for the book 'which I have been looking into with interest. Mrs C's [*sic*] talk is, I think, the best, as would be natural, she being such an amusing companion. This bears testimony to the honesty of your reports'.[54] After her death, on reading her *Life* (compiled by her father), Hardy's comment that she was a 'remarkable woman; & yet she achieved nothing solid or enduring'[55] seems rather uncharitable but it has to be balanced with the sympathetic view expressed in his autobiography:

Have just read of the death of Mrs Craigie in the papers.... Her description of the artistic temperament is clever; as being that which 'thinks more than there is to think, feels more than there is to feel, sees more than there is to see'. It reveals a bitterness of heart that was not shown on the surface by that brilliant woman.[56]

Hardy's final gesture of friendship towards this 'brilliant' woman was to be 'present at the unveiling by Lord Curzon of the memorial to his friend "John Oliver Hobbes" (Mrs Craigie) at University College', London, in July 1908.[57]

Apart from Pearl Craigie, the only other female personality who featured in Archer's *Real Conversations* was Mary St Leger Harrison, the daughter of Charles Kingsley, and better known by her pseudonym 'Lucas Malet'. In her talk she classed Hardy with Balzac, Flaubert, Zola, and Meredith in the 'realist' school of fiction and enthused over Hardy's 'exquisite eye for nature', the absolute truth of his pictures of country life, the fidelity and sensitiveness revealed in his drawing the 'English peasant from the inside, as... no other English novelist has.'[58]

Hardy must have been pleased to read all this, coming from a woman who had made an impact on him when he first met her. The candid entry in his autobiography reads: 'Called on "Lucas Malet". A striking woman: full, slightly voluptuous mouth, red lips, black hair and eyes: and most likeable.'[59] This 1892 reminiscence is very typical of his entire autobiography, where he constantly describes the literary and society women of his acquaintance almost entirely in terms of their beauty (or lack of it), especially their eyes and lips. Even before they had met there had been an exchange of letters; in the first of them (February 1892) Hardy said he had read two of her novels, '"Colonel Enderby's Wife", & "Mrs Lorimer", with the deepest interest. The former I consider one of the finest works of fiction of late years. There is not a threadbare place anywhere in it. You are one of the few authors of the other sex who are not afraid of logical consequences.'[60] When she sent him a copy of her most famous work, *The Wages of Sin* (1891), Hardy's letter of thanks had an interesting paragraph where he commiserated with her on the handicap of sex:

I have long seen what you say about a woman's disadvantages. And the worst of it is that even when, by accident, she does gain knowledge of matters usually sealed to her sex people will not believe she knows at first hand. However, you have a counterpoise in other matters: there being many scenes in life – though not so many as in the other case – wherein the knowledge is to the woman only.[61]

After reading *The Wages of Sin*, however, Hardy's original opinion of Lucas Malet as 'a thoroughly skilled artist' must have been considerably modified because he records his disappointment in a letter to Millicent Fawcett: 'But the wages [of sin] are that the young man falls over a cliff, & the young woman dies of consumption – not very consequent, as I told the authoress.'[62] This complete volte-face from his earlier verdict that in her novels she fearlessly exhibits 'logical consequences' could not have pleased Lucas Malet very much, if indeed Hardy had communicated his frank opinion to her. The absence of any quotation from this highly topical novel of the 1890s, in his 'Literary Notebooks', may perhaps be taken as a reliable indicator of Hardy's unflattering estimate of the work.

Another much-talked-of novel of the 1890s does, however, feature among the extracts in Hardy's 'Literary Notebook'. Frances Elizabeth McFall, better known as 'Sarah Grand', had sent Hardy a copy of *The Heavenly Twins* (1893) with the inscription: 'a very inadequate acknowledgement of all she owes to his genius.'[63] Hardy must have been sufficiently struck by it because he copied an abridged quotation from it, dated May 1893: 'We are long past the time when there was only one incident of interest in a woman's life, & that was its love affair.... It is stupid to narrow it [life] down to the indulgence of one particular set of emotions... to swamp every faculty by constant cultivation of the animal instincts.'[64] What Hardy's reactions were when one Monday in June 1893 he reached home to find 'the author of The Heavenly Twins' sitting in his drawing-room[65] can only be a matter of speculation, because he does not seem to have left any written impressions of this meeting. About three weeks after this visit Hardy loyally reassured Florence Henniker that her novel *Foiled* (1893):

as a transcript from human nature... ranks far above some novels that have received much more praise: e.g. The Heavenly Twins. If ever I were to consult any woman on a point in my own novels I should let that woman be yourself – my belief in your insight and your sympathies being strong, and increasing.[66]

It is obvious that to Hardy personal friendship ranked far above objective literary assessment because in September 1893 he repeated the same unfavourable comparison between these two women writers and, after sighing over Mrs Henniker's 'conventional views', he advised her:

If you mean to make the world listen to you, you must say now what they will all be thinking & saying five & twenty years hence; & if you do that you must offend your conventional friends. 'Sarah Grand', who has not, to my mind, such a sympathetic & intuitive knowledge of human nature as you, has yet an immense advantage over you in this respect – in the fact of having decided to offend her friends (so she told me) – & now that they are all alienated she can write boldly, & get listened to.[67]

The success of *The Heavenly Twins* had eclipsed even that of *Robert Elsmere* (1888), but if the number of extracts in Hardy's 'Literary Notebook' is any yardstick he was probably more impressed by Mrs Humphry Ward's book. As many as fifteen consecutive quotations from *Robert Elsmere* were copied by Hardy, and one of them – with which Hardy was obviously in perfect accord – bears marginal emphasis in red: 'Fate can have neither wit nor conscience to have ordained it so; but fate has so ordained it.'[68] Mrs Ward's observation that 'Truth has never been, can never be, contained in any one creed or system' surely touched a responsive chord in Hardy, and, almost as if to illustrate this fact that no philosophical system is *the* ultimate Truth, he also copied her conviction (so diametrically opposed to his own) that 'I cannot conceive of God as the arch-plotter against His own creation.' Nevertheless, she too could not completely ignore the:

> helplessness of human existence, which, generation after generation, is still so vulnerable, so confiding, so eager. Life after life flowers out from the darkness & sinks back into it again. And in the interval what agony, what disillusion! All the apparatus of a universe that men may know what it is to hope & fail, to win & lose!

As Hardy copied these lines he must have nodded in agreement, because in his subsequent poetry the persistent lament is that the impercipient First Cause has burdened humanity with consciousness which is a curse since without the perceiving consciousness there is no pain. Yet another quotation from the novel that Hardy copied reads: 'Christianity seems to me something small & local. Behind it, around it, including it, I see the great drama of the world sweeping on, led by God.' To this Hardy adds what Gittings calls 'his own satiric and agnostic twist'[69] and the idea surfaces in *The Dynasts* as:

> A local cult called Christianity...
> Beyond whose span, uninfluenced, unconcerned,
> The systems of the sun go sweeping on....

Hardy had first met the Humphry Wards in 1886 and he records that he found them 'both amiable people'.[70] When in 1892 Mrs Ward wrote to Hardy requesting him to join a scheme for commemorating Columbus's discovery of America, he responded quite warmly although later (in 1906) he characteristically excused himself from attending a meeting of a committee formed by Mrs Ward to settle a book sellers' dispute.[71] At the personal level Hardy was, as usual, always courteous and when Mrs Ward sent him her novel *The Marriage of William Ashe* (1905) he declared that his great pleasure in the book disqualified him from being able 'to write critically about it – as I suppose fellow-scribblers ought in wisdom to do with one another's books'.[72] Admitting that he liked the middle part of the book best, he hastened to reassure her: 'I don't mean to say that I think you fell off in the last third, but that the culmination & catastrophe of a story – which necessarily admit of fewer varieties of form than the development... – must to an old reader appear less novel.' This suggests that although Hardy had long abandoned novel-writing he still pondered on questions of novelistic technique. On a more personal level he told her that he could not understand why the women in the novel cared for Cliffe and added disarmingly: 'But I am not a woman, & bow my head.' Raising the knotty question of authorial intention he commented on her heroine: 'Kitty has, I think, more of my sympathy than you wished her to have...I know somebody like her, & so do you, & one day I will ask you in an unguarded moment if you had her in mind.'

When in 1913 she sent her novel *The Coryston Family* to Hardy (through her publishers) she must have been extremely gratified by his admission that he found the book so interesting that he had sat up in bed till '1 a.m.' finishing it. With its 'remarkably distinct & living' characters, Hardy considered it perhaps her finest work and he confessed to having read it with a complete suspension of critical disbelief.[73] To the student of Hardy, however, Mrs Ward's most interesting work is her book of literary reminiscences, *A Writer's Recollection* (1918). Here she says that she was first 'strongly affected' by *The Return of the Native* and that 'Tess marked the conversion of the larger public, who then began to read all the earlier books, in that curiously changed mood which sets in when a writer is no longer on trial, but has, so to speak, "made good"'.[74] Confessing to being a late convert, she ultimately came to value his books for 'their truth, sincerity and humanity, in spite of the pessimism with which so many of them are tinged'. Hailing *The Dynasts* as 'the noblest, and possibly one of the most fruitful experiments in recent English letters', she still has one reservation: 'I wish Mr Hardy had not written "Jude the Obscure"!' Although Hardy read this,[75] his friendship with the Wards continued and often when he was in London he took the opportunity of calling on them. Whenever he wrote to Humphry Ward he remembered to send his kind regards to Mrs Ward and when she unexpectedly died in 1920, Hardy's letter of condolence to her husband recalls 'how vigorous & zestful she seemed in all relating to literature'.[76]

Hardy's reaction to the death of another of his literary friends was more emotional and the intensity of feeling took even him by surprise. Chancing on an old photograph of Rosamund Tomson (later Marriott Watson) some time after her death, old memories of 'framing of rhymes/ At idle times' came flooding back, and Hardy instinctively kissed the dimmed portrait – an experience that he recounts with both tenderness and wry self-amusement in his poem 'An Old Likeness (Recalling R.T.)'. Hardy's association with this beautiful poet, wife of the landscape painter Arthur Tomson, stretched back to over two decades. In June 1889 Hardy recommended her for membership to the Incorporated Society of Authors, and his backing seems to have been successful, because she was able to attend the Society's dinner, the next month, as a member and not as Hardy's guest.[77] In June 1889 Rosamund Tomson (writing under the pseudonym 'Graham R. Tomson') had published her first volume of verse and she sent a copy of *The Bird-Bride* to Hardy with the inscribed words 'Thomas Hardy, with the sincere admiration of G.R.T. June, 89'.[78] A few months later she sent Hardy a copy of *Selections from the Greek Anthology*, edited by her, and while thanking her for the book Hardy coyly wrote: 'No: wild horses shall not drag it out of me – that estimate of a poetess's work which came to my ears – till I see her.'[79] That some mild literary flirtation was going on between them is suggested by Hardy's next surviving letter to her where he is probably sending out a feeler: 'It rains a drizzle here today, so that we cannot see the hills – But the lovers walk two-&-two just the same, under umbrellas – or rather under one umbrella (which makes all the difference).'[80]

Although briefly dazzled by her, Hardy retained his critical faculties and was able to tell her plainly that 'fiction would do such a publication no good' in response to her request for a literary contribution to her proposed 'painter's weekly'.[81] When she sent him her photographs he gallantly responded saying that 'neither of them does justice to the original' but he remained steadfast in his refusal to write an introduction to her 'Art-World'.[82] Till December 1891 the relationship remained cordial, and Mrs Tomson sent Hardy two volumes of poetry: *Concerning Cats: A Book of Poems by Many Authors* edited by her, which the animal-loving Hardy must have surely enjoyed, and her own collection *A Summer Night and Other Poems*. But subsequently the relationship soured, and in July 1893, alluding to his disenchantment with Mrs Tomson, Hardy wrote to Florence Henniker that he would:

> trust to imagination only for an enfranchised woman. I thought I had found one some years ago – (I told you of her) – and it is somewhat singular that she contributes some of the best pieces to the volumes of *ballades* you send. Her desire, however, was to use your correspondent as a means of gratifying her vanity by exhibiting him as her admirer, the discovery of which promptly ended the friendship, with considerable disgust on his side.[83]

Matters were exacerbated when Mrs Tomson published in the New York *Independent* a two-part article on Hardy in November 1894. Apparently, there was nothing to offend Hardy in what she wrote; indeed, he could only have been mollified by her characterization of him as 'the most modest of geniuses', by her description of his total 'absence of self-consciousness that is positively charming', of his 'infrequent smile of remarkable sweetness', and of his eyes which though 'keen as a hawk's' were 'full of a quiet *bonhomie*'.[84] But the ever-touchy Hardy took exception to her insinuation that, after being initially refused the land for Max Gate by the agent of the Duchy of Cornwall, he had used his personal influence with the Prince of Wales to gain his request. Hardy's annoyance with such newspaper 'gossip' is evident from his letter to the 'agent' assuring him that he had never found him 'in our dealings to be the disagreeable person described' and adding, 'A woman is at the bottom of it, of course! I have reason to know that the writer of the account is a London lady, pretty, & well known in society (The signature is not I believe her real name). Why she should have written it I cannot say – except that it was not to please me.'[85]

But all bitter memories were wiped clean by death, and when the publisher John Lane sent Hardy a copy of her posthumously published *The Poems* (1912) it was probably the beautiful photograph facing the title-page in this book that Hardy instinctively kissed. Two poems in this collection are openly dedicated to Hardy, entitled 'Two Songs/ To Thomas Hardy'. But these poems are curiously impersonal, and there is no annotation by Hardy to suggest that they were of special significance to him. Interestingly, another poem in this collection, 'In a London Garden', bears the pencilled words in Hardy's hand: '(20 St John's $W^d R^d$)'.[86] Did the memory of some long-forgotten romantic rendezvous in a London garden flash across Hardy's mind as he read this poem? Was there more to their relationship than is suggested by the meagre surviving letters but is hinted at in Hardy's own poem with its reference to 'a far season/ Of love and unreason'?

Among the younger generation, Hardy had become almost a cult figure, and many writers, both male and female, made their literary pilgrimage to Max Gate. Sassoon, Galsworthy, E. M. Forster, Kipling, Granville-Barker, Edmund Blunden, Walter de la Mare, Robert Graves, John Masefield, John Drinkwater, H. G. Wells, Middleton Murry all went to pay their homage. Among the many women writers, perhaps the foremost was Virginia Woolf. After reading Hardy's poem 'The Schreckhorn' and his reminiscences of her father in F. W. Maitland's *The Life and Letters of Leslie Stephen* (1906), Woolf wrote to Hardy in 1915 stating that they were 'incomparably the truest and most imaginative portrait of him in existence, for which alone his children should be always grateful to you'.[87] She also told Hardy that 'I have long wished to tell you how profoundly grateful I am to you for your poems and novels', and ended by adding that the 'younger generation, who care for poetry and literature, owe you an immeasurable debt'. Pleased, Hardy wrote back praising Leslie Stephen's editorial intelligence and saying that he had gladly suffered her father's 'grim & severe criticisms' and 'long silences' for the 'sake of sitting with him'.[88] Almost a decade later, when Virginia and Leonard Woolf published Stephen's *Some Early Impressions* (1924) – which contained a brief reference to the serialization of *Far From the Madding Crowd* in *Cornhill* – Hardy wrote to her to thank 'the daughter of my old friend'.[89] But despite his genuine courtesy, Hardy had his touchy pride too, because when in the previous year Virginia Woolf had requested a literary contribution, Hardy had responded melodramatically: 'alas I have fallen into the sere & yellow leaf, & fear I am unable to undertake writing now… But there are plenty of young pens available.'[90] Hardy's pique had been prompted by Woolf's ignorant statement in her 1923 essay 'How It Strikes a Contemporary' that 'Mr Hardy has long since withdrawn from the arena.'[91] However, when Virginia Woolf later visited Florence Hardy at a London nursing home (after one of Mrs Hardy's operations) and repeated her request for a literary contribution, Hardy relented and his poem 'Coming up Oxford Street: Evening' appeared in *Nation and Athenaeum* on 13 June 1925.

Although Woolf considered Hardy's *The Trumpet Major* 'the worst book in the language' and could never understand 'how his reputation ever mounted, considering the flatness, tedium, and complete absence of gift' in this novel, she concluded that 'he had genius and no talent. And the English love genius.'[92] However, she admired his poetry and did not agree with the view that they were 'too melancholy and sordid'.[93] In 1921, Virginia Woolf and her husband were among the 104 signatories to an address congratulating him on his eighty-first birthday, on which occasion he was presented with a 'first edition' of Keats's poems as a token of regard from the younger writers. But it was only in July 1926 that Woolf actually travelled to Max Gate to meet Hardy, partly out of literary regard and partly because she had been commissioned to prepare a tribute to this grand old man of letters. She came away from the interview with a rather unsympathetic view of Florence Hardy, but she was clearly impressed by his 'extremely affable' manner, his 'cheerful and vigorous' aspect, his 'quizzical bright eyes', and his kindness in seeing anyone who wanted to see him.[94] Despite his aversion later in life to signing copies of his books on demand, Hardy readily signed Virginia Woolf's copy of *Life's Little Ironies*, and when she told him that she had brought *The Mayor of Casterbridge* with her to read on the train to Dorchester, his only question was: 'And did it hold your interest?' To Hardy the teller of tales this was of supreme importance, and the 'Ancient Mariner' in him must have been pleased with her reply that she 'could not stop reading it'. Woolf's final impression as she came away was that of a man who himself withdrawn from the world of literature yet 'had sympathy and pity for those still engaged in it'.

In her 1928 memorial essay,[95] as befitting the occasion, Woolf's tone is adulatory in her assessment of Hardy, the man and artist. She and her husband had attended the ceremony at Westminster Abbey where Hardy's ashes were interred, and in July 1932 she wrote to his widow praising her two-volume 'biography' of Hardy which Macmillan had published in 1928 and 1930. In this letter she confessed to having 'loved [Hardy's] novels, poems, as long as I can remember' and is flattered by Florence Hardy's suggestion (in her letter praising Woolf's *TLS* article on Hardy) that Woolf might have undertaken to write Hardy's biography.[96] When Woolf compliments Florence Hardy, saying that nobody 'could have improved upon your biography' because 'nobody could have given the book the atmosphere and the unity that you did', one wonders if the thought ever crossed her mind that nobody could have 'improved' the 'biography' because nobody could write better on Hardy than Hardy himself.

Another young novelist who visited Hardy and seems to have struck a chord of genuine friendship (although she had little pretension to beauty) was May Sinclair. She and her American friend Mary Moss had come down to visit Hardy in 1908, and though rain prevented their proposed bicycle trip to Weymouth, Hardy seems to have taken to May Sinclair because he repeatedly kept inviting her to visit Dorset and give him 'another opportunity' to show her round the county. Although his literary engagements prevented him from accepting her tempting offer of lunching aboard a friend's yacht, and on a later occasion ill health forced him to miss her lunch invitation, he was not just making up excuses, as he often did to wriggle out of more formal (especially speech-making) engagements.[97] This is shown in his letter to her, in August 1909, where he writes: 'Will you be in Dorset this summer? If so, please let me know; we could put you up for a night or two *en passant*, with pleasure, if you would care to stay at such a dull house, where there would be nobody else.'[98] For Hardy to make this offer is the supreme act of friendship, because while Max Gate received an endless stream of distinguished visitors, only a very few select people had the honour of being house guests. May Sinclair, an active suffragist, could probably have been the 'girl-friend' Hardy referred to when he told H. W. Nevinson that he was present in the crowd when the suffragists – 'a girl-friend of mine was one of them' – attempted to present their 'Bill of Rights' petition to the House of Commons in June 1909.[99] Although Florence Hardy appears to have disapproved of her novels because of their 'sex-mania', Hardy – who had had similar accusations flung at him – was sufficiently interested and his reply to Sinclair, when she sent him her novel *The Creators: A Comedy* (1910), is worth quoting:

I am much interested in learning from the female characters the things that go on at the back of women's minds – the invisible rays of their thought (as is said of the spectrum) which are beyond the direct sight or intuition of man. I recollect Leslie Stephen once saying to me that he liked women's novels for that reason: they opened to him qualities of observation which could not be got from the ablest of novels by men.[100]

If Hardy, who had given up novel-writing for about a decade and a half, could be so enthusiastic still about women's novels, women's poetry stirred him even more deeply. In 1903 he had met the poet Adela Florence ('Violet') Nicolson – who wrote under the pseudonym 'Laurence Hope' – and was struck by this 'most impassioned & beautiful woman'.[101] It is difficult to decide what moved Hardy more: her personal beauty, her 'passionate' verses, or her romantic gesture of committing suicide by 'having poisoned herself in excessive grief at the death of her husband, Gen. Nicolson'.[102] She had sent Hardy presentation copies of two volumes of her poetry, *The Garden of Kama* (1901) and *Stars of the Desert* (1903), and when news of her suicide reached Hardy from Madras he was struck by the (Hardyan) 'coincidence' that, apparently, she had died 'on the very day' when Hardy and Gosse '(who had never spoken of her to one another before) were discussing her poems at Max Gate'.[103] The death of this 'gifted and impassioned poetess' prompted Hardy to write a brief obituary notice, published in *Athenaeum* in October 1904.[104] In it Hardy speaks of the 'tropical luxuriance and Sapphic fervour' of her 1901 'series of love lyrics from India' and of the 'firmer intellectual grasp, with no loss of intensity' revealed in her 1903 volume. Quoting a stanza from 'nearly the last page of her last book' where she speaks of her readiness for death, Hardy concludes that 'the tragic circumstances of her death seem but the impassioned closing notes of her impassioned effusions'.[105] Later, at the request of a lady friend, Hardy wrote a preface for her posthumously published volume of poems, *Indian Love* (1905), and was justifiably irritated with Heinemann for not printing this preface, which he had 'gratuitously contributed' to help the sales of the book.[106]

A couple of years after meeting Violet Nicolson, Hardy met another poet, Dora Sigerson Shorter, when he went to Aldeburgh in 1905 to attend the 150th birth anniversary celebrations of Crabbe. In 1896 Dora Sigerson had married the journalist and editor Clement

Shorter, with whom Hardy's correspondence stretches from October 1891 to January 1925, and whose initiative in getting the extant manuscripts of Hardy's novels professionally bound deserves our gratitude. In 1902 Hardy had been presented with a copy of Mrs Shorter's *The Woman Who Went to Hell, and Other Ballads and Lyrics*, and he wrote to Clement Shorter saying how charmed he was with the 'vague dreaminess' of one of the poems in this volume.[107] A few years later, when he received her *Collected Poems* (1907), he again wrote to Shorter, telling him, 'My wife is so interested in them that she has carried them off to her room, so that I have read only 2 or 3 as yet.'[108] However, it was only during his 1911 visit to Clodd at Aldeburgh that he really got 'to know Mrs Shorter much better than I had ever done till then' and expressed to her husband his delight in finding 'what a sweet woman she was'.[109] Again in 1912, Hardy and the Shorters were guests at Clodd's house and in July 1913 the Shorters and Clodd stayed at Max Gate and then went on to visit Hardy's siblings at Talbothays. Mrs Shorter enjoyed her visit very much, and in response to her letter Hardy wrote back saying: 'I shall tell my brother & sisters when I see them that you & Mr Shorter much enjoyed your visit to Talbothays.... Their meeting you was quite an event, as they have known of your poetry for years.'[110]

Even in the midst of his grief at the sudden loss of his wife, Hardy noticed Mrs Shorter's poem in *Westminster Gazette* and read it 'with much interest', as he courteously mentioned to Shorter while thanking him for their letter of condolence.[111] Subsequent letters to Shorter are sometimes punctuated with expressions of delight at reading a new poem of Mrs Shorter, or of concern regarding her failing health. In June 1917 he wrote to Shorter praising one of her poems: 'It is what you newspaper men would call "Strong". Her pen is more facile than it used to be. I hope she is drawing near health.'[112] But Mrs Shorter died only six months later and on reading the announcement of her death in *The Times*, Hardy immediately wrote to Shorter: 'I offer no consolation; there may be some, but I do not know it. If one has much feeling – & you have that I know – such a blow is heavy to bear.'[113] Perhaps remembering the pain of the early days of his own widowerhood, Hardy later commiserated with Shorter: 'Reentering old haunts is inevitably depressing when you have shared them with another who is no longer there.'[114] In response to Shorter's request, Hardy later wrote a brief 'Prefatory Note' to the posthumous collection of Mrs Shorter's sketches, *A Dull Day in London* (1920).[115] More spontaneously, however, he composed the poem 'How She Went to Ireland' in which he speaks of how 'Dora' was taken to Ireland without her being conscious of the journey or of her surroundings – a reference, presumably, to Mrs Shorter being taken to Dublin for burial.[116]

Hardy's enthusiasm for Mrs Shorter's poetry was on a more muted level than his gushing response to Mrs Nicolson. With another poet of the same generation (all three were born in the late 1860s), his opinion underwent a radical change from his initial irritation with the 'fashion for obscurity' which he felt spoilt much of Charlotte Mew's poetry.[117] Ultimately he came to regard her as the 'greatest poetess I have come across lately, in my judgement, though so meagre in her output', and he openly expressed his regret to J. C. Squire that his anthology, *A Book of Women's Verse* (1921), did not include any of her poems.[118] Sydney Cockerell had sent Hardy a copy of Mew's volume *The Farmer's Bride* (1916) and Hardy was so impressed by her poems that Florence Hardy wrote to Charlotte Mew conveying his eager desire to meet her, if possible.[119] In response to this invitation Mew visited Max Gate in December 1918, and despite her complete lack of physical charm, her poetry and conversation so captivated Hardy that he persuaded her to stay for two days and they seem to have spent the time reading out their own poems to each other.[120] Later, in spite of his lifelong aversion to joining any sort of signature campaign, he joined Cockerell, Masefield, and de la Mare in securing for her a Civil List pension. When Mew wrote, in January 1924, to thank him for his efforts, Hardy replied with characteristic self-deprecation: 'What I did was really infinitesimal: Others did more than I. You are merely to think the little event happened – a very small one.'[121] Earlier, Mew had joined forty-two other poets in sending a bound volume of their holograph poems as a gift to Hardy on his seventy-ninth birthday. Hardy was so touched by this gesture of homage from the younger generation of poets that he actually took the trouble of personally writing to each one of them to thank them for their efforts. To Charlotte Mew he wrote: 'I shall always value the MS & keep it for your sake, as will my wife also.'[122] Later, Mew sent the original manuscripts of two of her poems to Florence Hardy in fond memory of Hardy's appreciation of her poetry.

Birthday congratulations for Hardy as he stepped into his eighties came from as far afield as across the Atlantic. In 1920, fourteen American writers sent Hardy a congratulatory cable and among them was Amy Lowell who had visited Hardy in August 1914 at the beginning of the war. She had followed up her visit by sending him a copy of her *Sword Blades and Poppy Seed* (1914), and while commending her poem 'After Hearing a Waltz' for 'admirably' capturing the 'beat of the waltz' in its 'metre & rhythm' Hardy half-jokingly went on: 'but for the difference of sex, critics might be asking you when you committed the murder – that is, if they are such geese as some of them are here, who in my case devoutly believe that everything written in the first person has been done personally.'[123] In December 1918 Lowell wrote to Hardy reminding him of her visit and sending him her volume *Can Grande's Castle* (1918) with its argument for 'polyphonic prose' which completely baffled him. He wrote to her confessing:

> I have not yet mastered your argument for 'polyphonic prose'... I don't suppose it is what, 40 years ago, we used to call 'word-painting'. Curiously enough, at that time, prose having the rhythm of verse concealed in it, so to speak (e.g. in the novels of R.D. Blackmore and others) was considered a fantastic affectation. Earlier still, when used by Lytton, it was nicknamed 'the ever and anon style'.[124]

In her reply Lowell patiently explained, while conceding that 'polyphonic prose' was not a 'very good name for it':

> It is not intended to be prose at all, but poetry.... Of course the way to read it is just to take it the way it comes without accentuating either the rhythm or the rhyme, since they are only used to enrich the form.... Perhaps it is an impossible form, but when I read it aloud to my audiences...I have no difficulty in making them apprehend it.[125]

Hardy appreciated her point about the extra dimension added to one's experience of poetry when one hears the poet herself read aloud her work. 'I am sure it would make all the difference if I could hear you read it as you do at your lectures', he wrote to her in 1924.[126] But Hardy still could not reconcile himself to 'free verse'. In

1914, after mentioning the names of those of her poems which he had especially liked, he had added: 'Whether I should have liked them still better rhymed I do not know.'[127] Almost a decade later, he again frankly expressed his reservations:

> I suppose I am too old to do it [i.e. free verse] justice. You manage it best; but do you mind my saying that it too often seems a jumble of notes containing ideas striking, novel, or beautiful, as the case may be, which could be transfused into poetry, but which, as given, are not poetry? I could not undergo an examination on why (to me) they seem not. Perhaps because there is no expectation raised of a response in sound or beat, and the pleasure of its gratification, as in regular poetry.[128]

This 1923 letter was in response to Lowell sending Hardy a copy of *American Poetry 1922: A Miscellany* which contained, apart from Lowell's poems, eight sonnets by Edna St Vincent Millay. Hardy was so impressed by them that in the same letter to Lowell he expressed his high opinion: 'Edna Millay seems the most promising of the younger poets.' When Edna Millay sent Hardy a copy of her *The King's Henchman: A Play in Three Acts* (1927) she inscribed in it the words: 'with the admiration and love of many years.'[129] Hardy however preferred her poetry to her drama, and frankly told her:

> An opinion, from a reading, on a play meant for acting, is not worth much, & I do not attempt to write one: indeed I have not formed one. I have simply let you carry me back to those old times outshadowed, & enjoyed the experience.

> I think I was among the early readers on this side of the Atlantic to be struck by your lyrics: & I am not sure that I do not like you better in that form than in the dramatic.[130]

Although he did not approve of Millay's change of literary direction, when Amy Lowell sent him a copy of *John Keats* (1924) Hardy was all praise for her biography. He commended her on her 'skill & industry', on her careful sifting of 'the legends for & against him', and warned her not to 'take any notice of what our funny men of the newspaper press say' about it.[131]

However, not all the specimens of 'floating nebulous bright intel-lectuality'[132] who visited Max Gate carried away happy memories of the house and its inmates. When Cicily Isabel Fairfield, better known as Rebecca West, visited Max Gate with her lover H. G. Wells, they were struck by the air of depression about the place; and the subse-quent cartoon drawing by Wells, glossed by Rebecca West's com-ments, do not add up to a flattering picture of the Hardys in 1919.[133] Rebecca West had sent an inscribed copy of her novel *The Return of the Soldier* (1918) to the Hardys, and in response to Wells's query whether he could bring her to Max Gate, Hardy had rather endear-ingly replied:

> Will she be angry that I have not read The Return, although I have heard it so much & so well spoken of? But I feel sure she is one of that excellent sort (which I flatter myself I am, & I am sure you are) who don't care a d— whether friends have read their last book or not, or any of their books. Indeed I am rather glad some-times when they *haven't* read mine.

Rebecca West later sent the Hardys a copy of her book *The Judge* (1922) with the inscribed words 'in respectful homage'; and she cleared Emma Hardy's reputation from one of the malicious ru-mours that had accumulated over the years around her memory. It has been said that Emma Hardy was fond of reminding her husband that he had married a 'lady' and Rebecca West was supposed to have been a witness on one occasion. She denied this and since she first visited Hardy in 1919, long after Emma's death, this 'story' about Emma Hardy's snobbery is best discounted.[134]

Chance visits often fail to do justice to a reticent recluse, and a bet-ter picture emerges from the account left behind by one who had the opportunity of longer regular visits and the rare intimacy of working with Hardy. In her reminiscences, *Thomas Hardy: His Secretary Remembers* (1965), May O'Rourke portrays a benign, paternal figure who is so considerate towards his young secretary that he refrains from asking her to type out a poem of his containing an 'irreverent line' lest it should hurt her Roman Catholic sentiments. May O'Rourke had first discovered Hardy's poetry among some old magazines in her attic and she had become an instant devotee. When her own volume of poems, *West Wind Days*, was published in 1918, a friend sent a copy to Hardy hoping he would encourage this local poet (she was then living at Fordington Vicarage in the house once occupied by Hardy's friends, the Moules) and adding that she 'worships you afar off'.[135] Hardy promptly replied that this 'unknown young lady' would always be welcome at Max Gate although he had 'not yet come to any conclusion about her poetry, being a slow critic as well as a very unsafe one'.[136] When O'Rourke called at Max Gate in July 1918 she was immediately struck by Hardy's 'accessibility and charm', and this impression only deepened when five years later, in 1923, she took up the offer of acting as Hardy's occasional secretary because Florence Hardy's failing health made her unable to cope single-handedly with the sheer volume of typing work that needed to be done.

May O'Rourke very soon came to develop toward Hardy a 'personal loyalty – the devotion of a very little poet for a poet of supreme magnitude', and the experience of typing *The Famous Tragedy of the Queen of Cornwall* was, to a poet, pure 'bliss' because she could appreciate 'where the authentic touch lay bright as dew upon so many of the words'.[137] Their relationship did not suffer when she ignored Hardy's suggestion that she should write 'poems about nature' or told him frankly that she had not read *Jude*. That she filled an emotional void in the life of the childless Hardy is suggested by an incident which she records where Hardy, trying to explain Wessex's (their notorious dog) fondness for her, says: 'He likes to see a bright young face.' The 'sadness which vibrated painfully beneath those quiet words' gave O'Rourke a 'glimpse of that longstanding inward regret that no child of his had ever enriched his life'.[138]

The poet in O'Rourke led her to admire the craftsmanship so evident in Hardy's 'carefully spaced lines and stanzas', and when she ventured to comment on his 'feeling for design in his verse', he:

> was interested, and I think, pleased; and he asked if I would like him to show me how to do it with a poem of my own. One lay near at hand, so Hardy settled down to loosening the tight pattern I had achieved, it seemed to me, setting the words free as he moved a line a little further in, another line a little further out, till the balance he sought was achieved.[139]

Two touching gestures reveal O'Rourke's reverence for Hardy the man and Hardy the poet. When she visited Keats's grave she brought back for Hardy a violet plant which she had 'shielded and cherished' across Europe. On being offered a cutting from the plant for herself, she declined because 'for Hardy to have this token from Keats' grave was only fitting; to have a share myself would be vandalism.'[140] She continued to work as Hardy's secretary intermittently and after his death, with Florence Hardy's permission, she wrote a tribute which was published in *The Month* (September 1928). Surely, there could be no finer compliment to Hardy's poetry than her words: 'Thomas Hardy...heeded the cries and guessed the mute anguish of his fellow-citizens on earth. It was an inflamed compassion for his own kind that spurred him... into a Job-like argument with God.'[141]

# 10
# Conclusion : 'A Confused Heap of Impressions'

In 1906 Hardy sent his sister Kate a picture postcard with a couple of lines describing his attendance at a London women's suffrage meeting: 'One woman rapped out: "We shall have more difficulty in getting the vote than you men had: we have committed the crime of being born woman".'[1] After centuries of injustice and blatant sex-discrimination, women in the second half of the nineteenth century were articulately demanding to be absolved from the 'crime of being born woman'. What came to be known as the 'Woman Question' was really a fight for equality of opportunity at an all-embracing level: it included not just the demand for the vote, but also the campaign for access to higher education, for entry into the professions, for a redress of the iniquities in the marriage and property laws, in short, for the right of a woman to live with dignity as an individual and not just as a socially and economically dependent inferior. Literature cannot be divorced from life, and in order fully to understand Hardy's attitude to women it is necessary to complement the analysis of his presentation of women in his fiction with an examination of his varying reactions to these important feminist issues of his day.

Hardy's changing responses to the suffrage movement make a fascinating study. Although he ultimately sympathized with the demand for women's franchise, he was initially sceptical, and as late as 1892 the author of *Tess* declined an offer to become Vice-President of the Women's Progressive Society on the conscientious ground that 'I have not as yet been converted to a belief in the desirability of the Society's first object', presumably women's suffrage.[2] This statement is all the more surprising because Hardy's first wife Emma was an enthusiastic supporter of the suffrage movement and there seems to be sufficient justice in her 1894 complaint to Mary Haweis (another active suffragist): 'His [i.e. Hardy's] interest in the Suffrage Cause is nil, in spite of "Tess" & his opinions on the woman question not in her favour. He understands only the women he *invents* – the others not at all' (Emma Hardy's italic).[3] This is not merely an instance of what biographers

199

have seen as Emma's habitual denigration of her husband, because as late as January 1909 Hardy informed Agnes Grove that 'it would be really injuring the women's cause if I were to make known exactly what I think may be [the] result of their success.'[4]

Even after he was 'converted' to the suffrage cause, his attitude seems to be a classic instance of doing the right thing for the wrong reasons. In an interesting letter to Millicent Fawcett (November 1906) he declared:

> I have for a long time been in favour of woman-suffrage. I fear I shall spoil the effect of this information (if it has any) in my next sentence by giving you my reasons. I am in favour of it because I think the tendency of the woman's vote will be to break up the present pernicious conventions in respect of manners, customs, religion, illegitimacy, the stereotyped household (that it must be the unit of society), the father of a woman's child (that it is anybody's business but the woman's own, except in cases of disease or insanity), sport (that so-called educated men should be encouraged to harass & kill for pleasure feeble creatures by mean stratagems), slaughter-houses (that they should be dark dens of cruelty), & other matters which I got into hot water for touching on many years ago.
>
> I do not mean that I think all women, or even a majority, will actively press some or any of the first mentioned of such points, but that their being able to assert themselves will loosen the tongues of men who have not liked to speak out on such subjects while women have been their helpless dependents.[5]

This letter makes curious reading, because while Hardy seems capable of advancing the revolutionary idea that the father of a woman's child is nobody's business but her own, he never voices the simple justification behind the demand for women's suffrage: that if women are to be bound by laws equally with men, they have the inalienable right to share in the process of making those laws. Thus, in a 1909 letter to Clement Shorter, Hardy again airs his unconventional reasons for 'not object[ing] to the coming of woman-suffrage':

> As soon as women have the vote & can take care of themselves men will be able to strike out honestly right & left in a way they cannot do while women are their dependents, without showing unchivalrous

meanness. The result will be that all superstitious institutions will be knocked down or rationalized – theologies, marriage, wealth-worship, labour-worship, hypocritical optimism, & so on. Also some that women will join in putting down: blood-sport, slaughter-house inhumanities, the present blackguard treatment of animals generally, &c, &c. End of my sermon.[6]

Hardy seems to have been somewhat uncertain, if not apprehensive, of the ultimate consequences of women gaining the vote because in December 1908 he wrote to Helen Ward, declining her request to contribute to a prospective suffragist newspaper:

> Though I hold...that women are entitled to the vote as a matter of justice if they want it, I think the action of men therein should be permissive only – not cooperative. I feel by no means sure that the majority of those who clamour for it realize what it may bring in its train: if they did three-fourths of them would be silent. I refer to such results as the probable break-up of the present marriage-system, the present social rules of other sorts, religious codes, legal arrangements on property, &c (through men's self protective countermoves.) I do not myself consider that this would be necessarily a bad thing (I should not have written 'Jude the Obscure' if I did), but I deem it better that women should take the step unstimulated from outside. So, if they should be terrified at consequences, they will not be able to say to men: 'You ought not to have helped bring upon us what we did not foresee.'[7]

To Hardy, 'the position of women [was] one of the ninety-nine things in a hundred that are wrong in this so-called civilized time' and though he admitted that 'the vote is theirs by right', he had misgivings about 'whether it will be for their benefit at first'.[8] Therefore he scrupulously kept out of the fray, taking care not to allow his name to appear in public campaigns on either side of the controversial issue. In 1910 he thus solemnly reassured Emma by letter[9] that he had refused Lord Curzon's request to sign the 'Anti Woman-Suffrage Appeal' (published in *Times*, 21 July 1910), but at the same time he frankly confessed his 'dilemma' in private to one of the anti-suffragist signatories: 'I hold that a woman has as much right to vote as a man; but at the same time I doubt if she may not do mischief with her vote. Thus the query is, must we do a wrong thing (by with-holding it) because it may be good policy, or a right thing (by granting it) even though it may be bad policy?'[10] Such eternal soul-searching made Hardy constitutionally unfit to take 'any practical part in controversial politics' and this is the excuse he characteristically offered when in 1916 Evelyn Sharp wrote to him inviting him to become a member of the National Council for Adult Suffrage which was committed to securing votes for women before the end of the First World War.[11]

On the issue of women's education Hardy was less equivocal as he realized that 'Man is himself responsible for the vacuum in woman's brains'.[12] When Hardy was made a Governor of the Dorchester Grammar School what struck him 'in looking up its history of 350 years, & that of all the many other Grammar Schools of that age & standing, is that it never occurred to any of the pious & practical founders to establish a single Grammar School for women. Every one of these excellent institutions has been for males only'.[13] Thus the women of the age were intellectually starved, and Hardy's sympathy with their state of deprivation indirectly comes through in the passage that he copied into his 'Literary Notes II' notebook:

> The drama of a woman's soul; at odds with destiny, as such a soul must needs be, when endowed with great powers & possibilities, under the present social conditions; where the wish to live, of letting whatever energies you possess have their full play in action, is continually thwarted by the impediments & restrictions of sex.[14]

But women in the late nineteenth century were gradually overcoming the 'restrictions of sex' and with the Universities and the medical colleges – hitherto hallowed all-male preserves – gradually opening their doors to female students, educational opportunities for women were brighter than ever before. Also, training colleges for schoolmistresses had been set up – of the type attended by Sue Bridehead and Hardy's own sisters Mary and Kate, his cousin Tryphena Sparks, and his cousin's wife Annie Sparks (née Lanham) – with a view to providing women with professional training and, ultimately, economic independence. After visiting one such institution, the Whitelands Training College, Hardy recorded in his autobiography:

A community of women, especially young women, inspires not reverence but protective tenderness in the breast of one who views them. Their belief in circumstances, in convention, in the rightness of things which you know to be not only wrong but damnably wrong, makes the heart ache.... How far nobler in its aspirations is the life here than the life of those I met at the crush two nights back![15]

Apart from being a schoolteacher, which was a traditional feminine role, women were campaigning for entry into other professions and one field that they seem to have invaded in sufficient numbers was journalism – another traditionally all-male territory. Hardy actively promoted the journalistic aspirations of first Agnes Grove and then Florence Dugdale and he was willing to lend the weight of his name even to those who were not avowedly his 'pupils'. For instance, in 1890, he wrote to the editor of *Contemporary Review* on behalf of Mona Caird because she 'preferred this slight introduction to sending it [i.e. her article on Marriage] as a stranger'.[16] But for the nameless, faceless female journalist – or, more specifically, the female reviewer – Hardy seemed to have scant professional respect. In December 1916, for example, he lamented to Arthur Quiller-Couch regarding the absence of a 'school or science of criticism – especially in respect of verse. I cannot find a single idea in any one of them that is not obvious, but I suppose the verses that come to hand in newspaper offices are put into the hands of the youngest *girl* on the staff' (my italic).[17] About a year later, in February 1918, Hardy referred more scathingly to an unsigned review of his *Moments of Vision* in a letter to Florence Henniker: 'Did you see the super-precious review of the verses in the Westminster Gazette? It amused me much (having no weight or value as criticism) as it was obviously written by a woman. It condemned the poem entitled "The pink frock" because the frock described was old-fashioned & Victorian!'[18] It is probably this same hapless (female?) reviewer to whom Hardy sarcastically refers in his autobiography as 'the fair critic who pretended to be a man, but alas, betrayed her sex at the last moment by condemning a poem because its heroine was dressed in a tasteless Victorian skirt!'[19]

Hardy's complaint against female reviewers was not new. As far back as 1904 he had written to Henry Newbolt regarding 'some odd experiences of criticism' in respect of *The Dynasts*: 'For one thing, I find that my reviewers have largely been women, especially in America. Surely Editors ought to know that such a subject could hardly be expected to appeal to women.'[20] But one review, by a female reviewer, must have appealed to Hardy because this 1908 laudatory article by Grace Alexander was cut and pasted into Hardy's personal scrapbook and it stands unmarked by any of the dismissive marginal comments by Hardy which so often characterize some of the other newspaper clippings. Ever since he had entered the field as a novelist, Hardy's fictional women had drawn most of the critical attention and ire, and Hardy had to keep insisting that 'no satire on the sex is intended in any case by the imperfections of my heroines' (1874)[21] and nearly two decades later he is still lamenting that many of his novels 'have suffered so much from misrepresentation as being attacks on womankind' (1891).[22] Hence Grace Alexander's review, which drew attention to Hardy's 'delicate and unbroken, one might almost say... chivalric, sympathy' for women, must have pleased Hardy. The review opens with a quotation from *A Group of Noble Dames*, about how men are usually ungenerous to the women dependent on them, and then goes on to say: 'Looking into the world he [i.e. Hardy] has seen that it is the woman, usually, who suffers and the woman who pays, and seemingly with a kind of obligation resting on him he writes as though to offer her artistic compensation.' Therefore, the reviewer concludes, 'women owe to Thomas Hardy a unique debt of gratitude for the fullness and fineness of his comprehension of them'.[23] The personal satisfaction that Hardy probably derived from this sympathetic review must have been of the same kind as that derived from 'numerous communications from mothers (who tell me they are putting "Tess" into their daughters' hands to safeguard their future) & from other women of society who say that my courage has done the whole sex a service(!)'.[24]

If Hardy had little respect for the woman reviewer, his faith in the female editor seems to have been even less. For instance, in July 1921, when Ruth Head proposed to edit a selection of Hardy's writings, he expressed his wish that the extracts would be taken from both his prose and verse and then cautiously hinted: 'The difficulty of selections, in poetry particularly, is (if you don't mind my saying it) that though what a woman reader likes a man may usually like, what a man likes most is sometimes what a woman does not like at all. And this especially with my writings.'[25] Hardy must have heaved an immense sigh of relief when he learnt that Ruth Head's husband, the neurologist Henry Head, would be helping her in her editorial task because his next letter to Mrs Head candidly confesses:

> I particularly prefer it now that I learn that your husband is giving a kindly eye to your selections. (This is shockingly ungallant, but how can I be otherwise in a business of this peculiar sort!) In extenuation I humbly add that my writings, particularly in verse – & I don't care an atom what prose you select – suffer from the misfortune of being more for men than for women, if I may believe what people say.[26]

However, when a woman translated some of his poems into French, Hardy's sympathy for the translator was expressed in a letter to Edmund Gosse: 'I thought they [i.e. the French translations] were done with unusual fidelity of statement...I have been told recently that the translator is an invalid – a cripple I believe, & that she has worked very hard at them. I hope she will get something out of them to repay her for her trouble. She is quite a stranger to me.'[27] Hardy's generous instincts were always 'quickened', as he himself confessed to Florence Henniker in 1899, by the plight of 'a "woman-writer" struggling with a pen in a Grub street garret'.[28] But after attending a meeting of the Women Writers' Club in 1894, Hardy had to modify radically his mental image of the struggling woman writer. Knowing 'what women writers mostly had to put up with', Hardy was 'surprised to find himself in a group of fashionably dressed youngish ladies instead of struggling dowdy females, the Princess Christian being present with other women of rank. "Dear me – are women-writers like this!" he said with changed views.'[29] For this breed of woman writer Hardy seems to have had nothing but contempt; as he told Henry Nevinson, he did not much care for the title of 'novelist' 'since innumerable young ladies who have published a tale at their own expense call themselves by that name'.[30] Even more scornful is his reference to the 'ladies' who failed to turn up for the Lord Mayor's dinner to literature (July 1893) 'because their husbands were not invited – So much for their independence'.[31] But for the woman writer of genuine talent, Hardy's admiration was unqualified, as is evident from his copying of two poems by Emily Dickinson and pasting a cutting of a poem by 'H.D.' into his 'Literary Notes II' notebook.[32]

Towards the bright, independent, articulate modern women of the turn of the century – the 'New Women' – Hardy's attitude was again ambivalent. He appreciated them in literature, but in real life he probably found them somewhat overwhelming. When Florence Henniker sent him one of her stories in 1911, the creator of Sue Bridehead responded enthusiastically to the heroine: 'The girl, though so slightly sketched, is very distinct – the modern intelligent, mentally emancipated young woman of cities, for whom the married life you kindly provide for her would ultimately prove no great charm – by far the most interesting type of femininity the world provides for man's eyes at the present day.'[33] However, when these liberated city women went careering down London streets on their bicycles, it was a different proposition altogether, and one suspects that Hardy felt a sneaking sympathy for the indignant omnibus conductor whose words he related, with obvious relish, to his sister Kate:

> The young people seem to cycle about the streets here more than ever. I asked an omnibus conductor if the young women (who ride recklessly into the midst of the traffic) did not meet with accidents. He said 'Oh, nao; their sex pertects them. We dares not drive over them, wotever they do; & they do jist wot they likes. 'Tis their sex, yer see; & its wot I coll takin' a mean adventage. No man dares to go where they go.'[34]

However, Hardy was clear-sighted enough to recognize that this was an exception; in patriarchal society it was usually the woman who was meanly taken advantage of. His sympathy for victimized, exploited women, especially women marginalized by society, is repeatedly expressed through his writings. In 1891 he visited a private lunatic asylum, and was much affected by listening to women relating 'their stories of their seduction',[35] and his avowed purpose in writing *Tess* was that it had 'been borne in upon my mind for many years that justice has never been done to such women in fiction'.[36] Even though Hardy's local experience was that 'the girls who have made the mistake of Tess almost invariably lead chaste lives thereafter, even under strong temptation', social censure often turned such first-time offenders into permanent outcasts. In his autobiography, he recounts one such touching encounter while returning from an aristocratic evening party:

On coming away there were no cabs to be got...and I returned to
S.K. [*sic*] on the top of a 'bus. No sooner was I up there than the
rain began again. A girl who had scrambled up after me asked for
the shelter of my umbrella, and I gave it, – when she startled me
by holding on tight to my arm and bestowing on me many kisses
for the trivial kindness. She told me she... was tired, and was
going home. She had not been drinking. I descended at the South
Kensington Station and watched the 'bus bearing her away. An
affectionate nature wasted on the streets! It was a strange contrast
to the scene I had just left.[37]

Hardy's indignation at a society which not merely tolerated but tac-
itly sanctioned and even at times indirectly forced women to go on
the streets is evident from a quotation from Victor Hugo that Hardy
copied into his '1867' Notebook: 'It is said that slavery has disappeared from European civilization. This is a mistake.... It weighs
now only upon woman, & is called prostitution.'[38]

Hardy did what little he could for such unfortunate women. At
the lunatic asylum he appealed for the re-examination of a young
female inmate who seemed to him to be quite sane. As a member of
the jury at the Dorset Assizes, Hardy joined his compeers in acquit-
ting a woman on the charge of the manslaughter of her infant (a real-
life *The Heart of Mid-Lothian* situation), finding her guilty only of the
lesser charge of 'concealment of birth: which, of course, being a
crime, had to receive a punishment'. Hardy's relief and joy at the
light sentence handed out to the defendant are clearly revealed in his
report of the case in a letter to Florence Dugdale (1912): 'But as neither the judge nor a single person in court wished her to be punished
the judge got over the difficulty by sentencing her to one day's
imprisonment, & adding "the day being already begun you have
nominally undergone that, so you are free".'[39] Hardy's humane
response is quite in keeping with the character of a man who held
that: 'That which, socially, is a great tragedy, may be in Nature no
alarming circumstance.'[40] In a less veiled manner, Hardy had challenged the very concept of illegitimacy in his controversial poem 'A
Sunday Morning Tragedy' (*Time's Laughingstocks*, 1909) where the
poet in his own voice interrupts the first-person narrative to question parenthetically: '(Ill-motherings! Why should they be?)'. The
mother's lament in this poem – 'O women! scourged the worst are
we...' – is anticipated by the speaker in the poem 'The Coquette, and
After' (*Poems of the Past and the Present*, 1901) who regrets that 'Of

sinners two/ At last *one* pays the penalty – / The woman – women always do!' (Hardy's italic).

Hardy's sympathies were broad enough to include not just the 'ruined maid' but also the woman found guilty of murder. In his fiction he remained unflinchingly loyal to Tess even after her murder of Alec, and in real life he responded to the 1923 execution of Edith Jessie Thompson (found guilty of murdering her husband) by writing the poem 'On the Portrait of a Woman about to be Hanged', in which he accused the 'purblind vision' of the Prime 'Causer' who had implanted a 'worm', a 'Clytaemnestra spirit', in its fair handiwork. Hardy sent this poem to J. C. Squire with the challenging words (which unequivocally reveal his stance): 'If your paper is too moral to sympathize with a wicked woman, will you return the enclosed?'[41] This does not imply that he valued human life so little that he was prepared to condone murder. As he had tried to explain in a note of 1889, later incorporated into his autobiography: 'When a married woman who has a lover kills the husband, she does not really wish to kill the husband; she wishes to kill the situation. Of course in Clytaemnestra's case it was not exactly so, since there was the added grievance of Iphigenia, which half-justified her.'[42]

Hardy realized that women's images, both in life and in literature, were distorted by being refracted through the male point of view. He felt, for example, that Fanny Brawne had not received justice at the hands of Keats's biographers and that she did not really deserve the scorn that has been heaped on her.[43] A woman's story told by a man from a predominantly male perspective is significantly different from a woman's story told by a woman from an intimately female experiential standpoint. Therefore, although poets have dwelt briefly on the 'pathos of the woman's part in time of war', it is a matter of great regret that 'no poet has ever arisen to tell the tale of Troy from Andromache's point of view'.[44] Hardy himself at one point contemplated composing something analogous, because one of his many abandoned ideas for the 'Iliad of Europe from 1789 to 1815' (which finally shaped itself as *The Dynasts*) was to call the 'grand drama' 'Josephine'.[45] It would have been interesting if he had worked out this scheme; then, perhaps, *The Dynasts* would be more widely read today than it generally is. On a smaller scale, in his dramatic lyrics, he tried to make this imaginative leap by adopting the woman's point of view, by trying to think, feel and express himself as a woman: these poems range from the early 'She, to Him' sonnets (only four survive from this 1866 sequence) to the late poems of expiation, written and published after Emma's death as 'the only amends I can make',[46] quite a few of which were directly inspired by Hardy's reading of his late wife's prose memoirs (*Some Recollections*).

In this last instance, however, there is a suspicion that Hardy made good 'copy' out of Emma – both of her as a person, and of her creative attempts at literature. For instance, in the 'Notes' supplied for the revision of Samuel Chew's book, Hardy indirectly admitted that in *A Pair of Blue Eyes* 'the character and temperament of the heroine... [has] some resemblance to a real person'.[47] To George Dewar, however, Hardy was more forthcoming and in a letter of July 1913, he unequivocally acknowledged that in *A Pair of Blue Eyes* the 'character of the heroine is somewhat – indeed, rather largely – that of my late wife, & the background of the tale the place where she lived. But of course the adventures, lovers, &c. are fictitious entirely, though people used sometimes to ask her why she did this & that.'[48] Of Emma Hardy's literary efforts, 'The Maid on the Shore' is interesting because it offers two striking instances of parallelism in Hardy's own work. In one episode, the hero's wife Boadicea is presented with the family jewels as a wedding gift, and she adorns herself with these ornaments reminding the reader of Tess's similar action on her wedding night. In another episode, Boadicea's young sister is chased by a thoughtless boy on horseback and the little girl's fright makes her fall into a convulsive fit followed by a prolonged nervous prostration. In Hardy's story 'The Doctor's Legend' (1891), a similar incident occurs when a young girl, chased by an irate Squire, suffers an epileptic fit which is followed by a protracted nervous malady.

Of course, one cannot state with any degree of certainty just when Hardy read Emma's novelette, but there could well be some justice in Dale Spender's contention that 'Samuel Richardson, Thomas Hardy and William Wordsworth are among other great writers known to have similar propensities for taking the writing of women and using it for their own ends'.[49] Citing the examples of F. Scott Fitzgerald (who plagiarized from his wife Zelda's diaries) and D. H. Lawrence (who freely appropriated the 'solicited notes and reminiscences' of his wife and women friends), Dale Spender argues that throughout literary history male writers have often been guilty of stealing the fruits of women's creative labour. Remarkably enough, this feminist thesis is anticipated by Emma Hardy in her letter to the

Editor of *The Nation* in 1908: 'Such words [e.g. 'virility'] are untrue as denoting perfection to be an attribute of the masculine intellect, for a good deal that is carried out as original and finished work has been suggested, and often completely thought out, by a woman, though never so acknowledged.'[50]

A small example of such unacknowledged borrowing can be traced to an 1885 conversation that Hardy had with a 'sympathetic group of women', in which the discussion naturally turned to 'love', and 'Lady Camilla informed him that "a woman is never so near being in love with a man she does not love as immediately he has left her after she has refused him".'[51] In *The Woodlanders* (1887) Hardy's imaginative alchemy transformed this into the narrative comment on the fluctuating Grace–Giles relationship:

> If it be true, as women themselves have declared, that one of their sex is never so much inclined to throw in her lot with a man for good and all as five minutes after she has told him such a thing cannot be, the probabilities are that something might have been done by the appearance of Winterborne on the ground beside Grace.[52]

Apart from illustrating woman's fickleness, her chronic inability to know her own mind, this passage also reveals another time-honoured male (mis)conception of woman: that a woman's 'No' actually means 'Yes'. This is an arrogant assumption that many a suitor, both in fiction and in real life, has often made and this is the justification that Alec d'Urberville offers for having taken advantage of Tess. When Tess sorrowfully laments, 'I didn't understand your meaning till it was too late', Alec scornfully sweeps it aside with the dismissive generalization: 'That's what every woman says.' This suggestion of female hypocrisy stings Tess into vehement protest: 'How can you dare to use such words!... Did it never strike your mind that what every woman says some women may feel?'[53] Tess's 'No' had meant 'No', but Alec had simply not bothered to listen.

If Alec is trapped in traditional patriarchal attitudes, so (apparently) is his creator. The tendency of Hardy's narrator to indulge in negative and reductive generalizations about women has been widely noted. Such generalizations, however, are not just restricted to the novels or short stories, but feature too in Hardy's notebooks, his autobiography, and even his personal correspondence. Thus, an 1871 notebook entry declares: 'Nothing is so interesting to a woman as herself'; and a couple of pages later, in 1872, Hardy records a cynical comment about women that he professes to have overheard – 'She can use the corners of her eyes as well as we can use the middle.'[54] This bit of folk-wisdom was probably metamorphosed into the advice Dick Dewy receives from his father, in *Under the Greenwood Tree* (1872), about the nature of young maids: 'She'll swear she's dying for thee...but she'll fling a look over t'other shoulder at another young feller, though never leaving off dying for thee just the same.'[55] This proverbial (male) equation between 'fickleness' and 'woman' is implied in Hardy's 1865 comment, copied into his autobiography: 'Public opinion is of the nature of a woman.'[56] The very absence of elaboration suggests that the nature of woman is too well known to require explanatory amplification and also assumes that both writer and (male) reader share a common perspective on the 'other' half of creation.

A corollary to woman's fickleness was, reputedly, her vanity. Hardy's 1878 observation succinctly sums up this traditional perception of woman's preoccupation with her physical appearance: 'When a couple are shown to their room at an hotel, before the husband has seen that it is a room at all, the wife has found the looking-glass & is arranging her bonnet.'[57] From a relatively young writer who is trying to establish himself, such comments are hardly surprising. What *is* surprising, however, is that Hardy thought it fit to include these comments when he came to compose his autobiography, in secret, during the second decade of the twentieth century. In 1899 he had pasted into his 'Literary Notes II' notebook a cutting of an English translation by Arthur Symons of an original French poem dealing with woman's narcissistic worship of self in front of her mirror, totally unheedful of the perishable quality of her charms.[58] Two decades later, Hardy's conviction about woman's essential vanity remained unchanged, and he wrote to the president of the Oxford University Dramatic Society (in 1919) regarding its proposed dramatization of *The Dynasts*: 'My feeling was the same as yours about the Strophe and Antistrophe – that they should be unseen, and as it were speaking from the sky. But it is, as you hint, doubtful if the two ladies will like to have their charms hidden. Would boys do instead, or ugly ladies with good voices?'[59] Earlier in the same year, when Alfred Pope sent Hardy the proofs of his book recording the wartime contributions of his daughters (and sons), Hardy made a few 'trifling corrections' and offered the laconic comment: 'By the way will the girls like their birth dates to be mentioned?... I am too old to be a judge of the modern feminine mind.'[60]

Despite the negative tenor of such comments, Hardy's sympathy for women is clearly evident from an 1870 observation:

> When a young woman is eager to explain her meaning to a lover who has carelessly or purposely misunderstood her, there is something painful to an observer who notices it, although it is evidence of deep love. It somehow bespeaks that in spite of her orders to him to fetch & carry, of his devotion & her rule, he is in essence master.[61]

Hardy's sympathy for women can also be read into the quotation from *John Inglesant* (1881) that he copied into his 'Literary Notes I' notebook: 'From those high windows behind the flower-pots young girls have looked out upon life, which their instincts told them was made for pleasure, but which year after year convinced them was, somehow or other, given over to pain.'[62] One is reminded of that passage in *Jude* where the narrator, with Darwinian bio-determinism, brands the young girls 'The Weaker', but also speaks tenderly of the 'storms and strains of after-years, with their injustice, loneliness, child-bearing, and bereavement'.[63]

The same ambivalence, the indignation and pity for the 'injustice' that is woman's common lot, coupled with a tacit assumption of woman as being an inferior evolutionary species, is evident in Hardy's comment to William Archer in 1901: 'What are my books but one plea against "man's inhumanity to man" – to woman – and to the lower animals?'[64] On one level, it speaks positively of Hardy's passionate hatred for any form of cruelty practised towards man or beast. But the (unintentional?) descending order of the sentence structure lays it open to a less positive interpretation. The abrupt, disconcerting shift from the generic ('man's') to the gender-specific ('man') and the hierarchical placing of 'man', 'woman', and 'lower animals' seem to imply that woman occupies an intermediary position in the evolutionary ladder – not as lowly as the animals, but not yet quite as exalted as man. If such an interpretation seems to be an over-straining or falsification, one has only to go back a few years to Hardy's 1895 letter to Archer, where (in the context of *Jude*) he reiterates essentially the same idea in words that have an identical descending order: 'I suppose the times are still too barbarous to allow one to strike a blow – however indirectly, for humanity towards man, woman, or the lower animals.'[65] One would expect a *writer* to be more conscious of the possible implications of his word-order.

Hardy's use of language at times betrays his ideological limitations and reveals how hopelessly he is trapped in *man*-made language. For instance, in a letter explaining the impetus behind *Tess*, he declared: ' "Tess of the d'Urbervilles" was not written to prove anything, either about Heaven or Earth. A certain character was imagined to feel at a certain time of *his* life that God was not in his Heaven, & there was an end of it, without prejudice' (my italic).[66] Despite his sincere emotional commitment to Tess, and the testimony of an actress that he 'talked of Tess as if she was someone real whom he had known and liked tremendously',[67] Hardy could not rise above the conventional male pronoun which sounds so jarring in the context.[68] It is a good illustration (on a minor level) of the justice of Bathsheba's general complaint that language was made by men to express their feelings and, as such, men's language is an inadequate vehicle to express women's feelings, as often there are no precise verbal equivalents for uniquely female experiences.

However, it is not only women who find language a recalcitrant medium. In one of his marginal comments on George Egerton's *Keynotes*, Hardy tried to defend the undemonstrative male protagonist of the story 'Now Spring has Come' by suggesting: 'It was simply the lack of expressive power: not lack of feeling.'[69] Most of Hardy's annotations in this copy of *Keynotes* read like those of a man attempting to justify the ways of men to women. Thus, a few pages later in the same story, Hardy again remarked: 'He s.^d [*sic*] that because *she* was not impulsive enough' (p. 65; Hardy's emphasis). Throughout these stories in which Egerton powerfully projects the woman's point of view, one has the feeling that Hardy's commentary attempts to counter it by presenting the male point of view. For instance, where Egerton writes: 'A woman must beware of speaking the truth to a man; he loves her the less for it', Hardy's footnote reads: 'This bears only on sensualism. It is untrue of man in his altruistic regard of woman as a fellow-creature: untrue of his highest affection for her' (p. 29). However, Hardy was not content with merely defending his own sex; a couple of his marginal comments betray positive hostility to women. Where Egerton speaks of the 'untamed primitive savage temperament' lurking in woman,

Hardy queries: 'Hence her inferiority to man??' (p. 22). Egerton's thesis is that men, down the ages, have constructed a false ideal of womanhood, and therefore women, in their own self-interest, hypocritically have to live up to this ideal. Man 'has fashioned a model on imaginary lines... and every woman is an unconscious liar, for so man loves her'. Against this passage occurs perhaps the most devastating of Hardy's marginal comments: '*ergo*: *real* woman is abhorrent to man? hence the failure of matrimony??' (p. 23; Hardy's emphases).

Hardy read and annotated *Keynotes* in December-January 1893/4, and during this time he seems to have grown gradually disenchanted with women (it is useless to speculate whether Emma Hardy or Florence Henniker was responsible for this disillusion). An 1893 note incorporated into his autobiography reveals the same sense of mixed hurt and hostility: 'I often think that women, even those who consider themselves experienced in sexual strategy, do not know how to manage an *honest* man' (Hardy's italic).[70] Of the several extracts from Schopenhauer that Hardy copied into his 'Literary Notes II' notebook in 1891, one is headed '*On Women*'. It is a miscellaneous collection of abridged quotations, most of them negative: 'Women are childish, frivolous, & short sighted'; 'Dissimulation [is] innate in woman'; the natural feeling between women is 'enmity', because of 'trade-jealousy'; women have not produced any 'great, genuine, or original' work of art; women are 'a constant stimulus to ignoble ambitions' etc. On the lighter side, Hardy also copied out the philosopher's wonder about how men could 'give the name of *the fair sex* to that undersized, narrow-should.[d] [*sic*] broad-hipped & short-legged race'.[71] Nevertheless, despite Schopenhauer, men down the ages have continued to find women irresistible and Hardy certainly was no exception.

Like most male artists (and his fictional Jocelyn Pierston), Hardy was extremely susceptible to female beauty. The narrative of his adolescent years is punctuated with references to girls briefly glimpsed and adored from afar because for Hardy distance lent not only enchantment but also an idealizing halo. As in the case of his own creation, Ella Marchmill, it could be just a photograph which fuelled his romantic dreams and Hardy's autobiography contains a candid confession of his youthful passion for the Austrian Empress (Elizabeth, wife of Francis Joseph I): 'She was a woman whose beauty, as shown in her portraits, had attracted him greatly in his youthful years, and had inspired some of his early verses, the same romantic passion having also produced the outline of a novel upon her, which he never developed.[72] Age does not seem to have cured this extreme romantic susceptibility – the 'throbbings of noontide' persisted – and Hardy admitted to Harley Granville Barker in 1925 that although on principle he felt that 'to attempt to put a novel on the stage is hopeless, and altogether a mistake in art', he had nevertheless composed a dramatization of *Tess* because 'having been tempted by many "leading ladies" of the nineties I could not resist'.[73] These 'would-be Tesses' are named in the autobiography as 'Mrs Patrick Campbell, Ellen Terry, Sarah Bernhardt, and Eleanora Duse'[74]: a truly formidable list and any man can be forgiven for falling a prey to their combined charms. Ultimately, of course, it was a local beauty, Gertrude Bugler, whose 'request' resulted in the performance of *Tess* by the amateur 'Hardy Players'. As Hardy acknowledged to J. C. Squire in 1925, 'I no longer believe in dramatizing novels, & have no dramatic ambitions. Its appearance is entirely owing to the fact that our leading lady down here coaxed me to let her do Tess.'[75]

As a celebrity, Hardy 'found himself continually invited hither and thither to see famous beauties of the time'[76] but his eyes were never really dazzled by the aristocratic beauties on display. He realized that the veneer of beauty really depended on the exigencies of life, on the accidents of birth and fortune, and after attending a 'crush' (replete with a Princess, a Duchess, and diamond-studded aristocrats), Hardy commented: 'But these women! If put into rough wrappers in a turnip-field, where would their beauty be?'[77] Nevertheless, Hardy's artist's eye could not help noticing beautiful women: the '*too* statuesque girl' with 'absolutely perfect' features whom he saw in a railway carriage;[78] the 'young women... in fluffy blouses' who 'distracted' him on top of omnibuses;[79] or the girl in the omnibus whose 'marvellous beauty' and face of 'softened classicality' left him wondering – 'Where do these women come from? Who marries them? Who knows them?'[80] Hardy seems to have measured women's beauty in terms of their personal desirability as wives. Of Princess May he records, 'she is not a bad-looking girl, and a man might marry a worse.'[81] More interesting is his response to an unnamed socialite whom he describes as 'an Amazon; more, an Atalanta; most, a Faustine. Smokes: Handsome girl: cruel small mouth: she's of the class of interesting women one would be afraid to marry.'[82]

Marriage, of course, features very prominently in Hardy's fiction – especially the tragedy of indissoluble unions. To Hardy, 'a bad marriage is one of the direst things on earth, & one of the cruellest things',[83] and in the 1912 'Postscript' to the Preface of *Jude* he stated unequivocally that 'a marriage should be dissolvable as soon as it becomes a cruelty to either of the parties – being then essentially and morally no marriage'.[84] The marriage question had been very much in his mind in the 1890s, and in his autobiography he records a conversation in 1893 with Lady Londonderry, the Duchess of Manchester, and Lady Jeune, where 'four of us talked of the marriage-laws... also of the difficulties of separation, of terminable marriages where there are children, and of the nervous strain of living with a man when you know he can throw you over at any moment'.[85] Hardy was aware of the waywardness of the sexual instinct – hinted at, ironically, in the 1895 Preface to *The Woodlanders* and worked out more fully in *The Well-Beloved* – and he was appalled by the socio-religious system which imposed a permanent bond on what was essentially a transient physical attraction. Human nature tends to kick against compulsion, and he had offered a light-hearted solution to the problem in *Far From the Madding Crowd* where Bathsheba's father, troubled by his own roving eye, finds a novel remedy for his marital restlessness. He persuades his wife to take off her wedding ring and pretend that she is only his sweetheart and not his 'ticketed' wife: the pleasurable illusion that he is 'committing the seventh' subsequently keeps his fickle heart from wandering. That truth was even stranger than fiction was proved by a story related to Hardy by his friend Sir Francis Jeune, a judge in the Divorce Court, about a couple who 'being divorced they grew very fond of each other, the former wife becoming the husband's mistress, and living happily with him ever after'.[86]

But such fairy-tale endings were rare in real life, and the grim reality of marriage is recounted in Hardy's autobiography:

'Am told that — has turned upon her drunken husband at last, and knocks him down without ceremony. In the morning he holds out his trembling hand and says, "Give me a sixpence for a drop o'brandy – please do ye, my dear!"' This was a woman Hardy had known as a pretty laughing girl, who had been married for the little money she had.[87]

When a marriage reached such a stage, Hardy felt that some legal redsress ought to be available. As he told Florence Henniker in 1911, he had thought for many years 'that marriage should not thwart nature, & that when it does thwart nature it is no real marriage, & the legal contract should therefore be as speedily cancelled as possible. Half the misery of human life would I think disappear if this were made easy.'[88] Thus, Hardy seems to have been sympathetic to Lady Byron's situation in the breakdown of the Byron marriage;[89] however, in the case of Meredith's daughter, he felt that the couple's strained relations were 'her fault' and there seems to be an air of disapproval in his description of her taking 'a flat in London as a bachelor woman'.[90]

Although Hardy definitely hoped that the divorce laws would be made more easy and humane, he did not wish to undermine the institution of marriage altogether. In fact, he proclaimed himself quite 'offended' with Florence Henniker in 1896 for saying (probably in the context of *Jude*) that he was 'an advocate for "free love"'.[91] But Hardy must have modified his stance considerably because a decade later, in 1907, he wrote to Florence Henniker, commenting on the heroine of her novel *Our Fatal Shadows*:

> Of course *I* should not have kept her respectable, & made a nice, decorous, dull woman of her at the end, but shd [*sic*] have let her go to the d— for the man... But gentle F.H. [*sic*] naturally had not the heart to do that. The only thing I don't care much about is her marrying the Duke's son – whom she did not love; an action quite as immoral, from my point of view, & more so even, than running off with a married man whom she did love would have been. But convention rules still in these things of course.[92] (Hardy's italic)

If *The Woodlanders* had been composed in 1907 and not in 1887, would Grace Melbury have gone 'to the devil' for Giles Winterborne thus rendering his self-exile from his one-roomed hut (and consequent death) quite unnecessary? Would Jude have no occasion to accuse Sue of a mean save-your-own-soul-ism because she would be quite prepared to 'go to the devil' with Jude instead of returning to Christianity, Phillotson, and self-annihilation?

Furthermore, by his own professed moral standards (quoted above), Hardy stands self-convicted in *Two on a Tower*. The contemporary reviewers, including Mrs Oliphant, who found Lady Constantine's marriage of convenience to Bishop Helmsdale, whom she does *not* love, revoltingly immoral and indecent were perhaps not very wrong after all. But Hardy was incensed by the 'screaming' of Mrs Oliphant just as he was provoked by the screaming of another 'maiden lady' (regarding *Jude*), although he tried to laugh it out of court. Hardy's encounter with this female critic, Miss Jeannette Gilder, is described at length in his autobiography, and part of it is worth quoting as it crystallizes his mixed attitude to women. After (rather excessively) berating the 'immorality' and 'coarseness' of *Jude* in a review in the New York *World*, Miss Gilder had requested an interview with Hardy in order 'to get your side of the argument'. Hardy declined politely, but with thinly veiled 'sarcasm', which Miss Gilder failed to register because she wrote back thanking him for his 'goodness'. Hardy's comment on this episode is a mixture of self-congratulatory righteousness and a patronizing appreciation of women:

> Hardy must indeed have shown some magnanimity in condescending to answer the writer of a review containing such contumelious misrepresentations as hers had contained. But, as he said, *she was a woman,* after all – *one of the sex that makes up for lack of justice by excess of generosity* – and she had *screamed* so grotesquely loud in her article that Hardy's sense of the comicality of it had saved his feelings from being much hurt by the outrageous slurs. [93] (My italics)

The sequel to this story is even more interesting because when the 'unsuspecting' Hardy turned up at an evening party he noticed that while he conversed with the hostess, a 'strange lady' joined in – silent, but attentive. He later discovered that he had been outwitted, that Miss Gilder had indeed obtained her 'interview', as the silent lady was none other than his hostile reviewer who was a friend of his hostess and that the 'whole thing had been carefully schemed'. Hardy's sardonic comment on the whole episode was: 'But make the doors upon a woman's wit, and it will out at the casement.'

In the final analysis, it is extremely difficult to pin Hardy down as he himself was continually wary of any 'isms'. Although Hardy was capable of offering the suggestion – only half-jestingly – that since the British 'Constitution has worked so much better under queens than kings the Crown should by rights descend from woman to woman',[94] and although he recorded (with tacit admiration?) the story of a local girl who refused to adopt her husband's surname after marriage so that 'to the end of their lives the couple were spoken of as "Nanny P— and John C—" ',[95] he can startle modern readers by the morbid voyeurism of his description of the 1856 hanging of Martha Browne, recalled *seventy* years later: 'I remember what a fine figure she showed against the sky as she hung in the misty rain, & how the tight black silk gown set off her shape as she wheeled half-round & back.'[96] Thus, George Wotton is quite right in his assessment that although Hardy at times 'writes with great sympathy about the subjection of women, at others his comments appear to us now to display the typical male attitudes of his time which would certainly be called sex blind and perhaps sexist'.[97] The conflicting impressions left by Hardy's observations on women, in both his fictional and non-fictional writings, are perhaps best summed up in his own words as 'a confused heap of impressions, like those of a bewildered child at a conjuring show'.[98]

Hardy always insisted that his 'mood-dictated writing' recorded 'mere impressions that frequently change' and that he was 'only a mere impressionist'.[99] Art/literature was concerned with 'seemings only', with 'impressions, not convictions', and he repeatedly warned against trying to construct a philosophy/ ideology out of what were 'mere impressions of the moment'.[100] In the 1895 Preface to *Jude*, he spoke of 'a series of seemings, or personal impressions, the question of their consistency or their discordance, of their permanence or their transitoriness, being regarded as not of the first moment'; and in the 1911 'General Preface' to the Wessex Edition (1912) he reiterated that 'consistency' had never been his objective and that he was content with recording 'mere impressions of the moment, and not convictions or arguments'.[101] 'Unadjusted impressions have their value', he declared in the 1901 Preface to *Poems of the Past and the Present*, 'and the road to a true philosophy of life seems to lie in humbly recording diverse readings of its phenomena.' This is exactly what this book has attempted to do: to record Hardy's 'diverse readings' and conflicting observations on the nature of 'Woman' and his fluctuating and contradictory responses to women as revealed both in his fiction and in his real life.

These contradictory responses have shaped Hardy's presentation of his fictional women. Thus Viviette Constantine's noble transcendence of self-interest is portrayed with sympathy, but it is simultaneously undercut by the recurrent damaging allusions to the Fall and by the narrator's framing misogynic commentary. His other *femmes fatales* – Eustacia, Felice Charmond and Sue – are subject to the same ambivalence. While manuscript revisions suggest that Hardy ultimately took a sympathetic view of Mrs Charmond, in the case of Eustacia constant textual revisions reveal a gradual withdrawal of, if not authorial sympathy, at least authorial emotional commitment. He portrays Eustacia's rebellion with sympathetic understanding but somehow the rebellion itself seems trivialized by having as its object nothing worth striving for. In the case of Sue, who remains the inscrutable 'Other', the double perspective seems the result of the author/narrator being tugged in two opposite directions: he wishes to internalize Sue's experience and present it from the centre of her tortured consciousness, but he cannot resist silently aligning himself with Jude's male point of view and seeing her as a baffling spectacle from the outside, because despite Hardy's denials, Jude is a partial self-portrait. Of the heroines analysed in this study, only Ethelberta comes through victorious; but her success seems, at best, a Pyrrhic victory, because the price she pays is too high, and in any case Hardy deliberately chose to blind himself to the potential for tragic conflict in Ethelberta.[102] In the briefer compass of the short stories, his sympathy is less qualified and less complicated, and his protest on behalf of the victimized lives of Barbara and Sophy or the emotionally sterile and cramped lives of Ella and Edith is expressed in a more forthright fashion. However, if Hardy were asked to offer a theoretical exposition on the 'Woman Question', he would have declined, saying, 'I have troubled myself very little about theories.... I am content with tentativeness from day to day.'[103]

# Notes

## 1. Introduction: The Critics' Debate

1. Virginia Woolf, 'Women Novelists', *A Woman's Essays*, vol.1, ed. Rachel Bowlby (London: Penguin, 1992), p. 13.
2. R.G. Cox ed. *Thomas Hardy: The Critical Heritage* (New York: Barnes & Noble, 1970), p. 1. Subsequent references to this useful anthology will refer to it as Cox.
3. Ibid., p. 6.
4. Ibid., p. 14.
5. Graham Clarke ed. *Thomas Hardy: Critical Assessments* (East Sussex: Helm Information Ltd, 1993), vol.I, p. 72.
6. Cox, pp. 30-1.
7. Ibid., p. 33.
8. Ibid., p. 47.
9. Ibid., p. 58.
10. Ibid., p. 72.
11. Ibid., pp. 75-6.
12. Ibid., p. 95.
13. Ibid., p. 96.
14. Ibid., p. 221.
15. Ibid., pp. 258-60.
16. Ibid., pp. 268-9.
17. Samuel C. Chew, *Thomas Hardy: Poet and Novelist* (New York: Alfred Knopf, 1921; rpt. Russell & Russell, 1964), p. 133.
18. F. W. Knickerbocker, 'The Victorianness of Thomas Hardy', *The Sewanee Review*, 36: 3 (July 1928), p. 317.
19. T. P. O'Connor's 1928 article is reprinted as monograph no.54 in J. Stevens Cox ed. *Thomas Hardy: More Materials for a Study of His Life, Times and Works*, Vol.II (St Peter Port, Guernsey: Toucan Press, 1971), p. 234.
20. Quoted by W. L. Phelps in Cox, p. 402.
21. Cox, p. 180.
22. Ibid., pp. 62-3.
23. Ibid., pp. 105-6.
24. Ibid., p. 148.
25. Virginia Woolf, *The Common Reader*, Second Series (London: Hogarth Press, 1932), pp. 250-1.
26. 14th ed., Vol.XI, p. 192.
27. Henry Charles Duffin, *Thomas Hardy: A Study of the Wessex Novels, the Poems, and The Dynasts* (Manchester: Manchester Univ. Press, 1916; 3rd rev. ed., 1937), p. 238.
28. Albert J. Guerard, *Thomas Hardy: The Novels and Stories* (London: Geoffrey Cumberlege, 1949), p. 129.
29. Irving Howe, *Thomas Hardy* (London: Macmillan, 1967; rpt. 1985), p. 108. Subsequent page references to Howe are incorporated into the text.

30. Ian Gregor, *The Great Web: The Form of Hardy's Major Fiction* (London: Faber and Faber, 1974), p. 203.

31. Mary Jacobus, 'Tess's Purity', *Essays in Criticism*, 26: 4 (Oct 1976), p. 321. Subsequent page references to this article are incorporated into the text.

32. Mary Jacobus, 'Sue the Obscure', *Essays in Criticism*, 25: 3 (July 1975), p. 314. Subsequent page references to this article are incorporated into the text.

33. Elaine Showalter, 'The Unmanning of the Mayor of Casterbridge', in Dale Kramer ed. *Critical Approaches to the Fiction of Thomas Hardy* (London: Macmillan, 1979), p. 102. Subsequent page references to this essay are incorporated into the text.

34. Rosalind Miles, 'The Women of Wessex', in Anne Smith ed. *The Novels of Thomas Hardy* (London: Vision Press, 1979), p. 24. Subsequent page references to this essay are incorporated into the text.

35. Penny Boumelha, *Thomas Hardy and Women: Sexual Ideology and Narrative Form* (Sussex: Harvester Press, 1982), pp. 32-3. Subsequent page references to Boumelha are incorporated into the text.

36. Rosemarie Morgan, *Women and Sexuality in the Novels of Thomas Hardy* (London and New York: Routledge, 1988; rpt. 1991), p. 161. Subsequent page references to Morgan are incorporated into the text.

37. Maggie Humm, 'Gender and Narrative in Thomas Hardy', *The Thomas Hardy Year Book*, no.11 (1984), p. 43.

38. Desmond Hawkins, 'Thomas Hardy and the Ruined Maid', *The Hatcher Review*, 3: 29 (Spring 1990), pp. 421-2.

39. Martin Seymour-Smith, *Hardy* (London: Bloomsbury Publishing, 1994), p. 71.

40. Michael Millgate, *Thomas Hardy: A Biography* (Oxford: Oxford Univ. Press, 1982; Clarendon pbk, rev. ed. 1992), p. 356.

41. Hardy, *The Mayor of Casterbridge*, New Wessex Edition (London: Macmillan, 1975), p. 168.

42. Howe, *Thomas Hardy*, p. 84.

43. Frederick R. Karl, '*The Mayor of Casterbridge*: A New Fiction Defined', *Modern Fiction Studies*, 21: 3 (Autumn 1975), pp. 416, 427.

44. Katharine Rogers, 'Women in Thomas Hardy', *The Centennial Review*, 19: 4 (1975), p. 252. Subsequent page references to this essay are incorporated into the text.

45. Mary Childers, 'Thomas Hardy, The Man Who "Liked" Women', *Criticism*, 23: 4 (Fall 1981), pp. 329, 332. Subsequent page references to this article are incorporated into the text.

46. Patricia Stubbs, *Women and Fiction: Feminism and the Novel, 1880-1920* (Sussex: Harvester Press, 1979; rpt. London: Methuen, 1981), p. 59.

47. Judith Bryant Wittenberg, 'Thomas Hardy's First Novel: Women and the Quest for Autonomy', *Colby Library Quarterly*, 18: 1 (March 1982), p. 47. Subsequent page references to this article are incorporated into the text.

48. Janet Freeman, 'Ways of Looking at Tess', *Studies in Philology*, 79: 3 (Summer 1982), p. 323.

49. Kaja Silverman, 'History, Figuration and Female Subjectivity in *Tess of the d'Urbervilles*', *Novel*, 18: 1 (Fall 1984), p. 11.

50. George Wotton, *Thomas Hardy: Towards a Materialist Criticism* (Totowa, New Jersey: Barnes & Noble, 1985), pp. 172-3.

51. Marjorie Garson, *Hardy's Fables of Integrity: Woman, Body, Text* (Oxford: Clarendon Press, 1991), p. 3. Subsequent page references to Garson are incorporated into the text.

52. Howard Jacobson, *Peeping Tom* (London: Chatto & Windus, 1984; rpt. Penguin Books, 1993), pp. 76-7. Subsequent page references (Penguin paperback edn) are incorporated into the text.

53. Emma Tennant, *Tess* (London: HarperCollins, 1993; rpt. Flamingo paperback, 1994), p. 82. Subsequent page references (Flamingo pbk edn) are incorporated into the text.

54. Gertrude Bugler, a young and beautiful amateur actress, played the roles of Marty and Eustacia in dramatizations of Hardy's novels performed by the local 'Dorchester Debating and Dramatic Society' (later known as 'The Hardy Players'). But her most spectacular success was when she played Tess, and the octogenarian Hardy developed an infatuation for this flesh and blood incarnation of his beloved Tess. Gertrude was the daughter of a local dairymaid, Augusta Way, who is supposed to be one of the original inspirations behind the conception of Tess.

55. Peter Widdowson, *Hardy in History: A Study in Literary Sociology* (London and New York: Routledge, 1989), p. 216.

## 2. *The Hand of Ethelberta*

1. Hardy, *The Hand of Ethelberta*, New Wessex Edition (London: Macmillan, 1976), p. 242. All future references to the novel are to this 1976 (hardback) edition and page numbers are parenthetically incorporated into the text.

2. Perhaps this was a case of wish-fulfilment on Hardy's part because the title of Ethelberta's volume, in the serial version, was a naive *Metres by Me*. Among Hardy's earliest poems dating back to this period are the 'She, to Him' love poems where Hardy adopts the woman's point of view. Only four of these 1866 sonnets survived from a larger sequence and they were eventually published in *Wessex Poems* (1898).

   Interestingly, all the creative writers in Hardy's fiction are women. Apart from Ethelberta, there is the poetess Ella Marchmill in 'An Imaginative Woman' and Elfride in *A Pair of Blue Eyes*, who writes an Arthurian romance. Egbert Mayne, in *An Indiscretion in the Life of an Heiress*, is also a writer, but his line seems to be critical writing rather than creative.

3. That men have appropriated even language is a sore point with Bathsheba too. When Boldwood presses her to define the nature of

her feelings for him, she protests that it is 'difficult for a woman to define her feelings in language which is chiefly made by men to express theirs'.

4.   Guerard in *Thomas Hardy*, p. 109, calls attention to 'the masculinity of Ethelberta'. Richard H. Taylor also sees Ethelberta as 'a symbol of purposive masculinity' in *The Neglected Hardy: Thomas Hardy's Lesser Novels* (London: Macmillan, 1982), p. 65.
5.   Taylor, *Neglected Hardy*, p. 66.
6.   John Bayley, *An Essay on Hardy* (Cambridge: Cambridge Univ. Press, 1978), p. 151.
7.   Thomas Hardy, *The Life and Work of Thomas Hardy*, ed. Michael Millgate (London: Macmillan, 1984; rpt. 1989), p. 54. This disguised autobiography by Hardy will henceforth be referred to as *Life*.
8.   Ethelberta deserves the censure that Sir Walter Scott aimed at Elizabeth Bennet for falling in love with Darcy the moment she visits his impressive Pemberley estates.
9.   D. H. Lawrence, 'Study of Thomas Hardy', written in 1914 but published posthumously in 1936. See *Study of Thomas Hardy and Other Essays*, ed. Bruce Steele (Cambridge: Cambridge Univ. Press, 1985), p. 23.
10.  On one occasion when Christopher solemnly kisses Ethelberta by way of farewell, she gently draws Picotee forward and tells Christopher very simply: 'Kiss her, too. She is my sister' (p. 181). This scene perhaps anticipates that more famous one in *Tess* where, after her marriage, Tess generously tells Angel to kiss Marian, Izz and Retty in 'charity'.
11.  Michael Millgate, *Thomas Hardy: His Career as a Novelist* (London: Bodley Head, 1971; rpt. Macmillan, 1994), p. 112.
12.  Penny Boumelha, '"A Complicated Position for a Woman": *The Hand of Ethelberta*' in Margaret R. Higonnet ed. *The Sense of Sex: Feminist Perspectives on Hardy* (Urbana and Chicago: Univ. of Illinois Press, 1993), p. 252.
13.  In Hardy's first short story, 'Destiny and a Blue Cloak' (1874), he had used a similar plot device.
14.  Millgate, *Hardy: Career as a Novelist*, p. 110.
15.  Taylor, *Neglected Hardy*, p. 64.
16.  Hardy, *Tess* (London: Macmillan, 1975), p. 101.
17.  The parallel is not as outrageous as it may initially sound. After Ethelberta has tested her power over Lord Mountclere, she quotes from *Macbeth*: 'To be thus is nothing;/But to be safely thus.' (p. 248)
18.  Millgate, *Hardy: Career as a Novelist*, p. 110.
19.  W.H. Auden, *Collected Shorter Poems: 1927-1957* (London: Faber & Faber, 1966; rpt.1977), p. 147.
20.  Taylor, *Neglected Hardy*, p. 74.
21.  Richard Little Purdy and Michael Millgate eds *The Collected Letters of Thomas Hardy*, Vol.1, (Oxford: Clarendon Press, 1978), p. 190. This seven-volume work will henceforth be referred to as *CL*.
22.  *Life*, p. 224.
23.  *CL*, 7, p. 38.

**3. *The Return of the Native***

1.  *Life*, p. 122. However, for those who believe that Hardy's marriage to Emma was a disaster from the very beginning, there is no irony; rather, it is only natural that Hardy should write a novel focusing on marital disharmony.
2.  Peter J. Casagrande, *Unity in Hardy's Novels: 'Repetitive Symmetries'* (London: Macmillan, 1982), pp. 119, 126.
3.  Guerard, *Thomas Hardy*, p. 140.
4.  *CL*, 1, p. 53.
5.  Morgan, *Women and Sexuality*, p. 62.
6.  Leonard W. Deen, 'Heroism and Pathos in Hardy's *Return of the Native*', *Nineteenth-Century Fiction*, 15 : 3 (1960), p. 210.
7.  Many of Hardy's fictional women are orphans: Cytherea Graye, Bathsheba, Fanny, Paula, Viviette, Lucetta, Marty and (virtually) Sue.
8.  See Simon Gatrell ed. *'The Return of the Native': A Facsimile of the Manuscript with Related Materials* (New York and London: Garland Publishing, 1986). The facsimile of folio 28 of the MS (p. 37) clearly shows 'mother' corrected to 'aunt', and facsimiles of folios 64-5 (pp. 79-80) show 'father' corrected to 'grand-father'.
9.  Cox, p. 58.
10. Hardy, *The Return of the Native*, New Wessex Edition (London: Macmillan, 1975), p. 267. Future references are to this 1975 hardback edition and page numbers are parenthetically included in the text.
11. Eustacia's speech was originally more defiant and hubristic. 'I do not deserve my lot!' was initially, in the MS version, 'I am too good for my lot!', and her present modest 'I was capable of much' originally read 'I was capable of perfection'. See p. 427 of Gatrell's MS facsimile edition.
12. In his 1878 letter to Arthur Hopkins, Hardy stated:
    'The order of importance of the characters is as follows:
    1. Clym Yeobright
    2. Eustacia
    3. Thomasin & the reddleman
    4. Wildeve
    5. Mrs Yeobright.' *CL*, 1, p. 53.
13. Robert Evans, 'The Other Eustacia', *Novel*, 1 (1968), p. 251.
14. Richard Benvenuto, 'Another Look at the Other Eustacia', *Novel*, 4: 1 (1970), p. 77.
15. Writing to Hardy to offer his impressions of the MS of *The Return of the Native*, John Blackwood characterized the female protagonist as 'that she devil Avice'. See Gatrell's Facsimile edition, p.xi.
16. John Paterson, *The Making of 'The Return of the Native'* (Berkeley and Los Angeles: Univ. of California Press, 1960; rpt. 1963), pp. 29-30.
17. Gatrell, Facsimile edition, p.xvii. See also Simon Gatrell, *Hardy the Creator: A Textual Biography* (Oxford: Clarendon Press, 1988), p. 38. Here the last line reads: 'Never happy in her own', which is grammatically more consistent.

18. See R. E. C. Houghton, 'Hardy and Shakespeare', *Notes and Queries*, (Vol.206), New Series 8: 3 (1961), p. 98. The *Lear* parallel is strengthened by Hardy's addition of snakebite as contributing to Mrs Yeobright's death, apart from her weak heart, physical exhaustion and emotional stress. Surely this is meant to recall Lear's famous association of filial ingratitude with the venom of the 'serpent's tooth'.

19. Stubbs, *Women and Fiction*, pp. 72-3.

20. Paterson, *The Making of 'The Return'*, p. 134.

21. Stubbs, *Women and Fiction*, p. 73.

22. Paterson, *Making of 'The Return'*, pp. 113, 123. Strangely however, Eustacia's original defiant words to Wildeve – 'you may tempt me, but I won't encourage you any more' – were changed to a compromising 'but I won't give myself to you any more' in the 1895 edition; and this 1895 version remained unaltered in the 1912 edition.

23. Dixie Lee Larson, 'Eustacia Vye's Drowning: Defiance Versus Convention', *The Thomas Hardy Journal*, 9: 3 (1993), p. 62.

24. Gatrell, Facsimile edition, p. 221. This misogynic idea of women hampering men's plans and dragging them down will operate as a recurrent verbal motif in Hardy's next tragic novel *Two on a Tower*.

25. Casagrande, *Unity in Hardy's Novels*, p. 127.

26. Millgate, *Hardy: Career as a Novelist*, p. 125.

27. Millgate, *Hardy: A Biography*, p. 199.

28. *CL*, 4, p. 212.

29. Hardy underlined this Oedipal theme by a revision made in the 1895 edition. When Clym learns of Eustacia's role in his mother's rejection and death, the narrator says: 'his mouth had passed into the phase more or less imaginatively rendered in studies of Oedipus' (p. 328). Before 1895, the phrase had read: 'in studies of Laocoon'.

30. Garson, *Hardy's Fables of Integrity*, pp. 54-79.

31. In earlier versions, Wildeve decides 'to act honestly toward his gentle wife, and chivalrously toward another woman'. The qualifying word 'greater', with its consequent privileging of Eustacia over Thomasin, was a later 1895 afterthought. See Otis B. Wheeler, 'Four Versions of *The Return of the Native*', *Nineteenth-Century Fiction*, 14: 1 (1959), pp. 37-8.

32. D. H. Lawrence, *Study of Thomas Hardy*, p. 24.

33. Millgate, *Hardy: A Biography*, p. 200.

34. Paterson, *Making of 'The Return'*, pp. 15-16.

35. Ibid., p. 47.

36. Gatrell, *Hardy the Creator*, pp. 36-7.

**4. *Two on a Tower***

1. Hardy uses this phrase in *Two on a Tower*, New Wessex Edition, (London: Macmillan, 1976), p. 88. All subsequent references are to this hardback edition and page numbers are parenthetically included within the text.

2.    Cox, p. 100.
3.    Cox, p. 102.
4.    Apart from the picture of Samson and Delilah that hangs symbolically on the wall of the inn Jude and Arabella visit during their first courting, both Jude and Henchard (towards the end of their careers) are directly referred to as 'shorn' Samson.
5.    Strangely, Viviette too echoes the language of this negative gender stereotyping. When Swithin attempts to explain to Viviette his 'amazing discovery' in connection with 'variable stars', she responds with self-deprecating irony: ' I shall not understand your explanation, and I would rather not know it. I shall reveal it if it is very grand. Women, you know, are not safe depositaries of such valuable secrets' (pp. 85-6).
6.    The word 'ruin' echoes throughout the novel. Apart from the instances cited in the main text, other examples are Viviette's cry: 'O Swithin! Swithin!... I have *ruined* you! yes, I have *ruined* you!' (p. 225) and Swithin's realization that Viviette faces the cruel choice of 'repairing her own situation as a wife by *ruining* his as a legatee' (p. 235). In the next few pages of the main text, for the sake of added emphasis, all such negative words have been italicized.
7.    Hardy, *Jude* (London: Macmillan, 1975), p. 85 (my italics).
8.    In 1906, Hardy wrote to Millicent Fawcett that 'the father of a woman's child' is not 'anybody's business but the woman's own'. See *CL*, 3, p. 238. But whether Hardy held such radical views as early as 1882 is not known.
9.    This episode reminds us of Tess's encounter with the Biblical sign-painter and his half-painted seventh commandment on the wall. Again, ironically, it is while Jude and Sue are working on the relettering of the Ten Commandments that wagging tongues hound them out of home and employment. In 'Candour in English Fiction' (*New Review*, Jan 1890), Hardy stated that the 'crash of broken commandments' is necessary to tragedy.
10.   By contrast, Viviette *unwittingly* commits bigamy when she secretly marries Swithin, believing herself to be a widow.
11.   *Life*, p. 43.
12.   *Life*, pp. 104-5. In Florence Emily Hardy's version of this passage, *The Early Life of Thomas Hardy: 1840-1891* (London: Macmillan, 1928), p. 134, the long last sentence ('Thus though their eyes... upon her past') is missing. Florence Hardy probably felt that Hardy was being too indiscreet, but it is just such candid confessions that open up a whole new world of significance to the modern reader.
13.   We are reminded of the narrator's suggestion, at the end of *Far From the Madding Crowd*, that 'good-fellowship' or '*camaraderie*' is more permanent as a basis for love than 'evanescent' sexual passion.
14.   A similar 'poor man and the lady' motif is present in 'The Spectre of the Real', a story that Hardy co-authored with Florence Henniker. Here, Rosalys and Jim make a runaway marriage but they soon tire of each other and agree to a mutual separation. The narrator makes it clear that their love had been based on sexual attraction so that

when the novelty of 'sensuous' charms wears off, there is nothing
left to hold the pair together. This is emphatically *not* the case in the
Viviette–Swithin relationship.

15.    This interpretation (Bradley's) is just one among the many plausible
conjectures on the cause of Lear's death.

16.    Pearl R. Hochstadt, 'Hardy's Romantic Diptych: A Reading of *A Laodicean* and *Two on a Tower*', *English Literature in Transition, 1880-1920*,
26: 1 (1983), p. 29. Bishop Helmsdale's death may or may not be
causally related to the untimely birth of Viviette's child and his
doubts about its paternity. But in 'The Spectre of the Real', Lord
Parkhurst's suicide is in all probability caused by his discovery of his
wife Rosalys's past history. The narrative 'silence' leaves the reader
conjecturing whether Rosalys impulsively did a 'Tess'-act of
wedding-night confession.

17.    Rosemary Sumner, 'The Experimental and the Absurd in *Two on a
Tower*', in Norman Page ed. *Thomas Hardy Annual*, No. 1, (1982), p. 80.

18.    *CL*, 6, pp. 44-5.


## 5. *The Woodlanders*

1.    Cox, p. 142.
2.    Duffin, *Thomas Hardy*, pp. 232-3.
3.    Guerard, *Thomas Hardy*, p. 142.
4.    Millgate, *Hardy: Career as a Novelist*, p. 256.
5.    David Lodge, 'Introduction' to Hardy's *The Woodlanders*, New
Wessex Edition (London: Macmillan, 1975), p. 17. All subsequent
references to the novel are to this 1975 (hardback) edition and page
numbers are parenthetically included in the text.
6.    Stubbs, *Women and Fiction*, p. 86.
7.    Douglas Brown, 'Transience Intimated in Dramatic Forms', in R. P.
Draper ed. *Thomas Hardy: Three Pastoral Novels. A Casebook* (London:
Macmillan, 1987), p. 158.
8.    Apart from being forced to sell her hair, does Marty also sell her
father's body to Fitzpiers for his anatomical investigations? Fitzpiers
tempts Grammer Oliver to enter into a contract to sell her brain and
probably he uses his seductive arts on Marty too because in Chapter
18 Fitzpiers shows Grace a 'fragment' of old John South's brain' (p.
156) under the microscope. Grace's 'wonder as to how it should have
got there' is shared by the reader because this remains an unexplained mystery in the novel. Surprisingly, this incident has attracted little critical attention; and unless we are to add grave-digging to
Fitzpiers's other crimes, the only plausible explanation is that he
pressurized Marty into selling John South's brain.
9.    Robert Gittings, *The Older Hardy* (London: Heinemann Educational,
1978), pp. 45, 155-6.
10.   Merryn Williams, 'A Post-Darwinian Viewpoint of Nature', in
Draper ed. *Hardy: Three Pastoral Novels*, p. 173.
11.   Stubbs, *Women and Fiction*, p. 76.

12. Mary Jacobus, 'Tree and Machine: *The Woodlanders*', in Kramer ed. *Critical Approaches*, pp. 125-6.
13. The epigraph to *The Woodlanders* was composed by Hardy. See *CL*, 2, p. 85.
14. It is quite unnecessary to see lesbian implications in this scene. Rather, it is 'an instance of supportive female bonding' (Judith Wittenberg, 'Thomas Hardy's First Novel', *Colby Library Quarterly*, 18: 1 (1982), pp. 49-50). Interestingly, the conciliatory kiss does not feature in the MS of the novel; it was a later addition on the printer's copy for the 1912 Wessex Edition. See Dale Kramer ed. *The Woodlanders* (Oxford: Clarendon Press, 1981), p. 229n.
15. Hardy's novels offer a rich source of intertextuality. This interview between Mr Melbury and Mrs Charmond recalls the interview between Diggory and Eustacia, on a similar issue. Interestingly, although Melbury dogs Fitzpiers's steps almost as fanatically as Diggory stalks Wildeve, Melbury has been spared the charge of 'voyeurism' levelled by modern critics against Diggory.
16. Folio 333 of the MS of *The Woodlanders* in the 'Thomas Hardy Memorial Collection' at Dorset County Museum, Dorchester. I am grateful to the Curator of DCM, Mr Richard de Peyer, for granting me access to the MS.
17. Folio 357 of the MS of *The Woodlanders*.
18. Ibid., folio 359.
19. Boumelha, *Hardy and Women*, p. 108.
20. This phrase is not present either in the manuscript or the English first edition (1887). It appears in the 1896 Osgood McIlvaine edition.
21. Grace anticipates Tess as a victim of paternal social ambition and recalls Ethelberta in being suspended 'in mid-air between two storeys of society' (p. 235).
22. Quoted by Carl J. Weber, 'Hardy and *The Woodlanders*', *The Review of English Studies*, 15: 59 (1939), p. 332.
23. Cox, p. 154.
24. Gregor, *The Great Web*, p. 156.
25. According to Kramer, textual revisions 'suggest Hardy's continuing concern that Grace be recognized as a sexual being'. 'Grace's sexual interest in Fitzpiers is projected in all versions of the novel' and her 'reason for reaccepting Fitzpiers [is] sexual desire' (*Woodlanders*, 1981 Clarendon edition, pp. 45-6).
26. Grace's explicit '*Come to me, dearest!*' was added as late as 1912. For variant readings of Grace's appeal, in successive stages of the novel from MS to the 1912 Wessex Edition, see Kramer ed. *Woodlanders* (1981), p. 287n.

## 6. The Short Stories of the 1890s

1. George Wing, 'Tess and the Romantic Milkmaid', *A Review of English Literature*, 3: 1 (1962), pp. 22, 30.
2. *CL*, 1, p. 249.

3. Ibid., p. 245.
4. By Sept 1889 Hardy had completed half of *Tess* (then called 'Too Late Beloved') but after rejections from three magazines, he laid it aside to compose the 'Noble Dames' stories (Jan–May 1890) after which he resumed work on completing and bowdlerizing *Tess*.
5. *CL*, 7, pp. 117-18.
6. Sandra M. Gilbert and Susan Gubar, *The Madwoman in the Attic* (New Haven and London: Yale University Press, 1979; rpt. 1984), pp. 4, 6.
7. Hardy, *'Life's Little Ironies' and 'A Changed Man'*, New Wessex Edition (London: Macmillan, 1977), p. 12. Subsequent references to the stories in *Life's Little Ironies* (abbreviated as *LLI*) are to this (hardback) edition and page numbers are included in the text.
8. Hardy, 'The Tree of Knowledge', *The New Review*, X, no. 61 (June 1894), p. 681.
9. *CL*, 5, p. 283.
10. Hardy, *'Wessex Tales' and 'A Group of Noble Dames'*, New Wessex Edition (London: Macmillan, 1977), p. 253. Subsequent references to the stories in *A Group of Noble Dames* (abbreviated as *GND*) are to this (hardback) edition and page numbers are included in the text.
11. Hardy had himself written such proxy love-letters on behalf of the local illiterate maidens; see *Life*, p. 287.
12. This sentence was added in 1894 for the volume edition of *LLI*; it does not appear either in the manuscript or the serial version of 1891. In the magazine version, Edith is a widow and Anna's pregnancy is bowdlerized. Also, the sentence about marriage leaving Edith's 'deeper nature' unstirred was absent in the serial version.
13. The word 'ruin' reverberates throughout this story as in *Two on a Tower* (see Ch. 4). Edith is distressed at having indirectly pushed Charles into a 'marriage which meant his ruin' (p. 101); after discovering Anna's illiteracy when he is irrevocably married to her, Charles accuses Edith: 'You have deceived me – ruined me!' (p. 104). In her epistolary impersonation as Anna, Edith hopes that she is 'no *weight* upon him in his career, no *clog* upon him in his high activities' (p. 98; my italics).
14. Perhaps the only *male* creative writer in Hardy's fiction, Trewe is almost a self-portrait. Trewe's extreme sensitiveness to critical 'misrepresentation', his life-long pursuit of the 'unattainable' 'imaginary woman', the 'undiscoverable, elusive one' (like Pierston in *The Well-Beloved*), his shyness of strangers, are well-recorded aspects of Hardy's own personality. The narrator describes Trewe as 'a pessimist in so far as that character applies to a man who looks at the worst contingencies as well as the best in the human condition' (p. 15). This is surely Hardy of 'In Tenebris II' (dated '1895-96') where the poetic self is one 'Who holds that if way to the Better there be, it exacts a full look at the Worst'.
15. In his successive textual revisions of this story, contrary to his usual (reverse) practice in other novels and stories, Hardy toned down 'any words or scenes which might have indicated some kind of sexual or

passionate basis to Ella's obsession with Trewe'. See Martin Ray, '"An Imaginative Woman": From Manuscript to Wessex Edition', *The Thomas Hardy Journal*, 9: 3 (1993), pp. 76-83.

16. Hardy had earlier used music as a metaphor for compulsive sexual attraction, in *Desperate Remedies*, in the scene where Cytherea Graye is 'fascinated' and 'compelled' to sit 'spell-bound' in an atmosphere of 'unearthly weirdness' while Manston plays the organ.

17. From Hardy's subsequent textual revisions, a 'harsher and more critical portrait of Car'line progressively emerges', stressing her peevishness and her 'increasingly selfish' self-absorption. See Martin Ray, '" The Fiddler of the Reels": A Textual Study', *The Thomas Hardy Journal*, 9: 2 (1993), pp. 55-60.

18. Jude matures from his initial regret at 'the wilfulness of Nature in not allowing issue from one parent alone' to a fine scorn for biological parenthood (*Jude*, New Wessex Edition, 1975, pp. 195, 288).

19. *CL*, 3, p. 238.

20. *CL*, 4, p. 67.

21. Pertinent here is Launcelot Gobbo's witty comment: 'it is a wise father that knows his own child' (*The Merchant of Venice*, II. ii. 73-4).

22. Frances in 'Destiny and a Blue Cloak' (1874) and Rhoda in 'The Withered Arm' (1888) are other illustrations of the theme of female rivalry in love. Apart from Boldwood's crazed shooting of Troy, Hardyan examples of such treacherous *male* rivalry in love do not easily come to mind; however, as a counterbalance, there is the unselfish solidarity of Tess's dairymaid friends.

23. Hardy, *Woodlanders* , New Wessex Edition, 1975, p. 277.

24. This is yet another instance of the 'poor man and the Lady' motif recurrent throughout Hardy's fiction. Compare *An Indiscretion in the Life of an Heiress* (the bowdlerized survival of Hardy's original, unpublished novel 'The Poor Man and the Lady'), *Two on a Tower*, 'Barbara of the House of Grebe', 'The Waiting Supper' and 'The Spectre of the Real' which Hardy co-authored with Florence Henniker.

25. *CL*, 5, p. 196.

26. The use of the words 'victim' and 'pay' verbally link Leonora to Tess, who 'once victim' is 'always victim' and who is 'The Woman [who] Pays'.

27. *Life*, pp. 162-3.

28. Hardy, *Tess*, New Wessex Edition (1975), p. 107. Subsequent page references are to this edition and are incorporated into the text.

29. See Carl J. Weber, *Hardy of Wessex: His Life and Literary Career* (New York: Columbia University Press, 1940; rev. ed. 1965), p. 300.

30. T. S. Eliot, *After Strange Gods* (London: Faber & Faber, 1933), p. 58.

31. Rosemary Sumner, 'Hardy Ahead of His Time: "Barbara of the House of Grebe"', *Notes and Queries*, 225 (June 1980), pp. 230-1. Sumner elaborates this argument in *Thomas Hardy: Psychological Novelist* (London: Macmillan, 1981; rpt. 1986), pp. 23-8.

32. George Wing, '*A Group of Noble Dames*: "Statuesque Dynasties of Delightful Wessex"', in Norman Page ed. *Thomas Hardy Annual*, 5 (London: Macmillan, 1987), p. 82.

33. Ibid., p. 87.
34. The original proposed titles for 'On the Western Circuit' had been 'The Amanuensis' and 'The Writer of the Letters', both of which focus the tragic spotlight on Edith Harnham.


## 7. *Jude the Obscure*

1. *Life*, p. 216.
2. Joshua's motives appear suspect as he seems impelled more by 'pride of place' than by the pure desire for knowledge. Towards the end, both brothers become so warped by their desire for upward social mobility that they become guilty of parricide as they fail to respond to the cries of their drowning father – a sin of omission that recalls Gwendolen's frozen immobility when her husband Grandcourt is drowning, in George Eliot's *Daniel Deronda* (1876).
3. *CL*, 2, p. 93.
4. Hardy, *Jude the Obscure*, New Wessex Edition (London: Macmillan, 1975), p. 30. Subsequent references to the novel are to this (hardback) edition and page numbers are included in the main text.
5. John Paterson, 'The Genesis of *Jude the Obscure*', *Studies in Philology*, 57: 1 (1960), p. 98.
6. Patricia Ingham, 'The Evolution of *Jude the Obscure*', *The Review of English Studies*, 27 (1976), no. 106, pp. 159, 162.
7. Ibid., pp. 162, 161. With Phillotson absent from the original conception of the novel, the character inter-relationships in *Jude* resolve themselves into the familiar triangular pattern with an important gender reversal. Thus, D. H. Lawrence's comment that 'Jude is only Tess turned round about' is quite valid (*Study of Thomas Hardy*, p. 101).
8. Original version of this passage in *Jude*, as quoted by Ingham in 'The Evolution of *Jude*', *RES*, p. 166.
9. See R. L. Purdy, *Thomas Hardy: A Bibliographical Study* (London: Geoffrey Cumberlege and OUP, 1954), p. 87.
10. Hardy typically complicates the issue by stating in his 1895 'Preface' to *Jude* that the 'present and final title, deemed on the whole the best, was one of the earliest thought of' (p. 27).
11. See Millgate, *Hardy: Career as a Novelist*, p. 312.
12. *CL*, 2, p. 84.
13. Robert B. Heilman, 'Hardy's Sue Bridehead', *Nineteenth-Century Fiction*, 20: 4 (1966), p. 307.
14. *CL*, 2, p. 98.
15. Boumelha, *Hardy and Women*, p. 132.
16. John Goode, 'Sue Bridehead and the New Woman', in Mary Jacobus ed. *Women Writing and Writing About Women* (London: Croom Helm, 1979), p. 103.
17. *CL*, 2, p. 99.
18. Elaine Showalter, *The Female Malady: Women, Madness and English Culture, 1830-1980* (New York: Pantheon Books, 1985; rpt. London: Virago Press, 1987), p. 273.

19. *CL*, 2, p. 99.
20. Heilman, 'Hardy's Sue Bridehead', *NCF*, pp. 311, 313.
21. Ibid., p. 318.
22. Terry Eagleton, 'Introduction' to *Jude*, New Wessex Edition (1975), p. 19.
23. Jacobus, 'Sue the Obscure', *Essays in Criticism*, 25: 3 (1975) pp. 320-1.
24. Elizabeth Langland, 'A Perspective of One's Own: Thomas Hardy and the Elusive Sue Bridehead', *Studies in the Novel*, 12: 1 (1980), pp. 19, 22.
25. Morgan, *Women and Sexuality*, pp. 138, 154.
26. Anne B. Simpson, 'Sue Bridehead Revisited', *Victorian Literature and Culture*, 19 (1991), p. 55.
27. This is a variant of the 'what's-done-can't-be-undone' motif that runs through *Tess* and Hardy's short stories of the 1890s.
28. *CL*, 2, p. 93.
29. Ibid., p. 94.
30. John Lucas is surely forgetting all these marginal women in the novel when he asserts that 'we would need more in the way of women than the novel actually gives us' before we can decide whether Sue is a 'representative woman' or simply a 'pathological case'. See Lucas, *The Literature of Change: Studies in the Nineteenth Century Provincial Novel* (Sussex: Harvester Press, 1977; rev. ed. 1980), pp. 189-90.
31. In both these 'straw hat' passages (pp. 42 & 55), the boy Jude is lying down with his face covered by the hat and the sun's rays peering at him through the 'interstices' of the straw plaiting. Despite Hardy's persistent denials of any autobiographical element in *Jude*, the parallels with a passage in his autobiography are striking: 'He was lying on his back in the sun, thinking how useless he was, and covered his face with his straw hat. The sun's rays streamed through the interstices of the straw, the lining having disappeared. Reflecting on his experiences of the world so far as he had got he came to the conclusion that he did not wish to grow up.' Hardy was then about 8 years old. See *Life*, p. 20.
32. Eagleton, 'Introduction' to *Jude* (New Wessex Edition), p. 23.
33. In 1890, Hardy read Weismann's *Essays on Heredity*; see *Life*, p. 240.
34. Boumelha, *Hardy and Women*, p. 153.
35. *Life*, p. 448. Hardy's comment was, however, made in a different context: to explain his oversensitivity to adverse criticism.
36. Edmund Gosse, 'Mr Hardy's New Novel', *St James's Gazette*, 8 November 1895, p. 4.
37. Kate Millett, *Sexual Politics* (New York: Doubleday, 1970; London: Rupert Hart-Davis, 1971), pp. 130, 133.
38. Jude conceptualizes life as a 'constant internal warfare between flesh and spirit' (p. 210); at one point he calls Sue his 'good angel' (p. 204); later he appeals to Sue, his 'guardian-angel', not to desert him (p. 361).
39. See Phillip Mallett, 'Sexual Ideology and Narrative Form in *Jude the Obscure*', *English*, 38: 162 (1989), pp. 211-24.
40. *CL*, 2, p. 99.

41. Cedric Watts, *Thomas Hardy: 'Jude the Obscure'*, 'Penguin Critical Studies' (London: Penguin Books, 1992), p. 51.
42. *CL*, 2, p. 195; Hardy's parenthesis.
43. Ibid., p. 200; Hardy's parentheses. Although it would require some critical ingenuity to make Molly or Arabella into a seduced and betrayed rustic girl like Tess, Hardy's point about Hetty is valid. Hardy is here more concerned with class inequality rather than with gender injustice; but Hetty – as the woman who pays – is the locus where the politics of class and the politics of gender intersect. Despite living an unconventional life herself, George Eliot seems to have accepted the most sexist of the literary conventions of the day: the 'fallen woman' *must* die and thus expiate her guilt. Thus, at the end of *Adam Bede*, while Arthur is charitably reinstated within the community, Hetty conveniently dies while sailing back to England. Ironically, the charge that Hardy formulated against Fielding and George Eliot was levelled against Hardy too by D. H. Lawrence, who felt that Arabella's 'coarseness seems to me exaggerated to make the moralist's case good against her' (*Study of Thomas Hardy*, p. 106).
44. Watts, *Jude*, 'Penguin Critical Studies', p. 84.
45. The two divorces are obtained under false pretences; see William A. Davis, Jr., 'Hardy, Sir Francis Jeune and Divorce by "False Pretences" in *Jude the Obscure'*, *The Thomas Hardy Journal*, 9: 1 (1993), pp. 62-74.
46. *CL*, 7, p. 41. Interestingly, Sue does *not* feature in the list of possible 'villains', the other two alternatives being 'Jude's personal constitution' and 'blind Chance'.
47. Garson, *Hardy's Fables of Integrity*, pp. 161-2.
48. Stubbs, *Women and Fiction*, p. 81.
49. Katharine Rogers, 'Women in Thomas Hardy', *Centennial Review*, 19: 4 (1975) p. 251.
50. Cox, p. 260.
51. Bram Stoker, *Dracula*, Everyman Paperbacks, (London: J. M. Dent, 1993; rpt. 1995), p. 88. Interestingly enough, in *A Laodicean*, Paula literally runs after Somerset across almost half the Continent and, meeting him by his sick-bed, she makes almost a direct proposal.
52. *CL*, 2, p. 93.
53. Katharine Rogers, 'Women in Thomas Hardy', *Centennial Review*, p. 254.
54. Showalter, *The Female Malady*, p. 137.
55. Gail Cunningham, *The New Woman and the Victorian Novel* (New York: Harper & Row; London: Macmillan, 1978), p. 106.
56. Cedric Watts, 'Hardy's Sue Bridehead and the "New Woman" ', *Critical Survey*, 5: 2 (1993), p. 155. Watts points out the irony that while female writers allowed their heroines to break down, it was the 'male playwrights' – Ibsen and Shaw – who showed revolts successfully carried out.
57. Boumelha, *Hardy and Women*, p. 148.
58. John Goode, 'Sue Bridehead and the New Woman', Mary Jacobus ed. *Women Writing*, p. 104.

59. This novel, under the title *The Pursuit of the Well-Beloved*, was published serially in Oct. to Dec. 1892. For the book version, it underwent a thorough rewriting with changes so substantial that some critics accord equal status to both texts, treating the work not as one story with alternative endings but as alternative texts with an either/or structure.

60. Robert C. Slack, 'The Text of Hardy's *Jude the Obscure*', *Nineteenth-Century Fiction*, 11: 4 (1957), p. 272.

61. Hardy, *Jude the Obscure*, The Wessex Novels, Vol. VIII (London: Osgood, McIlvaine & Co., 1896), p. 42.

## 8. Hardy, his Wives, and his Literary Protégées

1. Hardy's copy of Brennecke's book is now in Dorset County Museum and I am grateful to the Curator, Mr Richard de Peyer, for allowing me to consult it.

2. *CL*, 6, p. 151.

3. Tennant, *Tess*, p. 127.

4. Emma Hardy, *Some Recollections* eds Evelyn Hardy and Robert Gittings (London: Oxford Univ. Press, 1961), p. 55. Subsequent page references are to this edition, unless otherwise specified.

5. *Life*, p. 89.

6. *Some Recollections*, p. 60. This is confirmed by Hardy's autobiography; see *Life*, p. 85.

7. *Life*, p. 150.

8. See Purdy, *Hardy: A Bibliographical Study*, p. 38 and Millgate, *Hardy: A Biography*, p. 395n.

9. Alan Manford, 'Who Wrote Thomas Hardy's Novels? (A Survey of Emma Hardy's Contribution to the Manuscripts of Her Husband's Novels)', *The Thomas Hardy Journal*, 6: 2 (1990), p. 92. See also Alan Manford, 'Emma Hardy's Helping Hand', in Dale Kramer and Nancy Marck eds *Critical Essays on Thomas Hardy: The Novels* (Boston, Massachusetts: G. K. Hall & Co., 1990), pp. 100-21.

10. Gatrell, *Hardy the Creator*, p. 48.

11. Simon Gatrell ed. *'Tess of the d'Urbervilles': A Facsimile of the Manuscript with Related Materials*, 2 vols (New York and London: Garland Publishing, 1986), vol.1, p.xi.

12. Michael Millgate ed. *Letters of Emma and Florence Hardy* (Oxford: Clarendon Press, 1996), p. 217.

13. Ibid., pp. 175-6.

14. Lennart A. Björk, *The Literary Notebooks of Thomas Hardy* (London: Macmillan, 1985), vol. i, p.xxxviii.

15. *Some Recollections*, p. 60.

16. *Life*, p. 250.

17. F. E. Hardy, *Early Life*, p. 313.

18. Raymond Blathwayt, 'A Chat with the Author of "Tess"', *Black and White*, 4 (27 Aug. 1892), p. 239.

19. Elfride's words to Knight – 'I suppose I must take you as I do the Bible – find out and understand all I can; and on the strength of that, swallow the rest in a lump, by simple faith' (ch. 19) – clearly echo Emma's words to Hardy: 'I take him (the reserved man) as I do the Bible; find out what I can, compare one text with another, & believe the rest in a lump of simple faith.' These lines from Emma Gifford's Oct 1870 letter were copied by Hardy into his 'Memoranda I' notebook; see Richard H. Taylor ed. *The Personal Notebooks of Thomas Hardy* (London: Macmillan, 1978), p. 6.
20. *Life*, p. 72.
21. Jacobson, *Peeping Tom*, p. 180.
22. *Life*, p. 74.
23. *Some Recollections*, p. 59. The MS of *Some Recollections*, now in Dorset County Museum, bears ample evidence of revisions in Hardy's hand. I am grateful to Mr de Peyer for granting me access to this MS.
24. See Purdy, *Hardy: Bibliographical Study*, p. 230n. See also *CL*, 6, p. 281n.
25. Thomas Hardy, *The Excluded and Collaborative Stories* ed. Pamela Dalziel (Oxford: Clarendon Press, 1992), pp. 332-47. While Dalziel sees it as a 'collaborative' work, Purdy includes 'Blue Jimmy' among Hardy's 'Uncollected Contributions'; see *Hardy: Bibliographical Study*, p. 314.
26. The typescript, prepared by Florence Dugdale, is now in DCM and I am grateful to Mr de Peyer for granting me access to it. Examples of Hardy's revisions include: 'motive' revised to 'motto', on p. 85; correction of 'great nephew' and 'Uncle' to 'grandson' and 'Grandfather' respectively, on p. 76.
27. This poem could well be Emma's reply to Hardy's own poem 'The Ivy-Wife' which Emma seems to have taken personally.
28. *Letters of Emma and Florence Hardy*, p. 50.
29. Ibid., p. 40 (Emma Hardy's italic); see also p. 38. Here Emma seems to anticipate the argument of Elaine Showalter's essay, 'The Unmanning of the Mayor of Casterbridge'.
30. *Letters of Emma and Florence Hardy*, p. 6.
31. Ibid., pp. 62-4.
32. Ibid., pp. 61-2.
33. *Life*, p. 392.
34. *CL*, 3, p. 261.
35. Ibid., pp. 261-2.
36. Ibid., p. 274. Hardy's letter contains an interesting postscript – 'My services to Lady Grove are really too small to be worth naming' – which suggests that Reginald Smith had guessed both the extent of Hardy's hidden contributions to the work of Agnes Grove and Florence Dugdale and also that Florence had replaced Agnes as Hardy's current favourite literary pupil.
37. *CL*, 7, p. 147.
38. *CL*, 4, p. 117.
39. Ibid., p. 45.
40. Ibid., p. 114.

41. Ibid., p. 13.
42. Purdy, *Hardy: Bibliographical Study*, pp. 314, 316, 317.
43. MSS in Hardy's hand for 'The Yellow-Hammer' and 'The Lizard' are now in the Purdy Collection in the Beinecke Library at Yale University. The ascription of 'The Calf' rests upon oral evidence, i.e. Purdy's being told by Florence Hardy's sister, Mrs Ethel Richardson, that she was 'sure' Florence had said that Hardy was its author. I am grateful to Professor Michael Millgate for providing me with this information.
44. *CL*, 4, p. 98.
45. *Letters of Emma and Florence Hardy*, p. 60; Florence Dugdale's italic.
46. *CL*, 6, pp. 138-9.
47. Ibid., pp. 144-6.
48. Ibid., p. 153; see also pp. 154-7.
49. Ibid., p. 269.
50. *CL*, 5, p. 275.
51. Ibid., p. 294; see also *Letters of Emma and Florence Hardy*, p. 155.
52. See *CL*, 5, pp. 346-7 and n.
53. *Letters of Emma and Florence Hardy*, p. 95. Before her marriage, as Florence Dugdale, she had collaborated with Detmold in three books: *The Book of Baby Beasts* (1911), *The Book of Baby Birds* (1912), and *The Book of Baby Pets* (1913). However, there is some controversy regarding the date of publication of *Baby Pets*. Traditionally, it has been assigned the date 1915, e.g. by Purdy, and this is the date given in the *British Museum General Catalogue of Printed Books* (1960). Pamela Dalziel, however, has pointed out that 'the Bodleian Library acquisition stamp is dated "14. 5. 1914" and the catalogue gives 1913 as the year of publication'. See Dalziel ed. *Excluded and Collaborative Stories*, p. 345n. In 1915, of course, Florence Dugdale would be Florence Hardy.
54. *Letters of Emma and Florence Hardy*, p. 99.
55. Quoted by Marguerite Roberts, *Florence Hardy and The Max Gate Circle*, *Thomas Hardy Year Book*, no.9 (Guernsey: Toucan Press, 1980), p. 36; this letter is not included in Millgate's edition of Florence Hardy's letters.
56. *CL*, 5, p. 215.
57. Ibid., p. 13 and p. 283 (Hardy's parenthesis).
58. Quoted in Robert Gittings and Jo Manton, *The Second Mrs Hardy* (London: Heinemann Educational, 1979), p. 90; this letter is not included in Millgate's edition. Florence Hardy's article, 'No Superfluous Women', did however appear in *Weekly Dispatch* as late as Sept 1922.
59. *CL*, 2, p. 38.
60. *Life*, p. 270; Hardy's italic.
61. *CL*, 2, pp. 14 & 26.
62. See Lennart A. Björk ed. *The Literary Notebooks of Thomas Hardy*, vol. ii, (London: Macmillan, 1985), pp. 57-60. The first poem with its regret – 'Oh! had I but wept that day!' – dated June 1893, could well have inspired Hardy's moving poem 'Had You Wept'.

63. See *CL*, 2, pp. 30, 36, 38.
64. Ibid., p. 40. The two subsequent quotations are from this same letter.
65. Quoted in Dalziel, *Excluded and Collaborative Stories*, pp. 285, 287.
66. *CL*, 2, p. 137.
67. *CL*, 7, p. 127.
68. *CL*, 2, pp. 71-2.
69. Taylor ed. *Personal Notebooks*, p. 69; *Life*, p. 452.
70. The MSS of Mrs Henniker's letter of appeal (23 May 1915) and her letter of thanks (28 May 1915) are now in DCM and I am grateful to Mr de Peyer for allowing me access to them. For Hardy's response (25 May 1915) see *CL*, 5, p. 99.
71. *CL*, 2, pp. 17 & 40 (Hardy's parenthesis). It was Hardy's recommended 'profile' photograph which served as frontispiece to *Outlines* (1894).
72. *CL*, 2, p. 39 ; see also p. 41.
73. Ibid., p. 37. Perhaps in a spirit of competition, Emma Hardy also independently appointed A. P. Watt as her literary agent but he does not seem to have had any success in placing her stories.
74. See Evelyn Hardy and F. B. Pinion eds *One Rare Fair Woman: Thomas Hardy's Letters to Florence Henniker 1893-1922* (London: Macmillan, 1972), pp. 209-10.
75. *CL*, 2, p. 29.
76. Ibid., p. 37. When the story was published in *Outlines*, its title was changed to 'A Sustained Illusion', perhaps based on Hardy's suggestion for changing the ending of the story.
77. *CL*, 2, p. 44. Mrs Henniker seems to have heeded Hardy's advice to avoid 'Gawd'; she used 'Gor-d' instead.
78. Ibid., p. 13.
79. Ibid., p. 245.
80. Ibid., pp. 252, 264.
81. Ibid., p. 140; pp. 197, 205.
82. Ibid., p. 84.
83. *Life*, p. 286.
84. *CL*, 2, p. 87.
85. *CL*, 3, p. 269.
86. Desmond Hawkins ed. *The Grove Diaries: The Rise and Fall of an English Family 1809-1925* (Wimborne: The Dovecote Press; New Jersey: The University of Delaware Press, 1995), p. 310.
87. *CL*, 4, p. 111.
88. Ibid., p. 246.
89. *Letters of Emma and Florence Hardy*, pp. 31-2.
90. Ibid., p. 36.
91. *CL*, 2, p. 91.
92. Ibid., p. 92.
93. Ibid., p. 95; see also p. 96.
94. Ibid., p. 101.
95. *CL*, 2, p. 44; *Jude*, New Wessex Edition (1975), p. 204.
96. *CL*, 2, p. 94.
97. Ibid., p. 91.
98. Ibid., p. 114.

99.   Ibid., p. 115.
100.  Ibid., p. 116.
101.  Ibid., p. 116.
102.  Ibid., p. 117.
103.  Hawkins ed. *Grove Diaries*, p. 314.
104.  *CL*, 2, p. 124.
105.  Ibid., p. 137.
106.  Ibid., p. 142.
107.  Ibid., pp. 189 & 190.
108.  Ibid., p. 196.
109.  Ibid., p. 226.
110.  Ibid., p. 247.
111.  Ibid., p. 251.
112.  Ibid., p. 253.
113.  *CL*, 3, pp. 108-9.
114.  Ibid., p. 266.
115.  Ibid., p. 269; see also p. 268. The wording of Agnes Grove's dedication seems to have faithfully followed Hardy's suggestions.
116.  Ibid., p. 271; see also p. 272.
117.  Ibid., p. 284.
118.  *CL*, 4, p. 82.
119.  Ibid., p. 89.
120.  *CL*, 3, p. 268.
121.  Ibid., p. 354; Hardy's parenthesis.
122.  *CL*, 4, p. 244.
123.  See *Letters of Emma and Florence Hardy*, p. 17.
124.  *CL*, 2, p. 157.
125.  Ibid., p. 148; see also *Letters of Emma and Florence Hardy*, p. 10.
126.  MSS of Florence Henniker's letters to Hardy are now in DCM and I am grateful to Mr de Peyer for granting me access to them.

### 9. Hardy and Some Contemporary Female Writers

1.   Quoted in Vera Buchanan-Gould, *Not Without Honour: The Life and Writings of Olive Schreiner* (London: Hutchinson & Co., 1949), p. 69.
2.   J. Stevens Cox ed. *The Library of Thomas Hardy, O.M.*, Toucan Press Monographs, no.52 (1969), p. 201, collected in *Thomas Hardy: More Materials for a Study of His Life, Times and Works*, Vol.II.
3.   S. C. Cronwright-Schreiner ed. *The Letters of Olive Schreiner 1876-1920* (London: T. Fisher Unwin Ltd, 1924; rpt. 1976), p. 14; editor's parentheses.
4.   Olive Schreiner, *The Story of an African Farm* (Oxford: Oxford University Press, 1992), pp. 151-2. Subsequent references are to this paperback edition and page numbers are parenthetically incorporated into the text.
5.   Hardy, *Jude*, New Wessex Edition, pp. 151-2. Subsequent page references, parenthetically included in the text, are to this hardback edition.

6. Quoted in Millgate, *Hardy: A Biography*, p. 351.
7. *CL*, 7, p. 38.
8. *CL*, 2, p. 47.
9. Ibid., p. 52; Hardy's parenthesis.
10. Quoted in Janet B. Wright, 'Hardy and his Contemporaries: The Literary Context of *Jude the Obscure*', *Inscape*, 14 (1980), p. 145.
11. *CL*, 2, p. 102.
12. Ibid., p. 102 and n.
13. *Literary Notebooks*, 2, pp. 60-1; Hardy's emphasis.
14. George Egerton, *Keynotes* (London: Elkin Mathews & John Lane, The Bodley Head, 1893), p. 22. I am grateful to William Hemmig, of the Beinecke Library, for sending me a copyflo of Hardy's annotated copy of *Keynotes*. I would also like to thank Vincent Giroud, Curator of Modern Books and Manuscripts, Beinecke Rare Book and Manuscript Library, Yale University, for granting me formal permission to quote Hardy's marginal comments in this copy of *Keynotes*. Subsequent page references to the stories in *Keynotes* are to this 1893 edition and are parenthetically incorporated into the text.
15. *'Life's Little Ironies'*, New Wessex Edition (1977), p. 97.
16. I am grateful to Mr Richard de Peyer for sending me photocopies of the galley proofs which are now at DCM.
17. However, this marginal comment may not be Hardy's.
18. *CL*, 6, pp. 153-7. The following quotations in the main text are from the same source.
19. *Life*, p. 100.
20. Ibid., p. 100 and p. 268; Hardy's parenthesis.
21. *Literary Notebooks*, 1, p. 152; Hardy's emphasis and ellipsis.
22. *Literary Notebooks*, 2, p. 208.
23. This phrase comes from Hardy's rival, George Moore's *Confessions of a Young Man*, (1917 rev. ed.). But the idea behind it had plagued Hardy all his life. Hardy's consolation lay in the fact that George Eliot had 'borrowed' the term 'Wessex' – which Hardy had first used in *Far From the Madding Crowd* (1874) – in *Daniel Deronda* (1876).
24. *CL*, 2, p. 299.
25. *CL*, 7, p. 111.
26. Harold Orel ed. *Thomas Hardy's Personal Writings: Prefaces, Literary Opinions, Reminiscences* (London & Melbourne: Macmillan, 1967), pp. 127, 129.
27. Eliza Lynn Linton, 'Candour in English Fiction', *New Review* (Jan 1890), pp. 10-14.
28. Quoted in George Somes Layard, *Mrs Lynn Linton: Her Life, Letters, and Opinions* (London: Methuen & Co., 1901), p. 277; all the italics and parenthesis are Linton's. Linton began writing her literary reminiscences late in life. Her incomplete *My Literary Life*, posthumously published in 1899, contains interesting (if sometimes negative) portraits of G. H. Lewes, Landor, Dickens, Thackeray, and George Eliot; but there is no reference to Hardy.
29. *Life*, p. 135.

30. However, Simon Gatrell challenges this general assumption and says that when *The Return of the Native* was offered to *Belgravia* it was no longer edited and owned by Miss Braddon and her husband John Maxwell (*'The Return of the Native': A Facsimile*, p.xix).

31. *Literary Notebooks*, 1, p. 92.

32. *CL*, 1, p. 133.

33. Ibid., p. 107. The full text of Mrs Oliphant's July 1882 letter to Hardy is quoted in John Stock Clarke, 'The "Rival Novelist" – Hardy and Mrs Oliphant', *The Thomas Hardy Journal*, 5: 3 (1989), p. 57.

34. See Cox, p. 203.

35. *Life*, p. 287; *CL*, 2, p. 105.

36. *CL*, 2, p. 106.

37. *Life*, p. 295. The veracity of this episode is questioned by John Stock Clarke in his *THJ* (1989) article, p. 60.

38. Cox, p. 259.

39. See Robert C. Slack, 'The Text of Hardy's *Jude the Obscure*', *NCF*, pp. 266-7.

40. *Life*, p. 258.

41. *CL*, 2, pp. 93-4.

42. Pearl Craigie's letter to Hardy, dated 19 Nov 1895, is now in DCM and I am grateful to Mr de Peyer for granting me access to this letter.

43. John Morgan Richards, *The Life of John Oliver Hobbes Told in Her Correspondence with Numerous Friends* (London: John Murray, 1911), p. 141.

44. *CL*, 2, p. 10.

45. *Life*, p. 272.

46. *CL*, 3, pp. 221, 239.

47. *CL*, 2, p. 185.

48. *Life*, p. 276.

49. *CL*, 2, p. 217.

50. *Literary Notebooks*, 2, p. 96; Hardy's emphasis.

51. Ibid., p. 117.

52. *Life*, p. 183.

53. William Archer, *Real Conversations* (London: William Heinemann, 1904), pp. 51-69.

54. *CL*, 3, p. 104.

55. *CL*, 4, p. 151.

56. *Life*, p. 357; Hardy's ellipsis.

57. Ibid., p. 368; Hardy's parenthesis.

58. *Real Conversations*, pp. 216-34.

59. *Life*, p. 258.

60. *CL*, 7, pp. 119-20.

61. Ibid., p. 120.

62. *CL*, 1, p. 264.

63. *The Library of Thomas Hardy*, Toucan Press Monograph no.52, p. 202.

64. *Literary Notebooks*, 2, p. 57; Hardy's ellipses and parenthesis.

65. *CL*, 2, p. 12.

66. Ibid., p. 18.

67. Ibid., p. 33.

68.  *Literary Notebooks*, 1, pp. 211-13. The four subsequent quotations are taken from the same source.
69.  Gittings, *Older Hardy*, p. 113.
70.  *Life*, p. 187.
71.  *CL*, 1, p. 263; *CL*, 3, pp. 233-4.
72.  *CL*, 3, p. 163. The three following quotations in this paragraph are taken from this same letter.
73.  *CL*, 4, p. 320.
74.  Mrs Humphry Ward, *A Writer's Recollection* (London: W. Collins Sons & Co., 1918), p. 359. The three subsequent quotations are from the same page in the same source.
75.  See *Letters of Emma and Florence Hardy*, p. 153.
76.  *CL*, 6, p. 12.
77.  *CL*, 1, pp. 192 & 193n.
78.  Michael Millgate, 'Thomas Hardy and Rosamund Tomson', *Notes and Queries*, 20: 7 (1973), p. 253.
79.  *CL*, 1, p. 199.
80.  Ibid., p. 201; Hardy's parenthesis.
81.  Ibid., p. 202.
82.  Ibid., pp. 206, 209.
83.  *CL*, 2, p. 24. Since twelve poems in *Ballades and Rondeaus* were by 'Graham R. Tomson', Purdy and Millgate identify the lady alluded to as Rosamund Tomson. Gittings however suggests that the lady 'may equally have been another woman poet he knew about this time, Agnes Mary Francis Robinson, who wrote verse in much the same style, and appeared in the same anthology as Rosamund Tomson' (*Older Hardy*, p. 65).
84.  Quoted in Millgate, 'Thomas Hardy and Rosamund Tomson', p. 254.
85.  *CL*, 2, p. 66.
86.  Hardy's annotated copy of *The Poems* of Rosamund Marriott Watson, now in DCM. I am grateful to Mr de Peyer for allowing me to consult this volume.
87.  Nigel Nicolson ed. *The Letters of Virginia Woolf*, Vol.2, (London: The Hogarth Press, 1976), p. 58. The two subsequent quotations are taken from this same letter.
88.  *CL*, 5, p. 76.
89.  *CL*, 6, p. 255.
90.  Ibid., p. 196.
91.  Andrew McNeillie ed. *The Essays of Virginia Woolf*, Vol.3 (London: Hogarth Press, 1988), p. 355.
92.  Nigel Nicolson ed. *Letters of Virginia Woolf*, Vol.6 (1980), p. 4. Anne Olivier Bell ed. *A Moment's Liberty: The Shorter Diary: Virginia Woolf* (London: The Hogarth Press, 1990), p. 391.
93.  Bell ed., Woolf's *The Shorter Diary*, p. 6.
94.  Ibid., pp. 216-18. Subsequent quotations in this paragraph are all taken from this diary entry.
95.  *Times Literary Supplement*, 19 Jan 1928; revised and rpt. in *The Common Reader*, Second series (1932).

96. Letter from Virginia Woolf to Florence Hardy, dated 21 July 1932, now in DCM. I am grateful to Mr de Peyer for allowing me to consult this letter. The subsequent brief quotations are from this same letter.

    Surprisingly, this letter does not seem to have been included in the 6-volume edition of Virginia Woolf's letters, ed. Nigel Nicolson.

97. See *CL*, 4, pp. 31-2, 45, 92, 101.
98. Ibid., p. 38.
99. Ibid., p. 39. The other possible candidate, according to Purdy and Millgate, is Florence Dugdale. But given that around this time Dugdale was writing critically of the women's movement, referring to it as 'Suffragitis', Sinclair seems the more plausible candidate.
100. *CL*, 4, p. 128; Hardy's parenthesis.
101. *Personal Notebooks*, p. 290.
102. *CL*, 3, p. 142.
103. Ibid., p. 144n.; Gosse's parenthesis in his annotation to Hardy's letter.
104. *Life*, p. 346.
105. Unsigned obituary notice on 'Laurence Hope' in *Athenaeum*, 29 Oct 1904, p. 591.
106. *CL*, 7, pp. 135n & 140.
107. *CL*, 3, p. 18.
108. Ibid., p. 319.
109. *CL*, 4, p. 151.
110. Ibid., p. 287.
111. Ibid., p. 242.
112. *CL*, 5, p. 219.
113. Ibid., p. 242.
114. Ibid., p. 320.
115. See *Personal Writings*, pp. 86-7.
116. See Purdy, *Bibliographical Study*, p. 260.
117. *CL*, 5, p. 275.
118. *CL*, 6, p. 113.
119. *Letters of Emma and Florence Hardy*, p. 146.
120. See Penelope Fitzgerald, *Charlotte Mew and Her Friends* (London: William Collins Sons & Co. Ltd, 1984), pp. 171-2.
121. *CL*, 6, p. 228.
122. *CL*, 5, p. 336.
123. Ibid., p. 67.
124. Ibid., p. 292; Hardy's parenthesis.
125. Quoted in *Life*, pp. 420-1. The first of the three ellipses is Hardy's.
126. *CL*, 6, p. 229.
127. *CL*, 5, p. 67.
128. *CL*, 6, p. 186.
129. *The Library of Thomas Hardy*, p. 212.
130. *CL*, 7, p. 64.
131. *CL*, 6, p. 313.
132. Hardy's description of the as yet unmet Rebecca West; *CL*, 5, p. 293. A substantial portion of this letter is quoted at the end of the paragraph (Hardy's italic).

133. Gordon N. Ray, *H.G. Wells and Rebecca West* (London: Macmillan, 1974), pp. 94-5.
134. See Gittings, *Older Hardy*, p. 131.
135. *CL*, 5, p. 271 n.
136. Ibid., p. 270.
137. May O'Rourke, *Thomas Hardy: His Secretary Remembers*, Toucan Press Monograph no.8 (1965), pp. 28, 34; collected in *Thomas Hardy: Materials for a Study of His Life, Times and Works*, vol.I.
138. Ibid., p. 38.
139. Ibid., p. 36.
140. Ibid., p. 43.
141. Ibid., p. 45. Although Florence Hardy had read and approved of O'Rourke's article in MS, she later wrote to O'Rourke accusing her of presumptuously taking a judgemental stand on Hardy's beliefs and castigating her article as 'a carefully veiled attack' (*Letters of Emma and Florence Hardy*, p. 282).

## 10. Conclusion: 'A Confused Heap of Impressions'

1. *CL*, 7, p. 142.
2. *CL*, 1, p. 266.
3. *Letters of Emma and Florence Hardy*, p. 6.
4. *CL*, 4, p. 3.
5. *CL*, 3, pp. 238-9; Hardy's parentheses.
6. *CL*, 4, p. 21.
7. *CL*, 3, p. 360; Hardy's parentheses.
8. *CL*, 4, p. 39.
9. Ibid., p. 106.
10. Ibid., p. 107; Hardy's parentheses.
11. See *CL*, 5, p. 186.
12. *Literary Notebooks*, 2, p. 106.
13. *CL*, 4, p. 3.
14. *Literary Notebooks*, 2, p. 12.
15. *Life*, pp. 246-7.
16. *CL*, 1, p. 208.
17. *CL*, 5, p. 194.
18. Ibid., p. 250; Hardy's parenthesis.
19. *Life*, p. 414.
20. *CL*, 3, p. 112.
21. *CL*, 1, p. 33.
22. Ibid., p. 250.
23. Grace Alexander, 'A Portrait Painter of Real Women: An Inquiry Into the Humanity and Femininity of Thomas Hardy's Heroines...', *New York Times Saturday Review of Books and Art*, 13 June 1908, pp. 328-9. The review is pasted in 'Scrapbook I' labelled 'T.H. (Personal)'. It is now in DCM and I am grateful to Mr de Peyer for allowing me to consult it.

24. *CL*, 1, p. 255; Hardy's parentheses.
25. *CL*, 6, p. 95.
26. Ibid., p. 96 (Hardy's parenthesis).
27. Ibid., p. 328.
28. *CL*, 2, p. 215.
29. *Life*, pp. 280-1.
30. *CL*, 3, p. 229.
31. *CL*, 2, p. 20.
32. *Literary Notebooks*, 2, pp. 175, 248.
33. *CL*, 4, p. 154.
34. *CL*, 2, p. 193 (Hardy's parenthesis).
35. *Life*, p. 248.
36. *CL*, 1, p. 251; the following quotation is from the same letter, on the same page.
37. *Life*, p. 281.
38. *Literary Notebooks*, 2, p. 479; Hardy's ellipsis.
39. *CL*, 4, p. 232.
40. *Life*, p. 228. This May 1889 note could well be an allusion to Tess's rape/seduction as during this time Hardy was writing *Tess*.
41. *CL*, 6, p. 178.
42. *Life*, p. 231.
43. See *CL*, 5, p. 248 n.
44. *Literary Notebooks*, 2, p. 155.
45. *Life*, pp. 110, 117.
46. *CL*, 5, p. 37.
47. *CL*, 6, p. 154.
48. *CL*, 4, p. 288.
49. Dale Spender, 'Women and Literary History', in Catherine Belsey and Jane Moore eds *The Feminist Reader: Essays in Gender and the Politics of Literary Criticism* (London: Macmillan, 1989; rpt. 1992), p. 30.
50. *Letters of Emma and Florence Hardy*, pp. 39-40.
51. *Life*, p. 177.
52. *Woodlanders*, New Wessex Edition (1975), pp. 121-2.
53. *Tess*, New Wessex Edition (1975), p. 106.
54. *Personal Notebooks*, pp. 8, 10 respectively.
55. *Under the Greenwood Tree*, New Wessex Edition (1975), p. 120.
56. *Life*, p. 50.
57. Ibid., p. 125.
58. *Literary Notebooks*, 2, p. 83.
59. *CL*, 5, p. 347.
60. Ibid., p. 296.
61. *Personal Notebooks*, p. 5.
62. *Literary Notebooks*, 1, p. 146.
63. *Jude*, New Wessex Edition (1975), p. 161.
64. *Real Conversations*, pp. 46-7.
65. *CL*, 2, p. 96.
66. *CL*, 4, p. 62.
67. *Life*, p. 463.
68. The issue is somewhat complicated by the fact that within the novel it is Angel who bitterly and deliberately misquotes these famous lines from Browning (Chapter 37). So, in his letter, is Hardy suggest-

ing that Angel Clare is the central consciousness of *Tess* rather than the eponymous heroine?

69. Hardy's annotated copy of *Keynotes*, p. 59. I am grateful to Vincent Giroud, Curator of Modern Books and Manuscripts, Beinecke Rare Book and Manuscript Library, for granting me formal permission to quote Hardy's marginal comments. Subsequent page references are to this 1893 copy and are parenthetically incorporated into the text.
70. *Life*, p. 273.
71. *Literary Notebooks*, 2, pp. 30-1.
72. *Life*, p. 313.
73. *CL*, 6, p. 362.
74. *Life*, p. 282. See also *Personal Notebooks*, p. 83 and n.
75. *CL*, 6, p. 359 (see also p. 369).
76. *Life*, p. 282.
77. Ibid., p. 235.
78. Ibid., p. 130; Hardy's italic.
79. *CL*, 3, p. 270.
80. *Life*, p. 229.
81. Ibid., p. 269.
82. Ibid., p. 221.
83. *CL*, 2, p. 98.
84. *Jude*, New Wessex Edition, p. 29.
85. *Life*, p. 273.
86. Ibid., p. 348.
87. Ibid., p. 133.
88. *CL*, 4, p. 177.
89. *Literary Notebooks*, 2, pp. 200-1.
90. *CL*, 3, p. 218.
91. *CL*, 2, p. 122.
92. *CL*, 3, p. 275.
93. *Life*, pp. 297-8. All quotations referring to this episode are taken from pages 296-8. Interestingly, 'screaming' is a word Hardy seems to have associated almost exclusively with women. In the 1912 'Postscript' to the Preface of *Jude*, Hardy referred to Mrs Oliphant's 'The Anti-Marriage League' article as 'the screaming of a poor lady in *Blackwood*' and in the novel itself he had commented: 'If [Jude] had been a woman he must have screamed under the nervous tension which he was now undergoing' (New Wessex edition, p. 145).
94. *CL*, 2, p. 264.
95. *Life*, p. 211.
96. *CL*, 7, p. 5.
97. Wotton, *Hardy: Towards a Materialist Criticism*, p. 122.
98. *CL*, 6, p. 48; see also *Life*, p. 441.
99. *CL*, 6, p. 48; 7, p. 162; 5, p. 70 respectively.
100. *Life*, pp. 405, 408, and 439 respectively.
101. Orel ed. *Personal Writings*, pp. 32-3 and p. 49 respectively; for the following quotation see p. 39.
102. In *Life*, (p. 116) Hardy declared: 'Laughter always means blindness – either from defect, choice, or accident.'
103. Ibid., p. 160.

# Index